SEASON III: DENZEL

The Draft Pick Series

Darie McCoy

Edited By
All That's Wright

ISBN Ebook: 978-1-961999-15-2

Paperback: 978-1-961999-18-3

For those who are shining and thriving in conditions where others thought they should shrink and fade into the background. I see you. Get it!

You are powerful beyond measure. Don't be afraid to shine.

— *TARAJI P. HENSON*

Prologue

Denzel stared at the monitor in his home office as his attorney went over the final details surrounding his acquisition of controlling shares of CleanSun, the solar energy company. Seated to his left, Wendy had her laptop open in front of her. His personal business manager was always checking and double checking, no matter who dispensed the information.

According to Derek, everything was in place. A meeting with the board had been arranged for the next week. Two days after Christmas, people were typically still in holiday mode. It was impressive how the team had managed to keep this moving forward so quickly. But, money was a great motivator.

When Denzel received the call from Andrei about the company, he'd joked that someone must have fucked up to get on the big Russian's radar. He was right, but the recommendation had been sound. With better leadership at the helm, CleanSun could more than double their profits and help the environment in the process.

The meeting was just wrapping up when Denzel's phone rang. Looking at the screen, a smile spread across his face. Waving to Wendy, he stood from the table.

"What's up, CJ? Did you miss me? We just video chatted two days ago."

Denzel plopped into the chair behind his desk and moved the mouse around to wake the computer. He was slightly exaggerating about the last time they'd spoken. It had been more than a week since he'd had to talk his friend down from going overboard with the buying for his and Alyssa's yet to be born child. Not that he totally succeeded, but at least he kept him from buying anything the baby wouldn't be able to use until age three.

"Miss you? You call me every other day. I could be just making sure your ass was still alive."

"Whatever, man. I know you're all broken up inside."

"Anyway..." Carver dragged out the word, letting it be known he was done with the joking segment of their conversation.

"I was checking to see when you're coming in for the thing at Andrei's place."

"Funny you should ask. I have some business in Vegas next week. So, I was planning to stay over since the festivities kick off on Saturday. Why? What's up?"

Denzel heard shuffling in the background and the closing of a door before Carver spoke again.

"I heard through the grapevine... the queen might be coming in early. I didn't know if you knew."

Denzel's pulse kicked up at Carver's revelation. He'd hoped, but it hadn't been confirmed that Dominique would be in attendance at the Russian Holiday/Christmas celebration Andrei and his lady were having at his place. Since they were cousins, there was a high probability Zaria would invite Dominique. Until now, he hadn't been certain.

He would've gone regardless. However, knowing she'd be there was the ice cream, cherry, and chocolate fudge on his sundae. Pumping a fist in the air, he sat up straighter in his seat.

"See. That's what real friends are supposed to do. Let a brotha know what's going on, so he can be ready."

"You're welcome." Carver's tone carried a cocky edge, but Denzel wouldn't let the razzing dampen his excitement. When he saw

Dominique Truman again, things would be different. He'd grown tired of their current dynamic. It was time to stop playing around.

"Question." Carver broke into Denzel's mental planning.

"What?"

"Do you intend to actually talk to her this time?"

"Fuck off. You act like all I do is stare at her whenever I see her."

"Because you do, creeper." Carver quipped wryly, prompting Denzel to flip him off. It didn't matter if his friend couldn't see him. That part was irrelevant.

⁓

Denzel worked to keep his fingers from tapping out a beat on the arm of the chair. He was seated in the festively decorated sunroom at Andrei's. And fuck Carver Jamieson. He *was* staring at the beautiful Dominique Truman.

The urge to tap was to squelch the desire to stalk across the room and rip off Vitaly Antonov's arm. His logical mind said the little shit was fucking with him by deigning to touch her, but logic didn't apply to this situation. Knowing he was Andrei's younger brother was saving the goalie from the consequences of being so forward.

Denzel had heard all the rah-rah about them being a family now since Andrei was with Zaria, but he called bullshit. The guy was clearly flirting with Dominique, and she was eating it up. Every time she giggled, Denzel wanted to knock out one of Vitaly's teeth. Let's see him smile pretty with big ass gaps where his incisors were supposed to be.

The conversational hum in the room was background noise to the thoughts in Denzel's head. Knowing Vitaly was doing this shit on purpose wasn't doing much to keep him from wanting to walk over there and tell him to get his hands off his fucking woman.

The problem was, if Denzel gave in to that urge, it would definitely set him back with Dominique. Not to mention what would happen with her parents being in the room. Hell, he'd just listened to her father rip into and Vitaly the night before because they hadn't included him in their little venture to eliminate a threat to Zaria.

The man had been dead ass serious when he told them not to do it again without telling him. While Denzel appreciated Neal Truman's protectiveness, he wasn't interested in being on the man's bad side before he had a chance to truly win Dominique.

Knowing he was bordering on being the creeper Carver accused him of, Denzel tore his gaze away from the small group gathered on the other side of the room. Since Carver and Ryker were engrossed in their own discussion, Denzel went over to where Andrei stood beside a man who almost matched Andrei in height, but not in bulk.

He'd been introduced as an associate by the name of Gregor. Considering he'd been invited to an intimate gathering of family and friends, Denzel figured Andrei was being his usual secretive self with the introduction. In all the years they'd known each other, he'd never met Gregor. But, that didn't mean much since there were probably tons of people in his own life Andrei didn't know existed.

Nodding at the two, he didn't have a chance to say anything before Andrei made a crack about Denzel coming over to stare at Dominique from a new angle. *Fuck his big ass too.* This time, his internal thoughts spilled from his mouth. Since when did Andrei Antonov have jokes?

Denzel could only conclude it was one of the side effects of having Zaria Coleman in his life. Hell, her family had even given him a nickname. A name which he quickly made known wasn't available for everyone to use. Shifting gears, Denzel mentioned CleanSun and his completion of the deal to secure controlling shares in the company.

He probably shouldn't have taken joy in showing Hiriam Baxter to the door. But after hearing what he'd attempted to do to Zaria and meeting the man in person, any molecule of sympathy he could've had was blown into the stratosphere. The man was a sexist, racist...hell, all the bad "ists." It had to be money and connections keeping him in control of the company for the number of years he'd been there.

"I guess I'll be seeing more of this city than usual."

When Andrei looked at him with a questioning expression, Denzel continued.

"Until I feel out the board, and get someone better at the helm. I'll probably have to be here a few times a month to keep an eye on things."

Travel wasn't new to Denzel. He'd been doing it for years as an athlete. Now, it was his business ventures which had him boarding a plane two to three times a month. However, that pace was nothing compared to the one he'd kept during his time playing professional football when he was building his brand and expanding his business interests.

Raised by a restauranteur and an economist, the concept of working hard, while also making your money work for you, was instilled in him from a young age. So, as many of his counterparts were partying and paying for bottle service at exclusive nightclubs, he was asking for stocks, shares and other forms of royalties in addition to lump sum payments for endorsements.

He partied, but he'd stuck with his plan to leave the field with his bank account and body intact. After ten years, his body was a little worse for wear, but more together than many of the guys who played alongside him. Even some who'd spent less time in the league hadn't fared as well physically. Financially, he could probably buy into a team at more than the minimum asking. But he wasn't interested in team ownership at this stage in his life.

Professionally, he was quite happy with where he was. It was his personal life which needed to be enhanced. It seemed like the men closest to him were all finding their one. He didn't begrudge them their happiness. It simply seemed to highlight what he didn't have. And it was past time that he did something about it.

Wandering away from Andrei and his *associate*, Denzel went by the buffet set up along one wall. Preparing a small plate, he strode across the room.

Chapter One

WHAT THE HELL WAS GOING ON?

Dominique released a giggle while simultaneously swatting at Vitaly.

"Stop it! You're a nut!"

"I'm serious. I wouldn't lie to you!"

The twinkle in his bright blue eyes said he was not to be trusted and would indeed lie his ass off if it suited him. She was certain he was afforded entirely too much leeway based on his looks alone. Add in his career as the starting goalie for a successful hockey team, and he could essentially say popcorn rained from the sky and some people would argue in his defense when it didn't happen.

Arching an eyebrow, she looked up at him skeptically. At five-ten, Dominique didn't have to look up to many people on a daily basis. But, leave it to her sister-cousin to get herself involved with a giant. So, they were now in a room filled with his giant friends and family.

To be fair, it was mainly the men who were larger than average. Not that she wasn't accustomed to tall men. Her dad was over six feet, as was her brother. It was likely because these men weren't just big. They gave off *big* energy. There was probably very little they couldn't have if they decided they wanted it.

Movement to her right drew her stare from Vitaly's mischievous face to the man approaching. Man was actually too tame a word for Denzel

Reyes. Unbelievably handsome and fit, sexiness oozed out of Denzel's pores. He was seriously like looking at the definition of hot, sweaty sex. The kind that ended in jelly legs, weak arms, and made a woman not care if her silk press was ruined.

Whenever they'd met in the past, she'd always required an adjustment period to even respond to him when he spoke to her.

She covered it well. Those years of acting training came in handy. Her theater professor would be proud of the way she hid her attraction to him. From what she'd seen on social media and heard through mutual associates, he wasn't one to stick and stay in one place. Dominique's years in show business had made her leery of men like Denzel Reyes. Too handsome. Too charismatic. Too rich. It was a recipe for heartache. The line of women looking to attach themselves to such a man was long enough to wrap around the globe a few times.

No. Dominique was good with not jockeying for position next to a man who would discard her like pop-up tissue as soon as a fresher piece presented itself to be used. That being said, he appeared to be coming toward their little group. Zaria had disappeared a few minutes ago, leaving her with Vitaly, Alyssa, and Ensley.

Alyssa was Zaria's bestie and Ensley was a friend Zaria met through the African American Women's Association for Nevada Attorneys. Or, as she called it, the Black Lady Lawyer group. Ensley was another southern transplant living right outside of Vegas. Both women were giving Vitaly the same expression of disbelief that Dominique had worn before she realized Denzel Reyes was heading in her direction.

Well, he could just be joining their group. It was a small gathering; there weren't many others to talk to unless he wanted to hang out with her parents. Cisco had abandoned them more than thirty minutes ago. Dominique didn't blame him; he had game film to watch. It had taken some maneuvering to get him free to come at all. He had coursework and an away game a couple of days after he returned to campus.

"This seems to be where the party is."

Denzel stopped next to her. He was so close she could feel the heat wafting from his body. Without conscious thought, she shifted toward him and away from the shelter of Vitaly's arm draped across her shoulder. An arm which suddenly felt heavy. Much heavier than it had only moments before.

When Dominique looked into Denzel's face, the smile stretching his lips didn't quite reach his eyes. No. His eyes held something entirely different. Soon the rest of his face joined in the stony expression directed at Vitaly. She couldn't call it curiosity, but something compelled her to look at Vitaly to gauge his response. The quirky grin he'd worn moments before began to slowly slide away.

The mood of their little group transitioned and Dominique wasn't certain what happened. Denzel's question was friendly enough, but she wouldn't call the way he was staring at Vitaly pleasant. Not remotely. Glancing at Ensley and Alyssa, Dominique saw that they'd noticed as well. *What the hell was going on?*

Shifting her attention back to Denzel, she looked between the two men. "Is something wrong?"

At her question, he redirected his stare to her face. The granite look faded from his eyes as he regarded her.

"Not at all. Right, Vitaly?"

The swiftness with which the hardness replaced his pleasant countenance when he looked back to Vitaly was enough to make Dominique think she'd imagined the softer expression. To make matters worse, Vitaly had grown stiff beside her. The two stared at one another for what seemed like eons, but what was actually only a few seconds.

The weight across Dominique's shoulders lifted, and Vitaly shifted away from her. Conflicting thoughts swirled in her mind. The two men were acting like they were in a damn pissing contest. *Over her.* She couldn't fathom why. It wasn't because she lacked confidence in herself, and her ability to garner a man's attention.

She knew Vitaly wasn't interested in her romantically. And Denzel had been playing the flirt since forever. With the rotation of women she'd seen hanging onto him, she'd never taken him seriously. It didn't matter how her body responded to his nearness. Her head had always placed him off limits.

When a cool feeling brushed her left side, she realized that Vitaly had not only moved his arm, but his entire body. Another person could now fit in the gap he'd left. He was standing much closer to Alyssa and

Ensley. There was no way Dominique could prevent herself from glancing up at Denzel. The mercurial shift in his demeanor was enough to make her head spin. His dark eyes appeared to sparkle and his smile revealed even white teeth.

"Your cousin outdid herself with this food. As long as I've known Triple A, I've never come to his place and been served traditional Russian food. This isn't bad at all."

Denzel bit into a golden-colored bun, consuming half of it in one bite. Humming around the food, he popped the other half into his mouth, quickly devouring the pirozhki. The bun stuffed with meat, mushrooms, and glazed onions didn't stand a chance. Dominique was so flabbergasted by the shift in his behavior, it took her a second to realize the other three members of their little group had stepped away.

"So, you're just going to stand there eating, and pretend you didn't just do...whatever it is you just did?"

Denzel paused with another pirozhki halfway to his mouth. His eyebrows shot up in surprise—like he had no clue what he'd done.

"What did I do? I walked over, mentioned that y'all seemed to be having a good time, and started eating my food. Do you want some? I haven't seen you eat anything."

As he verbally offered her food, he placed a fresh pirozhki in front of her lips. Dominique had no explanation for why she automatically opened her mouth to accept it. She'd been about to call him on his blatant skirting of the facts, but had somehow transitioned into letting him feed her from his own hand.

"Bite."

The command was low, but firm. And, her jaw responded without consulting her, closing around the bun taking a generous bite. The soft bread gave way and the flavorful mixture danced on her tongue. Her eyes widened when he popped what was left into his mouth and began to chew. The entire time, he regarded her silently.

Unable to hold his stare, her gaze skittered away. Heat crept up Dominique's neck, but it was far from embarrassment causing the flames to lick at her skin. She needed to get away from this man. Immediately. Before she could act on her internal mandate, strong, warm fingers clasped onto her hand, tucking it into the crook of his arm.

"I forgot to get something to drink."

He began walking as if it were a foregone conclusion that she would join him. Staring at his perfect profile did absolutely nothing to deter him. But what did she expect? Her own limbs were betraying her. Feet which had been firmly planted fell right into step with his strides as he took them from one side of the room to the other.

A few round tables had been added to the space to allow for conversational groupings. So, they did a little winding between them before Denzel placed his plate in an empty space and pulled out a chair.

"Here, have a seat, and I'll get us something to go with this food. Anything in particular you want?"

When she simply stared at him, he nodded. "I'll surprise you. Be right back."

He continued on to the bar, which was set up next to the food. As if her bum was glued to the chair, Dominique didn't move. She simply stared at him in disbelief. The disbelief was equally aimed at herself and him. Because...*what the hell just happened?*

Someone loudly clearing their throat snapped Dominique out of the trance. She stopped staring at Denzel's broad back and wide shoulders, looking around the room. When her gaze collided with her mother's, a different kind of heat rushed to her face. Belinda Truman didn't miss much, and the single eyebrow lift let Dominique know a conversation would be had. Sooner rather than later.

Vibrating against her hip offered Dominique a reprieve from her mama's knowing glance. Thank goodness her dad seemed oblivious as he conversed with Andrei's assistant, Frederick. Tugging her phone from the pocket of the chic blazer her stylist said was all the rage, Dominique looked at the screen.

Her pulse kicked up when she saw her agent's name. Standing, she rushed to the nearest door, which just happened to be the one leading outside toward the pool. Uncaring about the cold air wafting past her, she answered the call.

"Hey, Tammy."

"Hello. May I speak with Marissa Clarke? I was told I could reach her at this number."

It took Dominique a solid minute for the words to sink in. Marissa

Clarke was the name of the lead character for the nighttime drama set to be the anchor show for the Mosaic Media Network under the umbrella of Radiant Reels Studios. Her name had been on a very short list of actresses being considered for the role.

They were keeping things so hush-hush, they had each of the actresses shoot a pilot episode to be shown to the network execs. It was unheard of, but they had a kick ass team of producers and a sought-after director on board, which meant the creators had been given more freedom than usual to explore all the options.

Tammy saying the name, Marissa Clarke, meant Dominique had gone from under consideration to lead actress in a starring role. *Holy Shit!* The squeal of glee slipped from her lips and she bounced on the balls of her feet, dancing to music only she could hear.

"Are you serious right now? Don't play with me!"

"You know I wouldn't joke about something like this. Congratulations! This is the role of a lifetime. I've got a really good feeling about what this means for your career."

Dominique's heart was already thudding from the news, but hearing the excitement in her agent's voice added a new layer to her elation. When the first drop of warmth slid down her cheek, she didn't know what was going on. After the second occurred, she swiped at it, realizing she was crying.

Tammy launched into plans that needed to be made to get Dominique relocated to the Atlanta area to begin production. She was going on about those details when warmth surrounded Dominique's shoulders. Gasping, she shot a quick look back to see who'd draped a coat around her to ward off the chill of the night air.

Denzel stood behind her wearing a smile which slowly transformed into a look of concern. His long fingers cupped the sides of her face as his thumb swiped at the tears Dominique had forgotten about.

"Hey...What's wrong?"

His dark eyes searched hers. At his initial touch, Dominique forgot all about her agent talking away in her ear. That was until Tammy, repeatedly calling her name, pulled her back into the conversation.

"Dom. Dom!"

Placing her free hand on Denzel's chest, she shook her head before answering her agent.

"Hey, Tammy. I'm still here. This is just a lot. My emotions are all over the place."

"I know. I know. I'm dumping a ton of information on you at one time, but you know how things work in this business. We have to jump on it. I've already contacted Doug, and let him know a copy of the final contract from the studio should be in his hands tomorrow morning. After he goes over it, we'll all get together to confirm things. The main thing to know is you'll have to be in or around the ATL before the end of the month."

"The end of the month? That's quick."

"It's the business." Tammy quipped.

"I know, Tam."

"Cool. I'll let you get back to your family thing, and I'll call you after I talk to Doug in the morning."

Dominique couldn't ignore Denzel's quiet, probing stare as she finished her conversation with her agent. He hadn't said a word after asking her what was wrong. It appeared he'd accepted her touch and silent plea as a temporary hold to getting answers to his questions. However, as soon as she said goodbye to Tammy, all bets were off.

"So, you're moving to Atlanta?"

"How did you know?"

Reminding her of their current position with his touch, he tilted his head closer to hers. He'd transferred his hold to wrap his arms around her shoulders, holding the coat he'd draped across them in place.

"I heard Tammy talking about searching for rental properties."

"Oh. Well, yeah. I'd been waiting to hear back about a role in a new series, and she just got the news. As long as the contract is okay, I'll have to be in the area before the end of the month for rehearsals. We start shooting in early February."

"Really? That's amazing!"

Before Dominique could recover from the dazzle of his smile, Denzel literally swept her off her feet, spinning them in a circle. Unbidden giggles spilled from her lips along with her thanks. It felt like the most natural thing in the world. *Too natural.* Once he set her back on her feet, she attempted to put some space between them.

The combination of the sensual scent of his cologne, the feel of his hard body pressed against hers, and the way he looked at her like she'd hung the moon... It was too much. She was on sensory overload. Only Denzel didn't seem inclined to allow for distance between them.

Dominique was once again given a reprieve when the sound of excited voices coming from the sunroom infiltrated their bubble. They both turned toward the windows to investigate. Whatever was going on had everyone on their feet gathered around Andrei and Zaria.

The moment Denzel's embrace slackened, Dominique took a step back. Glancing up at him through her lashes, she murmured her thanks. The breathiness of her voice only hinted at the effect their closeness was having on her senses. Between the exhilaration of landing the part and the sexual tension between them, her head was in a losing battle with her feelings.

Finally, she was able to string consecutive words together. "Um...I think we should probably go back in."

Extending his arm toward the door, he nodded. "After you."

Hoping she could slip into the room unnoticed, Dominique tried to shrug off Denzel's warm coat the moment she crossed the threshold into the room. Letting her know he was right there, he lifted the garment, folding it over his arm as he pulled the door closed behind them. Her hopes were dashed when her mother called out her name.

"There you are, Dom! Come look! Zee-Baby and Dray are engaged!"

Smiling genuinely at her cousin's good news, Dominique rushed to join the cluster of people gathered around Zaria and Andrei. Zaria's face was brighter than ever. Even the normally stoic looking Andrei wore a softer expression. His eyes were trained on Zaria, and she was never more than a few inches away from his side.

Getting closer, Dom offered her congratulations to them while listening to her mama chatter on about how she just knew it and her dad co-signing every word.

Chapter Two

BOUT DAMN TIME

Denzel regarded the celebratory atmosphere in the aftermath of the couple's announcement. He wasn't surprised Andrei had popped the question. Knowing him, he'd probably bought the ring months ago. Denzel wouldn't knock his friend for being a planner. He'd seen the woman he wanted, and didn't stop until he had her at his side. It wouldn't hurt to take notes.

Although all things don't typically work for all people. And Denzel recognized that, while they were family, Dominique and Zaria were not the same woman. What worked for Antonov might not work for him. Besides, he and Dominique had a different beginning. They'd met some years ago when he made an appearance on the sitcom she worked on. She'd played the part of the quirky best friend and he'd been on the show as the temporary love interest of the main character.

Six years ago

Denzel walked onto the main set after spending the past half hour being primped, plucked, and powdered by the make-up artist. While this was his first time on the set of 'She's It Girl', it wasn't his first time on the set of a television show. He'd made a few cameo appearances in the past. He'd also had a small role in a movie playing a character other than himself.

No starring roles, but being a serious actor wasn't where he wanted his career to go. He'd been working hard to establish himself as a legitimate businessman. And, for the most part, he'd accomplished his goal. Being behind the desk discussing the sport he loved was now something he did because he wanted to—not because he needed the seven-figure salary he'd garnered when he'd signed on with the network.

Being on a set did pique his interest though. He watched the crew scurry around performing last-minute tasks. The person they assigned to babysit him was at his side waiting for any indication that Denzel needed something. The kid seemed nice enough. Young, eager, and hardworking. Hopefully, the industry wouldn't chew him up and spit him out. Although Denzel did wonder if they assigned this particular kid because of their shared Latino heritage. Where Denzel was biracial with a Mexican father and an African American mother, Cristiano was of Columbian descent. Most likely, to the people running the show, they were the same.

"Are you sure I can't get you anything, Mr. Reyes?"

Cristiano rolled the R in Denzel's name the way he'd only heard it when he visited his Pop's side of the family. Not taking his gaze off the cookie cutter décor of the set, Denzel shook his head.

"Nah. I'm good. Thanks."

Holding up the insulated mug the younger man had pressed into his hand, he gently shook it. "I still have water in here."

The PureGlacial water was Denzel's only request. They had Craft Services food trucks set up. If he was on set long enough, he'd give them a try. However, at the moment, his only need was to acclimate himself to his environment.

A throaty giggle drew Denzel from his perusal of his surroundings and the show activities. He damn near forgot how to breathe when he discovered the owner of the voice creating the sultry sound. Seated on a sofa off to the side was a familiar dark-skinned beauty. Her smile revealed deep dimples. It was possibly unfair to other women for her to be so beautiful and possess those coveted attributes.

Seeing Dominique Truman in person was an unexpected gut punch. All the hours he'd spent watching the show to familiarize himself didn't prepare him. Not even a little bit.

It wasn't as if Denzel hadn't seen a stunning woman before. From the minute he was old enough to understand what was happening, he'd been on the receiving end of advances from a variety of attractive women— models, movie stars, and their other glamorous counterparts.

Most days, Denzel would consider himself smooth when it came to women. While he didn't often have to approach someone, it wasn't a foreign concept. And, he usually didn't have an issue going for what he wanted, but Dominique Truman wasn't just any woman. He knew it from the moment he heard her laughter.

He probably lost all of his cred with Cristiano when he stared at the woman so intently, he didn't hear a word being said to him. It took Cristiano tugging on his sleeve for Denzel to realize he'd been trying to get his attention.

"Would you like to meet her?"

Trying to regain his composure, Denzel looked at Cristiano with lifted eyebrows.

"Meet who?"

He'd already been introduced to Kelly Franks when they'd done a virtual table reading of their scenes together. It hadn't been in person, but they'd been introduced and interacted.

"Miss Franks. I read the script and you two have quite a few scenes together."

Hiding his disappointment that Cristiano wasn't talking about Dominique, Denzel nodded. Instead of telling Cristiano anything about his prior meeting with Kelly Franks, Denzel went along. Primarily because Kelly was the other occupant of the sofa with Dominique. And, being closer to her was a win in his mind.

While they walked over, Denzel mentally ran lines in his head, trying to remember if there was any interaction between himself and the lovely starlet. If memory served him correctly, they did. During the table read, someone else had stood in for her as it was only Kelly, himself, and one of the producers on the video chat.

So, Denzel allowed Cristiano to take him over to Dominique and Kelly, introducing him to the duo.

"Nice to finally meet you in person."

Kelly's smile showed all thirty-two of her teeth. She was pretty, in a glammed up to glam down mid-western way.

"It is." Responding politely to Kelly, Denzel shook her hand, releasing it as quickly as possible without being rude. Then, he turned his attention to Dominique.

"It's nice to meet you as well, Miss Truman."

When she accepted his handshake, while courteously replying in kind, Denzel had to grit his teeth to keep from pulling her to him and biting those full lips of hers. She was even more stunning up close. Without thinking, he stroked his thumb across the back of her hand as he reluctantly allowed her to pull it free.

"How does anyone get any work done around here with two such beautiful women in the cast?"

He'd meant it as a joke, but the minute the words left his lips, he saw the light behind Dominique's eyes fade. He didn't know how, but he'd fucked up. Pasting a determined smile on his face, he continued to make chit chat, pulling both women in by asking them questions about the show. When it was time to shoot the first scene, Dominique wasn't as standoffish, but the previous warmth hadn't returned to her eyes when she looked at him.

Present

Drawing closer to the small crowd, Denzel didn't take his eyes off Dominique. It was obvious she was genuinely happy for her cousin. So much so that she made no mention of her own good news. He was certain her family would want to celebrate her achievement as well, but she remained mute about it. Selfishly, he kind of liked being the first to know and offer her congratulations and support.

Staying on the outskirts, allowing those closest to Zaria to be near the center of the action, Denzel purposely ignored Carver sauntering over to stand next to him. Denzel didn't have to wait long to find out what was on his mind.

"So, I see you decided to stop staring and do something."

"I did."

Both men continued to look straight ahead as they spoke to one another.

"Bout damn time."

At Carver's comment, Denzel finally tore his eyes away from Dominique.

"Excuse you. I know the man who waited more than fifteen years to claim his woman isn't talking shit to me."

"Fuck you. At least I made myself known. She just got scared and ran from me. Can you say the same?" Carver wore a knowing smirk.

Flipping him the bird, Denzel leaned in closer to make sure he wasn't overheard.

"Yeah…You made yourself known, but it was after you sabotaged any potential relationship she could've had in college."

"Why are you bringing up old shit?"

"Why are you over here poking me about what I'm doing concerning my woman?"

"Your woman? Does *she* know that?"

Returning to devouring Dominique with his gaze, Denzel lifted one shoulder.

"If she doesn't, it won't be much longer before she understands."

"Uh huh…If you say so."

"I know so." Denzel nodded as if the motion made every word spoken covenant.

Chuckling, Carver nudged Denzel with his elbow. "That's what I like about you, man. You're confident. Even when you're being delusional as fuck, you do it with complete faith in your abilities."

Tearing his gaze away from Dominique, Denzel stared at Carver.

"Why are we friends again?"

"Don't play. You know you love me. I'm the brother you never had."

Shaking his head, Denzel left Carver standing to approach the happy couple, and offer his congratulations. If doing so put him closer to the woman he wanted to be near, all the better.

After some of the excitement died down and it seemed the party was waning as well, Denzel found himself seated in a different chair in a different room. But the results were similar. He was once again watching

Dominique. Only this time, he was waiting to see when or if she'd clue her family in on her own good news.

While her cousin was busy talking her mother off the big extravaganza wedding cliff, Dominique sat next to her, smiling and backing up the wishes of the bride-to-be. Occasionally, her eyes would find his, but quickly dart away. Those moments were when he knew for sure he hadn't been wrong about her feeling the chemistry between the two of them.

She was an excellent actress, but something had changed; and she couldn't seem to hide behind a nonchalant exterior anymore. Not when it came to him. After what felt like eons, the conversation shifted when Dominique's phone pinged.

"I thought we said no phones." Her mother looked at her with a semi-stern expression.

"When did we say that?"

Zaria came to Dominique's rescue. Belinda Truman looked at her like she'd committed the ultimate betrayal.

"This is family time. We don't have our phones out during family time."

"I'm sorry, Mama. It might be Tammy. She said she would let me know when she got in touch with Doug. I thought it would be tomorrow though."

"Tammy? Your agent Tammy? Why is Tammy calling you on the holiday?"

Denzel had to cover his mouth to hide his chuckle at the expression on Dominique's face when she responded to her mother's questions.

"Mama... You remember this is a holiday we *chose* to celebrate, right? For most Americans, January seventh has no significance. It's just another day."

Swatting at her, Mrs. Truman sucked her teeth. "Don't get fresh with me. I know that. It's still Sunday night. If she's calling and messaging you on a Sunday night, it must be important, right?"

Denzel settled into the cushioned comfort of the chair, watching his Una squirm under her mother's knowing look before she finally spilled the beans.

"She called to tell me I got the part. I still can't say much until they make the official announcement. But, assuming everything works out with the contract, I'll be moving to Atlanta for a while to start rehearsals before we go into full production."

"What?"

"Why didn't you say anything?"

"How long have you known?"

Zaria and Mrs. Truman tripped over one another's questions, not giving Dominique a chance to answer. Their loud exclamations drew the attention of the others, who came closer to find out what was going on.

"What's happening over here?" Neal Truman stopped next to his wife, putting a hand on her shoulder.

"Dom just told us she got the part in that show in Atlanta. She's coming home!"

Not listening to Dominique's corrections regarding coming home, her mother squeezed her in a hug.

"I can't believe you didn't tell us immediately! You know how much I've been praying to have you closer to home. Zee-Baby ain't never coming back, but I was hoping Atlanta being the new Hollywood might get you closer."

Accepting her mother's embrace, Dominique patted her arm. Once she released her, Dominique's father reached in to hug her as well.

"That's great news, baby girl. When do you get started?"

"It's going to move pretty quickly. I have to find a place to live, if I don't want to live out of a hotel the entire time."

Dominique's face scrunched at the possibility of an extended stay in a hotel.

"Well, Atlanta can be pretty rough. So, maybe you wanna look for a place on the outskirts?"

Her father had the right idea, giving Denzel the perfect segue to enter the conversation.

"I can help with that."

"I'll bet you can..." Belinda Truman mumbled the words, but Denzel heard them. Shooting her a smile, he returned his attention to Dominique.

"I own several properties in the area. Many of them I use specifically to rent to celebrities and people who will be there for less than a year, but longer than a month. They typically want a place outside of the city, but close enough to get around. And they're all in gated communities or a building with on-site security."

"So, you're saying you can put Dom up while she's in town?" Mrs. Truman leaned forward, crossing her legs and propping her chin on her folded fingers.

"I can check with the property manager to see what's available. But, I'm sure I can help. The Atlanta area has been my home base for a few years now. We can work something out."

"Uh-huh..."

Denzel avoided the penetrating gaze of Dominique's mother. Her response to his offer to help was drawing her husband's attention. Neal was now staring a hole in the side of Denzel's head as if he'd turned into a different creature, and wasn't the same man he'd shared drinks and played cards with the previous night.

Pulling his own phone from his pocket, Denzel unlocked it and passed it to Dominique.

"Put your number in, and I'll let you know what I find out when I talk to my guy in the morning."

Blocking out anyone not in his direct line of sight, he worked to keep his expression all business while he watched Dominique enter her number into his contacts. Considering the access he had, he could've secured her number a long time ago, but having her give it to him was far better than getting it from somewhere else. Besides, getting it on the sneak tip felt stalkerish.

When she was done tapping at the display, she surprised him by calling herself from his phone. Ending the call, she passed the device back to him. Until then, he hadn't been sure she'd believed him when he said he could help with her housing situation. Her mother had done most of the talking after he'd brought it up.

"Now that we got housing worked out, I think it's time for one more toast."

The remainder of their celebratory group gathered near the bar. Those who were able to drink had alcoholic beverages in their hands as they raised their glasses to toast Dominique. Chatter and laughter followed the toast, and the group began to slowly disperse.

The moment reminded Denzel of home. If he hadn't just spent the Christmas holidays with his own family, he was sure the scene would've sent him to his phone to call his parents. For Denzel, the only thing missing was him being closer to Dominique instead of several feet away.

His one consolation was knowing she would soon be much closer to him. When he'd started the night, he'd already planned to end it with Dominique Truman being more aware of his intentions. He'd felt the crumbling of the barrier between them when they were outside next to the pool. Denzel intended to completely obliterate that wall very soon.

As the group dispersed and non-family members were saying goodbye to their hosts, Denzel nodded to Andrei in farewell before approaching Dominique. She was standing next to Alyssa, who was more animated than Denzel was used to seeing her. Carver stood nearby with her coat in his hands, staring at his wife indulgently.

Approaching, Denzel realized she was going on about the comic book character, Queen Neferata. Alyssa was an avid fan of the series. Once Carver learned the image on the majority of the covers and the star of the series was modeled after Dominique, he'd started referring to her as *the queen* whenever her name came up in conversation with Denzel.

Denzel caught the tail end of Alyssa trying to pry any inside information from Dominique regarding the rumors that major studios were looking to turn the series into a live-action movie or short serial for a streaming services. Shaking her head, Dominique smiled.

"As far as I know, they're just rumors. But if I did know something, you know I couldn't tell you."

Dropping her voice, Alyssa stepped closer. "I wouldn't tell anyone. Who would I tell? Carver? Zaria? It would go in one ear and out of the other with those two. Come on, Dom." Alyssa dragged out Dominique's nickname.

"I wish I had something to give you, but I really don't know anything." Dominique touched Alyssa's shoulder.

Pouting, Alyssa finally held out her arms to let Carver help her into her coat. Casting one last hopeful glance at Dominique, she waved goodbye. Bumping forearms with Carver as he passed by, Denzel said goodnight to both.

He knew a driver was probably parked outside, waiting to take him to the local apartment he'd recently acquired. However, he wanted a minute alone with Dominique. They'd been surrounded by people most of the night, with the exception of their brief moment next to the pool. Capturing her hand before she could walk farther into the house, he kept her near him as his friend lead his wife through the door.

Questions swirled in Dominique's eyes as she looked up at him.

"Walk with me for a second."

Chapter Three

WALK WITH ME

She tried it. Dominique had attempted to get away from Denzel Reyes and his magnetic presence, but he'd caught her. The heat of his hand clasped around hers sent a shiver skating along her spine. It felt entirely too good to have his large hand enclosing hers. Those hands had made him a formidable opponent when he played football.

Dominique recalled hearing a sports analyst say Denzel had one of the lowest fumble rates in league history. Once he had his hands on the ball, it was secure. No one could get him to let it go until the whistle blew, ending the play. The way his fingers curled around hers, she understood why. His hold was firm, but flexible enough to allow him to move with her, if necessary. There was no getting away.

His lifted eyebrow reminded her that he'd used those kissable lips of his to ask her a question. Wait. He hadn't asked. He'd made a statement. More like a command. *Walk with me.*

"Umm...Okay... Walk with you where?"

Dominique looked around the foyer. The rest of Zaria's and Andrei's guests were gone. Her parents had called it a night, and were in their room upstairs. Zaria stood with Andrei next to the front door. Dominique caught Zaria's questioning gaze and gave the slightest shake of her head. She didn't need a rescue. At least she hoped not.

Denzel had volunteered to help her find a place in Atlanta. That's probably all he wanted to discuss.

"This way."

His ease with navigating the property made Dominique wonder how often he'd visited Andrei. From what she'd learned about her sister-cousin's new fiancé, he wasn't big on visitors. But, Denzel was one of the few people he considered a friend. With one last look back at Zaria and Andrei, Dominique allowed him to lead her away.

When he led her to a door which opened to the outside, she was surprised. She hadn't realized it was possible to get outside that way. The chill of the night air didn't have a chance to set in because Denzel once again draped a coat around her shoulders. His scent enveloped her. She couldn't stop herself from breathing in the masculine aroma.

For a few moments, they walked in silence along the path between the house and the outer buildings on the property. Since he'd initiated this little outing Dominique held her tongue, waiting to see what he had to say. Finally, he broke the silence.

"Congratulations again. I know you've been grinding for years to make your mark. So, I'm sure it feels really good to have your hard work pay off."

Nodding, Dominique shot him a quick glance before she refocused on the winter foliage along the stone walkway.

"It does. It feels great. But the work isn't over. The hard stuff is coming. Being the lead is a lot of pressure. More spotlight. Which means more people thinking they have the right to know every little thing about what goes on in your life."

Until she'd said it aloud to Denzel, Dominique hadn't permitted herself to dwell on that aspect. Some things in her life would have to change. She wasn't thrilled about it, but it wasn't going to bring her down. There was little chance Tammy or Doug wouldn't bring up the changes when they met in the morning.

"I understand. People be peopling way too hard when it comes to celebrities and public figures they like. And don't let them dislike you. They'll damn near go broke trying to prove to everyone else you aren't all that."

Dominique stopped and looked up at him. "Was this supposed to be a pep-talk? Because it's taking a turn."

Denzel's lips stretched into one of his signature grins. "It's not-not a pep talk. But if nothing else, I'm gonna keep it real with you." He recaptured her hand, giving her fingers a squeeze.

"I'm just saying that this is a great opportunity, but people are gonna people harder than ever, when the announcement drops. You've probably already seen some changes with the success of the comic, and them talking about possibly making it into a live-action movie."

Dominique had been staring down at their joined hands, but her eyes flew to his when he brought up the comic she was the title character for, Queen Neferata. Although it was gaining more attention, it was still kind of niche. So, she was shocked he knew about it. Apparently, her thoughts were written on her face. Denzel chuckled, bumping her lightly with his arm.

"What? You thought I only cared about football?"

Shaking her head, Dominique tightened her grip on his fingers before relaxing her digits.

"No. I know there's more to you than sports. I just didn't take you for a comic-head."

"I'm not. But I'm a Dominique Truman head."

Dominique nearly stumbled and fell flat. Looking into Denzel's face, she was confronted with the honesty in his expression. He wasn't running game. His dark eyes peered into hers, projecting nothing but honesty. *Well damn...* How was she supposed to respond?

The intensity of his stare held her captive. She wanted to look away, to hide from what she saw there, but she couldn't. Earlier, she'd wondered what the hell was going on when he'd interrupted her conversation with Vitaly. Now, there was no hiding from it. Denzel Reyes wasn't simply flirting. This wasn't like the previous times they'd met.

"Um...I'm not sure what to say to that."

"You don't have to say anything. It wasn't a question. It was a statement. I've followed your work. I think you're amazingly talented. Being beautiful and fine as fuck is just icing on an already delicious smelling cake."

The warmth Dominique felt when he first began praising her

became a heat snaking down to her center. The passion undergirding his words was... a lot. She wasn't sure how to navigate the situation. They'd never been completely alone before. They always encountered one another through work or socially in a room full of people. Having Denzel's undivided attention was simultaneously intoxicating and distressing.

"Do you need an understudy in the bushes to call out your next line? Because you look like you want to say something, but you forgot your lines."

Denzel chuckled lightly, then slid his arms around her back, gently pressing their fronts together. "This isn't a gig, baby. Like I said. You don't have to say anything. I'm just putting it out there. I've paid attention. And I'll keep paying attention."

Nodding mutely, Dominique allowed herself to enjoy his embrace. Her heart thundered in her ears so loudly she was astonished she heard a word. No amount of reminding herself about his reputation could squelch the feeling. Besides, she had no proof any of the things said about him were true. People loved to make up things about the rich and famous. It had become an American pastime that was also a lucrative business for some.

"Let's go back."

Denzel turned them toward the house with one arm lying across her shoulders.. They'd stopped near the front of the ice rink, but didn't even step onto the landing. As they walked, Dominique found her footing again.

"Question."

"Answer."

Bumping him with her hip, Dominique couldn't suppress her grin.

"Smart ass. I meant, I have a question."

"And I meant, I have an answer to your question."

"Whatever."

Dominique pursed her lips, looking away from the broad smile on his face. She held the pout until he stepped in front of her, stopping her in her tracks.

"Okay. No joking around. What's your question?"

Now that he'd confronted her and once again given her his undivided attention, her tongue seemed to glue itself to the roof of her mouth. Denzel didn't nudge or prod her to speak up. He simply stood in front of her with his hands on her shoulders, sending warm tingles emanating from where they rested. The drive to know the answer was what forced her to ask, despite the heat licking up her neck from being so close to him.

"Don't get me wrong. The walk was nice, but...What was the purpose?"

Without missing a beat, Denzel responded and snatched her breath with his bald honesty.

"I wanted a moment alone with you."

"Why?" Dominique was proud of herself for gathering enough air to push out the single syllable.

"Because, it seems like whenever I see you, there are always a ton of people around. I didn't want the opportunity to pass me by."

"If that's the case, why are we going back in so soon?"

Lowering his head until their eyes were mere inches apart, he stared directly into hers. Dominique could see the light reflected off his dark brown irises.

"I just wanted a few minutes before I had to go. Since you'll be in my city, I'm sure we'll have more opportunities to see one another."

Pulling back slightly, he gave her the space she needed to rediscover how to exchange oxygen for carbon dioxide. Rubbing along her arms, he continued speaking.

"Besides, we'll talk before then. I need to know what kind of place you'll want to live in while you're there. My property manager will need the details to find the perfect place."

Dominique started to say she could have her assistant communicate with the property manager, but something warned her it might be the exact wrong thing to say. So, she kept it to herself. Instead, she simply dipped her head in acknowledgement.

When Denzel ran his tongue along his bottom lip, her heart started doing that thing again—pounding in her ears. She'd been in enough pretend romantic scenes and real ones to recognize his expression. What he wasn't saying with his words, he was saying with his eyes and the wetting of his bottom lip. He wanted to kiss her.

With a hand to his chest, Dominique put the brakes on the moment. As attracted as she was to the man, things between them had gone from zero to Speed Racer, and she needed a minute. He acknowledged her unspoken request by stepping away. Then he turned, taking them back down the path and into the house.

He didn't stop until they were once again at the front of the large double doors leading to the canopy where everyone's driver waited for them. Sure enough, when he opened the door, a man was leaned against the passenger side of a dark SUV.

Cupping the side of her face, Denzel leaned forward, dropping a kiss on her cheek. The breath Dominique inhaled when he touched her was released as he pulled away.

"Talk to you soon."

With her nod of agreement, he released her. She was helpless to prevent herself from watching him walk away. The man had swag oozing from his pores. After he reached the vehicle, he stood before the door the other man opened for him. Turning to her, he lifted two fingers in the peace sign, then mouthed, "Go inside."

Glad no one was around to see how she folded for him, Dominique backed into the house and closed the door. Resting her back against the sturdy wood, she stared into space. After she gathered herself, she took the stairs on the left, going up to her room. This night had been a doozy.

~

"Are you sure this is the right place?"

Dominique's brow dipped as she looked from her cellphone screen to the passing landscape. Her assistant Madison was on the other end of the video call, giving her an expression Dominique had become quite familiar with.

"I have no idea, since all I can see is your pretty face, ma'am." Madison quipped.

"Don't be a smarty pants." Dominique rotated the phone view so it displayed what she saw.

"It looks like the pictures to me. Just...bigger."

"That's what I mean!"

Dominique switched the display back around. The driver, hired to bring her from the airstrip to the house which would serve as her home base, had turned onto a long driveway after she tapped her phone against the box at the gate to use the passkey she'd been sent via an app.

Instead of the subdivision she expected, there was only one house in the distance and it was obvious the buildings in close proximity were a part of the same property.

"Something isn't right here Maddy. Do you still have the property manager guy's number?"

Dominique and Denzel had spoken a lot during the two weeks it had taken her to get things together to make the move. He'd relented and connected her assistant with his property manager. Yet, somehow, she still didn't have the man's contact information.

"I'm sure I do. Let me look." While Madison went through her messages and contacts, Dominique stared at the sprawling estate she was getting closer to by the second.

"Oh shoot! I'm so sorry, Dom. I have to call you back."

"Excuse me? You can't do me like this, Maddy. For all you know, this could be a kidnapping situation."

"Ma'am, don't be dramatic. You used the passcode to get into the gate. You aren't being kidnapped. I'll text you the number, but I really have to go. Paige Knight just messaged me."

Pouting, Dominique looked at the phone. "Fine. Be like that. Run off to your richer, more famous client."

"Ma'am, don't play with me. I'll call you back as soon as I can."

Madison ended the call. A smile tugged at the corner of Dominique's lips. Despite the bout of uncertainty in the situation, she wasn't really upset with Madison for seeing what Paige needed. Dominique wasn't her only client. She had a couple of others she assisted.

Of the three, Paige had the more demanding schedule. With the way roles were coming in for Paige, Dominique was certain she'd have to start looking for a new assistant soon. Paige would keep Madison so busy she wouldn't have time for more than one client.

The vehicle rolled to a stop in front of the sprawling Mediterranean style estate. Dominique still felt like something had to be off. Then, she looked to the left, and she saw the cute little bungalow from the pictures. Finally! Something looked familiar. She didn't recall Madison mentioning the place was someone's guest house, but maybe she had, and Dominique hadn't internalized the information.

Considering how busy she'd been since finalizing the contract, it was a definite possibility she was given the information and had let it go in one ear and out the other. The driver opened Dominique's door, then went to the back of the SUV to unload the small rolling luggage she traveled with.

Her other belongings, she felt she'd need, had been shipped in advance. The man declined the tip Dominique offered. Her ride had been arranged through a service. So, there wasn't a rideshare app she could use to give it to him automatically.

Shrugging, she looked at the little attached bungalow and considered going there, but she didn't actually see the entrance. The driver had placed her luggage near the double doors of the main house. So, essentially, the decision had been made for her.

Ascending the short flight of stairs, the front door opened when she reached the top.

"Hello! Hola, Senorita!"

A trim Latina woman with smooth light brown skin and a ready smile was framed in the doorway. Her black hair was swept away from her face in a bun. Returning her smile, Dominique admired the way silver strands shot through her hair, as if they didn't dare land in any location that took away from her attractiveness.

"Hello..." Although she was smiling, Dominique was still somewhat confused.

"Come in! Come in! I'm Silvia, the house manager. I've been expecting you, Senorita Truman."

"Please, call me Dominique."

Following the other woman into the house, Dominique had to clench her jaw to keep it closed. Throughout her career, she'd been in some extraordinary mansions and estates. So, it was rare for her to be overly impressed. But, whoever designed and furnished the place was a very talented individual.

The entryway was grand while still somehow managing to project warmth. The marbled tile led to a sweeping, curved staircase leading to the second floor. From the open doorway, Dominique glimpsed the plush furniture of a living room. Large colorful pillows were strategically placed on a light tan sofa. It appeared to be oversized, similar to some of the pieces at Andrei's.

"Okay, Dominique." Silvia smiled; the apples of her cheeks rose so high her wide eyes became barely open slits.

"It's so nice to finally meet you. Your things arrived. I didn't know how you wanted them. So, I had them put in your rooms, but I didn't put anything away. I hope that's fine."

Slightly dazed, Dominique nodded. "It's no problem. I appreciate you taking care of it."

As much as she wanted to be polite, she was too confused and concerned to continue to act as if she knew what was going on. Sure she was busy, but she was positive she would've remembered Maddy telling her the new place came with a house manager. She didn't have a house manager at her place in Cali.

To be fair, though, her house in L.A. could fit inside this one at least three times and there would still be room to spare. It was large enough for her as a single person who didn't have many visitors aside from her immediate family. So, there were enough bedrooms for when they visited, but it wasn't large enough for the lavish parties people believe all celebrities throw at their homes.

"Miss Silvia?" Dominique's steps were slow as she moved farther into the house.

"Please, just Silvia."

"Silvia, I'm confused. My assistant did most of the coordination with the property manager, but I think there's been a mistake. This place is much bigger than what I expected."

Dominique didn't add that there was no way she was willing to pay the price tag to rent something this large—even if it was only for six months. Had she considered renting out her own house, she knew she wouldn't garner enough proceeds to cover half of what this house was worth. It was obvious Denzel was cutting her some kind of break.

The short-term lease she signed wasn't the cost of what he could get for an estate like this. From talking to her associates in the business who'd worked out of Atlanta recently, the housing market was overwhelming to navigate. She was lucky she knew someone with properties who could help her find something in the time frame that she needed. But, she couldn't allow him to go to such lengths.

"No, ma'am. You are in the right place. If you'll follow me, I'll show you to your rooms."

Knowing Silvia was simply doing her job, Dominique followed the older woman. But she still had questions, especially once she latched onto Silvia say 'her rooms'. What rooms? She was supposed to have a little bungalow similar to the one she saw when the driver dropped her off.

Despite not being the best with directions, Dominique was certain they weren't walking toward the little semi-attached house. Instead, she was led up the stairs and to the left at the top. Following Silvia, Dominique's eyes were drawn to the large windows on one side of the long hallway.

Outside, she could see the outline of more structures in the distance. However, it was the huge swimming pool that garnered her attention. While not Olympic sized, it was still long and wide enough for someone to get some decent laps in. Fingering the back of her phone, she itched to call Mr. Denzel Reyes and find out what the hell was going on.

Stepping through the arched doorway behind Silvia, Dominique's gaze raked over the furnishings of a sitting room. Similar, but not identical, to the sofa downstairs, it was light colored with large colorful pillows. A large flat screen television was mounted on the wall above the gas fireplace, which gave the room a cozy feel.

"These are your rooms." Silvia stretched her arm to the right, then the left as she spoke. "Through that door is your bedroom. There's a full bathroom, and a half bath over in the sitting area."

Drumming up a smile, Dominique thanked her. She managed to nod in the appropriate places in response to being told where her boxes and other luggage were located, and when Silvia said she'd be happy to show her around the property once she'd had a little time to get settled.

"If you would like, I'd be happy to help you unpack."

"Thank you, Silvia. I appreciate the offer, but I think I have it under control."

"Okay." Reaching into her pocket, Silvia produced a business card. "Well, if you change your mind, here's my information. Just give me a call. I'll stop by in a little while to check on you. I didn't get a list of any dietary requirements or allergies you have, but if you'll send them over, I'll make sure the chef is made aware."

"The chef?" Dominique hadn't meant to sound so sharp, but this was getting out of hand.

"Yes. He's only here a few days a week, but he does meal prep and can make whatever you'd like."

"Oh. Okay. Thank you, Silvia."

"You're more than welcome. Let me know when you're ready for your tour!" Leaving with a bright smile on her face, Silvia closed the door behind her.

She'd barely heard the snick of the latch when Dominique unlocked her phone and stomped into the bedroom, closing the door behind her. Just in case she got a little loud, she wanted to put another barrier between herself and the hallway.

The phone only rang twice before Denzel's voice flowed through the line. *Voicemail.* Dominique wanted to scream. Instead, she waited until the requisite beep to leave her message.

"Denzel...This is Dominique. We need to talk."

She was so flustered she ended the call without uttering another word. The last thing she wanted to do was have a one-sided disagreement with the man's voicemail.

Chapter Four

WELCOME TO ATLANTA?

Denzel's phone buzzed in his pocket, but he didn't answer. He'd neglected to silence it completely and was happy there was enough background noise from the replay of the game footage that it couldn't be heard. He really didn't want to hear Harvey's mouth about bringing electronics onto the set. They'd already had a round on the subject when he'd flat out refused to leave his phone in his dressing room.

Most of the time, when he was at the studio, it was on silent and he'd check his messages once shooting was done for the day. However, today, he'd been anxious. He'd expected to be done with this interview with Kaylen Payne an hour ago, but he'd actually enjoyed his conversation with the young quarterback. And, as it turned out, they had a mutual acquaintance.

Kaylen and Vitaly shared the same sports agent, Jamie Shannon. Jamie was doing the damn thing, having secured two premiere players in different sports and negotiating lucrative contracts for both. She was single-handedly proving a woman could be successful and thrive in the male dominated side of the sports world.

"So, for the second year in a row, your team has a chance to advance to the Championship game. What's the one thing you want to focus on to turn that chance into a definite thing?"

Denzel leaned in slightly with his elbows resting on the arms of his chair, staring at the young man a few feet away from him. The affable quarterback smiled, but managed to maintain a serious expression.

"I don't know if there's just one thing. But, I will say this, as long as we continue to play together as a team, and go onto the field with the same level of intensity we've given every game this season, we'll make it there again. And this time, we'll walk away with the ring."

Nodding, Denzel extended his hand to give him a fist bump. Instead of accepting, Kaylen burst into laughter. Widening his eyes, Denzel pulled his hand back.

"What? What's so funny?"

"Come on, man. You couldn't help yourself, could you?" Kaylen shook his head, then lifted his own fist.

"I don't know what you're talking about, man. I'm just offering you encouragement." Bumping his knuckles against Kaylen's, Denzel dropped his hand on the armrest of his chair.

"Yeah... with the hand sporting one of the three Championship game rings you won during your career."

Denzel lifted his right hand, looking at the big jewel on the ring finger. It was the ring from the last Championship game he and Carver played in together before Carver retired.

"What? This old thing?"

Kaylen was a good sport. So, Denzel knew he wouldn't have any hard feelings about the move he'd pulled. Smiling at him, he thanked him for coming on the show. Then, he went through his normal closing before the director said 'cut', putting an end to filming.

Once the cameras were off, Denzel shook Kaylen's hand, thanking him again for taking time away from his schedule to be onsite for the interview instead of doing it remotely. After he'd done what was necessary before he could leave, Denzel nodded to Juan letting him know he was ready to go.

Acknowledging various people on his way out, Denzel fished his phone from his pocket. When he saw the missed call from Dominique, he unlocked the screen. They'd texted back and forth the past couple of days, but hadn't spoken. He didn't like that shit, but he didn't press her. Knowing she'd be in town soon was his consolation.

Checking his voicemail, he was certain he didn't mistake the quiver of anger in her voice. She probably thought she was being reserved, but he heard it. *Shit*...That meant she'd already landed and was at the house. She was early. He'd planned to be home when she got there. Silvia was aware she was coming, and he'd given his house manager instructions on what to do if Dominique arrived before he did.

He debated on if he should return the phone call or follow his original plan and have Juan take him home. Landing somewhere in the middle, he shot her a text telling her the interview had run long, and he'd contact her soon. It wasn't technically a lie, since he would be in contact with her soon. Face-to-face contact.

What he'd done was risky. Denzel was well aware of it. He hadn't confided in even his closest friends when the idea occurred to him. Originally, when he'd learned of Dominique's impending move, he'd had every intention of doing exactly what he said. He even went so far as to call Terry and speak to him about what was available for a short-term lease.

The problem came in when Terry told him about the available units. Denzel wasn't a slumlord. He didn't own properties in bad areas, but he didn't like any of the proposed units for Dominique. They were too close to being inside the city. She'd never struck him as a person who liked to be in the middle of things. Even the times they'd met socially, she usually was only at the event long enough to be polite before she disappeared.

So, Denzel's next option was to put her in his pool house. It was separate from the main house with its own entrance, affording her privacy. Then, he'd gotten a call from his Tia Isabel about his cousin Rafael. Denzel had been in touch with him when he learned his younger cousin was moving to the area to complete his PhD studies. But, according to his aunt, he was having some issues finding adequate housing.

Denzel couldn't very well tell his tia he didn't have room for Rafael. So, he switched up at the last minute and had a suite of rooms prepared for Dominique. He was more comfortable with her under the same roof with him anyway. It would make it easier security-wise.

When Juan pulled the vehicle into the garage, Denzel snapped his attention away from staring at his phone screen. He hadn't realized his thoughts had consumed him to the point he'd zoned out. If anyone asked, he'd deny being nervous about his reception with Dominique. He'd had a plethora of opportunities to tell her what was up, but he didn't.

At least he wouldn't lie to himself about the reasons why. He had a chance to have her with him, and he took it. Plain and simple. Well...plain, but probably not simple. Not if the tone of her voicemail message was any indicator.

The moment Denzel crossed the threshold into the foyer, Silvia was there waiting for him. Her arms were folded across her middle and her foot tapped a staccato beat on the tiled floor.

"Denzel Alejandro Reyes. Please tell me you told that young woman she would be staying in this house with you."

Well...fuck... It appeared he had more than one disgruntled woman to deal with. Silvia Flores had been hand selected by his mother, since Denzel knew next to nothing about what a house manager did at the time. He should have known then his mama was essentially hiring someone like her.

Silvia would take care of his household efficiently, but she'd also call him on his shit without a second thought. What was he going to do? Fire her? He'd never hear the end of it from his mama if he did.

"Listen, Silvia. It's not what you think."

The foot tapping continued as she stared at him with one raised eyebrow. They both knew it was exactly what she thought—mostly.

"Ok. It's not completely what you think. I didn't plan it like this, but this way is better."

Only a quick step back kept him from feeling the full sting of the blow when she swatted his arm.

"Have you lost your mind?" Silvia looked at him as if she truly believed he'd taken his brain out, left it somewhere, and had forgotten where he'd placed it.

"Don't worry. I have it under control."

"You better more than have it under control. She looked so confused. It was all I could do not to call one of the boys and ask them to take her wherever she wanted to go. But, since I hadn't talked to you yet, I held off."

Denzel's jaw hardened. Only respect for his elders kept him from lighting into Silvia when she said she'd put Dominique into a car and help her leave. *The fuck she would.* He was able to hold his tongue, but his facial expression spoke volumes.

"I'm just saying I thought about it. I didn't say anything to her other than to offer to give her a tour once she was settled."

Denzel nodded and moved towards the stairs. Stopping at the bottom of the landing, he turned back to her.

"Silvia, it goes without saying that I value your opinion, and you are integral in this household." Holding her gaze, he continued, "But, let's be clear. I'm a grown man. Whatever is between me and Dominique is between us. You should know me well enough to know I wouldn't intentionally cause her harm."

Rotating back toward the stairs, he started up. "You don't have to worry about giving her the tour. I'll take care of it."

Saying nothing further, he climbed the stairs. It went without mention that Silvia could consider her day complete. He didn't listen for the sounds of her fading footsteps. His mind was already on the woman occupying the guest suite at the end of the hall.

As he drew closer to the arched doorway leading into the suite of rooms he'd asked Silvia to prepare for Dominique, Denzel almost convinced himself the older woman was just being overprotective. There wasn't anything nefarious in his decision to have Dominique in this suite instead of at one of his other properties. Even though her voice had an edge to it in her voicemail, it didn't necessarily mean she was angry.

He almost believed that. Right up until she opened the door following his knock, Denzel thought he might have read too much into the three short sentences she'd left, telling him they needed to talk. However, when the door swung open, and he saw the fire blazing behind her eyes, he knew he was monumentally wrong in his assessment. Dominique was pissed. Seeing her expression, all of his smooth words vanished. A single word dropped from his lips.

"Hey."

"Hey? Hey? That's all you have to say to me?"

Releasing the door, she folded her arms across her middle. The action pushed her breasts higher, giving him a peek at her creamy dark brown skin above the vee opening in her sweater. Reminding himself he wasn't some horny teenaged boy, Denzel jerked his attention upward, meeting her furious stare.

"What would you like me to say? Welcome to Atlanta? Well...technically, this isn't Atlanta, it's just considered part of the Atlanta area."

Muttering words he couldn't quite make out, Dominique spun on her heels and stalked away from him, offering him a delicious view of her ass encased in form fitting jeans. Her rounded curves called out for his touch. *He was so fucking unfocused right now.* Stepping into the room, he turned as he closed the door behind him to get a moment to sever his ogling of her plush body and pull himself together.

She wasn't nearly in the right headspace for the shit floating through his mind. And, if he ever wanted her to be, he needed to get his shit together. The first step on that path was to squash this and get her to stop being mad about moving her into his home.

When she made it to the L-shaped sectional, she stopped in the corner and faced him. She didn't sit. It simply seemed like she wanted to put some distance between the two of them. Striding forward, he eliminated it.

"You know good and well that's not what I meant. Don't play. I've spoken to you countless times since you offered to let me rent one of your properties while I'm here. None of those times did you say it wasn't an option. Yet the driver, you also arranged, left me on the doorstep of this fucking mansion. Tell me the truth. Is this your house?"

"Yes."

"Why am I in your house, Denzel? Is this also your bedroom? Because if it is—"

"It's not my bedroom." Cutting off her tirade, he took another step closer. "It's just like Silvia told you. These are your rooms to use as long as you're here in the area."

Pacing away, Dominique once again put space between them. He guessed when she felt like she'd achieved a large enough buffer, she prodded him again.

"What about my other question? *Why* am I in your house? The pictures I have were definitely not of this place."

"Technically, they were."

"Stop fucking saying technically! Don't skirt the truth. I was annoyed before, but if you keep saying that..." She let the rest of her words trail off.

"I'm telling the truth. The pictures you were sent were of the pool house. I use it as a guest house and allow close friends and family to use it when they come to the area."

Slowly, Denzel advanced to where she stood next to the fireplace. "I'd planned for you to stay there because it's safer than the other properties I have available right now. But at the last minute, I had a family thing come up. So, I had to move you into these rooms instead."

When he got almost within arm's reach, Dominique started shifting away from him. For every step he took forward, she took two, moving away.

"And what exactly kept you from mentioning any of this to me before I showed up?"

Stopping, Denzel quit trying to get closer to her. "If I'd told you I had plenty of room at my place, what would you have said?"

Folding her arms across her middle again, she tilted her head to the side scoffing, "Thanks, but no thanks."

"Exactly. You would've cut off your nose to spite your face and spent the next month or more adding unnecessary stress to your life trying to find a place while living out of a hotel. Why go through all of that when I have all this space? If you're worried I'm doing this to get at you, I'm not."

Well...not entirely. Denzel kept the internal thought to himself. He absolutely set himself up for them to be together, but he had no expectation of her immediately falling into his bed.

"I was born at night, but it wasn't last night." Dominique pursed her lips, giving him a classic Black girl expression. All that was missing was her asking him if she looked like Boo-Boo the Fool.

"Am I interested in you? Absolutely. I've made no secret of my desire to get to know you better. But my main concern in this situation was your comfort and protection. The places Terry first told me about were too close to the Atlanta night life. I felt like the party scene wasn't really your thing.

So, the next best option was the pool house. When I had to let my cousin stay there, this suite of rooms became the final alternative."

"No it's not. I can still book a room at a hotel. I'm sure there's a place secure enough for me to use as my home base while I'm here."

"Dominique...Are you trying to piss me off right now?" If she wasn't, she was doing a damn fine job by suggesting she was going to plant her fine ass anywhere which wasn't here.

"Piss you off? I can't say it's my goal, but why should it matter if it happens? You misled me. No matter which way you try to slice it, that's what happened, and it's so far from being cool!"

In some part of Denzel's mind, he knew he had no right to be mad about her making her own choices concerning where she laid her head. But he wasn't operating from there at the moment. Now, all he heard was a string of words leading him to the conclusion Dominique was doing more than simply *threatening* to leave.

He needed her to stop talking. Just for a minute. Long enough for him to figure out the right thing to say to diffuse the situation. But she didn't. And he didn't have the ability to prevent what happened next. Before he could rein himself in, he had her face captured between his hands and his lips were on hers—stopping the stream of her words.

The things she'd said weren't sweet, but she was. Moaning at the minty saccharine flavor of her mouth, Denzel deepened the kiss. Dominique's sigh, and the softening of her body against his were all the encouragement he needed to gather her closer. If he'd known she tasted this good, he would've flown his ass to Cali to see her before she ever set foot in the state of Georgia.

Her tongue tangled with his, making him wish they had far fewer barriers between them. He wanted to feel her skin against his. Transferring his hold from her face, he wrapped his arms around her, splaying his fingers along her back just above the rise of her plush ass. She felt fucking amazing pressed against his much harder frame.

Knowing he couldn't allow things to get out of control, Denzel started tapering the kiss off with gentle pecks. Loosening his grip, he rested his hands on hers. He wasn't sure if her stunned expression was due to her surprise at being kissed, or at seeing her fingers curled around his lapels. Her gaze was glued to his chest.

She slowly relaxed her digits. Denzel experienced a twinge of regret at ending the kiss once her eyes came back into focus. Apparently, temporarily occupying her mouth hadn't completely erased what she was feeling. It had simply bought him a short reprieve.

"Okay. You're right. It wasn't cool of me to not be straight up. But, I seriously only want you to be somewhere safe. A place where you can relax and know that you won't be bothered. You might not believe me when I say it, but you're about to blow up. You're already a celebrity in your own right, but this show with Mosaic is going to put your name in a lot of mouths.

You probably think you're ready for it, but life as you know it is about to change quickly, baby. Paparazzo will be looking for any opportunity to catch you unawares. Fans are going to get too excited and start overstepping. Out here...None of those people will ever get close enough to breathe in your direction."

Cupping her face again, he lifted her chin until her eyes connected with his.

"You have a right to be upset, but don't paint a target on yourself. Okay?"

Denzel watched the play of emotions dance across her face until she finally seemed to come to a conclusion. The tension in his shoulders released when she silently nodded in agreement. Kissing the tip of her nose, he clasped one of her hands in his.

"Come on. I'll show you around the place."

Chapter Five

IMMEDIATELY NO

Dominique wasn't sure how she was putting one foot in front of the other. According to the way her body felt, she should still be in the center of the room in a melted puddle of want. Denzel Reyes was a very skilled kisser. It led her imagination to wondering what other talents he possessed. Whatever they were, she ought to be terrified to find out.

She hadn't been pretending to be angry. She was furious with him and building up a head of steam to really let him have it, when he'd essentially told her to shut up by way of planting his lips on hers. And damn...It was effective. So effective she'd stopped trying to convince herself she needed to grab her shit and get out of Dodge.

Instead, she was walking beside Denzel with her hand covered in the warmth of his, half listening as he gave her a brief history of the house, pointing towards the windows to the structures detached from the main house.

"We can walk out there too, if you want." Not waiting for a reply, he tugged her in the direction to the right. They'd reached the landing at the top of the stairs. Instead of going down to the first floor, he was leading her in the direction away from her suite of rooms.

As they walked, Dominique's eyes were drawn to the paintings on the walls. They were a mixture of cultures. However, the collection of

Indigenous, African, and Mexican art didn't clash. It added to the overall warmth she'd experienced when she first entered the house.

"These paintings are gorgeous." She'd meant the thought to remain internal, but when it slipped out, she didn't regret offering the compliment.

"Thank you, but I can't take credit. My mama and my Tia Isabel are responsible for the bulk of the decorating. The most I had to do with the process was paying the designer they worked with."

Dominique found herself enamored by the smile stretching his lips when he talked about his mother and his tia. It was obvious that he loved both women dearly.

"They let me think I was in charge though. They showed me options and kept saying things like, 'It's your house, son.' 'You have the final say, sobrino.'"

His chuckle was contagious. She found herself joining in as he pitched his voice differently to mimic each woman. The conversation was light as he showed her the remaining guest rooms before leading her to another set of stairs.

"Good Lord, how big is this place?"

This time, Dominique hadn't intended to keep the thought to herself. It wasn't the quantity of the rooms he'd shown her, it was the size. Each rivaled a hotel suite with space for seating and complete bedroom sets—even if all of those things weren't there.

"It's only three levels above ground. There's an elevator, but I wanted you to see everything."

Nodding, she followed him up the stairs, trying to ignore the fact that he hadn't released his hold on her hand the entire time. It wouldn't hurt her to get some steps in. She'd missed her work out for the day. So, this would have to count as cardio.

The naughty little voice inside her made a cardio suggestion, which Dominique immediately squashed—even as her eyes ate up the way Denzel's suit was contoured to his muscular frame. *Damn.* She may need to find another place simply to preserve her sanity.

As if he'd heard her slip back into her original stance, he shot a glance over his shoulder. He didn't need words to convey his feelings. *Don't even think about it.* Any fight Dominique had in her was left behind in the suite of rooms when he'd kissed the fire out of her words and moved it into her pulsing center.

She honestly didn't want to consider how far things would've gone if he hadn't pulled away. Maybe Syd was right. Dominique's bestie had told her she needed to get laid. According to Syd, Dominique's self-imposed hiatus from men was addling her brain. She might be on to something.

Denzel came to a stop. To Dominique, it happened so abruptly, she almost ran into his back. In reality, she'd been so wrapped up in her thoughts, she hadn't noticed them slowing down until he stopped. Similar to the doorway leading into her suite, there was a curved arch above the door. The difference was, there were two doors barring the entrance. Pushing open one of them, he gave her fingers a tug, pulling her into the room with him.

"**This**...is my bedroom."

His emphasis on *this* was a call back to her question, asking if he'd set her up in his bedroom. Looking around, Dominique wondered why he didn't laugh in her face at the suggestion. Her suite was really nice. Better than many five-star hotels she'd frequented.

But Denzel's suite of rooms was the stuff a homebody's dreams were made of. If the homebody also had very particular, more than a little bougie, taste. Her gaze wandered around the space, landing on the furnishings and entertainment set up. The bar built into one wall was impressive.

Dominique didn't trust herself to walk more than two steps inside. It was enough for her to have seen it. It had been more than fifteen minutes since their lip lock, but the tingles returned to her center if she stared at him too long. Roaming within feet of a useable surface wasn't in her best interest.

"This is really nice. It looks like you have everything you need."

Glancing away from the wall of windows offering a view of the front side of the property, with its green grass and manicured foliage, she returned her gaze to his.

"Thank you. You can look around more if you'd like." Denzel gestured to the open doorway.

Immediately no. Dominique gave a quick headshake. "No, that's okay. I'm good here."

Seemingly unaware of her internal battle, Denzel shed his suit jacket and strode through to what she assumed was his bedroom. Her imagination kicked into high gear when she watched the play of muscles beneath the light blue button-down shirt he wore under the jacket. She wasn't ashamed, but the blaring red light was flashing, saying she was courting danger.

He wasn't even in the same room with her anymore, and his presence filled it to the brim. Checking around for good measure, she made certain she was still within reach of the nearest exit. When she twisted back around, he was standing in front of her again. *How the hell had he done that?*

"What's wrong?" The mirth which normally seemed to dance in his eyes was gone. A dip appeared between his eyebrows.

"Nothing's wrong." Determined not to fold under the effect of his nearness, she tilted her head back and returned his stare. She patently ignored him releasing the buttons at his cuffs.

"Are you sure?"

"Yes. Positive."

Continuing to roll up his shirt sleeves, Denzel assessed her quietly for a few seconds, then nodded in response to a question only he seemed to hear. Folding her hand in his, he guided her from the room, pulling the door closed behind him.

"Why don't we head downstairs? Then, we can go out by the pool, and I can show you the firepit.

"Sounds good."

Going full on denial of whatever was sparking between them was the only way Dominique was able to ignore his now exposed forearms. His tawny skin defied the winter weather when most people with lighter complexions tended to get a little pale.

Taking her on a different route than he'd used to bring them to his bedroom, Denzel led her to the elevator tucked into a corner. Dominique stepped into the car once the door opened, but after it closed, she was sure it wasn't the smartest thing she'd done. They were now in an enclosed space.

His body threw off enough heat that she couldn't help but feel it, and the masculine scent of his cologne assailed her. He didn't drench himself in it. His natural body chemistry just seemed to enhance it. She recognized the fragrance. She'd encountered a few other men who'd worn it. None of them made it smell as delicious as it did on Denzel. Not one.

Relief flooded her when the doors parted and she was able to leave the elevator. They ran into Silvia, who was on her way out for the day. She reminded Dominique to text her about any dietary restrictions or allergies to pass on to the chef. As soon as Silvia was out of sight, Denzel halted their progress through the downstairs.

"What dietary restrictions is Silvia talking about?"

His question was so sudden, Dominique didn't even think before responding.

"She told me earlier the chef would be able to meal prep around any restrictions or allergies I might have and asked me to let her know. Why?"

Denzel's gaze raked over her from the top of her head to her feet, then back up to her eyes once more.

"Are you on a diet or something? Did the studio say some bullshit about you needing to lose weight to keep the role?"

Dominique's breath caught in her throat. The steel laced in his voice combined with the fierceness of his gaze caught her off guard. The implication she'd need to change anything about her physical appearance for the job clearly angered him. *That was unexpected.*

Rushing to reassure him, she instinctively placed both palms on his chest.

"No. Nothing like that. At least they haven't said anything to me about it."

Without thinking, she trailed her fingertips along the outline of his collarbone before lingering at his shoulders.

"If they do, you can tell them to fuck all the way off." Warmth bloomed along her hips as his large hands landed there.

"You're perfect exactly the way you are. Only you get to decide if something about you should change. Even then, I would still land on the side of don't change a thing."

Taking slow, measured breaths, Dominique studied the firm set of his jaw and barely checked fury in his eyes. Other than her family and best friend, no one had voiced their thoughts quite so fiercely. She'd been in the business for years. Body image and self-esteem issues were par for the course among most people in her profession.

It was only the combination of her amazing foundational upbringing and a kick ass therapist which kept her from yielding to the pressures of trying to fit into some mythical mold constructed by people who could never measure up to that standard themselves. In the beginning, she'd tried.

As a theater student, knowing she killed her audition, and having the role go to someone who could barely string three consecutive words together, hurt like a son of a bitch. Having them make no secret of the fact they'd chosen the other actress for aesthetic reasons and not talent hadn't helped. But killing herself in the gym and barely eating wasn't the life Dominique wanted.

Of course, she wanted to be successful in her field. However, she also wanted to be able to actually enjoy the fruits of her labor. Besides, it only took one come to Jesus talk with Belinda Maryann Truman to make it known that she wasn't allowed to be anyone but the fabulous person she was raised to be.

Denzel's fingers flexed against her hip, keeping Dominique tethered to the moment. It was as if he were silently prompting her to verbally agree with his statement. The glint in his eyes and his raised eyebrow were confirmation.

"I'm not dieting, nor do I intend to. I have an exercise regimen. I don't eat crazy because I want to be healthy. But, I don't deprive myself of good food trying to fit into a Hollywood standard."

A curt nod followed her statement. His fingers lingered at her side before he stepped back and recaptured her hand.

"Speaking of exercise, let me show you the gym."

Dominique wished she could say she was surprised by Denzel's home gym. Considering he looked just as fit as he had during his playing days, it was obvious he put in time there. There was an all-in-one tension weight machine along with free weights, treadmill, elliptical and various yoga equipment.

Essentially, almost anything one could be find at a fitness center was present. Including two large televisions mounted on the wall between the windows. After she'd decided to stay, Dominique figured she could use the extra space in her suite to do yoga and maybe the path she'd seen from her window to jog or walk. Now, she had additional options.

"My trainer comes in a few times a week, but I work out on my own most days."

Dominique nodded as she walked over to the bar resting on the Squat Rack. There was no weight on it, but the free weights were arranged on a separate rack nearby. Denzel stood behind her, capturing her gaze in the mirror.

"One thing. If you're going to lift, let me know. I'd prefer you not be down here doing things like that alone. It's not safe. Do you normally work out with a trainer?"

He didn't touch her. But, to Dominique, he might as well have. His voice caressed her as surely as if he'd skimmed her skin with his lightly calloused digits. Why did it send warmth throughout her body when he seemed concerned about her safety? Was she so starved for genuine affection?

Or was it because it didn't match the man she'd decided he was when they met all those years ago? The man she'd observed smiling in photos with various beautiful women didn't appear cruel and uncaring. Yet, it was taking her a minute to merge the two into the person standing behind her, projecting sincere concern for her well-being.

Clearing her throat, she broke eye contact and moved away from the rack. "I'll keep that in mind. I probably won't do any lifting until I find a local trainer or get on my trainer's schedule for virtual sessions."

"If you'd like, I can ask Rob if he knows someone who can work with your schedule."

Dominique's lips quirked in a wry grin at his suggestion. "Is Rob's schedule too busy to add me?"

"I wouldn't know. I figured you'd want to work out with another woman."

Dominique didn't miss the way his fingers flexed before he slid his hands into his pockets, hiding them from her.

"I'm open to any gender for a trainer as long as they're good and understand what my fitness goals are."

"Mhm. Well, Rob typically trains former professional athletes. So, I'm not sure his workout routines would be suitable for what you need."

Whirling on him, Dominique propped her hands on her hips. "What's that supposed to mean?"

"Woman...I know you heard me a few minutes ago when I said you were perfect exactly the way you are." Denzel stepped into her space, sliding one arm around her waist, anchoring her to him.

"I'm not saying you couldn't hang with Rob's workouts. If we don't want our bodies to completely betray us, former professional athletes have to keep up a certain level of activity. It takes a long time to get our body in a condition where we can start to back away from the rigorous training we've done for years to remain in playing shape. What I said has everything to do with him and his methods and nothing to do with you."

"Mhmm...If you say so."

Dominique's voice was breathier than she intended. A couple of quick taps to his biceps and he loosened his hold, allowing her to step away. She needed the distance to remind herself of their current status—which was **not** in a relationship.

One, extremely hot, kiss did not mean they were a thing. And, she didn't permit this level of familiarity with men she hadn't even gone on a proper date with. Even then, it took a while. Deciding a change of scenery was in order, Dominique switched the subject.

"I thought we were going outside to see the pool and the firepit."

Extending a hand, he grasped hers again, leading her out into the hallway. Who knew giving your tenant a tour required hand holding?

"We have to make it quick. It'll be dark soon."

Stopping next to a closet, he removed a coat, holding it up to her. Responding to the silent command, she turned, slipping her arms into the sleeves. How it was possible for her to drown in, and not be completely covered by a garment was an interesting dichotomy. Dominique stood there like a child being dressed by a parent for cold weather while Denzel took care of her. He pushed the sleeves up to expose her hands and rebuttoned the cuff to keep them in place.

Zipping the coat wasn't happening, so he pulled a knit scarf from a hanger and draped it around her neck. When he pulled a fleece hoodie out and slipped it over his head, Dominique stared between the two of them.

"I know you didn't just bundle me up like that little boy from the Christmas movie, then turn around and put on a little hoodie to go out into the same exact climate."

Fixing the collar of the hoodie, Denzel looked unbothered by her comparison.

"I don't get cold very easily. It's almost fifty degrees outside. This will be fine for as long as we're out there."

"If that's the case, I can wear a hoodie too." Dominique tugged at the scarf to take it off.

"Stop that. For more than a decade you've been living in a city which rarely gets below fifty-five degrees. You aren't used to the wind and humidity added to the cold down here."

Cocking an eyebrow, Dominique stared at him.

"You don't know my life."

"Maybe not, but did I lie?" Denzel returned her raised brow with one of his own.

Pursing her lips, Dominique declined to respond. Instead, she searched for the door leading outside. She refused to acknowledge the truth of his statement when she stepped onto the expansive patio and the wind whipped around her, forcing her to gather the edges of the coat and shove her hands in the pockets.

Remarkably, he didn't poke fun at her. However, when she looked up at him, he wore a knowing expression. Mouthing the word, *whatever*, she looked around. Most of the outdoor furniture was stacked along one wall and covered. Decorative bins next to the neat stacks were where she assumed the cushions for the pieces were stored.

A splashing sound drew her attention to the pool. Dominique had noticed earlier that it wasn't covered. She found it curious as most homeowners, in areas where the weather dipped below freezing, covered their pools during the winter months. Frowning, she looked for the source of the splash.

There was a hot tub built into one end of the massive pool with water flowing into it, but the waterfall wasn't tall enough to elicit splashes as loud as what she'd heard. When she finally found the source, she looked from the water to Denzel in disbelief.

"Is he crazy?" Whoever the 'he' was, wasn't important. What she found more urgent was him swimming in these low temperatures.

"I can't say he's completely sane, but the pool is heated. So, as long as he's in there, he's fine."

"Yeah, but he has to get out at some point."

Giving the pool a wide berth, Denzel led her to the first of what he said were two fire pits and gathering areas outside. Close to the little semi-detached bungalow she initially thought she'd be staying in was a cozy set up with a sectional and two chairs. At the center of the grouping was a circular firepit.

Dominique could imagine coming out on a night similar to this one and sitting around the fire just relaxing. It was something she hadn't much opportunity to do at home. Looking at the set up made her consider adding a firepit to her own backyard.

"Hey, Jandro. What's up?"

Dominique turned to see the insanely handsome man who had just greeted Denzel. His wet hair was spiked in certain areas where he'd likely run his hands through it. And, the terry cloth robe he wore was open in the front, revealing his well-defined chest and chiseled abs. His bronzed skin seemed to glisten in the low light.

Well Damn.

Chapter Six

AW HELL NAW

Denzel looked from his cousin, Rafael, to Dominique, who was obviously enjoying the view. Normally, he wouldn't give a shit if a woman looked at another man and found him attractive. But Dominique was *his* Una, and it rubbed him the wrong way for Raffi to stand there with his robe open, glistening like he was on a porn set or some shit.

Of course, he couldn't say any of his internal thoughts aloud. It would make him look like an insecure asshole. He did, however, give his cousin a pointed look which the younger man interpreted perfectly and pulled the edges of the robe together, tying the belt.

"I was just showing Miss Truman around." Shifting closer to Dominique, he rested a hand on her lower back.

"Dominique, this is my cousin Rafael. Raffi, meet Dominique Truman."

Denzel clocked the moment Raffi realized exactly who Dominique was. One hand flew to his mouth and his jaw dropped.

"Oh shit! You're that actress from that movie! Oh wow..."

The eyes, which they'd both inherited from their grandmother, pinged between Denzel and Dominique. They stood watching him cycle through his fanboy moment. Denzel's chest puffed up a little at the awe filled glance his cousin shot him before extending a hand toward Dominique.

"This is wild. It's really nice to meet you, Miss Truman."

Accepting his handshake, Dominique smiled. "Please call me Dominique. I hear we're going to be roommates—sort of."

"No you're not. He's living in the pool house."

Denzel didn't give two shits how snappy he sounded when he said it. It was one thing to let Rafael stay in his pool house. It was something different for him to get the impression the three of them would be hanging out together. And hell, the fuck, no would he be hanging out with Dominique as 'roomies'. That shit had to be nipped in the bud.

Ignoring the nudging elbow from Dominique, Denzel simply stared at her. He meant exactly what he said. He was going to have to talk to his Tia Isabel about her son. For all of his book smarts, he didn't know how to read the room. Denzel scowled as his cousin's face brightened and he smiled, showing every tooth in his head—in Denzel's opinion.

"Yeah! Sweet! Listen, have you guys had dinner? I forgot to order groceries. So, maybe we can order something."

As if in total agreement with the suggestion, Raffi's stomach growled loudly, drawing a giggle from Dominique. Denzel's jaw clenched at the sound. He loved her laugh, but he'd recently discovered he didn't like any other man being the cause of it. Before he could squash the plans he saw written across Raffi's face, Dominique answered.

"We haven't. Denzel has been showing me around. I think Miss Silvia said something about the chef preparing food, but I don't know what it is. Do you know?"

Dominique looked up at Denzel as if she hadn't just invited someone into their private time. Despite fuming below the surface, he didn't deny her.

"I don't, but he knows you're here. So, it's likely he left more than usual in the warmer. We'll have to check."

Looking at Raffi, he knew his tia would give him an earful if she heard he was 'starving her baby'. Pointing over his shoulder to the pool house, he suggested his cousin get dressed and join them.

"If you already have a list of the groceries you want, leave it for Silvia, and she'll make sure your fridge and cabinets are restocked."

Denzel knew Silvia had made certain there was food when Raffi first arrived. Apparently, in the few days he'd been there, he'd already gone through it. Not surprising. Reyes men tended to have high metabolisms. Although Raffi was technically a Lopez, he'd taken that after his mom's side of the family.

It had gotten darker quicker than Denzel anticipated, so he postponed the rest of the tour and led Dominique back to the house. Separating at the downstairs closet, he reluctantly let her go back to her rooms while he went to his to shower and change into something more comfortable.

Twenty minutes later, he stood in the kitchen looking over the food the chef had left for them in the warmer. As he expected, there was more than usual. But, it wasn't enough for three. Not with Raffi's appetite. Lucky for him, all Denzel had to do was get the meal prep containers from the refrigerator to add to what was there.

He was considering what wine to pair with the meal when Raffi appeared. At least he had the courtesy of wearing jeans instead of the sweatpants to match the hoody he wore.

"Que pasa, primo?" Raffi plopped onto one of the chairs on the other side of the island from Denzel.

Denzel glanced up at him before putting his attention on the bottles of wine.

"Nothing much. Trying to pick a wine to go with dinner."

Raffi leaned forward, propping his elbows on the countertop. "Wine? Are we eating fancy? Do I need to go change?"

Denzel quirked an eyebrow before looking down at himself and back at his cousin.

"I'm going to ignore that question, because you're too smart not to see I'm in joggers and a t-shirt. Also, having wine with a meal isn't eating fancy. It's exactly what it is. Having a drink with dinner."

Laying his palms on the marble countertop, Raffi shrugged. "If you say so. I didn't know you had gotten so bougie. What happened to a bottle of cerveza with a meal?"

Covering the distance between them with two steps, Denzel used a flat hand to deliver a swiping smack to the back of Raffi's thick skull.

"Hey! What's that for?"

"A reminder of who you're fucking with." Denzel gave Raffi a sharp look before returning to his selection process.

"I don't know who you've been listening to, but experiencing the variety life has to offer doesn't make you bougie. Even if it does, who gives a fuck? What's not gonna happen is you living in my pool house trying to judge me for enjoying the money I worked hard to make. You can always try your luck at graduate housing."

Putting up his hands, Raffi squirmed in his seat. "Whoa, primo. No need to start talking about me moving out. I was just making an observation."

"No, you weren't. You were passing judgment. And if anyone shouldn't be yielding to that kind of crap, it should be you. Or did you forget the way some of our cousins looked at you when you said you wanted to study astrophysics? When was the last time they tried to talk shit to you about still being in school at twenty-five while some of them are already on their second or third baby momma with full-time jobs?"

Nodding, Raffi's expression was somber when he met Denzel's gaze. "You're right. I don't know why I said that. I'm just..."

"Trying to come off as regular to fit in."

Denzel completed his cousin's sentence. Deciding on the slightly sweeter red, he placed the other bottle of wine back into the rack beneath the counter and closed the door. Stepping in front of Raffi, he relaxed his posture. Placing a hand on his cousin's shoulder, he gave it a quick tap.

"I know it's hard to get out of the mindset, but you don't have to do that here. Just be yourself. How many times do I have to tell you not to worry about impressing those fools? If they don't want anything more or different for themselves, it's not your problem."

"Yeah...I know. Old habits." Raffi dipped his head and tapped his fingers on the countertop.

"Time to let those habits die, cuz." Denzel passed him the bottle of wine. "Here, put this on the table over there."

He'd decided to eat at the table in the kitchen area. The formal dining room was rarely used unless he had a large gathering. With it just being the three of them for dinner, the round five-seater table would work just fine. It was near the bay window offering a view of the pool area and the expansive back yard. Although it was now dark outside, the area was still visible due to the soft solar lighting illuminating the pool and the path leading to the pool house.

When Raffi returned, Denzel handed him plates and utensils to set the table. Looking at his watch, he wondered if he should wait for her or call Dominique to remind her of dinner. They hadn't set a specific time, but he'd told her it shouldn't take him long to shower and change.

He'd just pulled out his phone when she rounded the corner into the room. It appeared she'd taken the opportunity to get more comfortable as well. A loose blouse, along with roomy lounge pants, covered her from neck to toes. Pocketing his phone, he smiled.

"There you are. I was just about to call to let you know dinner was ready."

She returned his smile as she came farther into the room. "Well, I'm here." Looking from Raffi setting the table to Denzel, she raised her eyebrows. "Do we all have assignments?"

Glancing at his cousin, Denzel shook his head. "Not this time. We've got it covered. You just have a seat."

Dominique selected her seat while Denzel and Raffi put the food on the table. Despite his bout of saltiness when his cousin invited himself to dinner, Denzel thought the evening progressed well. Maybe Raffi wasn't as oblivious as Denzel thought he was. While they discussed a variety of topics, Raffi was polite and composed. And most of all, he refrained from grinning in Dominique's face like he didn't have home training.

"That's it. Last one. Good workout."

Rob tapped Denzel on the shoulder. The trainer stood behind him to spot him as he lowered the weight back onto the rack. Sweat rolled down Denzel's face. Grabbing a nearby towel, he captured the salty wetness before it could drip into his eyes.

"Thanks, man."

The sports drink quenched his thirst, but Denzel chased it with some cool water to finish the job. While Rob gathered his things, Denzel wiped down the equipment he'd used. Even though he knew the staff would come in and give it a thorough clean, habit controlled his movements. Soon, the two were walking down the hall engaged in a light banter about the final teams in contention for the upcoming Championship game.

"I know they pay you the big bucks to give your expert opinion, but I still say the *Red Tails* aren't gonna go the distance this year. Last year was a fluke."

Denzel shot Rob a glance of disbelief. "Have we been watching the same team for the past two seasons? Besides them going nearly undefeated both seasons, they'd been showing steady improvement before Kaylen Payne rounded out the team as quarterback."

Rob shook his head. "So, I guess they're your pick this year?"

Denzel held up a hand. "I didn't say all that. I was just pointing out some stuff for you to consider."

"Uh-huh..." Whatever else Rob was planning to say trailed off.

Denzel followed the path of his stare to see Dominique at the top of the stairs. His steps faltered, and he came to a stop. Wearing another pair of hip-hugging jeans belted at the waist along with a crisp white button down, she placed one hand on the railing. His eyes moved to the sliver of skin exposed when she took her first step down the stairs.

Her shirt was knotted in the front for a casual look which, revealed the slightest hint of her stomach when she shifted. The sparkling belt buckle called even more attention to the area, pulling the outfit together. *Where the fuck was she going looking so delicious?*

It wasn't until the question filtered across his mind that Denzel remembered Rob's presence. *Aw hell naw.* Rob's stare was glued to Dominique as she continued down the stairs, unaware.

There probably wasn't a soul living who could've prevented Denzel from putting an elbow to the man's ribs to stop him from gawking at Dominique. Denzel felt no guilt when the trainer grabbed his side and gave a startled yelp.

"What the hell, man?"

"Watch your eyes." Denzel grumbled.

"What? That doesn't make any sense. I see things with my eyes. How am I supposed to watch them?"

Turning on the man, Denzel pierced him with a hard glare. "Don't act like you don't know what I mean. Put 'em somewhere else, and don't stare at her."

Rob's eyes widened and understanding washed over his face. "Oh. That's you?"

"Is this my house?"

"Well...yeah." Rob's response was tinged with mild confusion.

Denzel didn't explain further. From his peripheral, he noticed Dominique within hearing range. Giving her his full attention, he struggled not to push Rob out the front door and drag her back up the stairs. When she was closer, he noticed she held a pair of stiletto heeled ankle boots in her other hand. The shiny color matched the topaz stones in her belt buckle.

"Good morning." Her smile was bright, but reserved.

"Good morning, U—beautiful." Denzel quickly covered his near slip. He'd only referred to her as Una in his thoughts. She wasn't ready to hear that aloud. No matter how much he wanted to stake his claim, he held his tongue.

Extending his hand, he helped her down the last few stairs until she stood between him and Rob in the foyer. Manners dictated he introduce the other man. So, Denzel performed the introductions quickly. The sooner he was done, the sooner Rob could get his ass out of Denzel's home.

"Rob, meet Dominique Truman. Dominique, this is my trainer, Rob Morton."

It was safe to assume Rob had caught on since he simply greeted Dominique without attempting to shake her hand. That was fine, because Denzel couldn't promise he wouldn't take measures others might consider drastic if the trainer attempted to touch her.

"It's nice to meet you, Rob. Denzel was saying you might know someone I could work with while I'm in the area."

"I'm sure I can help if you let me know what your goals are. I work with a couple of ladies who I'm sure would be happy to take you on."

Holding Dominique's hand firmly in his grasp, Denzel worked to keep his expression neutral while the two spoke. It wasn't as if Rob wasn't professional. Denzel had to admit after he got over his stunned staring, the trainer reverted to his business persona.

However, Denzel didn't care for the way Dominique's gaze swept over Rob's fit frame. It was so quick, if he hadn't been looking directly at her, he would've missed it. She didn't gawk, and to anyone else, he was sure it appeared she was only being friendly. His logical mind said that's all it was. But, he'd established logic didn't always apply when it came to her.

Looking at his watch, Rob started to back away.

"I'll put some names together and send them to Den—if that's okay."

"Sounds like a plan." Denzel responded, relieved the other man was leaving before he put his foot in his mouth, trying to get rid of him.

Releasing Dominique's fingers with a light squeeze, he walked Rob the rest of the way to the door. Dominique called out her thanks and goodbyes before turning in the direction of the kitchen.

Standing next to the door, Denzel opened it ushering his trainer out with a wave of his hand.

"After I check with Jessica and Kam, I'll shoot you a message."

"Thanks. I appreciate it."

"No problem." Rob stepped out onto the porch, then turned to face Denzel. "I know what you said, but it doesn't really seem like you've locked that beauty down."

"Rob, we've been cool a long time. Don't make me fire your ass and cut you off."

Chuckling, Rob turned away and trotted down the short flight of stairs toward his vehicle parked in the circular drive. Denzel closed the front door and set off in the direction Dominique had taken. As he got closer to the kitchen, he picked up the traces of a conversation between her and Silvia. Rounding the corner, he saw Dominique leaning against the island while Silvia stood on the other side in front of the coffee maker, offering her a cup.

"I'm sure I can get it myself. Thank you though."

Dominique straightened to her full height in her sock feet. Without his consent, Denzel's eyes raked over her figure before he could stop them. Coming to a stop next to her at the countertop, he finally looked up at Silvia.

"Buenos Dias, Denzel."

"Buenos Dias, Silvia."

His lip quirked in a slight smile at her attempt to be formal. She'd softened some since the previous day, but Silvia remained a little stiff. Internally shrugging, Denzel brushed it off. She'd get over it. He wouldn't apologize to anyone for making sure his Una was safe and protected.

Besides, Silvia couldn't stay mad at him. Before the end of the morning, she'd be back to her old self. She was more than halfway there. The fact that she was in the kitchen preparing to cook breakfast was proof.

Despite Dominique's assurances she could fix her own coffee, Silvia waved her off—just as Denzel expected. In less than a minute, a mug along with creamer and a sugar dish were placed on the counter in front of Dominique. Murmuring her thanks, she slid onto one of the tall bistro style chairs in front of the island.

After washing his hands, Denzel sat on the seat next to her. Observing her fixing her coffee to her liking shouldn't have been so mesmerizing. Yet, he couldn't take his eyes off her. Accepting his own mug of morning brew from Silvia, he focused his attention on it for a moment.

"You're up pretty early and already dressed." Denzel glanced at Dominique, then back to his cup, stirring in a cube of sugar. "So, what's on your agenda today?"

Pausing after taking a sip from her mug, Dominique put it down and cleared her throat.

"I have an appointment to take care of my credentials and a few small things at the studio this morning."

"Oh yeah? You didn't mention it last night." He wasn't keeping tabs on her, but he thought he had another couple of days before she'd be ready to venture out.

"I didn't realize I had to run my schedule by you." Dominique lifted one perfectly arched eyebrow.

Releasing his mug, Denzel placed one hand on her jean clad thigh, giving it a light squeeze.

"Don't be like that. I never said anything about you clearing your schedule with me. I'm just surprised you didn't mention it when we were talking last night."

Dominique's gaze pinged between the hand on her leg and his face. Neither moved for a beat until she relaxed her shoulders and went back to her coffee cup.

"I thought I'd have a couple of days, but Tammy called this morning and said I was cleared to go in and get it over with. It would leave my weekend free before things really got rolling on Monday."

Mentally calculating, Denzel nodded as she spoke. While his mind worked, he stroked her outer thigh with his thumb. He seemed incapable of not touching her when they were close to one another.

"Monday is good. That gives us time for you to meet Nikki and the team from GPS. I'll give them a call to move things up a little."

"Excuse me? Meet who? When?"

Chapter Seven

CLAUDE HAVE MERCY

Dominique stared at Denzel with wide eyes, waiting for his response. She was certain he hadn't just insinuated he'd made arrangements, yet again, without talking to her about it. When she finally blinked, it was a slow blink of disbelief.

"Don't look at me like that. I didn't go behind your back to do anything. I was planning to talk to you about it this morning. There was no way for me to know you had something else on your schedule."

"So, this is my fault?" Dominique tilted her head to the side, staring at him.

"There is no fault here, baby. Okay?"

Denzel squeezed her thigh and Dominique tried to ignore how good his hand felt on her leg, or the tingle she experienced when he called her *baby*. She also blocked out Silvia standing at the stove. The older woman was most assuredly ear hustling, but she didn't say a word to either of them.

"Well, since you now know I have things scheduled for today, do you mind cluing me in on the latest way you're planning my life here?"

Before Dominique caught on to what was happening, Denzel had her hand in his as he stalked out of the kitchen.

"Excuse me!" Not wanting to cause more of a scene in front of Silvia, Dominique whisper yelled as she walked quickly to keep up with his long strides.

"Nope."

Denzel's one word response was tossed over his shoulder as he continued down the hallway, not stopping until he reached a door nearly halfway down the corridor. Pushing it open, he led her inside. Once she was over the threshold, he closed it. The snick of the lock got her full attention.

"Was that really necessary?"

Before she could fold her arms across her middle and pierce him with the full force of her glare, she found herself in his embrace. With one hand on her back, he used the other to lift her chin so they could maintain eye contact.

"Yes. It was necessary. We need privacy so we can get a few things cleared up."

Dominique's mouth went dry, and she clamped her lips closed in an attempt to regain some moisture. She didn't have to wonder where the wetness had gone. The tightening of her core wasn't the least bit subtle. Although unexpected. The line from his firm jaw and the growl in his voice to the relocation of her body's natural fluids was clear. Not what she expected. But absolutely a straight line to her under used lady bits.

Thankfully, he didn't expect her to form words. The way his gaze bore into hers rendered her speech capabilities useless. Which was a feat within itself, because she always had something to say. The most she might be able to drum up was a breathy moan. She would've felt some kind of way about that, but Denzel was all up in her space and she couldn't remember why she was upset to begin with.

"We're both grown here." The fingers he splayed on her back flexed as if to emphasize his point. "But, you seem to take issue with me looking out for you."

Dominique was proud of herself when actual sentences formed and spilled from her lips. "I don't have an issue with you wanting to look out for me. It would be nice if you let me in on the plans."

Lowering his head, Denzel's voice was just above a whisper. "What do you think I'm doing here, baby? I haven't made any decisions on your behalf. I simply got the ball rolling, because I'm more familiar with who's available in the area. That's all."

Dominique heard the sincerity in his voice, even though she attempted to break away from the intensity of his gaze. However, her eyes refused to obey her, and continued to stare into his. Her lower lip protruded, but she couldn't stop the pout. Why did he have to pull her close to his hard body then start making valid points? Who asked him to do all that?

Appearing to take her silence as a green light, Denzel loosened his grip as he explained GPS was Grant Protective Services and Nikki was the head of personal protection for high-profile clients. Her brow lifted when he used the words high profile, but she had the good sense not to contradict him. They obviously didn't have the same criteria for who the term applied to.

"I understand the adjustments you'd have to make, so I thought Nikki and her team would be a great option. They aren't typical bodyguards."

"How so?"

"Their team includes women and men. They're great at blending in. So, to anyone on the outside, it simply looks like you have a couple of friends tagging along with you."

"That doesn't sound bad, but I was planning to contact the parent company for the Ryd app I used when I was in L.A. The app isn't available here yet, but I think At Your Service has an office. I was hoping they'd be able to squeeze me in since I'm a regular Ryd client."

Denzel's brow lifted as if he was surprised she had a plan of her own.

"I've heard of them. But now you don't have to worry about whether someone can fit you in. GPS has already confirmed availability. They just need to meet with you and get a start date."

His statement spawned a series of questions in Dominique's mind. Considering what he'd just said, she had no doubt GPS offered elite services. Elite services typically required hefty contracts and fees. She wasn't in the poor house, but she hadn't budgeted for dropping six figures on personal security for the next six months.

As she did in many situations which called for serious contemplation, she considered what her parents would say if she told them about it. The moment the thought entered her mind, she dismissed it. Those two hadn't gotten over her being in California alone. So, they would prefer she had security like she was the first lady of the United States. Dominique hadn't missed how easily they accepted the detail Zaria had, courtesy of Andrei.

Her dad had even asked her why she didn't have someone with her all the time the way Zee did. He wasn't convinced her use of Ryd was enough when she went out in Los Angeles. Knowing their advice would be to accept the meeting and figure out how to make it work, Dominique couldn't draw on their normal sage counsel.

Finally able to tear herself away from Denzel's assessing gaze, Dominique noticed her hand placement. Her palms rested on Denzel's impressive, sports shirt covered, chest. The shirt was still slightly damp from his morning exercise, but she couldn't bring herself to be concerned about him transferring the wetness to her.

"You're awfully quiet. Does that mean you're thinking, or I can confirm a time with GPS for you to meet Nikki?"

Ending her inspection of her digits on his broad chest, she allowed herself to be trapped by his penetrating stare again. Asking the question at the forefront of her mind, Dominique didn't concern herself with posturing.

"GPS sounds nice, but they also sound expensive."

Denzel's hold tightened, and the tiny distance between them shrank even more.

"Don't worry about expense. I already have a contract with them."

Shaking her head, Dominique pressed against him to get some space, hoping it would help her keep her sanity.

"I can't ask you to do that."

"You're not asking. I've got it. Next topic. You're dressed to leave the house. Do you have a set time they're expecting you at the studio?"

Quirking an eyebrow, Dominique prepared to assert herself. Because, no he didn't just tell her to shut up again without saying shut up. Not to mention he didn't at least kiss her to soften the blow.

"Don't look at me like that. We can agree I've got it covered and discuss your plans for the day. I have someone I can free up to take you to the studio and wherever else you wanted to go today. I just need to know what time you have to be there."

"Why are you so insistent on having someone with me?"

The hand Denzel had on her nape dipped into her hair and her face was tugged closer to his.

"Come on, baby. What would I look like having you down here without someone to look out for you when I'm not able to be there? I'm not that man. When you set foot out of these doors, there will always be someone with you to watch your back, front, and sides."

The shiver which shot down Dominique's spine was in competition with the heat blooming in her center. The man she'd spoken to on the phone over the past few weeks had been amiable with pockets of serious-ness. But the man holding her in his arms was a whole different animal. His determination reminded her of the conversation she had with Zee after Andrei assigned her first lady detail fairly early on in their rela-tionship.

Her cousin hadn't put up a significant fuss with Andrei, but she'd groused about it a little when she and Dominique spoke. Being on the outside, it was easy for Dominique to see Andrei's perspective. Besides him wanting Zaria protected, he was an extremely wealthy man in a business with a chunk of its roots in organized crime. Which meant some people still solved their problems with violence.

Her advice had been to remind Zee of her importance to him, and she just had to suck it up and let the man protect her. Now, Dominique's own words were coming back to haunt her. She couldn't even pretend there wasn't something between her and Denzel.

That delusion had sailed long before he walked her to the door of her rooms the previous night. As undefined as it was, there was defi-nitely something blossoming between them.

Belinda Truman hadn't raised her to be a person who planted her head in the sand. So, Dominique determined this wasn't an issue she needed to fight. Was it really so bad to have someone with her in an unknown space whose sole purpose was to watch out for her well-being? No. It wasn't.

Other than the teeny-tiny part of her which wanted to object to see what Denzel would do next, Dominique conceded his points. Immediately picking up on her relaxed stance, Denzel dipped down covering her lips with his, coaxing her to open and allow him entry. Being surrounded by him while he slipped his tongue into her mouth was a heady feeling, drawing a sigh from Dominique.

Damn. This man can kiss. The heat at her center began to spread, causing her to clench her thighs in an attempt to hold herself together. When Denzel's arm tightened, she couldn't ignore the stiffness poking her just below her belt buckle. *Claude have mercy.* That felt like a whole lot to handle, but her neglected core was campaigning for the opportunity to try it.

Only when he pulled away did Dominique realize she was hanging on to him just as tightly as he'd held her. Her fingertips brushed against the close-cropped hair at his nape.

"Now...what time do you need to be at the studio?"

It took a few seconds for his question to penetrate her lustful fog, but Dominique eventually got it together.

"I told them I'd be there by mid-morning. So, ten thirty-ish."

Nodding, he finally gave her the space she needed to fully concentrate. Releasing his hold, he walked over to the desk she hadn't even noticed was in the room. Her surprise at seeing an actual landline phone was only squelched when he pressed a few buttons and began a conversation with a man he referred to as Juan.

There was something in the way his demeanor shifted when he gave the other man instructions and asked questions. The command in his presence caused a stir in her nether regions. What was it they said about powerful men? She'd never been in a position to see this side of Denzel Reyes, but it looked damn good on him.

So good, she forgot she was supposed to be upset with him for making plans for her life without consulting her. That little nugget was swept to the back of her mind as she listened to him discuss who Juan thought would work best to take her where she needed to go today. She was caught up in her stare fest, to the point she didn't notice when he ended the call.

"Juan is going to send Vic around with the car in about thirty minutes. It should be long enough for you to have breakfast."

By the time he finished speaking, Denzel was back in front of her. Happy he didn't mention her ogling him like some lovesick teenager, Dominique snapped out of her trance when she could once again feel the heat wafting from his body.

"Um...yeah. It should be plenty of time. I don't normally eat a big breakfast anyway."

The frown forming on Denzel's face prompted her to explain before he went off on a tangent about her watching her weight for no reason.

"It has nothing to do with trying to count calories or anything similar. I'm just not much of a big eater in the mornings. I usually have a bowl of oatmeal or yogurt with fruit and grains."

"That doesn't sound like nearly enough to give you the energy you need to make it through the toughest part of the day." Denzel stroked her biceps with his fingertips while he stared at her as if he expected her to refute his statement.

Why did it sound as if there was something else he wanted to say regarding eating and energy? Despite the undertone in his voice, he didn't make any inferences. Instead, he led her back to the kitchen where Silvia was plating breakfast.

Attempting to make a liar out of her, Dominique's stomach growled when she smelled the savory aroma of sausage and saw the steam wafting off the fluffy eggs on the plates. As if they'd done so every morning for years, Denzel pulled out a chair for Dominique at the table. When he came back with their plates, she was done pouring orange juice into both of their glasses.

They slipped into general conversation about their activities for the week as they ate. It was very domestic. Dominique reminded herself not to get caught up. She was only there for a limited time. According to the production schedule she was given, it shouldn't take the entire six months for them to shoot all the episodes and wrap on the first season of *The Clarke Files*.

However, Tammy had received the contract for a feature film which should be ready to begin filming right around the time she was done with the show. Being the title character of a show was a first for Dominique, but she was hopeful playing the unconventional detective would allow her to spread her acting wings more.

Taking the last bite of her toast covered in peach marmalade, Dominique looked up to see Denzel watching her.

"What?" Speaking around the bite, her eyebrows lifted. A quick glance at his plate showed he'd finished eating.

"Nothing. I'm just enjoying seeing you enjoy your food. Especially considering you said you don't normally eat much for breakfast."

Wiping her mouth, Dominique finished chewing before she replied.

"I was hungrier than usual today. Now, I'm gonna be struggling to stay awake. I'll need constant stimulation until this lump in my belly stops trying to make me take a nap."

She smiled, holding in her laugh at the inside joke only she caught. Her mama was always saying the quickest way to get an over active or irritable child to settle down was to put a lump in their belly. Feed them something hearty, and they'd be out in less than twenty minutes. Why she remembered the saying at this moment, she couldn't say.

"Constant stimulation?" Denzel's gaze raked over her face before dropping.

Why was he like this? Dominique pursed her lips and lifted one eyebrow, giving him a classic, 'really?' expression. Her face projected something totally different from what was happening in her center. Her statement had been completely innocuous to her, but hearing those two words repeated back in his deep voice sent heat straight to her middle with the implications of **what** *constant stimulation* he could provide.

Thankfully, she didn't have to answer. A knock against the door-frame broke through the moment, and they both turned to see an unassuming man standing in the doorway.

"Hey, Vic. Come in and meet Miss Truman."

Denzel stood and was behind her seat, helping her to stand before Dominique could push away from the table. Up close, Vic was taller than he'd looked in the doorway, but she stuck by her original assessment of him being unassuming. If she didn't know he was a bodyguard, she wouldn't necessarily have guessed it was his profession.

"Miss Truman. Nice to meet you."

Nodding politely, Dominique returned the greeting. "I forgot my purse, but as soon as I get it, I'll be ready."

"No problem, ma'am. I'll wait for you outside."

"Okay. Thank you, Vic."

Vic left the room, leaving Dominique and Denzel alone once more. Although she was aware there was staff, Dominique still reached for her plate. Since Denzel brought them to the table, she grabbed his as well.

"You don't have to do that."

When he placed his hand on her arm, the warmth of it penetrated the fabric of her shirt. But instead of heating her skin, his touch caused goose pimples to sprout on her flesh. How the hell was she going to survive sharing space with this man without climbing him like a jungle gym? She held out very little hope the size of the house would be a barrier.

"It's fine. Miss Silvia cooked, and you brought the plates to the table. Putting the dirty dishes in the dishwasher isn't going to send me to my bed with the vapors."

Denzel's chuckle reached right into Dominique's center and wrapped around her core. *Why the hell is he sexy doing normal shit?*

"The vapors? Have you been binge watching period shows or some-thing? I haven't heard that phrase since my mama went on a kick with some show set in ancient Rome."

Putting space between them, Dominique took their empty dishes to the dishwasher.

"I'll have you know, it's a very common phrase."

"For an eighty-year-old, which you definitely are...not."

Dominique whirled around only to find herself face to chin with Denzel. Her height usually meant she was equal to or taller than many of her male co-stars, but Denzel Reyes was six foot four inches of virile man. Who was standing entirely too close for her to keep her wits about her. Clearing her throat, she stepped around him.

"Well, I don't have time to debate the regular use of vocabulary words. Vic is waiting for me."

The words had barely left her mouth before Denzel's fingers wrapped around her wrist and they were once again facing each other. He'd released her wrist, sliding his hand along her lower back. His beard tickled her upper lips before he connected their mouths in a kiss which couldn't be called chaste, but wasn't deep enough to be a prelude to anything more.

"Vic can wait, but that couldn't." With another soft peck, he pulled away. "Have a good day."

With her fingers absently caressing her bottom lip, Dominique watched Denzel as he left the room. He'd been long gone from the empty doorway before she remembered herself.

"Umm... Yeah. You have a good day, too."

Chapter Eight

WHAT'S THAT'S SUPPOSED TO MEAN?

Denzel thought he deserved a pat on the back for having the ability to walk away from Dominique. She looked mildly dazed, but his body was making suggestions neither of them had the time to follow through on. Although he'd wanted Dominique in his life and his bed for longer than he cared to admit, he had no intention of rushing her into anything.

What was it they said about the road to Hell and good intentions? Yeah...he'd have to figure out his next move, and soon. Being under the same roof with her, knowing she was one floor below his, had made it nearly impossible for him to get to sleep the previous night. He was surprised Rob hadn't said something about how long it took him to get into the groove of things during their session.

After he dressed, Denzel went to his home office. Traces of Dominique's perfume lingered in the air. The scent wasn't strong, but he'd become so attuned to her already that it stood out to him. The lightly floral scent had fruity undertones which made his mouth water to seek out and kiss every place she'd applied it.

When his dick plumped in his pants, Denzel had to quickly redirect his thoughts before he ended up in the bathroom rubbing one out. His reaction to her being so near had him feeling like a teenager again—all hormones with poor impulse control.

Plopping into his chair, he lifted the lid on his laptop, then pulled out his cellphone to check in with his assistant. He'd found it worked better for him to not maintain an office outside of his home. So, some of his employees worked from home as he did. For those who performed better in an office environment, he reserved a section in one of his commercial properties. He didn't carry a large staff, so it wasn't an issue. Also, it gave him a place to gather with everyone when necessary.

The screen of his cellphone lit up with an incoming call. Tapping the display, he answered.

"Hello, Ms Reed."

"Hey yourself, Mr. Reyes. I'll give you a pass on the Ms Reed stuff, but we both know it's not necessary."

"Oh no. It's definitely necessary. Me and Ash are cool, and it's gonna stay that way."

"Mr. Reyes. I didn't call you to discuss Asher Peterson. He has no say in how friendly I am or am not with anyone. Besides, this is business."

Denzel's lips tipped up in a grin as he thought about the first time he met Nikki Reed. He'd been out at a lounge with one of the guys from the station. They were sitting at the bar when Nikki took the seat next to him. Without effort or acknowledgement, she had the attention of every man in the vicinity—his included.

As stunning as she was, Denzel had done nothing more than issue a polite hello before they were interrupted by his former teammate Asher Peterson. Or as they'd called him in San Diego, Big Bama Boy. The chemistry between those two was off the charts. So, it took very little encouragement for Denzel to back off. Truth be told, his main attraction to her was because she reminded him of Dominique in a way.

What could he say? He had a type. They were both tall with smooth, dark brown skin. While Nikki topped six feet, Dominique was just under that mark, with more abundant curves. It was completely by chance he learned she was in private security. They'd met again when he visited the GPS offices before signing a long-term contract with them. The two had become friendly afterward over the course of Denzel using GPS services.

Leaving the topic of their mutual acquaintance behind, Denzel shifted gears. "Thank you for getting back to me so quickly."

"Not a problem. I had a feeling that we'd need to speak sooner rather than later, when we initially set things up."

"Your instincts were correct. Dominique wants to get out and about before things officially kick off. I want her people in place as soon as we can arrange it."

"Did you speak with her about it? I know this is on your tab, but you know how we do things."

Much like Jasper Hunt, who handled security for Carver, it was rare for GPS to take on contracts to protect people who weren't on board with having private security. They'd make accommodations for being discreet and not so in-your-face with their protection style. However, they made it clear they weren't the kind of firm for people who habitually put themselves in dangerous situation by sneaking away from their security details.

"Of course, I spoke to her. It's the reason I wanted to move the meeting up so the two of you could meet, and we could get the ball rolling sooner."

"Great. Just had to check the box to make sure. Give me a second."

The call went silent as Nikki apparently placed him on hold. She didn't keep him waiting long. Before he could open his email to read the first message, she was back.

"Thank you for holding."

Regardless of their friendly acquaintance, Nikki was all business when they discussed the timing for Dominique to meet the suggested members of her security team. When Nikki proposed an early evening appointment, Denzel shot Dominique a message. Once he received a response, he locked in the time.

Done with the business portion of the call, Nikki's professional persona slipped once again.

"I can't wait to meet Miss Dominique Truman."

"Oh yeah?" Denzel leaned into his high-backed office chair. "You work with celebrities often, don't you? I would think getting star-struck was a thing of the past."

Nikki's light laughter filtered through. "I do work with famous people regularly. But that's not why I'm looking forward to meeting Miss Truman. To be clear, I do love her work. But I want to meet the woman who inspired you to make these kinds of moves."

Frowning, Denzel looked at the phone like it was a foreign object in his hand.

"What's that supposed to mean?"

"Denzel, don't pretend we haven't run into one another around the city on many occasions. And each time you've had a different woman on your arm. None of those times have you contacted AG about getting any of them their own bodyguards."

Tapping his desk, he wanted to ignore her calling him out, but he couldn't. She was right. At least partially. While only Andrei and Nikki had brought it up, Denzel was tired of people throwing his affiliation with beautiful women in his face.

He was aware of the optics, even if the majority of the time he wasn't connected to the women he'd been seen with. More often than not, he was simply the nearest body when the cameras came out. Could he have made it clear he wasn't with those women? Yes. Did he? No. He didn't think it was necessary.

"I'm going to pretend you didn't go there and end this conversation here. Dominique and I will see you this evening."

He didn't miss Nikki's hearty laugh as he ended the call. It was obvious she didn't give two fucks about him being short with her. Denzel wasn't angry, but he refused to go into his history with anyone aside from Dominique. Even then, he would only go so far.

However, Nikki bringing it up highlighted a potential issue. One he should prepare himself to navigate. But, not right now. At the moment, he had business interests requiring his attention. Opening a chat window with his assistant, he officially got his day started. Working steadily, he didn't come up for air until his cellphone rang again. Looking at the display, his lips stretched into a wide smile.

With a tap to the screen, he accepted the video call. Placing his phone on a stand, he grinned at his father.

"Hey Pops!"

"Hijo."

Slipping into Spanish, Denzel stared at his father's face on the small screen. He didn't appear sad, but he wasn't his normal jovial self either.

"What's going on?"

Raking a hand down his face, his father shook his head. "Not much, son. Other than your tia calling me nine hundred and eighty times a day to ask if I've spoken to you about Raffi, and if he's settled in okay. It's almost like she doesn't have a phone of her own to call her twenty-five-year-old son and ask him all of those questions. No. Instead, she calls me. She could even call you, but no. She calls me. Always me."

Chuckling, Denzel relaxed his shoulders. "You know why she calls you, Pops."

When his father simply stared at him, Denzel shook his head and laughed even harder.

"I don't see anything funny. Your tia is trying to make me bald like her husband."

Stroking his hand over the salt and pepper hair he had smoothed back in a low ponytail, his father frowned.

"It's funny because this isn't anything new, Pops. And just so you know, your sister has been calling me too. I just don't answer every time. And when I do, I remind her of two things. One, she has her son's phone number. Two, he's in school—not a war zone."

His father's response was a deeper frown. Sitting back, Denzel slowly swiveled his chair from side to side.

"Tia only calls you like that because you spoil her. You're her big brother who fixes everything for her. She's anxious, and you're supposed to fix it."

Denzel's parents were both the eldest child in their respective families. They'd purposely only had one child because they'd already spent so much of their life helping their parents raise their siblings. As far as they were concerned, one was enough. It hadn't been so bad being an only child. He was the eldest of all the grandchildren, which gave him a special place with his abuela.

It did, however, come with the drawback of being expected to carry the mantle, just as his parents had. Which is how he ended up with Raffi in his pool house. He could've put him in one of the rental units, but his mama had taught him family and business didn't mix. So, the pool house was the option he could live with. He didn't rent space at his home. He had guests. That way, there were no expectations.

"Hey, Pop. Does Mama know Tia Isabel is blowing up your phone?"

The way his father quickly checked over his shoulder was all the answer Denzel needed. He figured she didn't. He'd also hazard a guess his aunt only called during the day when his dad was taking care of things at one of his restaurants.

Because they were both the consummate older siblings, his parents had come to an agreement years ago to always put each other and their child first. Denzel was certain his aunt was avoiding having his mama find out. If she knew, Diana Reyes would have no problem telling her sister-in-law to bother her own husband about their child.

"There's no need to worry your mother with Isabel's nonsense."

"I'll take your response as a no."

His father mumbled, but Denzel caught it. *Just like your mother.*

"Yeah, Pops. That's not an insult. My mama is amazing. Beautiful. And smart. So..."

Steepling his fingers, Denzel grinned at his father's frowning face.

"Why did I call you again?" A grumpy Ricardo Reyes was better than a stressed out or pissed off one, so Denzel maintained his smile as he offered suggestions.

"I'm guessing so you could be honest when you told your little sister you'd talked to me, and you were certain her baby boy wasn't being starved or mistreated."

"Watch yourself, Jandro." His father groused. Denzel squelched his chuckles and cleared the smile from his face. Mostly.

"For real though, Pops. You've gotta stop giving in to Tia Isabel."

"If you didn't avoid her, she wouldn't call me." His father snapped.

"Whoa, Pops." Denzel put his hands up. "You can't blame this on me. This ball is one hundred percent in your hands. I told you how I deal with it. If you don't want to hurt your little sister's feelings, then talk to Luis."

Scoffing, his father stared at him in disbelief. "As if her husband will do anything about Isabel. He gives her whatever she wants."

"I wonder where he learned that..." Denzel's comment was muttered mostly to himself and under his breath.

Tapping his fingers on his desk, Denzel checked his watch. "Look, Pops. I don't know what to tell you other than you could try my method, or text her Raffi's phone number every time she calls you. Either way, you'll get a little peace."

A chime sounded, letting Denzel know his next meeting was starting soon.

"Sorry, Pops. I gotta go. I have a meeting."

Waving a hand toward the camera, his father nodded. "Yeah, yeah. Handle your business. Don't forget to call your tia and get her off my back."

Before Denzel could remind the older man he hadn't agreed to do any such thing, his father ended the call. He couldn't do anything but laugh. *It's probably where he got that shit from. Probably? Definitely.* Shaking off the conversation, he moved to the nearby executive table and turned on the wall mounted monitor to begin the video conference.

After his meeting, Denzel's day wasn't as busy. With extra time on his hands, he noticed Dominique hadn't made it back from her trip to the studio yet. He restrained himself from checking in with Juan to see where they were. The urge prompted him to make a mental note regarding the normal report outs he received from Juan. Unlike the others, Juan worked directly for Denzel.

Juan was typically always with Denzel whenever he left the house. In addition to being Denzel's personal bodyguard, he was the primary point of contact with GPS when it related to the security personnel. There were times when there was a need for fewer or more guards. In those cases, Juan coordinated the changes.

As the time drew closer to the meeting with Nikki, and Dominique still hadn't arrived, Denzel stopped caring about how it looked. He messaged Juan, instructing him to find Vic's whereabouts. To keep himself busy, he went to the kitchen to look through the meals the chef prepared for the rest of the week.

With Ricardo Reyes as his father and Miriam Reyes as his abuela, Denzel knew his way around the kitchen. So, he could prepare his own meals. Though he would admit, his tamales didn't come close to his abuela's. However, knowing how and having the time to do it regularly were two different things.

Once he heard the chime of the front door opening, all thoughts of food were forgotten. Striding through the kitchen, he stepped into the foyer in time to see Dominique cross the threshold with the door being held open by Vic. Denzel clamped his lips closed and clenched his teeth to stop himself from commenting on the way the two were smiling, as if they shared some secret.

"Thanks again, Vic. I appreciate it." Dominique turned to face the other man, not giving Denzel any of her attention.

"You're welcome, ma'am. It's my pleasure."

"And his job." Denzel added as he stalked forward.

Whirling around to face him, Dominique gave him the stink eye before she turned back toward Vic.

"Regardless. I appreciate you. I know there was something else you were probably assigned to do today besides drive me all over Atlanta."

Holding out his hand, Denzel gestured toward the bags dangling from Vic's fingers. "I'll take those."

Shooting him another tight look, Dominique mirrored his movements.

"No thank you. I'll take those, Vic."

Denzel didn't look at Dominique. Instead, he kept his eyes on Vic. The other man quickly transferred the bags into his outstretched hand.

"Here you go, boss. If you need anything else, I'll be in the office with Juan for the rest of my shift."

With a barely perceptible nod of acknowledgement, Denzel watched Vic until the door closed behind them.

"Unbelievable." Dominique's feelings were clearly projected in the single word.

Since he didn't see a problem with anything he'd done, Denzel simply watched and waited. He knew she probably thought he was being an ass to Vic, but Denzel wasn't blind. While she was being her normal polite, positive self, Vic was ogling her and angling for another chance to be her personal escort for the day.

Instead of indulging her in the argument she was stewing for, Denzel pointed toward the hallway leading to his office.

"Our meeting with GPS starts in five minutes."

Pursing her lips, Dominique turned on her heels and stalked away from him. If she knew what was good for her, she wouldn't poke out her lips like that around him. He had all kinds of ideas for what she could do with her plush mouth. Following behind her silently, he didn't even attempt to keep his eyes from watching the sway of her hips. The jeans encased the rounded globes of her ass perfectly.

Once they reached his office, he pushed the door open and placed her bags on the chair next to it. Without a word to him, she seated herself in one of the chairs at the center of the table. Her purposely staying away from the end wasn't lost on him. The joke was on her, though. He rarely sat at the head of the table. His seat of choice was the one she currently occupied.

Rather than tell her so, he simply pulled out the next available chair. As if she had a camera in the room watching him, his assistant called to let him know she had GPS on the conference call and was ready to connect them.

"Thank you, Tiffany. We're ready here. Go ahead and connect us."

A moment later, the monitor on the wall came to life. Seated at a table similar to the one he and Dominique occupied were Nikki, two young women and a young man. Before they could do more than say hello, another person entered the conference room at GPS.

With his dark hair, liberally sprinkled with gray, still cut in a buzz style, Arlington Grant looked like he could put his uniform back on and go out onto the battlefield at any minute. Nodding, he didn't speak. He simply sat to Nikki's right and folded his hands on the tabletop.

Chapter Nine

TOUCHING NO-NO PLACES

Dominique sat staring at the people on the large screen with her arms folded across her middle. She'd shed her jacket and placed it on the chair next to her. She was fuming mad at Denzel, but she kept herself contained. The incident earlier that morning between the two of them in the kitchen, notwithstanding, it wasn't her first instinct to cause a scene.

Whether it was due to her upbringing or it was simply part of her nature, Dominique tended to shy away from such displays. Denzel had a way of making her forget herself though. In more ways than one. Still, she smiled politely when he introduced Nichelle Reed. Nichelle, who preferred being called Nikki, introduced the people she planned to assign to protect Dominique.

"Of course, on occasion, I may be there to fill in. Only when it's necessary, though."

Nikki stopped talking when a tall, broad-shouldered man entered the camera's view. He took the seat next to her, but remained silent. So, she went back to explaining her plan for keeping Dominique safe while not interfering with her daily activities.

Something about the other woman put Dominique at ease. She admitted her back went up when Denzel declared he had it handled, as if Dominique didn't have a plan of her own. After meeting Nikki, she conceded, only to herself, his idea had merit.

"Do you have any questions for us, Miss Truman?"

"Please call me Dominique." Unfolding her arms, Dominique sat up taller in her chair. "I do have a question. Regarding when I have to be at the studio or shoot on site, how would that work?"

Nodding as if she expected the query, Nikki replied.

"GPS has relationships with most of the studios around the country. Our staff has very high national security clearance, so it's not hard for us to get individual team members on the approval lists when we have clients working there. Once you let us know you're okay with the service, then we'll make contact with the appropriate people to get things in place. You won't have to worry about any member of your protection detail being denied access or put off the set."

Dominique's shoulders dropped slightly, releasing the tension she hadn't been aware she was holding. Nikki's confidence and attention to detail went a long way in easing her concerns. That's not to say she wasn't still peeved with Denzel though. Nikki's competence didn't let him off the hook for his behavior with Vic.

After she asked a few more questions to help them with the logistics of getting things settled, they wrapped up the call. She never did find out who the silver fox was who'd joined the meeting late. Since no one else commented, she assumed he was an important person in the company. Likely the *G* in GPS.

Denzel ended the video conference with a few taps to the controller, which was placed at the center of the table. The moment he did, Dominique popped up from her seat and grabbed her coat. As quickly as she moved, she wasn't fast enough to make it to her shopping bags before him. Staring from his fingers wrapped around the handles to his face, then back again, she reached for her purchases.

"I'll take those."

"I've got 'em."

"I see, but I'm perfectly capable of carrying a few shopping bags. So, you can just give them to me."

"I can. But I'm not."

"Excuse me?"

Dominique's head rocked back as she shot him a disbelieving glare. The infuriating man did nothing more than stare at her in response. Counting wasn't working, but Dominique inhaled deeply, then released it slowly in an effort to calm herself. Earlier, she'd been ready to give Denzel a piece of her mind. Now, she just wanted to go up to her rooms, throw on a pair of joggers and relax.

When she felt like she could speak without popping off, Dominique tried again. "Denzel?"

A single raised eyebrow was his response. Ugh! Internally rolling her eyes, she continued.

"I appreciate your offer to assist me, but I'm fine. I can handle these three little bags."

Denzel's response was immediate.

"I'm sure you can handle this, and much more. It doesn't mean I'm gonna let you."

Narrowing her eyes, Dominique shot him a glare. "I don't recall you being in charge of me, Mr. Reyes."

"Oh, it's Mr. Reyes now?" Putting the hand holding the bags behind him, he placed them on the next available surface farthest from where she stood.

"Why not? You seem to think you're the boss of everything and everyone."

Dominique folded her arms again. She was well aware that her anger may be slightly misplaced, but she was beyond caring.

"Baby, I don't know what you heard, or you thought you heard, but I *am* a boss. I never said I was the boss of you though."

He took a step closer to her. Reflexively, Dominique stepped back. They continued the dance until the conference table hit the back of her legs. Her bum landed on the surface as Denzel leaned over her with his face scant inches from hers.

"You're spoiling for a fight. So, why don't you tell me what's really going on?"

Unlike some men, Denzel didn't fill in the blanks with possibilities. If he had, she would've been able to latch onto something to fling back at him. Instead, she had to use her own words to tell him what was bothering her. But, words were fucking failing her, and the ones which did come sounded flimsy and petty.

Shivers skated along Dominique's spine when Denzel dropped his head, skimming his nose along the column of her neck. Heat bloomed outward from where his skin grazed against hers. If she was having difficulty forming words before, things had just gotten monumentally harder.

"What's the matter, baby? Cat got your tongue?"

All she could manage in response was a breathy whimper. With his hands flat against the table next to her, their only physical connection was when the tip of his nose glided along her skin. That small contact was enough to make coherent thought a distinct impossibility for Dominique. Normally, she wasn't this chick. Slick words and a handsome face didn't move her much. Even when you add in a body which would make a Greek god jealous, she wasn't fazed.

But...Denzel Reyes...She'd spent years staying out of his orbit. Now, she'd been tossed into the fire—pussy first. At least it was how Dominique felt when moisture gathered in her channel and tingles radiated from her core. Squeezing her legs together offered zero relief. Denzel didn't help matters when he spoke directly into her ear. His voice held a gruffness, which made her wish for him to stop talking and keep talking at the same time.

When his low beard lightly scrapped against the side of her face, Dominique released a gasping whimper.

"What was that? Did you have something you wanted to say to me?" If seduction had just one sound, it would be his voice. It did things to Dominique she couldn't begin to name.

"Don't worry, Una. I know what you need."

Dominique was unable to process his words because his lips captured hers, stealing the rest of her thoughts. Acting on instinct alone, her mouth opened, allowing him entry. He wasted no time stroking his tongue in to mate with hers.

While he kept her mouth occupied, his hands were busy as well. Nudging her legs open, he placed them on the rounded globes of her ass tugging her forward the short distance required to have her pressed against him. She had no control of her own digits as they curled into the fabric of his shirt.

He wasn't wearing a full business suit, but the button down had just enough slack for her to grab on to him. When he eliminated the space between them, she couldn't miss the bulge poking her. Without conscious thought, her fingers slid lower until the tips made contact with the turgid protrusion. *Damn.*

A growl rumbled from his chest when she touched him, even though her touch was slight. It gave her a rush of power to hear her effect on him was just as potent as the one he had on her. Releasing her from the lip lock, Denzel rained kisses across her jaw and down her neck.

"So, we're touching no-no places now?" The sensual lilt to his chuckle belied the innocence of his words. As did his nimble fingers, flicking open the buttons of her top.

The anger she'd experienced mere minutes prior had morphed into something else. She no longer wanted to give him a piece of her mind. In a ridiculously short amount of time, Denzel had redirected her energy toward giving him a piece of something entirely different—and taking a portion for herself.

Their location meant nothing as she fumbled with his belt, buttons and zipper in an effort to meet her new friend while Denzel untied the knot of her shirt, exposing her bra.

"Fuck..." The single word seemed to be dragged from his lips as he pulled back, gazing down at her breast.

For a moment, they were a tangle of arms with him trying to remove her shirt while she attempted to reach for his dick. When he finally achieved his goal and held her mounds in his hands, he didn't spend time ogling them. Instead, he leaned down to capture one stiff peak in his mouth.

"Ahh!" Dominique wasn't prepared for the intense pleasure she experienced when he wrapped his lips around her nipple.

He applied the perfect amount of suction, sending a gush of warmth to her core. His rumbling chuckle at her response sent vibrations along her skin, causing goose bumps to sprout in their wake.

As Denzel lavished kisses across her chest to reach her other breast,

Dominique remembered her mission. Gripping the waistband of his boxer briefs, she slipped her fingers inside. She'd just attempted to wrap them around the velvet encased steel of his shaft when he pulled his hips away robbing her of her new treat.

She had no control of the frowning pout on her face when she looked up at him. Now standing at his full height, he shook his head as if he were trying to shake a thought into place.

"Nope. Not here. If I let you touch me here, we'll end up fucking on this table. I mean...We're definitely gonna fuck on this table—probably everywhere in this office. But not for the first time we're together."

Zipping his pants, he quickly directed her in putting on her shirt. Forgoing the bra, he got her covered in less time than it took him to uncover her. Even while doing so, Dominique noticed he didn't allow her arousal to wane. He dispensed kisses and touches to keep her tethered to the moment, even though he was doing the exact opposite of what she wanted to do.

He kept her so enthralled, she couldn't recall the journey from his first-floor office to his third-floor bedroom. Nothing in between mattered once her bare skin hit the soft duvet covering the mattress on his custom platform bed. Having undressed her first, he stood beside the bed shedding his clothing without regard for if damage was done to the expensive material.

The more of himself he revealed, the wider Dominique's eyes stretched. He was always larger than many of his position contemporaries when he played football, but seeing all of him up close was...spectacular. When he lowered the waistband of his underwear and his thickness flopped against his stomach before pointing directly at her, she instinctively squeezed her legs together to assist with the ache in her core.

"What are you doing, Una?" Denzel grasped her ankles, tugging her closer to the edge of the bed and opening her legs at the same time.

"For what I have planned for this sweet pussy, these..." He gripped her inner thighs in emphasis. "will need to be open. Wide."

Dominique didn't have a chance to respond before Denzel dipped low, delivering a suckling kiss to her exposed mons.

"Oh shit!" Her back bowed off the bed, and she reflexively moved her hips away. His grip on them kept her in place.

"The fuck you think you're going with my pussy?" Denzel's growling words vibrated against her sweet spot, making her clench even harder.

She was no match for his strength, so Dominique could only thrash ineffectively as he feasted on her. Her moans drowned out his groans, but she felt each sound of appreciation he made against her sensitive folds.

Fireworks exploded behind her closed eyelids as she was tossed mercilessly into an orgasm. She was so overwhelmed with the feeling she didn't have the bandwidth to be embarrassed at how quickly she reached her climax. The man devouring her offered no consolation as he moaned in appreciation while lapping at the reward for his efforts.

When Dominique had nothing left to give beyond twitches as the aftereffects coursed through her, he finally placed a parting peck on her pearl. She watched him behind partially lowered lashes as he made his way up her body, stopping to kiss and worship randomly before they were once again face to face. Bracing himself above her with his hands planted on either side of her head, his dark eyes seemed to visually consume her.

Languidly, he joined their lips together, slipping his tongue inside her mouth, sharing her taste with her. Moaning, her fingers clamped onto his wrists before exploring the powerful muscles in his arms and back. As if she hadn't just experienced one of the most powerful orgasms of her life, Dominique's core slickened again.

Once Denzel lowered his hips into the cradle of her thighs, it was the most natural thing in the world for her to wind against the turgid length pressing into her pelvis. It seemed no matter how much pleasure she'd already experienced, her body wouldn't be satisfied until they were joined together completely.

Releasing her lips, Denzel kissed a path to the crook of her neck. His strong hands grasped her hips, stilling her movements.

"What is it you want?"

Pulling back, he rested on his knees with her legs thrown over his thighs. His thumbs traced circles on her hips while he kept her from grinding against him. Dominique released a frustrated grumble at being prevented from achieving her goal. *Why was he being stingy with the dick?*

It took her a solid minute to understand he wasn't simply talking; he'd asked a question and was waiting for a reply. Through her lustful fog, she tried to latch onto the words again. A light smack to her inner thigh brought her gaze to his face.

Rubbing the spot in soothing circles, Denzel's lips tipped up in the corner in a knowing smirk.

"Are you with me, Una? Use your words. Tell me what you want."

Desire was the commander of Dominique's vessel. The only word it permitted past her lips was a breathy "you."

Denzel's smiled stretched wider. "That's my good girl. Now..." Leaning over her, holding himself up with one arm, he stroked the tip of his dick through her folds.

"What part of me do you want? Hmm? Where?"

Gritting her teeth, Dominique wanted to scream, but the pressure he applied on her pearl with the mushroom shaped crown of his shaft hindered her ability to do anything beyond feel. She needed relief and if he wouldn't provide it, she'd do it her damn self.

So, instead of responding to his request, she slipped her fingers down her fupa. Forming a vee with her digits, she tried to stimulate herself. Before she could get in one good rub, her arms were pinned above her head.

"Who told you to touch my pussy?"

Fire shot from Denzel's eyes. Not waiting for her answer, he continued. Beneath lowered lids, she listened as he ranted about her audacity in thinking anyone was allowed to make her come except him.

Dominique lost all concept of focus when Denzel penetrated her weeping core. The bulbous head of his dick parted her folds, invading her channel in excruciating slow increments. The speed belied the heat of his words as he informed her of the new hierarchy of things.

Once he was fully encased inside her quaking walls, she would've agreed to anything to keep him there. He stretched her so deliciously, with a slight edge of pain. Even through her haze, she could tell he'd made certain not to hurt her. The slight discomfort was simply a byproduct of him being blessed in the dick department.

Closing her eyes, Dominique allowed the feeling of fullness to wash over her. Although he was completely sheathed in her channel, he didn't move. *Why wasn't he moving?* Having his thickness unmoving inside her was a new brand of torture. One she couldn't endure. The moment she tilted her hips away to initiate the movement she craved, Denzel's hand landed on her hip and more of his weight pressed her into the mattress.

"What did I just say, baby? Hm?"

Piercing her with a look of determination, he held her immobile with one hand at her hip while the other kept hers locked above her head. When he spoke, his normally deep voice carried a gruff edge.

"Stop trying to do my job. I've got this. *I* make *you* feel good. *I* give *you* orgasms. Understand?"

As he laid down his law, he started a slow, but pounding rhythm, withdrawing, then feeding her his length in tandem with his words. When she didn't respond to his question fast enough for his satisfaction, he shifted. Reaching behind her thigh, he pushed her leg toward her chest while levering himself onto his knees. The new angle sent him to new depths inside her.

The possibility that he was knocking something out of alignment was feasible, but it felt so good, Dominique couldn't bring herself to care. Once he released her hands, Dominique thought he'd given her a reprieve and she could now touch him as well. She was sadly mistaken.

As soon as he let go of her hands, he performed the same move with her other leg, lifting her lower half off the bed while he angled his hips until he was hitting her spot on every down stroke.

"I asked you a question, Una. Do. You. Understand?"

Each word was accompanied by a firm stroke against the sensitive nerves inside her slick tunnel. *How the hell did he expect her to form words while he literally fucked her senseless?* Her next orgasm hit her with so much strength, a scream tore from Dominique's throat. The incoherent string of babble she released seemed to galvanize Denzel. His thrusts took on an erratic rhythm. He soon followed her over the precipice into release.

Through partially closed lids, Dominique watched him lower her legs, then drop down over her again. This time, he blanketed her with his comforting weight as he rained gentle kisses across her collar bone, making his way up her neck until he finally reached her lips.

Sweat rolled down from his brow, but he didn't swipe it away. Instead, he brushed her hair back from her forehead while gazing at her. When he spoke again, his voice lacked the gruffness from moments before.

"Now. Do you wanna tell me what was bothering you?"

Chapter Ten

MY MAMA DIDN'T RAISE A HEATHEN

Denzel zipped around the kitchen gathering the things he needed and placing them on a tray. More than once during his hurried movements, he wished he'd had the dumbwaiter installed when it was suggested to him. But no, he didn't see the point, and he didn't want to create wasted space by adding the tiny elevator.

It was a rarity for him to take full meals in his suite of rooms, but this was a special occasion. Just the memory of the way it felt to have Dominique's tight heat wrapped around his length had him rushing even more. Besides his eagerness to experience it again, he didn't want to leave her alone for too long.

Too much alone time led to thinking. Thinking opened a path to regrets. There could be no regrets. Because they damn sure couldn't turn back the clock. And he didn't want to. The only option was forward. To get there, he needed to feed his woman and keep her sated for as long as possible.

Once he had everything they needed, he quick stepped to the elevator. Juggling the tray, he managed to get the door open without spilling anything. After placing the tray on the table in the outer room, he walked through to his bedroom to the ensuite bathroom. The patter of water hitting against the tiles reached his ears before he stepped over the threshold.

Instead of standing beneath the shower spray as he expected, Dominique was in front of the center sink. She appeared transfixed, staring at her reflection in the mirror. *Shit!* He'd been gone too long. Approaching her, Denzel didn't stop until the rounded cheeks of her ass brushed his sweatpants covered dick. Steeling himself against the pull of those plush temptations, he focused on her face in the reflective glass.

"Do you need something, baby?" He didn't want to pierce their bubble by asking a question which dipped too deep. Not yet. They'd get to that conversation.

Sliding his arms around her, Denzel rested his hands on her midsection. He wasn't sure if he should be grateful she hadn't redressed or at least slipped into his robe. Her distracting curves nearly had him bending her over the vanity to fuck away any doubts that may have crept in.

Her skin was silk beneath his lips as he pressed a kiss to her shoulder. He nuzzled the crook of her neck before trying again to capture her gaze in the mirror. Her rich, dark earth tone complexion no longer held the flush present when they'd come together earlier, but she still looked freshly fucked. Which gave Denzel a little prideful boost.

The springy coils of her hair were noticeably less tamed than before he'd put his fingers in it just a short time ago. When she simply stared at their likeness without answering, Denzel considered pushing, but decided against it. Taking a different tack, he reached into a nearby drawer.

Producing a shower cap still in the packaging, he proceeded to gently gather Dominique's mass of thick hair and tuck it beneath the satin-lined vinyl. When she quirked an eyebrow, he mimicked the gesture.

"Don't look at me like that. I bought this for you." It was out of his mouth before he realized how it would sound.

"What I mean is, I wanted to make sure you had what you needed, so I thought ahead."

Shit. That sounded even worse. Taking a deep breath, Denzel refocused on his task—although he was essentially done.

"I like being prepared. Okay? I didn't want you to need something and not have it."

Turning in the small space between him and the countertop, Dominique braced herself against the surface and stared up at him. Since he'd developed a case of foot-in-mouth syndrome, Denzel kept his lips sealed.

After a few moments, she finally broke the silence. Pointing at her now covered hair, she quirked one eyebrow.

"So, this is all about being a good host?"

Relief dropped his shoulders as he released the tension. Nodding, he lightly grasped her hips.

"Of course, baby. My mama didn't raise a heathen."

Unable to resist temptation any longer, Denzel yielded to at least snagging a kiss. A gentle peck quickly turned deeper. Encouraged by her soft whimpers, he tangled his tongue with hers as his hands began exploring her body anew. If he lived to be one hundred, Denzel didn't think he'd ever lose the desire to be surrounded by her velvet heat—feeling her plush softness pressed against him.

Not wanting to be left out of the party, his shaft hardened between them. He may have been able to control himself if she hadn't slipped her hand into his sweats, wrapped her fingers around his length and swiped her thumb over the tip. Who was he kidding? She could've simply stood there breathing, and he'd want to fuck her senseless. Having her participate was just the excuse he needed to escalate things more quickly. He wasted no time shucking off the pants giving her unfettered access.

Denzel's lips stretched into a grin after Dominique released a cute little squeak when he grabbed her thick ass, lifting her off her feet. Catching on quickly, she wrapped her legs around him and wound her arms about his shoulders. The pebbled peaks of her nipples grazed his chest, drawing a tortured groan from his throat. He needed those beauties in his mouth again. Soon.

Transferring them from the vanity to the shower was done in a few scant seconds. Denzel finally released her lips, but he didn't allow her feet to touch the tiled floor until she was exactly where he wanted her. Water pelted against his back as he shielded her from the spray. Lifting a fresh towel from the rack, he snagged the shower gel from the nook.

Dominique's gaze tracked his movements, but she didn't speak. Doing his best to keep the lustful fog expression on her face, Denzel squeezed a generous dollop of the cleansing gel onto the towel.

"Turn around, baby."

When she hesitated and opened her mouth to speak, he shushed her. "Sh... It's okay."

Holding the bottle up for her inspection, he allowed her to see it was safe for feminine use. Replacing it on the shelf, he worked the cloth to a lather, then began his own personal torture session. His dick was threatening to drop him to his knees, but Denzel maintained his focus on taking care of Dominique.

With a will he hadn't ever tested so thoroughly, he managed to cleanse her body without utilizing the built-in bench to sink inside her, or dropping to his knees to dine on her sweet nectar. He deserved another MVP trophy for that shit.

However, once he rinsed the soapy bubbles from her body, all bets were off. Only rudimentary attention was given to washing his own privates before he backed her into the tiled bench. Keeping her steady when she stumbled, he pressed her shoulders until she sat.

"That's it, Una. Rest on your throne. There's worshipping to be done."

Uncaring about the hardness of the surface, Denzel sank to his knees, tossed Dominique's legs onto his shoulders, and planted his face in her already leaking core.

"Mmm! Why do you taste so fucking good?"

He didn't expect an answer, and his Una didn't give him one. Her only response was gasping moans and fingers gripping the back of his head. His hair was too short for her to get a firm grip. Denzel had a fleeting thought of growing it out for her, but he quickly pushed it aside in deference to giving her pleasure in the moment.

"Oh! Oh my! Oh shit!" Disjointed phrases dropped from Dominique's lips and Denzel lapped up the resulting sweetness issuing from her channel as she climaxed.

He didn't stop until her trembles tapered off to intermittent jerks. Even as he placed one last kiss against her folds, he didn't want to stop displaying his adoration at the altar of the queen. But his shaft had hardened to painful proportions. Kissing his way up her body, he captured her lips, sharing her own decadent taste with her.

A thumping jerk from his dick reminded him they weren't done. Moving to sit beside her on the wide seat, he pressed his back into the warm porcelain.

"Commere, baby. I need that sweet pussy on my dick."

Dominique watched him beneath half lowered lids for a few beats before she responded to his command. Helping her straddle his lap, Denzel couldn't resist running his hands over every part of her he could reach. Letting her somewhat control the pace was killing him, but he didn't rush her. Instead, he incentivized her.

Holding one heavy, rounded globe of her breast in each hand, he leaned forward and fulfilled his desire from moments before.

"Ah!" Dominique's back bowed as she cried out.

When her hips began winding, rubbing her heated snatch against his swollen shaft, Denzel wanted to weep. *So close.* Releasing the nipple with a light pop, he stared at her lust filled face. Her teeth captured her bottom lip and her eyes were tightly closed.

"You like that? You want me to do it again?"

Denzel's voice sounded harsh and raspy to his own ears. Taking her whimpers as agreement, he latched on to the other turgid peak, giving it the same lavish treatment. This time, he nibbled and flicked his tongue against the pebbled flesh. Unable to stop them, his hips punched up slightly, seeking her slick heat.

Answering his unspoken demand, Dominique lifted slightly. Denzel's hands immediately relocated to her hips before he realized she was simply maneuvering to align his dick with her opening. The moment she slid down, his head dropped back on his shoulders, banging against the tile.

"Damn, baby." His fingertips pressed into the top of her ass cheeks as he unconsciously guided her movements. "It don't make no fucking sense how good you feel bouncing on my dick."

The way his words came out in a grumbling growl, Denzel could barely understand himself. So, it was quite possible she didn't understand what he said. It didn't matter. Their bodies spoke the same language.

"Mmm...Den."

The words came out in a guttural moan as Dominique picked up a faster rhythm. Gritting his teeth, Denzel's grip on her plush ass tightened, and he joined her in pounding their bodies together. It wasn't long after that he felt the telltale tingle at his spine.

Her walls fluttered around his shaft, signaling she was close. But, he wanted to make sure she went over the cliff before he did. Snaking one hand between them, he located her slick pearl and applied pressure as he pumped up into her grasping heat. It only took a few more well-placed flicks before she crested.

The scream she released bounced off the tiled walls and his grunted shouts soon joined in. Gripping her hips with both hands, he kept her impaled on his stiffness as his dick jerked inside her, releasing his entire load into her depths. *This damn woman had his whole soul in her hands.*

The rest of the evening was spent with the two of them having dinner, then falling back into bed. As much as he wanted to spend the remainder of the night buried inside her, he knew her body required a break. He gave her a reprieve on one front, but there was still his question hanging over them from earlier.

Part of him had an idea of why she was upset before, but experience had taught him not to make assumptions. He'd never compare his Una with Melody. However, his train wreck of a relationship with the R&B singer had some lasting effects. Their break up got messy. While some of the complaints she lodged were complete fabrications, others held notes of truth. Truths he'd been blissfully unaware of until she'd said anything.

They were difficult to hear—especially since they were issued through social media instead of through a face-to-face conversation or even a phone call. The delivery system made it harder for him to accept. Time and distance from the situation allowed him clarity. It didn't excuse what she'd done. Nevertheless, he was able to recognize where he'd gone wrong and needed to improve to be a better partner.

Not to Melody. Never with her again. But, with the woman he

considered having in his life exclusively. That wasn't to say he didn't have a spell when he rightfully earned his reputation for being in the streets. He absolutely did. The running around got old though. Quickly. However, the wheels were set in motion. So, to keep from being tied to anyone in particular and having the microscope turned on him again, he avoided even the appearance of long-term commitment.

Regardless of what had occurred in the distant or recent past, he refused to allow it to affect what he wanted to build with Dominique. Lying in the bed he typically slept in alone, Denzel trailed his fingertips along Dominique's side. Her bonnet covered head rested on his chest as she seemed to absently trace invisible patterns on his skin.

He smiled when he recalled the expression on her face when he volunteered to go down to her room to retrieve the hair cover. While he had shower caps and elastics at the ready, he was aware how particular some women were about their bonnets and sleep caps. Talking down her protests, he'd located the hair cover exactly where she said it would be. It took him less than five minutes.

Denzel was aware she didn't realize there was more than one way to get to her suite of rooms from his. He'd simply taken the rear stairs, and he was in front of her door in less than a minute. He didn't bother to look around at anything else while he was there. As far as he was concerned, their separate sleeping arrangements were temporary.

"I haven't forgotten what I asked you earlier, Una. I gave you a pass, but we aren't going to sleep without airing things out."

When Dominique shifted, he stopped his light touch, resting his hand at her hip, gripping her soft flesh. Looking down, he met her upturned gaze.

"Air things out?" The question was loaded. Denzel knew it. Yet, he couldn't back down.

"Yes. Talk to me. Don't say it was nothing. It was enough for you to try to skip dinner and spend the evening in your rooms alone."

The dip between Dominique's perfectly arched eyebrows deepened. "You're serious?"

"Absolutely."

"Denzel, you know what you did. Why should I give you a play-by-play?"

Cupping the side of her face, he stroked her cheek with his thumb.

"Even if I know what I did to contribute to you being upset, I don't know it from your perspective. How you felt as a result. Or what needs to happen going forward."

"What needs to happen going forward is for you to not act like every man who's friendly to me is trying to get into my panties. You were an ass to Vic."

She was cute as hell when she was giving him the business. Denzel couldn't resist tilting her chin up and planting a kiss on her plush lips. Pressing into his chest, she pulled back.

"I'm serious, Den."

"I know you are. You're just so damn cute when you're laying down the law." Her face pinched, but before she could launch into her response, he placed a finger on her lips.

"I think we may have to agree to disagree about what it means when a man is nice to you. Vic may have been simply doing his job, but the way he was watching your ass had nothing to do with his responsibilities. And he's no different from a large part of the male population.

Most of us have to work hard to unlearn lessons taught by society and some in their homes. More often than not, niceness and friendliness with someone we find physically attractive is transactional. There aren't nearly as many men as there should be who are friendly just for the sake of being friendly. Nine times out of ten, they're hoping to get something out of it. Even when they're doing the job they're paid quite well to do."

Dominique's lips twisted, and he was certain she didn't totally believe his explanation.

"You're a beautiful, sexy, desirable woman. Even if every man within your orbit doesn't have good enough taste to recognize it, you can't tell me you haven't experienced anything similar to what I just said more than a few times in your life. You didn't get fine overnight. This beautiful face and banging body have been a part of your package for a long time. Don't play coy with me, woman. You know I'm speaking the truth."

"I'm not playing coy. I sincerely didn't believe Vic was being anything but cordial. It had to be boring as hell for him to wait around for me to do administrative things at the studio. I know going to a beauty salon for me to buy my hair and skin care products wasn't on the top of his list either."

"He doesn't get paid to be excited about the places you go. He gets paid to protect. Any enjoyment he gets should be from knowing he did his job well."

Denzel clasped one hand over the fingers Dominique used to deliver a pinch to his pectoral.

"Ouch, woman! Why are you abusing me?"

"That was not abuse."

"What do you call it, then?" Denzel kept the offending fingers clasped in his, bringing them to his lips, delivering a kiss to the tips.

"Retribution."

"For?" One eyebrow lifted with Denzel's question.

"Making me question what I thought was a genuinely friendly inter-action. Also, you were, and still are, being an ass."

Using her unrestrained hand, she delivered a lighter pinch to his side. The move tickled more than it stung, and he quickly captured that hand as well. Rolling until he was braced over her with her hands pinned above her head, he dipped his face into the crook of her neck. Leaving a trail of kisses up to her ear, he growled his words.

"Keep playing with me and you're going to end up getting fucked. I was trying to give her highness a break. But if you keep acting up..."

Denzel let the rest of his sentence trail off. Pulling back, he regarded her with a challenge in his eyes. Dominique's chin tilted defiantly, making his dick hard.

"I'm not afraid of you, Denzel Reyes."

"Fear is never my goal, Una. I would never want you to be afraid of me."

Shifting, he aligned his shaft with her folds, but didn't enter the heated paradise he knew waited for him. Meeting her rebellious gaze, he flexed his hips.

"Cautious? On occasion. That might be wise. But never fear, baby. Never that."

A low moan escaped Dominique's lips, almost as if it was ripped from her throat. Her fingers flexed in his hold and her hips gyrated as much as he allowed with his lower half resting against hers. Unable to resist, he captured her lips again, slipping his tongue into her mouth, initiating a dance with hers.

Once again, his good intentions flew out the window. Delivering short thrusts, he rubbed his thickness between the puffy folds of her labia, stimulating her clit. Dominique's responding mewls were driving him crazy. Still, he managed to refrain from plunging inside her, pounding her sweet pussy into oblivion. No matter how much she appeared to want it, she was definitely going to be sore from their activities.

Of course, he'd be more than happy to kiss it and make it better. Ignoring the demands of his aching length, Denzel kissed his way down her torso. When he reached her belly button, he finally released her hands. Spreading her legs to accommodate his shoulders, he situated himself on his stomach sniper style.

Before he allowed himself a taste, he stared at Her Highness until he could no longer restrain himself. Leaning closer, he smiled at Dominique's unconscious hip tilt. Looking up at her, he observed her watching him with a lust filled expression. Placing a kiss on her folds, Denzel rubbed the tip of his nose along her slit.

"Hey, baby. I think I want you to sing for me." It was an odd time to make the request, but Denzel suddenly desired to hear her melodic voice.

"What?" The single word was delivered in slurred disbelief.

"Yeah, baby. You remember that high note you hit when you performed in your last Broadway play? I want to hear it."

Grasping the inside of her thighs, he held her legs flat against the mattress. Licking his lips, he glanced up at her one more time.

"You look like you need a little incentive. Let me help you."

With his offer of assistance, Denzel dove back into his new favorite treat. He didn't stop until he'd delivered on his promise and Dominique's high G hit the air.

Chapter Eleven

ARE WE GOOD?

The next day dawned with Dominique waking to Denzel entering his bedroom already fully dressed. In his hands was a small tray holding a bottle of water and a mug of the magic elixir better known as coffee. It's possible her brain was telling her body to sit up so she could partake of said elixir, but her limbs weren't in the mood to cooperate.

"Good morning, Sunshine." Denzel's smile was entirely too bright and his gaze far too clear. He looked like he'd been up for hours.

Shooting him a disgruntled glare, Dominique didn't respond. Instead, she watched him approach and place the tray on the nightstand nearest to her. As she observed him, she noticed her cellphone face down next to it. She didn't recall putting it there, so he must have gone down to retrieve it once she'd fallen asleep.

"Come on, sleepyhead. It's almost nine. I let you sleep as long as I could, but I didn't want to leave without talking to you a little and saying goodbye."

That got her attention. Jerking to a sitting position, she pulled the sheet with her to cover her breasts. Ignoring the small frown on Denzel's face as he tracked her movements, she pinned him with a look of disbelief.

"Leave? To go where?"

Was it possible she was overstepping? Yes. Did she care? No. This man had just blown her back out and turned her every which way but loose mere hours ago. Now, he sat on the side of the bed, dressed in what was obviously part of one of his expensive business suits, telling her he was about to leave.

The warmth of his hand on her thigh offered a modicum of comfort, but she still wanted answers. Anxiety was real, and it didn't matter if she'd gone to sleep and awakened in his bed or that her things occupied a suite of rooms in his house. He could still discard her.

"I have to go to Vegas on business. I'll be back tomorrow evening after my last meeting. I thought I could put it off until next week, but the numbers yesterday weren't what I wanted to see."

"Oh."

So much was in the single word response, but it was all Dominique could muster. Her feelings were all over the place. They'd made no promises to one another, but she felt some kind of way about them spending the night together only for him to hop on a plane the very next day.

This was too much to digest without her first cup of java. Avoiding his gaze, she picked up the mug and looked down at the contents. When she noticed the light color of the liquid inside, her gaze shot back up to his.

"How did you know?"

Tapping the tip of her nose, Denzel's lips stretched into a dazzling smile. Not like the one he used when he was on camera or even when he was interacting in polite company. In the short time they'd spent one on one, she'd learned this was his real smile.

"I pay attention. That's how I know. Now, drink your coffee so your brain can absorb the information you need to know."

With her synapsis only partially firing, Dominique followed his directive. She needed the clarity having her first cup usually brought. After she'd had a few sips, the tension in her shoulders lessened. Letting the flavor of the magic juice and the aroma finish the process of waking her up, she stared into the rapidly emptying mug.

"Do I need to leave you two alone?" The twinkle in Denzel's eyes matched the cheer in his voice.

"Why are you so chipper?" The coffee was still working on her, but Dominique simply wasn't a morning person.

"Why wouldn't I be? I have a good life." Leaning in, he cupped the side of her face, stroking her cheek with his thumb. "But I see you aren't the same person waking up on your own versus when someone wakes you up. I'll file that tidbit of info away for future reference."

Lifting one eyebrow, Dominique took another sip before placing the nearly empty mug on the tray. Denzel pulled his hand back, resting it on her thigh. The barrier of the bedcovers kept her from feeling the fullness of his warmth, but the weight was there.

"Thank you for bringing me coffee. It was sweet."

"You're welcome. It's part of my survival technique."

Dominique tried not to be distracted by the absent way he gently massaged her leg. The moment itself wasn't awkward, but she found herself searching for words. Something which would let him know she didn't regret what happened between them, but she was apprehensive about what it meant.

Only, broaching such a discussion would require time to have genuine discourse. Since he'd just said he was leaving soon, such a conversation was off the table. At least for the moment. Maybe his business trip was what she needed. It would give her some space to clear her head without his larger-than-life presence and back blowing dick game clouding it.

"What time do you leave?"

"I have a plane waiting for me now. I leave as soon as I know we're good." Leaning in, he narrowed her vision to include nothing beyond him. "So... are we good?"

Dominique searched his expression. Denzel was a confident man, but she saw the hint of vulnerability. It made her wonder if he thought she'd run the moment he set foot out the front door. She wouldn't. But, she guessed he didn't know that.

Placing her hand on his where it rested on her leg, she squeezed his fingers.

"We're good. I have some exploring and prep to do. We're supposed to get the first script in the next day or so and table reads start next week."

Tangling their fingers together, he made circles on her palm with his thumb. He seemed to be unable to not touch her in some way. Dominique didn't mind. It felt nice. Better than nice. If she didn't watch it. She could become addicted.

"Why don't I put something on and walk you out?"

She had an idea where the suggestion came from. Behaving like a sitcom housewife from the nineteen sixties wasn't hard coded in her DNA. While her mama had always been supportive of her dad and his career, Dominique rarely witnessed an instance of her walking him to the door to kiss him goodbye when he was off to work. Besides, she wasn't Denzel's wife, and it was way too soon to be thinking along the lines of permanent when it came to whatever this was they were doing.

Relationship status notwithstanding, Denzel wasn't simply going off to work. He was getting on a plane to fly over a thousand miles away. The way his face brightened at the suggestion said he'd more than like it if she saw him off. However, that's not what his mouth said.

"It's nice of you to offer, but not necessary. We can say our goodbyes right here. You can get some more rest. I hear you didn't get much sleep last night."

"I wonder why?" Dominique returned Denzel's smirk with her own, adding a gentle shove to his shoulder.

The man was like the pink bunny with the battery in its back. He just kept going and going... She was in awe of how he managed to look as if he'd gotten a full night's sleep while she was the very definition of dragging ass.

"Una, it sounds a whole lot like you're blaming me for your lack of sleep. I take offense. I did everything I could think of to help you meet the sandman."

"You have an interesting definition of 'helping'." Dominique used air quotes while struggling to hold back laughter.

"Are you saying I wasn't helpful? Do you want to file a complaint with customer service?"

At his question, Dominique gave herself over to the giggles she'd held at bay. Denzel's laughter joined hers. When they were able to get themselves together again, he announced that he really had to get going.

With one last parting kiss, he left her in his bed. Picking up the jacket she hadn't noticed draped across the back of a chair, he left the room.

As she watched him leave, part of her wanted to ask him why he called her Una, but the other part of her didn't want to know. Not yet. Living in California going on ten years, she'd made it a point to brush up on the Spanish she'd studied in high school and college. She'd become relatively fluent in the language, so she knew the literal meaning of the word.

However, just as she knew their available time was too short for a discussion on what they were doing, there wasn't room to examine why he'd moaned that single word in her ear the previous night when he orgasmed. Nor why he used it now, in the bright light of day.

With Denzel gone, Dominique looked around the bedroom, unsure of what to do next. While she wasn't a morning person, once she was up, she was up. So, going back to sleep wasn't an option. There was nothing formally on her schedule for the day, making it a great opportunity to simply explore.

Picking up the mug of coffee Denzel had brought her, she sipped the rest of the brew. Left with nothing but her thoughts to keep her company, Dominique couldn't avoid what had transpired over the past twenty-four hours. Not only had she allowed Denzel Reyes to bend her body like a pretzel, she'd been an active participant in the carnival show. A willing, enthusiastic participant. Just the thought of the way they'd come together was enough to make her squeeze her thighs tightly to stem the ache.

It wouldn't work. And she wasn't in her rooms with access to her BOB to take care of it. Her trusty purple friend would likely disappoint her now that she'd been privy to Denzel's carnal delights. The man knew his way around a pussy and wasn't shy about it. Unlike some men who looked like they should be able to throw down in the bedroom, only to end up being selfish pricks who blame their partner when they shoot off after three pumps, Den put in work.

Emitting a startled gasp and clutching the coffee cup close to her chest, Dominique looked at the nightstand. Her phone buzzed as it sang out a tune. Releasing her death grip on the mug, she picked up the device.

"Hey, Syd. What's up?"

"Hey, Girlie. What's up with you? I thought you would've called by now. How's Hotlanta?"

"Syd, I told you they stopped calling it Hotlanta in the early two thousands."

"Whatever. They don't get to tell me what nicknames I use. I'm grown."

"You're a mess." Dominique chuckled as she arranged the pillows behind her back.

"I never said I wasn't. I didn't lie though. I am grown."

"Yeah, Syd. You are grown."

"Mhm."

In her mind's eye, Dominique could see her bestie wearing a resolute expression and bobbing her head in agreement. Technically, Dominique wasn't in Atlanta. Denzel's home was in a suburb in Logan City.

"Anyway, Atlanta is fine, but I've barely been here three days. Actually, not even three days. So, there's not much to say. I did go to the studio yesterday to take care of some admin things."

"Oh yeah? How'd it go?"

"On the one hand, business as usual and on the other...not."

"How so?"

"I went in to get my credentials to get onto the property. But they seemed surprised I was there at all. So, I couldn't look around much in the offices we'd work out of when we start table reads or even the main set they planned for us to use.

Since they didn't really seem prepared for my level of interest, I didn't stay there as long as I thought. I met with a few people, got my stuff and was out of there by lunch. After that I had Vic drive me around, then take me to Murphy's to get some hair and skin care products."

Sydney moaned at the mention of Murphy's Salon and Spa. "Please tell me you bought enough to send me a little something?"

Smiling at her friend's antics, Dominique shook her head. "I may or may not have secured a couple of extra bottles of the curl cream you're addicted to."

"That's because you love me."

"I do."

"I really wish Murphy's, or at least the products, were national." Sydney groused.

Placing the call on speaker, Dominique laid the phone next to her on the soft duvet cover.

"I actually met the owner while I was there yesterday."

"Don't you play with my feelings, Dominique Truman."

"I wouldn't do you like that, Syd."

Sydney had stumbled upon the exclusive hair and skin care products during a business trip to Atlanta a few years ago. In the midst of a hair emergency, someone suggested Murphy's Salon and Spa. It had been love at first shampoo for her bestie, who in turn got Dominique hooked on their line of natural hair and skin care products.

"When I was unpacking, I realized a chunk of my hair stuff wasn't where I thought it was. It was easier to just go get more. Stephanie stepped out while I was speaking with the lady at the desk. She was super cool."

"Did you shoot your shot?" Excitement filled Sydney's voice.

"You know I did."

Once she knew she was in serious contention for the role of Marissa Clark, Dominique started making inquiries about makeup and hair stylists in the area to work with. Because, what was not going to happen, was them having her in these series streets looking like nobody loved her enough to tell her that her wig looked busted.

The series head stylist, Jerricka, had already put her on to a makeup artist. Then the MUA, Candy Hampton-Holmes, put her onto Stephanie Barker at Murphy's. She did warn Dominique, getting Stephanie might be a long shot.

"Don't leave me hanging! What did she say?"

"She said she'd have to think about it, but to send her a contract and she'd look it over."

"I'm so jealous!"

"You really don't have to be. It's not like you haven't had her magic fingers in your hair before."

"Yeah, but you have a chance to get to know her."

"Mmhmm... Get to know her and drop a bug in her ear about going national, so my bestie won't have to stalk her website like a fiend in search of a fix."

"I mean..."

Dominique didn't have to see Sydney to know she likely wore a sly grin as she shrugged.

"Anyway, we'll see. Enough about me. What are you doing calling me so early? Aren't you at work?"

"Yes, Miss Nosey. I'm working from home today. I'm downstairs in my office. You were on my mind, so I thought I'd check in."

"Well, that was nice of you."

"I'm a dope friend like that." A light shuffling was heard in Sydney's background before she spoke again. "You sound awfully bright eyed. Is your body still on L.A. time? Have you already been up making use of the gym at your new condo? I know how you like to work out early in the morning and get it over with."

Dominique captured her bottom lip between her teeth as she considered how to answer her friend. She'd gotten in a very early morning workout, but it hadn't been in a gym.

"Ummm... No. Actually, I've been awake for less than an hour."

"Excuse me, what? That's not like you."

"Maybe the excitement of the past few days took a lot out of me."

"Lies."

She tried it. Knowing she wouldn't get away with it, Dominique still tried to get out of having the conversation take this turn.

"What? I *was* up pretty late. So, I slept in. It's been known to happen."

"Dominique. Latoya. Truman."

"I know you didn't just pull out my whole name like you're my mama." Knowing it wasn't a video call, Dominique frowned at the phone as if Sydney could see her.

"And I'll do it again. Stop holding out on me. What did you do? Did that big sexy Blaxican come over and blow your back out last night? I told you when you said he was helping you find a place he was gonna help you alright."

Heat crept into Dominique's cheeks at the accuracy of her friend's guess. She had to take a deep breath in an attempt to moderate her voice when she responded.

"First of all, don't use that term. I've never heard him refer to himself as Blaxican. Second...not exactly."

Sydney didn't allow Dominique to remain silent for long after she dropped her little bomb. As was fully expected, she prodded.

"Not exactly what? He didn't exactly blow your back out?" Whispering her next question as if she were afraid of being overheard, Sydney asked, "Was he lame? All talk, no action? I'm sorry, friend."

"What? No! And why are you whispering? You live alone."

"If your feelings are hurt, I didn't want to make it worse by talking all loud."

Sucking her teeth, Dominique looked away from the phone. Grabbing the bottle of water Denzel left for her, she cracked the seal.

"I won't go into detail, but he was far from lame. *So* far."

"So, he ***DID*** blow your back out last night?!"

"Maybe."

"Whatever. I'm happy you got the cobwebs knocked off. You've had an exceptionally long drought."

"Excuse me, kettle. I'd like you to meet pot." Dominique could only laugh at her friend's ability to pretend they didn't share similar dating experiences in California.

"Pfft! Whatever. This isn't about me. It's about you."

"If you say so." Dominique let it drop, but they both knew she was right.

"I do. Real quick though. Let's circle back to something."

Dominique sat up straighter against the pillows. She'd been relieved, thinking Syd wasn't going to dig too deeply after getting a little info. Keeping things from her bestie wasn't Dominique's strong suit—not when asked a direct question.

"Circle back to what?"

"Earlier, when you mentioned stopping by Murphy's, you said you had Vic drive you. Who's Vic?"

Chapter Twelve

THIS ISN'T DRAMA

Denzel scribbled a few notes on the pad as he reviewed game footage from the last match up between the Red Tails and the Kodiaks. He was on his return flight after spending two days in Las Vegas in meetings with CleanSun executives. He was hoping only Hiriam Baxter and maybe a few of his cronies would have to be ousted in his effort to get things more firmly on the right track. He was wrong.

The company was profitable. Denzel wouldn't have invested as much if it weren't. However, they could be performing a minimum of four times better if they weren't so devoted to maintaining the status quo. How people working in such a forward-thinking industry as solar energy could be so resistant to change was a mystery to him.

Needing to prepare himself for Sunday Night Football, Denzel turned his attention back to analyzing the similarities and differences between the Red Tails and Kodiaks. On the face of things, he considered the Red Tails the better team. But he couldn't completely count the Kodiaks out. They'd been known to pull a few surprises out of their hats.

"Sir, the pilot asked me to let you know we'll be landing soon."

Looking up at the flight attendant, Denzel nodded to the young man. Shutting his laptop, he stowed it in his backpack. Securing his seatbelt, he turned his gaze to the night sky visible outside the window. It was late, but he'd refused to spend another night away from home.

Earlier, he'd been forced to leave a message for Dominique when his call went to voicemail. Preventing his thoughts from running away with speculations was a task within itself. As long as he had something else to focus on, he was okay. But, they hadn't held any lengthy conversations while he'd been gone. It wasn't due to lack of effort on his part.

He'd called, but they'd mainly texted. To her credit, she didn't ignore him. With the way he had meetings stacked up, there wasn't a great deal of time for long conversations. Also, the two-hour time difference worked against him. By the time he was free to talk the previous evening, she was winding down. He ended their chat after her third yawn in less than five minutes.

What had Denzel more than a little anxious was the fact they hadn't really talked about the change in their dynamic. As far as he was concerned, they were together, but it was the kind of thing which deserved a real conversation—not an assumption. So, he watched the lights of the city grow closer as he counted the minutes until they touched down.

It was after midnight when Denzel strode into his bedroom. Not turning on any lights, he walked straight through to his closet. Stripping out of his clothes, he placed the garments in their respective hamper. Being as quiet as possible, he closed the door to keep the noise from the shower from filtering out of the bathroom.

Skin tingling from the quick vigorous shower, Denzel left, dropping the damp towel into the linen hamper right before turning out the light. Guided only by the light of the moon filtering in through a gap in the curtains, Denzel approached the bed. It wasn't until he was standing beside it that he had a clear view.

Nothing but pillows lay atop the plush mattress. Dominique wasn't there. *What the fuck?* Flicking on the beside lamp, he confirmed what the dim lighting told his eyes. Clenching his jaw, he walked back into his closet. Grabbing the first pair of sweats his fingers touched, he jerked them on, slipped his feet into a pair of slides and stalked out of the room.

Taking the back stairs two at a time, Denzel was in front of the door to the suite of rooms he'd given Dominique. Ignoring the little voice trying to reason with him, he delivered two firm knocks on the mahogany wood. Barely counting to ten, he knocked again. When he lifted his fist to do it again, the door swung open.

Holding a satin robe closed with one hand, Dominique peered up at him.

"Denzel? What's wrong?" To add insult to injury, she sincerely looked confused. As if she hadn't expected to see him after he left her a message letting her know he was on his way home.

"What's wrong?" Repeating the question back, he arched an eyebrow, looking from her face to her hand on the door, holding it partially open.

"It's late. I assume something is wrong for you to knock on my door at this time of night."

"I just got in."

"Okay..."

Since she didn't seem to get the message, Denzel simply started moving forward. He didn't stop until he was far enough into the room to close the door behind him.

"Sure. Come on in."

He didn't miss the sarcasm in her tone. Denzel just chose to ignore it. Instead, he walked past her into the bedroom area. She didn't follow him immediately. It took a minute or two for her to appear in the open doorway. By then, he'd stripped off his sweats and slid beneath the covers.

The bed wasn't as large as the one in his room, but it was comfortable. Sitting with his back against the headboard and the covers draped across his lap, he watched her as she stared at him incredulously.

"Den... it's too late for drama."

"Drama? This isn't drama, baby. I'm just trying to get some sleep. Same as you. Now, if you don't get over here and get in this bed, I'll assume you brought up drama because that's what you want."

Flipping the covers back on the opposite side, he tapped his palm against the empty space.

"Which one do you choose, sleep or drama?" Piercing her with a determined stare, he waited.

Just when he thought she was going to buck, she dropped the robe onto the tufted bench at the foot of the bed. She wore nothing beneath the shiny satin. Not even panties. Denzel's dick plumped with lightning speed. This wasn't what he came for. His only goal had been to hold her as he slept. But seeing her heavy breasts, rounded hips and neatly trimmed pussy had him reconsidering if he was really that tired.

Not uttering a word, she climbed onto the bed, turned her back to him and tugged at the covers. Letting go of the bedding, Denzel gave her a small victory. As soon as she settled, he wrapped an arm around her waist and tugged, plastering his front to her back.

Leaning on one elbow, he peered over her shoulder into her face. After a few seconds, her eyes popped open, and she looked at him from the corner of her eye.

"What, Den? You asked me to choose, sleep or drama. I'm choosing sleep."

"Yeah...that choice was offered before you pulled your Lady Godiva routine."

Flexing his hips, he rubbed his thickening shaft against her softness, making it even harder. Rotating slightly, she looked at him directly.

"Are you serious right now? You show up at my door late at night, waking me up out of my sleep, and acting as if I should've expected you. Now you think I'm gonna have sex with you?"

One side of Denzel's lips tilted into a smile. Her mouth said all the right things to make him think she wasn't interested. The problem was, he'd gotten to know her body really well when they were together.

"I don't just think, baby. I know." Pressing her shoulder until she was flat on her back, he looked from her exposed breast to her face. "I know from the way your nipples pebbled when you dropped the robe. From the way you looked at me right before you tried to turn your back on me. And last but not least."

Flexing his fingers against her hip, he reached beneath her and squeezed one plump ass cheek.

"When I pulled you close to me, you couldn't resist throwing this ass back just a little. So, don't play."

Dominique's tongue darted out, swiping across her bottom lip. Her gaze skittered away before she brought it back to his.

"I can't stand you."

"Uh-huh. That's what your mouth says. Let's see what Her Highness thinks about me."

Tossing the covers back, Denzel captured Dominique's lips. Damn, he missed her taste. *All* of her taste. Releasing her lips with parting pecks, he kissed his way down her body—stopping at her breast to pay homage. When he finally pressed her thighs apart and settled between them, he was salivating.

"Hey, Your Highness. I bet you missed me. Didn't you?"

Grinning at Dominique's eager hip tilt, he put them both out of their misery. The first swipe of his tongue against her seam made him close his eyes to savor the flavor. The next had him ready to see if it was possible to bury his whole face in her fragrant pussy.

"Oh shit! Den!"

Hooking his arms around her legs, Denzel gripped and tugged to keep Dominique exactly where he wanted her—at his mercy. He wasn't anywhere near done with her.

Distracting Dominique with sex wasn't his original plan. He sincerely intended to get some sleep, and he wanted said sleep next to her soft form. But when she dropped her robe, exposing her voluptuous body, all bets were off. Sleep be damned. He had to have a taste of her. His dick was protesting not getting the chance to go first, but the greedy bastard would have to wait. Pleasuring her orally had a twofold purpose.

The primary reason was to prepare her to take him. His size made foreplay a non-negotiable. Secondly, and it was a very tight race, he loved pleasing her that way. He'd quickly become addicted to her flavor, the sounds she made, and the way she wound her hips, trying to get closer to him.

It was the biggest fucking turn on to have her be so responsive. When she moaned his name again and tried to clamp her thighs around his head, he tightened his grip and redoubled his efforts to send her over the edge.

Capturing her clit between his lips, he applied suction while flicking his tongue rapidly against the little bundle of nerves. Dominique's body tensed. Knowing she was close, Denzel increased his torment of her pearl before dipping into her honeyed walls to capture her essence as she reached her peak.

"Holy fuck! I'm gonna—MMM!!"

Smiling against her mons, Denzel accepted his reward from Her Highness. He didn't stop until Dominique's body subsided to intermittent tremors. Licking his lips, he rose to his knees with her legs draped over his thighs.

"See. I told you she missed me. If I wasn't an excellent swimmer, I would've drowned in all of that juice."

Dominique didn't respond. She lay limply staring at him through her lashes covering her barely open eyes. Her inability to form words made him proud, but he still thought he could do better. Planting his fists on the mattress, he kissed his way up her torso until he reached her lips. Her mouth opened to him immediately, allowing him to share her sweetness with her.

As his tongue tangled with hers, he lined the tip of his shaft up to her slick opening. Slipping into her pussy was indescribable. The way her velvet walls massaged his dick had him gritting his teeth in an effort not to come too fast.

"Fuck..." Dragging the word out, he withdrew from her depths before immediately sliding back in. "Damn, baby. What the fuck you got in here?"

Dominique's lack of response to his question didn't deter him. Her gasping whimpers were enough. Denzel hissed from the sting of her nails digging into this flank. Words may have escaped her, but his Una's body knew exactly what to do. Tipping her pelvis, she rocked into each stroke. The way her pussy gripped then relaxed around his dick felt like the most decadent massage he'd ever experienced.

The feeling was so amazing, Denzel forgot himself. Forgot his goal. Hooking one arm beneath her left leg, he brought it up to his shoulder. The move allowed him to sink deeper inside her, drawing a strangled gasp from Dominique.

The sound was like a starting pistol. His pace and the power in his strokes increased. Soon, he couldn't hold back the orgasm burning to be released. Seeking her clit with his thumb, Denzel stroked until her internal muscles clamped down on his thickness in an attempt to trap him inside.

"Gotdamn!" Denzel's grunts joined Dominique's moans as they both crested into their release.

His hips continued to jerk spasmodically until he was completely spent. Only then did he release her leg and drop to one side, tugging her along with him to keep them connected. Breathing heavily, he rubbed along her exposed skin. Soft puffs of air tickled his neck as Dominique did the same.

Once their breathing returned to somewhat normal, Denzel delivered two light taps to her hip, dropped a kiss on her forehead, and left the bed. He went to the bathroom and returned with a towel to clean her with. A shower was what he really wanted, but his Una looked like she was about to drift off to sleep at any moment. So, it would have to wait.

Gathering her against his side, as he'd wanted to when he first arrived home, Denzel tucked the covers around her shoulder before allowing sleep to take him.

Waking before the sun, Denzel opened his eyes but didn't move a muscle. He was lying on his side being the big spoon with Dominique asleep in front of him. She slept so peacefully, and it felt so amazing holding her, he didn't want to move. However, his body was on a schedule. He didn't need to see a clock to know it was already after six a.m. His session with Rob was at seven a.m. sharp.

Groaning internally, about not having time to wake Dominique properly, he placed a gentle kiss on her shoulder. Taking care not to wake her, he eased out of the bed. Tugging on his discarded sweat pants, he couldn't stop himself from staring at her.

She looked so peaceful. Even with her bonnet hanging on for dear life, she was beautiful in her repose. As carefully as he could, he fixed the hair cover. Then, he pressed another kiss to her forehead before leaving the room. His baby slept like she was getting paid and in line for employee of the month.

Grinning, he climbed the back stairs to reach his rooms. In less than twenty minutes, he was downstairs in the gym warming up as Rob walked in.

"What's good?" Rob dropped his backpack on a bench.

Walking closer to where Denzel jogged on the treadmill, the trainer extended his fist for a bump. Tapping his knuckles against Rob's, Denzel shook his head.

"I can't call it."

Rob looked at the time on the treadmill display, then up at Denzel. "Five more minutes. We're working upper body today."

Nodding, Denzel kept his pace for another three before dropping the speed. By the time he stepped off the machine, Rob had the free weights lined up next to the bench. It was business as usual once Denzel walked over to them.

He was wrapping up with Rob when Dominique walked in. Wearing loose joggers and an oversized sweatshirt with an asymmetrical neckline, she paused at the entrance. Seeing her hesitation, Denzel called out to her.

"It's okay. We were just finishing up. Besides, there's always enough room for you." Ignoring the look she shot him, Denzel grinned as he helped Rob set things right.

"It's good to see you again, Miss Truman."

"Good Morning." Dominique murmured politely as she walked farther into the room.

Denzel's gaze tracked Rob as he went to his bag and opened the outer zippered pocket. He wasn't bothered by Rob's comment, but he did wonder what had him stopping mid-cleanup to go to his bag. His curiosity was satisfied when Rob pulled out the pink and lavender business card.

"Miss Truman, I spoke with Kam. She has openings and would love to work with you. Just give her a call whenever you're ready."

"Thank you."

Dominique placed the card on the window ledge along with her water bottle as she stepped onto the mat beside the treadmills. Grabbing her elbows above her head, she started preparing her muscles to workout. While Denzel tracked her movements, he wasn't exactly smooth with the way he wrapped things up with Rob. Instead of walking with him to the door and chatting as they normally did, Denzel waved to his trainer before turning his attention to Dominique.

If he didn't know better, he'd swear she waited until Rob walked out to bend her sexy ass over continuing her stretches. She behaved like she didn't know he was there, but Denzel wasn't fooled. She'd come to be as in tune with him as he was with her. When she stood back upright, she glanced at him as she balanced herself with one arm on the treadmill while she held her heel to the back of her thigh, stretching her quad muscles.

"What?" Both eyebrows lifted with her question.

"You look much more alert this morning than you did when I woke you up before I left for Vegas."

Denzel stopped when she was within arm's reach, but he didn't touch her. One side of her mouth twitched like she wanted to smile, but it didn't develop.

"I'm not good with other people waking me up. I tolerate an alarm, but I prefer to wake up naturally."

"Oh, I noticed."

Denzel couldn't resist at least running his fingertips along the sliver of skin exposed by the over-cut of her sweater's neckline. Releasing her bent leg, Dominique stood to her full height. Her dark eyes were filled with questions. Questions Denzel knew could no longer be avoided.

"We need to talk." Normally, he detested those four little words. But, this time, he was the one to say them. He refused to go any further without things being abundantly clear between them.

Chapter Thirteen
HOLY FUCKING SHIT

We need to talk. Dominique's breath caught in her throat as her heart began to pound in her ears. She was an adult. Most of the time, a sensible adult. But, those four little words made her anxious. Especially since she hadn't worked out in her head what the hell she was doing with Denzel Reyes—beyond getting her back blown out.

Knowing the conversation was necessary, and actually having said conversation, were two different things. When he'd left for his business trip, neither of them spoke about the elephant in the room. In fact, he'd left her in his bed, in his bedroom, as if it was where she was supposed to be. Judging from his reaction once he came home to find her back in her rooms, he thought she'd be waiting for him there.

Folding her arms across her middle, she looked up at him and tried to ignore his enticing scent. Because, how the hell did he still smell good after a vigorous workout? That wasn't even close to being fair.

"You're right. We do need to talk."

Her voice was steady, belying the jittering nervousness twirling in her stomach. Thinking maybe what she needed was a little bit of distance, she went to the bench and sat down.

Returning her gaze to his, she held out one hand. "So... Talk."

Flashing her an indiscernible half smirk, he approached the bench, filling the available space next to her.

"I guess that's fair. I did bring it up."

Dominique tracked Denzel's movements without turning her head. His fingers spread wide on his quads. Long and thick, they evoked memories which made her redirect her attention to the wall opposite them. Her attempt at evasion wasn't much help, since that section of wall was composed entirely of mirrors. So, instead of being distracted by his hands, she had the visual of the two of them side by side to contend with.

They almost looked like a couple from one of those ads where the much fitter man was attempting to get the woman interested in exercise or about to give her a motivational talk about not giving up. Only, Denzel had made it abundantly clear he appreciated every dip and curve of her plus sized body. After he'd shown her where the home gym was located, he never mentioned it again. So, he wasn't in the midst of spouting the benefits of exercise to her.

Denzel caught her gaze in the mirror. "I think we should be on the same page about what's going on between us."

Averting her eyes from their reflection, Dominique looked at him directly. "What exactly is going on between us, Den?"

Denzel met her stare head on. The determination in his expression spoke before he did. "What's going on, is whatever we want to go on. We're consenting adults. The only rules on what we do together are the ones we make for ourselves."

The slight edge of nerves had Dominique tugging at the bottom of her sweatshirt. She'd challenged him to talk, and he obliged—getting straight to the point. But, he hadn't actually answered clearly.

"You're saying a lot without being plain."

"How much plainer do you need it, baby? I don't think I'm saying anything you disagree with. I haven't exactly been subtle about wanting to be with you."

The question hovering at the tip of Dominique's lips was, *"For how long?"* But she didn't ask him that. To be honest, she was terrified of his answer. They'd gone from casual acquaintances to her screaming down the walls from orgasms in a very short span. While they'd known each other for years, it seemed the moment they had any significant time alone, things started going at warp speed.

"Denzel, what are your expectations here? Because, based on last night, you seem to be under the impression we're people who share a bed every night. Like a couple."

The muscle working in Denzel's jaw drew Dominique's attention before his blazing eyes made her forget how to exhale.

"Are you saying you don't want to share my bed?"

There was no mistaking the hint of steel mixed with something else lacing his words.

"I'm not saying that, and please don't answer my question with a question. We're supposed to be talking. Really talking. Not playing, *guess what I really mean.*"

Denzel's right hand left his leg, tugging her folded arms free. Once they were, he tangled their fingers together.

"I already said what I mean, Una. You just don't want to hear it. I want to be with you. And after knowing what it feels like to go to sleep and wake up next to you, I don't want to go back to the other way. Not when we're under the same roof."

Cupping the side of her face with his other hand, he leaned in, closing the gap between them.

"And let me be one hundred percent transparent about this next part."

His dark eyes searched hers and she read the sincerity of his next words prior to him speaking.

"We aren't *like* a couple. We *are* a couple. Unless you can look at me right now and say you don't want me, that's my answer to all the questions. We're together."

Holy. Fucking. Shit. The words thundered in Dominique's head. Denzel was dead ass serious. The normal flippant, sometimes sarcastic lilt to his voice was absent, as was his trademark engaging smile. She'd been in the city less than five days, and Denzel had successfully turned everything she thought would happen on its ear.

She wasn't living in her own place. Instead, she was given a set of rooms in his house. Now, he was sitting next to her basically saying those rooms were to be decorative, because he wanted them in the same bed every night. So, essentially, they weren't just living under the same roof. They were living *together*.

The words slipped out before Dominique could think better of speaking them aloud.

"Are you for real crazy? Or do you just say things to see how people respond?"

Rather than being offended, as she thought he would be, Denzel's lips stretched into a devastating smile.

"Me being crazy depends on who you ask, but I'm completely sane. And, while I've been known to poke at people on occasion, I'm not doing that with you. Especially not now."

The fingers he tangled with hers tightened and the heat of his other hand warmed the side of her face. Both provided comfort. A tether keeping her in the moment, yet making her pulse increase with the intimacy of it all. It was one thing for them to yield to sexual attraction. It was another to formally admit they weren't simply indulging in harmless fun.

While it was fun, if things didn't work out, it would be far from harmless. She was already in deeper than she wanted to admit. Cheap beach chairs didn't fold as easily as she did when it came to Denzel Reyes. He had the potential to destroy her emotionally. Did she really want to take that risk? Even as the question flashed across her mind, she knew she was already too far gone. The risk had been taken when she didn't immediately leave the very first day.

Capturing her bottom lip between her teeth, she struggled to maintain his gaze. The intensity coupled with her current revelation was... a lot. When Denzel's eyes dropped from hers to track the motion, her core clenched. Cursing her body's response to him, she released her captive and cleared her throat.

"Does us being a couple necessitate us sharing a bed every night? It doesn't seem a bit fast to you?"

"Six years. It's been six years from the first time we officially met. How much slower do you want to go? Should I wait another five to hold your hand in public?"

Their proximity diminished the fire in the side eye she gave him. Dominique tried it anyway, pressing against his chest with her free hand.

"We may have met six years ago, but we'd barely had a conversation lasting longer than a few minutes at a time up until a couple of weeks ago. You can't count that time."

"Who says?"

Denzel dropped his head to the crook of her neck. The way the collar of her sweatshirt was cut exposed more skin on left side, and he took advantage, nipping at the exposed area. The spot normally wasn't a hot spot for Dominique—until he made it one. The scruff of his beard added a sensual layer to his touch, stealing her rational words.

"Umm... *I* say. We still have so much we don't know about each other."

"Mm... and plenty of time to learn everything there is to know," Denzel countered as he kissed his way up to her ear.

Somewhere inside her, Dominique had to find the strength to stop this seduction. Besides the fact that they still needed to come to an agreement, her love box was tender from Denzel's over abundant blessing. Her problem was, neither her sore pussy nor Denzel was on her side. Moisture gathered in her folds in preparation. He added to the production by gripping her hair in his fist. He'd discovered she liked her hair pulled and used the knowledge ruthlessly.

Dominique's sharp inhale was smothered by Denzel's lips covering hers. The tug against her strands was a direct pipeline to her pussy. Squirming against the solid bench beneath her bum, she latched on to the front of Denzel's shirt. Tugging at the soft material, she wasn't sure if she was trying to remove the offensive cotton or holding on to keep herself from falling.

Denzel seemed to take her actions as the former. Dominique's fingers were soon empty as he whipped his shirt off over his head. His dark eyes held her in a thrall. Whatever she'd thought moments before about not being able to withstand another round so soon was tossed into the wind. A pulsing ache spread outward from her core. Even the snug fit of her sports bra couldn't suppress the pebbling of her nipples.

"You can see mine. Time to show me yours."

The lustful intent in Denzel's expression was hot enough to melt the clothes from her body. Still, Dominique held up a hand as if her palm and five digits could stop what was coming.

"Wait...Umm..." Her clouded brain took a few ticks to release the rest of her thought aloud. "I came down here to exercise. Maybe we should save the other stuff for later."

It was worth a try. But, the way Denzel tilted his head to the side, said it didn't work. Dominique was in no way dressed for seduction with her oversized sweatshirt and baggy joggers. The only things hugging any part of her frame were her underwear and socks. Yet, Denzel's eyes raked over her like she was wearing the sexiest lingerie money could buy.

"Exercise? I can help with that."

His voice dipped with a deep, devilish timbre, sending a shiver of anticipation gliding up her spine. It made promises and declarations, causing Dominique to question why she would deign to suggest they stop. The thickness of his fingers didn't prevent them from nimbly slipping beneath the edge of her sweatshirt, quickly having it join his t-shirt in parts unknown on the floor.

She didn't have time to respond to the cool air against her skin, because Denzel's warm hands and lips seemed to be everywhere at once —kissing, touching, and branding her with his desire. Dominique couldn't feign innocence, since her hands were doing their fair share of exploring him.

While there was no longer the sheen of sweat from his workout, his tawny skin still seemed to glisten beneath her fingertips. As she traced his muscles, she admired the beautiful contrast in their skin tones. However, when he latched onto her nipple, Dominique's eyelids slammed shut and thoughts beyond receiving pleasure flew from her mind.

She didn't even notice he'd released the front closure of her bra until that moment. The man was a damn magician. The bow in her back thrust her breast into him, which seemed to suit him just fine. Moaning around his treat, he tweaked her other turgid peak, keeping it from feeling neglected.

All the while, his free hand was working its way into the waist band of her sweats. Considering the loose fit, it wasn't an insurmountable task. Her hiss was quickly followed by a pleasured moan when his digits located their target, stimulating her sensitive pearl. Rocking into the sensation, Dominique encouraged his exploration of her pulsing heat. When he dipped a finger inside her walls, she nearly bucked off the bench into his touch.

Cool air hardened her nipples further when Denzel suddenly pulled back, giving her a heated stare.

"Stand up."

It wasn't a request. And he didn't wait for her to comply. His hands were suddenly at her waist, lifting her from the bench. She had no choice but to brace herself on her shaky limbs. The moment her feet were planted, her pants and underwear were unceremoniously yanked down. She barely had time to toe off her sneakers before she was being lifted again.

Once she was seated, straddling his lap, Denzel resumed his assault on her senses with his mouth blazing a trail from her lips to her breasts and back. Dominique's core clenched. The winding motion of her hips was instinctive. The aching in her core had to be assuaged. Denzel's dick was right there, hard and ready. But the exercise shorts remained a barrier between them. A low rumbling noise issued from his chest before he shifted. Between two breaths, Dominique went from rubbing her pussy against his covered length to being impaled by it.

"Oh shit!"

Her exclamation was rewarded with a swat to her ass.

"Don't just sit on it, baby. Ride. You came down to exercise, remember?"

Dominique's response was delivered without the heat she'd hoped to return, but he filled her so full she couldn't muster fire.

"You're such an asshole sometimes."

"Mm-hm, baby. I'm your asshole though." Another swat was delivered to her other ass cheek. "Now ride. We're burning calories this morning."

The light sting caused her internal muscles to tighten around his thickness. Her responding moan was joined by his groan as it jolted her into motion. Lifting and lowering herself on his length to her own rhythm while listening to Denzel's sounds of approval, gave Dominique a heady sense of control. She liked how it felt, and she wanted more.

While she balanced herself with her hands on his shoulders, his large warm palms rested against the globes of her ass. Arching her back, Dominique stared into Denzel's eyes and snapped her hips in a tilting motion that made her ass bounce on his lap. She knew she'd wrested control when his gaze left hers to focus on the mirrored wall.

His dick seemed to get harder and larger inside her while he stared at the reflection of her riding his turgid length. Denzel's fingertips gripped her flesh, and he started breathing in heaving puffs. Grabbing his chin, she brought his attention back to her face.

"Give it to me."

She'd no sooner said the words than Denzel slid forward, balancing her on his hips with his shoulders against the wall and bench supporting his back. Assuming the reins of their tempo, he pumped upwards, making her take every inch of him. The change in position took Dominique by surprise and sent her careening into her orgasm.

Screaming her release, her walls clamped down on his dick like her pussy was trying to keep it forever. The feeling of his shaft swelling was followed by his length jerking inside her. *Shit*. She was gonna have to stop letting this man shoot up the club.

Without conscious thought, Dominique's hips whirled, grinding her mound against his pelvis, drawing out the moment. Resting against Denzel's chest, she didn't give one care about the sheen of sweat on his skin. She simply tucked her head beneath his chin as he lowered them both to the floor. This was absolutely going to count as her morning workout.

Neither of them said a word. Dominique lay draped on top of Denzel with his length still buried inside her. His breathing evened out and the sound of his heartbeat beneath her ear slowed. This exercise routine was hell on her delicate folds, but it wasn't a horrible option.

Her lips quirked into a sly grin as the thought flitted across her mind that a woman could get used to starting her morning with a toe-curling orgasm. As evidenced by how quickly she acquiesced, she couldn't foresee turning down the option when it was available.

"What are you grinning about, woman?"

Biting her lower lip, Dominique stretched the fingers of the hand lying on his chest.

"I don't know what you're talking about. I'm just laying here."

"Yeah, laying here patting yourself on the back for completely draining me of energy. I'm not going to be any good for at least an hour."

Levering herself until she could look into his face, Dominique quirked one eyebrow. "How is that my fault? I had every intention of using the treadmill and maybe doing some yoga until your little exercise suggestion."

Denzel's arms tightened around her and his eyebrows furrowed in a mock glare. "There is nothing *little* about my exercise suggestion."

To add to his statement, he flexed his hips, reminding her of their connection. It felt like his semi-hardened length was stiffening inside her, as if to back up Denzel's claims. Dominique's eyes widened. There was no way this man was ready for another round so quickly.

Had he taken one of those pills? Because nothing about his recovery time was normal. At least not in her experience. As good as she knew it would feel. She seriously didn't think her poor pussy could take anymore at the moment. Although the way her fingertips glided across his chest was in complete contradiction to those thoughts.

Nor did the way her walls pulsed around his thickening length agree with her assessment of her physical condition. Her hips simply outright called her a liar when they began rocking on his turgid shaft.

"I swear I'm gonna need to soak in Epsom salts because of you."

"I'll run the bath for you, baby. Now, be a good girl and take this dick. We're not done exercising."

Chapter Fourteen
WHAT DO I LOOK LIKE?

True to his word, Denzel ran Dominique a bath in the larger massaging bathtub in his room. In his opinion, the side eye she gave him was half-hearted at best. They both knew the one in his bathroom was better, not just bigger. It had more jets and double head rests. So, they could lounge in there together if they liked. If he didn't have meetings lined up, he'd have been more than happy to aid in soothing her sore muscles.

Flipping the end of his tie over one shoulder, Denzel braced himself on the side of the tub, leaning over to kiss Dominique's full, inviting lips.

"Try not to fall asleep in here."

"Mm. I make no promises."

Dominique sighed, sliding deeper into the water covering her berry-colored nipples. Denzel bit his lip in memory of having those beauties in his mouth. It was just as well she removed her body completely from his sight. He'd probably cancel his meetings and fuck her until they were both raw. Nothing like that had happened since he'd first discovered sex and went a little pussy crazy.

As a damn near forty-year-old man, he'd thought the uncontrollable part of his desire was past him. But, with his Una, restraint was damn near a blasphemous suggestion. Reminding himself of his responsibilities, he pilfered another quick kiss and left her lounging in the scented water.

Running into Silvia in the kitchen, he noticed his house manager was back to her old self when they interacted. She let him know she'd restocked the pool house with groceries for Raffi and asked Chef to increase meal prep to take both his cousin and Dominique into consideration. Denzel was fine with the increase for Dominique, but shot the woman side eye about Raffi.

"Didn't you just say you restocked groceries for Raffi? If he has groceries, why does he need Chef to cook for him?"

Silvia's expression perfectly matched her voice when she replied, "I keep this place stocked with groceries, but Chef still meal preps."

"I *pay* him to use the groceries *I paid for* to cook meals for me. You're spoiling Raffi. At this rate, even when he's done with school, I'll never get him to leave."

Waving a hand of dismissal, Silvia passed him the tumbler containing the juice blend she'd just finished making. Sitting it next to his water, Denzel tucked into his breakfast.

"You're nothing but talk. You know you like having your cousin here."

Denzel's response was a grunt issued around a mouthful of Huevos Rancheros. Closing his eyes, he let the flavors of the smothered chiles rellenos dance on his tongue. Once he'd swallowed the first bite, his eyes popped open, pinning Silvia with his stare.

"Why are you buttering me up?"

Staring at him with wide eyes, Silvia's jaw dropped, and she tilted her head as if she were offended. *Not likely.* Just not prepared to be called out so quickly. They usually made it halfway in before he let her drop whatever bombshell she was holding.

"Why do you think every time I make you Huevos Rancheros that I'm buttering you up? Sometimes I think you miss a taste of home and your abuela's cooking."

"Sometimes I do, but I also know there weren't any pre-made tostadas lying around. So, that means you had to make them. From scratch. While not hard for you, it required more effort than you normally put into breakfast around here."

Putting his fork down, Denzel propped his elbows on the countertop, resting his chin on his fists. "Spill."

Standing up to her full barely over five feet height, Silvia pushed her shoulders back. "I have no idea what you're talking about, Jandro. But, if you're going to act like this every time I make one of your abuela's recipes for breakfast. I'll just stop."

Tipping his head toward his plate, he stared at her from beneath his furrowed brow. "That's how you're going to play it? Okay. Fine. You know I'll find out, eventually."

Fluttering around the kitchen, Silvia tossed him a glance. "No you won't, because there's nothing to find out."

Lapsing into Spanish, she complained under her breath about not being able to do something nice without him being suspicious. He let her go on with her rant while he ate, and she set the kitchen back in order. He cleaned his plate like he was in the military with limited chow time. When he stood to take his plate to the sink, Silvia swiped it up.

"I've got it. You go on with your day. You're slightly behind schedule."

She was fishing. Denzel knew it, but decided not to bite. It had been on the tip of his tongue to let her know Dominique would be down later, but he changed his mind. It was likely what she wanted—for him to open the door to discussing what was going on between the two of them. He wasn't going there.

"Thank you for breakfast. It was delicious." Grabbing the tumbler, he took a sip as he turned to leave.

"Is Miss Dominique not coming down for breakfast?"

And there it was. Denzel almost smiled at how predictable Silva was.

"I'm sure she'll come down when she's hungry." Stopping in the doorway, he glanced back. "Silvia, while I appreciate you cooking breakfast from time to time, you know that's not why you're here, right?"

"Of course, Jandro. I know. I enjoy it."

Despite her mining for information, Denzel recognized the sincerity in her statement. With a curt nod, he left. She was right. He was slightly behind schedule. He wouldn't have as much time before his first meeting of the day as he'd originally planned. However, he couldn't bring himself to regret the reason for his delay. Not even a little.

Leaving Silvia with questions still burning behind her eyes, Denzel went to his home office. He was barely settled behind his desk when his phone dinged. Turning it over, he checked the message. Smiling, he tapped the screen to call his assistant. Tiffany picked up on the first ring.

"Good morning, Mr. Reyes. Your conference call with Mr. Ortiz will begin in five minutes."

Smiling at the not-so-subtle reminder, Denzel moved from behind his desk to the conference table and turned on the monitor as he spoke.

"Yes, Tiffany. I'm aware. That's not why I called. I just got a message from my guy about the thing I told you I wanted to set up in a couple of weeks around the same time as the Championship game."

Why was he being secretive in his own office, behind a closed door? Denzel couldn't say. He just knew he didn't want anything to spoil the surprise. His ever-efficient assistant simply rolled with it, assuring him everything else would be handled.

"Is there anything else you need before I connect the video conference with Mr. Ortiz?"

"No. I'm good for the moment. I'll hang up and you can get Cristiano on the line."

Without any further chitchat, they ended the call. The monitor mounted on the wall came to life, and soon Denzel was looking at Cristiano Ortiz. Sitting behind a desk, it was obvious the other man was in his home office as well. There was a slight view of the beach visible just over one shoulder.

"Buenos Dias!" Cristiano greeted Denzel with a wide smile.

"Buenos Dias." Denzel returned the greeting with a smile, but with slightly less bounce in his words.

Cristiano was in some ways still the friendly guy Denzel met on the set of *She's It Girl*. Though, it wouldn't be in anyone's best interest to assume his friendly smile was an indication he was a push over. Far from it. The kid was savvy. And connected.

"You were missed at the last meeting. A few people were asking about you, wondering if you ever planned to do more than a few commercial spots anymore."

Denzel hadn't been to a Silver Screen Association meeting in over a year. He kept his membership current. But, as of late, the meeting dates had conflicted with other things he had going on. The last time being Carver and Alyssa's wedding in October. He wasn't likely to miss being at his best friend's wedding to have people press business cards in his hand and offer him cameo appearances for agreeing to finance their films.

"I hope you didn't get their hopes up." Denzel lifted an eyebrow, regarding Cristiano's conspiratorial expression.

"I'd never speak for you. What do I look like? Your agent?"

"You're way too pretty to be my agent. That guy looks like the chewed end of a cigar and a combat boot had a baby."

Running a hand over his mop of curly hair, Cristiano shook his head. "I'll let you have that one, but I won't take too many of those pretty jokes."

"Whatever, man. Let's get down to business."

"I've been waiting for you," Cristiano quipped as he flipped open the binder in front of him. Denzel did the same, and the two turned their focus to the real reason for the conference call.

～

Once Denzel finished up with Cristiano, he dove into some other work reviewing files he needed to go over with his business manager. He had a meeting with Wendy during the afternoon to discuss current and future investments. Buzzing on his wrist pulled him from the task.

He never thought he'd turn into one of those people who had to be reminded to eat. But, when he was focused on a task, he could be single-minded to the point he didn't come up for air unless some outside influence prompted him to remember the rest of the world existed. He was pushing back from his desk when an alert flashed across his monitor.

Clicking it, the security feed from the front gate filled the screen. A tap to the volume button allowed him to hear the exchange between the person at the gate and a member of the security team.

"I have a package for Miss Dominique Truman. It requires a signature." A youngish-looking man spoke into the speaker with his gaze trained on the display.

"Wait right there."

Denzel finally recognized the voice and clicked off the screen. Justin would drive out to meet the delivery person and sign for the package. If the guy thought he was going to catch a glimpse of Dominique and any part of the inside of the house, he was sorely mistaken. The gate was as far as he would make it.

Just as he made it to the foyer, Denzel saw Dominique descending the stairs. Stopping at the bottom to wait for her, he couldn't resist stealing a kiss when she reached the last stair.

"Hey." He lingered for a moment before straightening, allowing her to leave her temporary perch.

"Hey, yourself."

"Did you have a nice bath?"

A smile stretched her lips, displaying the deep dimples in her cheeks. "I did. Your tub is amazing."

"Well, you can use it any time you like." He knew his tone and the tilt of his lips projected exactly what he wanted, when Dominique shoved his shoulder lightly.

"Stop it. *She* is out of order until future notice."

Wrapping his arms around her, he tugged her close. "I don't think you can speak for Her Highness. She'll have to tell me that herself."

Shaking her head, Dominique pinned him with an expression which was a cross between amusement and exasperation.

"You are a complete mess. What am I gonna do with you?"

"My suggestion?" Denzel lifted one eyebrow as he stared into her face. "Keep me."

Her response to his idea was delayed by Justin's entrance through the front door.

"Sir. Ma'am." He tilted his head in greeting. Holding out a large parcel envelope, he extended it toward them. "Miss Truman, this came for you from the studio."

"Thank you..." Dominique looked between Denzel and Justin in question.

"Justin, ma'am."

"Thank you, Justin." Nodding, the other man walked away. Dominique turned the envelope over in her hands, looking at the information printed on the outside.

"That was quick. I just got the notification the package was on its way less than an hour ago. They must have sent it the moment it was picked up."

"Oh yeah? What is it?"

"It's the script for the first episode. We shot a pilot, and it tested well. But they wanted to make a few changes for the next episode. I guess I know how I'm spending my weekend now. I'll have to get as familiar as possible. They want us to come in to the studio on Monday. I don't want to not be prepared if they want to start table reads."

Guiding her with a hand on her back, Denzel escorted her toward the kitchen.

"Well, let me know if you want some help. I'm decent at running lines."

When Dominique gave him side eye, he returned it. "What? I'm a registered actor with the Silver Screen Association. I'm pretty sure I can handle running lines. I don't have to be perfect, right?"

Tilting her head in agreement, Dominique gave him a curious expression. "You have a point. We'll see. I don't want to distract you. I know this is an important weekend with the playoffs leading up to the big game. I'm sure you have stats and other things you need to look over to be prepared for Sunday."

In all the things she said, what Denzel keyed in on was she'd been keeping up with the goings on with professional football. And, she knew the games were being broadcast on the network that aired his show. He wasn't the only one who'd been paying attention.

"You let me worry about those stats. There are people who compile most of the statistical information for me. I do a final check over and watch some game footage, but it shouldn't stop me from helping you out if you need it. Why don't we discuss it further over lunch?"

They entered the kitchen to see the chef standing at the stove with a couple of woks and a pot on the cooktop. One wok was covered, the same as the pot, and the other wasn't. Steam wafted up from whatever he was cooking in it.

"Hey, Chef Bo." Denzel called out as he pulled out a chair for Dominique to sit in front of the island separating the cooking area from the eat in portion of the space. Two table settings were already in place, as if either Silvia or the chef was anticipating them having lunch together.

"Hey, Reyes. How's it going?"

Chef Bo turned from the stove to nod at him before his face stretched into a smile when he saw Dominique.

"Good afternoon, Miss Truman."

"Chef, I told you to call me Dominique."

"Excuse me. Good afternoon, Dominique."

Grunting, Denzel shot him a glare. "Stop flirting with my woman, Bo."

Dominique gasped, but Denzel kept his eyes on the personal chef, who simply smiled even brighter. Cheeky fucker.

"Den..." Dominique murmured softly. Her request for him to stop it was implied in what she didn't say.

Knowing she didn't like what some women called his Neanderthal displays was enough for him to tone it down, but not enough for him to refrain from shooting the flirty bastard a warning glance. Clapping his hands together, Bo turned back to the stove, grabbing the handle of the uncovered wok.

He lifted it, giving it a back-and-forth shake, causing the contents inside to flip high enough for Denzel to see the vegetables. His stomach rumbled, reminding him of why he came to the kitchen in the first place. Asking Dominique what she wanted to drink, he went to the fridge.

By the time he'd poured them both tall glasses of water and returned to take his seat, Chef Bo was walking toward them with two plates. Authentic Chinese dumplings were on one plate while another was filled with a stir fry vegetable medley. Going back to the stove, he returned with spring rolls and rice. With one final trip, he carried a small tray containing his custom sauces to dip or drizzle as they desired.

Since his mama taught him manners, Denzel thanked the cocky chef before serving Dominique, then plating his own food. He was proud to see she didn't try to do it herself. It had taken a couple of false starts, but she seemed to understand that he preferred to do those things for her.

Thanking him, she waited until he served himself before picking up her fork and starting a different conversation from the one they were having in the foyer.

"So, how's your day been so far?"

"You don't want to talk about my boring morning."

Denzel dipped a dumpling into the soy dipping sauce and took a bite. The flavors burst on his tongue and it took actual effort for him not to hum in appreciation. Chef Bo was a terrible flirt, but he could cook his ass off.

"Of course I want to know. I was taught never to ask questions I didn't want to know the answer to, and don't bullshit people wasting their time by pretending you're interested." With a shrug, she picked up a spring roll. "But if you don't want to talk about it, that's cool. We don't have to."

Swallowing his bite of deliciousness, Denzel covered her hand with his own. "Sorry, I thought you were just making small talk."

"I'll let you in on a secret." Dominique looked around like she was about to reveal level ten confidential information. "I don't know how to make small talk. I never have. It's made for some very awkward interactions at industry gatherings. I prefer genuine conversations where I learn something—either about the person or what they do."

He didn't say it aloud, but her statement explained a lot. Over the years, Denzel had considered her either direct to a fault or completely closed off. It appeared he'd been at least partially mistaken about the reasons she sometimes seemed withdrawn. Squeezing her fingers, he rubbed the back of her hand before releasing it. With a wide smile, he picked up his fork again.

"I can probably help you with that. But for now, since you asked, prepare to be dazzled by the intricacies of business projections and future trends."

Chapter Fifteen
DETECTIVE MARISSA CLARKE

After listening to Denzel talk about how he'd spent part of his morning, Dominique made a mental note to phrase her question differently the next time. Most of what he said went in one ear and out the other—although there was the occasional gem she tucked away for future reference. Despite being bored to tears, as he'd predicted, she'd listened attentively.

The weekend passed with each of them doing their own thing during the day and coming together in the evening for dinner. Other than on Sunday. On that day, Denzel rose early to go into the studio. She would've thought he'd have to fly out to the game, but he wasn't a part of the onsite team for the playoffs. Only the big game. For that one, he'd leave a couple of days before and wouldn't be back until the day after—or late on game night.

She was standing in front of the mirror finishing with her light makeup when Denzel entered the bathroom. Crowding her back, he wrapped his arms around her before dropping a kiss on the sliver of skin exposed by the neckline of her sweater.

"Mm... You smell delicious."

"Don't start, Den."

Placing the tube of lip gloss back into the small makeup pouch, Dominique fought to keep her eyes open and remain focused.

"I'm not starting anything—just making an observation."

"Mhmm. And you had to cuddle up next to me and put your lips on me to do it?"

With a squeeze to emphasize his point, he placed his chin on her shoulder, putting his face next to hers. Meeting her eyes in the mirror, he asked, "how else am I supposed to do it? From across the room? Downstairs?"

"Don't be a smart ass." For a split-second, Dominique felt like one of the older ladies from church when she pinched Denzel's wrist. Of course, she didn't do it nearly as hard as Sister Eloise.

"Ow! We're gonna have a talk about you trying to abuse me."

Squirming in his hold, Dominique was finally able to turn around. Of course, Denzel didn't allow her to leave his embrace fully.

"Do we need to discuss the definition of abuse again?"

Her question was immediately followed by a gasping squeak when Denzel suddenly lifted her onto the countertop after shoving her cosmetics aside. Stepping into the vee he created with her legs, he lowered his face to hers.

"I can think of other things to discuss. Like ways you can make it up to me."

Shaking her head, Dominique dug deep for the inner fortitude to lean away. Placing a hand on his chest, she straightened her arm to keep him at bay.

"Nope. No, sir. We don't have time for your kind of suggestions. My ride will be here soon to take me to the studio, and I still haven't had breakfast."

She was grasping at straws, but Dominique would use whatever methods she had in her arsenal. One of the things she'd learned pretty quickly was his dislike of her skipping breakfast. He'd tried to play it cool, but failed miserably. She got away with it on Friday. Dominique knew it was likely because he'd assumed she'd come down at a decent hour to eat on her own.

If given the choice between sleeping or eating, Dominique usually chose sleep. And Denzel had worn her all the way out. Sleep was calling her name in a big way. However, he was one of those people who believed in starting the day with a good breakfast. So, she played on that to get him to display the strength she wasn't sure she had in order to keep them from ripping each other's clothes off again.

It wasn't like they hadn't started the morning with him waking her with an orgasm before he went down to work out. Their chemistry was scary strong, and Dominique really required a little space to not feel like a walking bundle of sexual hormones. Only, she needed him to be the one to back off. From her behavior in the gym a few days ago, she didn't have it in her to hold firm.

The breath trapped in her lungs came out in a relieved sigh when he snagged a quick kiss and backed away to lift her from her perch.

"Fine. You win this time."

When she was once again on her feet, he placed a stilling hand on her hip.

"You get a delay in the game, but it's not over."

Warmth spread from where his hand lay, and Dominique quickly took advantage of the reprieve, gathering her things to leave the bathroom.

"You can just leave those there, unless you think you'll need them during the day."

At his insistence, she was using his bathroom to finish getting dressed. Yet another testament to her inability to tell this man no. Her belongings were slowing migrating from downstairs up to his suite. She hadn't brought it up. Dominique told herself it was because his rooms were much nicer than her already beautiful accommodations.

If there wasn't time for a quickie, there definitely wasn't time for them to get into the discussion of where she left her personal items and laid her head each night. That can of worms was a slippery squirmy pile of 'this is gonna take a while.' With her decision made for the moment, Dominique simply picked up the smallest pouch containing lip treatments and her emergency compact.

The smell of bacon reached her prior to Dominique entering the kitchen. Ignoring her complaints about cooking for her every day, Silvia waved them to seats at the island and slid hot plates in front of them. Whatever her thoughts on the situation between Dominique and

Denzel, the older woman never said a word or implied she was anything but pleased to have Dominique there. She seemed to enjoy giving Denzel a hard time, but she was otherwise kind. It helped that she was very efficient at her job and kept the house running so smoothly it felt like there were magical elves at work keeping things neat and orderly.

A chirping from Denzel's phone interrupted their light morning conversation. Unlocking the device, he looked at the screen. Dominique didn't bother to peek at the display. She forked the last bite of her eggs into her mouth and chewed.

Even though she didn't bother to look, he tapped her forearm and held the phone where she could see the screen.

"Your ride is here."

The image of the dark SUV driving through the gate being driven by the dark-skinned beauty from the conference call with GPS was displayed. She hadn't expected Nikki to show up personally for her first day at the studio. She knew Haley and Erik were coming, but Nikki was a surprise.

Thanking Silvia for the breakfast, she excused herself only to be followed from the kitchen by Denzel.

"I forgot my bag upstairs. I'll be right back."

Not waiting for his response, she went up to grab her messenger bag. After making sure the script was safely tucked inside, she was at the top of the flight of stairs in a matter of minutes. As quick as she thought she was, her new security team was apparently faster.

As she stepped onto the landing to descend the stairs, Dominique heard Nikki and Denzel exchanging pleasantries as she introduced him to Erik and Haley again. All three were dressed casually and would easily fit in with the rest of the cast and people, whom she expected to be milling around the studio.

The ladies pulled off the, 'I'm not a bodyguard' look better than Erik. Unfortunately, no degree of jeans and pullover wearing could hide the nearly military erectness in his posture. Considering what she'd learned about Grant Personal Security, it was quite likely he was a veteran of some branch of the military.

"Good morning."

Dominique called out to the group when she made it to the bottom of the stairs. Accepting Denzel's hand to clear the last few steps, she greeted her security detail with a bright smile.

"Good morning, Miss Truman. You remember Haley and Erik, correct?"

Nikki gestured to the average height Black woman, who had her long hair swept up into a high ponytail, and the taller man with a light bronze tan and a low haircut resembling a fade. Reaching out to shake their hands, Dominique nodded.

"Of course. Nice to meet you in person, Haley, Erik. And please, everyone, call me Dominique or Dom. I'll answer to both."

Returning her handshake, the two only nodded their agreement. Neither went so far as to actually use her first name. Dominique wondered if they'd need some kind of team building exercise to relax. Because, how were they supposed to come off as *not* being bodyguards if they couldn't even call her by her first name? Pushing the thought aside, Dominique turned to Nikki.

"I didn't expect to see you today, Nikki. I thought you would only fill in as needed."

Nodding, Nikki looped her thumbs into the waistband of the jeans hugging her body like they were getting paid top dollar.

"I will, but I wanted to be around for the first day to make sure everything got off on the right foot. Just in case wires got crossed at the studio or something. I also wanted any of the new people the show brought in to see my face and associate me with you in the future."

"That's smart." Dominique dipped her chin in agreement. "Well, I'm ready if you are." Holding up her bag, she tapped it. "I have everything I need."

As soon as the words left her lips, Denzel slipped an arm around her waist. Bending, he spoke directly into her ear.

"You *almost* have everything you need."

Lifting a brow, she stared up at him.

"You need a goodbye slash good luck kiss."

While spoken lowly, it wasn't a whisper and was definitely overheard by the others.

"On that note, we'll wait for you outside."

Nikki issued her statement before opening the front door and ushering the rest of the team out to the car.

Yielding to the pressure of Denzel's fingertips at her back, Dominique turned in his embrace. The kiss he touted as a combination good luck and goodbye kiss had a decidedly carnal slant. Pride tinged with disappointment flowed through Dominique when she pulled away.

Pride because she'd surprised herself with being able to put an end to the kiss, but disappointed because it ended. It didn't make sense, but it didn't have to. Her feelings were mirrored in the slight crease of his brow when he stared at her.

"I really need to get going." Patting his chest, Dominique smoothed her hands over his pecs before resting them on his shoulders.

"Yeah. I know."

"You're gonna have to let go of me."

"Yeah. I know." Denzel's fingers flexed against her lower back before he reluctantly released her.

Clasping her hand in his, he walked them the few steps to the front door. Opening it, he dropped one final peck on her cheek.

"Have a great day, Baby."

"You too."

Dominique smiled up at him as she stepped over the threshold. Once she was settled in the back seat, she looked around to see he was still standing in the doorway. He didn't close it until the vehicle pulled away from the house. It was only when she turned her gaze to the other occupants of the car that she noticed the sly grin on Nikki's face. Despite her knowing expression, the other woman made no comment about Dominique and Denzel parting as if days instead of hours would pass before they saw one another again.

As it so happened, it was a good idea for Nikki to join them on the first day. Despite her careful planning, someone had dropped the ball regarding the team accompanying Dominique in all areas while she was on the premises. They'd made it through the gate just fine, but at the offices, one of the security guards attempted to stop them.

Dominique almost felt bad for the person on the other end of the call once Nikki was done with them. She didn't take anything out on the security guard who was simply doing his job, but she lit into the head of security since he was responsible for making certain their credentials weren't questioned. By the time all was said and done, profuse apologies were being issued.

Again, Dominique wondered about the whole 'blending in' aspect of her security detail. But her question was soon answered when they entered the conference room. She'd expected a trailer would be assigned to her when production started, but she hadn't known she'd have an office, of sorts, while they were rehearsing and going through table reads.

In her office, Dominique stood to one side as they literally swept every inch of the space, looking for listening devices and hidden cameras. She never would've thought of doing that. Honestly, she couldn't fathom anyone wanting dirt on her so badly they'd go to such extremes. While her success had risen significantly in the past few years, she still wasn't a huge name in the business. Someone making a big payday from photos or recordings of her wasn't something she considered a viable option at the moment.

She was in awe of their thoroughness in her office, but floored by the chameleon like way they integrated themselves into the group once they entered the conference room. Haley stuck close to Dominique, but she gave off more of a personal assistant vibe than bodyguard.

"There she is!" Wearing a wide smile, his signature wire-rimmed glasses and ever-present black cardigan, Adam Waters approach her with his arms stretched open.

"Hey, Adam."

Dominique returned the smile as well as the hug. It was no secret Adam was the reason she was chosen as the lead for The Clarke Files. He'd used his clout to make sure she landed the role. She only knew because people talk, and her agent filled Dominique in the minute she heard about the background machinations.

If it were possible, Adam's eyes brightened even further when he noticed Nikki. Taking Dominique's elbow, he escorted her closer to where Nikki was speaking with Jerricka Bishop, the head stylist for the show. They made a striking pair, with Jerricka being only slightly shorter than Nikki, but rocking similar abundant curves.

"Well, hello, Miss Reed. I didn't expect to see you today. Have you met our star?" Not giving Nikki a chance to answer, Adam launched into the introductions. "Dominique Truman, this is Nikki Reed. Nikki, meet Dominique. She's the Clarke in The Clarke Files."

Nikki's smile could only be described as indulgent when she looked at Adam. It was obvious he not only knew who she was, but what she did for a living. The director looked at her like he wouldn't need a plate or a biscuit to sop her up. Her towering over him by at least four inches didn't matter.

"Thank you, Adam. But, I've met Dominique. I drove her here this morning."

Adam's jaw dropped, but he quickly recovered. "Oh. Well, that's good to know." He wasn't at all subtle about the way he scanned the room, following Nikki's response.

"You know how we do things, Adam. We won't disrupt your process."

"Of course." Adam's dark mass of tousled shoulder length hair bounced lightly with the bobbing of his head.

Jerricka bumped Adam to the side to get closer to Dominique. Tossing him and Nikki an admonishing glance, she pulled Dominique into a hug.

"Since these two have forgotten I'm here, I'll just make room for myself. Hey, girl! I'm so happy you're here. I can't wait to dress you! I have *so* many ideas. We're gonna keep it cute, sassy, and sexy. Because, what they ain't finna do is hide all this fine in baggy, frumpy clothes."

One would think that as long as she'd known Jerricka, Dominique would've expected the praise, since the stylist wasn't stingy with it. Yet, she still ducked her head a little and blushed. Before Jerricka could go into things more deeply, knocking drew everyone's attention to the open doorway. Douglas Fowler smiled once he knew every eye was on him.

"Hello, everyone. It's great to have you all here. And before we get started, I'd like to take this opportunity to say how pleased I am we've assembled such a talented team. I feel like The Clarke Files has every-thing needed to make for an excellent show."

Walking further into the room, the executive producer stopped at the head of the long conference table where he began his spiel regarding the logistics of how the show would operate and who the contact persons were for particular needs. As he was wrapping up, a light commotion caused everyone to shift their focus back to the open doorway.

The young lady standing there was stunning, but it was obvious by her carriage, her knowledge of her appearance exceeded confidence. Standing behind her like a shadow was another young lady who was likely a personal assistant.

"I'm so sorry I'm late. This place is so big, I got turned around." Her apology was delivered with an airy giggle as she pressed one hand to the breasts, which looked like they might topple her small frame if she was even an inch taller. As it was, she appeared to be barely over five feet.

Extending his arm as he approached her, Douglas brushed off the apology. "It's no problem." Once he had her hand in his, he turned to face the rest of the group. "You're just in time for the formal introductions. So, why don't we start with you? Everyone, this is Bliss Meadows."

Dominique kept her expression neutral, but she noticed the way Jerricka's whole body stiffened when Bliss made her appearance. Even without her inside track from having worked with Jerricka previously, Dominique would've been able to put two and two together and come up with exactly four. She recognized the name and the face, but Dominique hadn't worked with Bliss before. However, Jerricka's reaction combined with her little performance were enough for Dominique to know Bliss was about that bullshit.

Great. Just great. Dominique tried to shrug off the feeling of foreboding. But considering Douglas's reaction to the younger woman, she knew she would do well to keep her eyes open and not turn her back. Douglas making Bliss the center of attention as if she were playing the title character of the show instead of Dominique, didn't escape her attention.

Knowing the only way to deal with bullies was to face them head on, Dominique pasted her most genuine fake smile on her face and stood to her feet.

"It's very nice to meet you, Bliss." Pulling everyone's gaze to her,

Dominique nodded to each person in turn. "I believe I've met almost everyone here. But, for those who don't know me, I'm Dominique Truman."

"Don't be shy, Dom. Tell them who you really are." Adam's chest puffed out with pride as he stood beside her. "This, ladies and gentlemen, is Detective Marissa Clarke."

Clapping erupted around the room despite most of the occupants knowing exactly who Dominique was and her role on the show. Pushing her hands down to calm the applause, she once again swept her gaze around the room. Ignoring the pout on Bliss's face, she smiled at each of them.

"Thank you all for the warm welcome. I look forward to working with each of you. And, I just know we're going to create something great together."

"Damn right we are." Adam chimed in before taking his turn introducing himself, then passing the baton to the person sitting next to him.

Once it was obvious the attention wouldn't return to them, Douglas escorted Bliss to an empty seat where she sat with her lip poked out. Catching Jerricka's eye, Dominique tilted her head in silent conversation. The other woman's nod was the response to Dominique's silent request for the whole scoop. She needed to know what she'd gotten herself into.

Chapter Sixteen

DOMINIQUE DAY

For Denzel, the past week had flown by in a blur. Why the fuck had they started scheduling the big game so close to Valentine's Day? It was like they didn't know football fans, players, and those associated with the industry had other obligations. He brushed off the fact that, until Dominique, it hadn't mattered. However, since they were together, his focus had shifted.

It had to. Because, not only would this be their first holiday as a couple, it would be their first time spending her birthday together. Years ago, when he learned Dominique was a Valentine's Day baby, he thought it couldn't be more appropriate for her to be born on the day of love. From his perspective, she was Oshun, Aphrodite, and Inanna all rolled into one beautiful package.

He'd been working on a surprise for her from the moment he knew she was temporarily relocating to the Atlanta area. If he had anything to say about it, the move would be permanent. But, he'd cross that bridge when he got to it.

Standing up straight, he looked around the bathroom at his handi-work. He'd cancelled his morning workout session with Rob to begin Dominique Day by pampering his woman. Sweeping his gaze around the room, he made sure everything was in place.

Steam wafted up from the scented water beneath the white sea of bubbles in the large jetted tub. Since it was morning, he decided against candles, but added strategically placed rose petals. On a small table within arm's reach of a person lounging in the water, were breakfast finger foods, along with water and juice.

Nodding to himself after finishing his mental checklist, he exited the bathroom to wake the woman sleeping in his bed. The sun was barely peeking above the horizon when he opened the curtains, allowing the dim natural light to fall over his sleeping beauty. His Una clearly wasn't a morning person, but he'd devised a wake-up strategy that didn't result in a grumpy woman.

Easing the covers off her lush body, he took a second to admire the expanse of mesmerizing dark skin. Without fully waking, Dominique began to squirm. Obviously missing the warmth of the sheets and duvet, she rolled from her side to her back, scooting toward where he would be if he hadn't already risen from the bed.

Taking advantage of her new position, Denzel eased her legs open and began kissing a path up the inside of her thighs. When he reached the apex, he almost forgot his mission when Dominique's pelvis tilted as if Her Highness was offering herself to him for morning worship. Licking his lips, he accepted the offering, placing a suckling kiss on her mons.

He'd learned the trick of waking her with an orgasm purely by greedy accident. He'd wanted to taste her and hadn't been able to resist. Much like this morning. Groaning at the flavor of the cream leaking from her slick walls, he gripped her thighs when they tightened in an attempt to clamp around his head.

Denzel didn't mind a nice pair of thigh shaped earmuffs. But he was on a mission, and suffocating wasn't on the agenda. A gasping moan escaped Dominique and fingers magically appeared in the short strands of his hair, tugging him closer to her center.

"Oh shit! Den! What?! I'm gonna!"

Her sleep rasped, tangled, incomplete sentences tumbled from her lips as a spurt of her essence landed on his tongue. Lapping up his prize, Denzel smiled against her fragrant pussy. Delivering kisses as her body trembled lightly while she came down from her orgasm, he patted himself on the back for success in nearly record time.

When the fingers raking through his hair gentled, he knew she was sufficiently sated for the moment. So, he gave Her Highness one final kiss before rising above Dominique. Leaning over her, he admired her morning glow. Crawling up her body, he settled between her legs, resting part of his weight on his elbows.

She was so relaxed he couldn't resist smiling before kissing her pillowy soft lips. "Happy Birthday, Baby."

"Mm... Thank you."

Once again, Denzel almost got distracted when Dominique lifted her legs, bracketing his sides with her soft heat. Gritting his teeth, Denzel steeled himself against going off script. With a few well-placed internal curses, he pressed against her thighs and sat up. Grasping her hands, he tugged her up with him.

"Come with me. I have a surprise for you."

"For me?" Staring at him with wide eyes, Dominique was the picture of genuine shock with one hand pressed to her chest.

"Yes, birthday girl. For you."

Another gentle tug got her to the edge of the bed. Once her feet dangled off the sides, he scooped her into his arms bridal style, earning himself a tight hug and a tickle from puffs of air skimming his skin with her giggles. He loved the sound of her happiness and aimed to make them constant.

The moment they crossed the threshold into the bathroom, Dominique's giggles transformed into a gasping sigh.

"Oh, Den... This is so sweet." Her words were accompanied by the kisses she rained on his face until he reluctantly placed her on her feet.

A bonus to sleeping naked was her being able to immediately step into the heated tub. When he sat on the side, she looked up with questions in her eyes.

"Aren't you getting in with me?"

"No. This is all about you." Shaking his head, he used a fork to pick up a chunk of fresh pineapple. Extending the piece to her, he issued a command.

"Open."

Accepting the sweet tangy fruit, she puckered her lips as she chewed. Leaning back, she allowed the built-in cushion to support her head. Opening without prompting for another piece of pineapple, she lifted an eyebrow as she stared at him.

"If it's about me, I should get what I want, right?"

"In theory." Denzel responded slowly as he broke off a piece of croissant, spread strawberry jam on it, and offered it to her. Despite her pout, she parted her lips to receive it.

"So, *all about me* has conditions? How is that fair?"

Using a cloth napkin to wipe the edge of her mouth, Denzel leaned in, resting a forearm on his leg.

"The conditions are there to make sure it remains all about you. Making your day easier, stress free, and happy. If I get in there with you, you know what's gonna happen, right?"

Wet fingers landed on his leg, wetting the sweatpants he wore.

"That's what I'm counting on, Mr. Reyes."

Closing his eyes to have a private conversation with his dick, Denzel didn't open them again until he thought he had himself somewhat under control. Piercing her with a heated stare, he was finally able to respond.

"Do you think there's a chance in hell I'll get into this tub and not fuck you? And in the process, fuck your hair all the way up, which will likely make you late getting to the studio."

Leaning away, he lifted her fingers from his leg. "Now, if you'd taken the day off, I'd be happy to join you and spend as much time as you want worshiping every inch of your beautiful body. But..."

"Being an adult sucks ass."

A hearty chuckle escaped Denzel's lips at the pout on Dominique's face following her declaration. Taking a chance, he leaned in to kiss away the frown.

"You're right. At times it does."

Pulling away before he took things too far, he reached for the juice to offer her a sip. After he was done feeding her, he left her to soak for a bit while he went to retrieve the first of the gifts he had for her. Returning, he helped her from the tub. When she walked in the direction of the shower, he followed.

"Now... If you want some help in the shower, I might be able to oblige." Grabbing her shower cap from the hook, he removed her bonnet and replaced it.

Tipping up her cute little nose, Dominique shocked him with her refusal. "Nope. That ship has sailed. I was gonna ride you until my legs gave out. I'm over it now."

A growl announced Denzel's intentions before he grabbed her around the waist, lifting her in front of him, and marching into the shower. His pants were shucked off while he maintained his hold on her squirming giggling form.

Her breathless denials were ignored as he twisted the handles to start the spray of water while stalking her until the backs of her legs hit the cool porcelain bench along the back wall. Sitting next to her, he quickly relocated her to his lap.

"Nah, Una. You don't get to sit your pretty ass down now. You wanted a birthday ride. You're getting a birthday ride."

Feats of willpower should be rewarded with actual medals. Dominique's giggles faded as she wrapped her soft fingers around his stiff length and slide her wet pussy down his shaft. His control only went so far. So, when she bottomed out and remained still, the smack he delivered to her rounded ass couldn't be prevented.

"Where's my good girl?"

Rubbing the affected area, he dropped a kiss on her lips before trailing pecks along her jaw and down to the crook of her neck. Coolness wafted over the base of his shaft when Dominique raised herself up before dropping back down on his cock.

"There she is..." Their sounds of carnal appreciation bounced off the walls as he guided her in the celebratory ride. When her climax clamped his dick within the vice of her silky walls, Denzel didn't attempt to stop the flow of his cum into her tight channel.

She laid slumped against him while he leaned his back into the cool tiles as they got their breathing under control. Gently rubbing his hands from her shoulders down to the curve of her ass and back, he placed a kiss on her damp forehead.

"Happy Birthday, baby."

"Mmm..."

Denzel's face stretched into a lazy smile at her satisfied response. He deserved another pat on the back for waking her early enough to allow her a quick nap before she had to get dressed for her day.

"Thanks Wendy, let me know if there's something I need to look into while I'm in Vegas this week."

"Sure thing, boss."

Ending the video call with his business manager, Denzel closed his laptop to end his workday. The only upside about leaving at the ass crack of dawn to fly out to Las Vegas would be he could kill two birds with one stone while he was there. He could check in on CleanSun in between his pre-game obligations.

As a sports fan, he always enjoyed the pre-game analysis and other activities leading up to the main event. Now that he was on the other side of the desk, he found some of it more than a little redundant. How many times did the same stats need to be repeated anyway?

Just as he removed his phone from vibrate mode, it dinged with a notification. A smile spread across his face when he saw it. Even if he'd have to leave Dominique in bed sleeping in less than twenty-four hours, Denzel felt good about his plans for the day.

Earlier, once they'd finally peeled themselves apart to shower, he'd presented her with her first gift. The platinum filigree bracelet with inlaid jewels looked magnificent against her dark skin. She put it on immediately after showering him with kisses.

A short time later, her phone began to ring with birthday wishes from her family and friends. Stepping away to continue to dress, Denzel was certain he wore a goofy smile from simply watching the joy she displayed at the affection she received from her loved ones.

People born on holidays tended to get a raw deal when it came to commemorating their birth. So, he was happy to learn the Trumans were holding true to form. He'd observed the way they treated one another during the Novy God celebration at Andrei's the previous month. From what he saw, they were a tight-knit, loving family.

The six dozen roses he'd had delivered to the studio had earned him

a very sweet text message from Dominique, followed by a phone call.
The flowers were the first of her Valentine's Day gifts. Some might say
he was going overboard, but Denzel didn't give a shit. There was no
such thing when it came to his Una.

As he was getting ready to leave his office, he encountered Juan in
the hallway.

"The people are here. Did you want to come out and take a look?"

"Yeah. Thanks, Juan."

The unseasonably warm weather would work to their advantage for
the plans he had for him and Dominique this evening. After inspecting
everything and making minor adjustments, Denzel checked in with
Chef Bo once more before he went up to finish packing. By the time the
sun was on the decline, everything was set and waiting for Dominique
to get home.

Meeting her at the door was mandatory for tonight. So, Denzel was
standing there when she exited the car, waving goodbye to Haley and
Erik as they drove away. Meeting her on the short flight of stairs leading
to the door, he relieved her of the vase she held before kissing her
inviting lips.

"Mmm... Hey, Baby. Did you have a good day?"

"It wasn't bad. Thank you again for the flowers."

"You're more than welcome."

Stealing another kiss, he grabbed her hand and escorted her into the
house, skillfully keeping her pointed in the direction he wanted.

"Why did you bring these home?" Denzel questioned as he lifted the
vase of flowers slightly higher.

"I wanted at least one here where I could see and enjoy them."

Placing the vase on a table in the hallway, he tugged her toward the
elevator using their joined hands.

"Come with me."

Dominique stared at him in speculation, but she didn't resist—
despite giving him side eye on the way up to the third floor. When he
pushed opened the door leading to the bedroom suite, Denzel stood to
the side to allow her to enter first.

"Oh! Den..."

Her hands covered her gaping mouth as she took slow, measured steps into the room. Various arrangements of flowers, including roses, were strategically placed in the sitting area. Taking her hand again, he led her into the bedroom, which was similarly adorned with fragrant bouquets.

"You have plenty of pretty flowers to look at here, Baby."

Dominique's eyes glistened with what he hoped were happy tears before she placed her soft hands on his face, guiding his head closer to hers to receive a kiss.

"Thank you. This is too much, but thank you."

Gripping her waist, he pulled her body flush with his.

"There is no such thing as too much when it comes to you, Una."

After another slow kiss, he steeled himself to pull away before his carefully thought-out plans were derailed. A tap on her hip, and another peck and he was able to put some distance between them.

"The day isn't over, Baby. Why don't you get changed for dinner?"

"Changed? Is it fancy?" The small crinkle in Dominique's nose was there and gone in an instant, but Denzel saw it.

"No. Not fancy. I took the liberty of picking something for you. It's laid out in the closet."

Her eyes widened for a second before she covered that expression as well.

"Let me just hop in the shower. I'll be right out."

Denzel somehow managed to keep himself busy so as not to give into the temptation to join Dominique in the shower. The image of the water gliding over her satiny skin was too vivid in his mind, and he had to step all the way out of the room to hold himself back.

When he returned, Dominique was exiting the closet wearing the jeans and lightweight sweater he'd laid out for her. She jumped slightly and put her hands behind her back when she noticed him, but she was too late. He'd seen the rectangular box.

Slowly approaching, he tipped his head from one side to the other.

"I know you aren't trying to hide things from me. Are you?"

Attempting to sidestep him, Dominique tilted her chin up. "I have no idea what you're talking about."

Sliding in front of her to block her path, Denzel stared down at her with one raised eyebrow. *Really?* The silent question was written on his face, but not spoken aloud.

Releasing a frustrated huff, Dominique removed the item from behind her back.

"Here, Mr. Nosey. I was going to give it to you after dinner."

Looking at the box wrapped in navy wrapping paper with a silver bow tied around it, Denzel kept his hands at his sides.

"You still can." At her lifted brows, he added, "give it to me later. I didn't mean to spoil your surprise."

Trailing a finger down the side of her face, he couldn't resist kissing her gloss-covered lips. He'd been so focused on making the day special for her, he'd never considered that she might want to do the same for him. Playing the events of the past half hour back, he realized something.

"Did you think I'd already found this when I said I'd laid out clothes for you?"

"Yes, but when I looked in the drawer, it was exactly where I left it."

Cupping her face, he kissed her lips, then her nose and finally her forehead.

"I would never go through your things. If I want to know something, I'll ask. I'm not that kind of person."

He maintained eye contact as he allowed himself to be soothed by the firm strokes to his chest from her rubbing hands.

"I didn't think you were snooping. But I didn't exactly bury it under a mound of clothes. If you'd looked in the drawer to get something out, it was in plain sight."

Nodding, Denzel moved them past the subject. He was ready to get their evening started. Taking the elevator down to the first floor, he led her through to the French doors leading out to the pool area. Lit softly by the strategically placed solar lights, it was the beginning of the romantic atmosphere.

Large lotus flowers ranging in shades from light pink to purple floated in the pool, adding a tropical edge to the ambiance. Dominique's fingers tightened in his hold, and he brought her hand to his lips to kiss the back. Leading her around the pool, they walked to where two attendants stood next to a table.

Situated near the fire pit, the elegantly set two-person table was covered with a floor length table cloth with candles placed at the center.

"Den, I thought you said it wasn't fancy."

Squeezing her fingers in return, he tapped the back of her hand. "It's not, Baby. We're essentially in my back yard."

"If you say so..."

"I do. Now, come sit. Our night is just beginning."

Accepting the seat he pulled out for her, Dominique's gaze continued to sweep the area. Even if she hadn't said a word, Denzel felt her appreciation and awe of the thought he'd put into the evening.

"Now, just so you know. This is part of Valentine's Day. Not Dominique Day."

"Dominique Day?" Quirking one eyebrow, she gifted him with a confused half smile.

"Of course, Baby. The rest of the world might not have come around to making it official—including you. But your birthday is a holiday within itself."

Raising the glass of wine the attendant poured for them, Denzel gestured for her to lift hers as well.

"To Dominique Day."

With her lips tilted in a smile and her cheeks high with the cutest blush, Dominique clinked her glass against his. "To Dominique Day."

Chapter Seventeen

WHO DOES THAT?

Dominique's face hurt from smiling. She couldn't believe Denzel had gone through so much effort to celebrate her birthday separately from Valentine's Day. She'd been wined and dined by men before, but Denzel Reyes was cutting new ground. They didn't even have a month under their belts and he was making himself an extremely tough act to follow.

Having dinner arranged outside near the fire pit, decorating the pool —not to mention the bedroom—might seem simple to some. But, she preferred activities where she didn't have to put on a public face and be concerned with having her privacy invaded. It was as if he knew it and was catering to the homebody part of her, while still giving her the attention she deserved.

Seeing how all out he went, made her a little nervous about the simplicity of the gift she'd gotten for him. However, the way his eyes lit up when he learned she'd bought him something eased her anxiety a little. Something she'd learned from observing Zaria and Andrei was that wealthy men get accustomed to showering others with material things without usually having their actions reciprocated.

It's not how she was raised. So, as she clinked her wine-filled glass with Denzel's, she resolved to remember to give and not just receive. If they were really going to give this relationship thing a go, he couldn't be the only one making such efforts.

Conversation over dinner was easy, even though Dominique was eager to learn what else he had planned. From the goat cheese and fig Crostini appetizer, to the palate cleansing citrus and arugula salad, to the braised short ribs over truffle mashed potatoes, dinner was excellent. Clearing her plate, Dominique was forced to wave off the chocolate lava cake dessert offering.

"I couldn't possibly eat another bite. This was amazing."

Folding her cloth napkin, she laid it beside her empty plate. The attendants quietly cleared the table of everything, save the candles and their wine glasses. Sensing the moment was now right, Dominique slid the box, she'd placed to the side, to the center of the table.

Allowing his fingers to linger over the package, Denzel finally pulled it closer to him. He didn't immediately open it. Instead, he held up one hand. One of the young men who'd been attending them placed an envelope into Denzel's palm. With a quick word of thanks, he mimicked her action, sliding the envelope closer to her.

"Same time?" A slight smile lifted his lips as he asked.

"Sure." Dominique fingered the edge of the slender white package before lifting the lip at the same moment Denzel released the bow from the top of his box.

Curiosity formed a crease in her forehead as she read the words on the page. She'd just reached full understanding when Denzel's voice broke the silence.

Holding up the black silk tie with the gray diamond pattern stitching, he turned it over in his hand. Running his fingertip over the custom jewel inlaid tie pin, he whistled as he traced his initials in sparkling gems.

"This is really nice, Baby. Gorgeous. Thank you."

"You're welcome."

Although Dominique didn't think the tie and pin came close to the things he'd given her already, she was pleased he seemed to like them. She on the other hand, was at a loss for words regarding the contents of her envelope. Denzel noticed her silence.

"Is there something wrong? Do you not like it? I know it's more practical than sexy, but I thought—"

"I love it. I'm just not sure how to respond."

Carefully placing his gift back into the box, Denzel put the lid on it and set it aside to grasp her hands in his.

"Thank you would be appropriate. What other way did you think you needed to respond?"

Lifting and lowering one shoulder, Dominique slid her thumb over the back of his hand. He'd given her shares in two companies. Not enough for controlling interest. But based on the listed estimated value, enough to offer her decent residuals. *Who does that?*

"It feels like, *thank you,* isn't enough. Your gift isn't just thoughtful, it's generous."

"So is yours. Besides, this isn't a contest."

Standing when he lightly tugged her fingers, she met him at the midpoint between their seats, next to the table. The warmth from his large hand cupping the side of her face prompted her to close her eyes and enjoy the moment. While her eyelids hid the world, Denzel's lips captured hers in a sweet, sensual kiss.

Once he pulled away, she followed him with her gaze. His dark eyes said so much in their silence. Turning her head, she placed a kiss in the center of his palm.

"Thank you."

"You're welcome, Una."

Guiding her with a hand on her back, they circled the table. "Now, for the final surprise of the evening."

Dominique's steps faltered, but Denzel was right there to catch her.

"There's more?"

"Absolutely. Come with me."

His smile was contagious and Dominique added to the aching cheeks in her future by joining him. After they struck out over the grass past the pool house, she understood why he'd chosen the outfit he'd selected for her down to the sneakers on her feet. Coming almost to a complete stop, she walked on stiff legs toward Denzel's latest surprise.

"Are you serious right now?" Dominique had to remember to close her mouth after she asked the question.

Instead of a verbal answer, Denzel responded by nudging her toward the giant hot air balloon sitting directly in the center of his back yard.

"How long has this been here? How did I not see it?"

Dominique's peppered questions were answered as they got closer to the big red balloon with two wide horizontal white stripes. Ropes anchored it into the ground kept it from floating upwards. Standing next to the basket attached to the balloon was an older man with a striking shock of white hair and a Santa Claus-like beard.

"Clarence." Denzel greeted the older man, who stepped closer, extending his hand.

"Good evening, sir, ma'am."

Nodding in greeting, Dominique couldn't seem to tear her eyes away from the basket and balloon. A nudge to her side brought her gaze to Denzel.

"Are you listening, Baby? Clarence is going over the safety information."

Properly chastised for zoning out, Dominique gave the pilot her undivided attention. Once he was done, he opened the door on the side of the basket to usher them inside. Assisting her up the block stairs placed at the base of the basket, Denzel immediately presented her with a coat, zipping her in. A satin lined beanie was placed on her head, a scarf was knotted around her neck, and gloves were put on her hands. He was outfitting her as if she was a small child, before he moved to cover himself in any way.

Knowing as mild as the temperatures were, it would be much colder once they took off, Dominique didn't complain. She even returned the favor by knotting his scarf once he shrugged into a jacket and donned his beanie.

Benches were built into two sides of the basket. According to the rules Clarence rattled off, they had to sit during take-off and landing, but could stand during the time in between. Sitting on the tufted seat with Denzel's arm wrapped around her, Dominique was briefly overcome with emotion. He'd given her a gift she would've never thought to ask for. *She was **so** gonna fuck him good tonight.*

The feeling of weightlessness caused Dominique's stomach to drop, but she quickly adjusted as Clarence pulled the lever to send heat shooting into the balloon to lift them higher in the sky. As they rose, she peeked over the side to see the property get smaller and smaller.

Soon, they were high enough that Clarence gave them leave to move around the basket. Gazing over the side at the lights of Atlanta in the distance, Dominique was completely entranced. Denzel's arms snaked around her waist and she snuggled into him as she basked in the view.

"This is so beautiful. Thank you again."

Denzel managed to locate an exposed sliver of skin next to her ear to place a kiss.

"It's not nearly as beautiful as you, but you're welcome."

As they floated toward the city, he pointed out various structures which looked completely different from their new angle, lit up against the night sky. When they reached the area typically seen when you do an internet search for the city of Atlanta, Dominique remembered to pull out her phone for pictures. Lifting it from her fingers, Denzel took over when she started to struggle.

He snapped pictures and dutifully showed them to her for approval after each one.

"I think that's enough. Thank you. I love trying to take pictures, but mine would've probably been blurry. I don't know why I can't seem to stay stable enough to get a good shot."

Grinning at her own expense, she held out her hand for the device. Instead of giving it to her, Denzel swiped her arm down and leaned his face close to hers.

"Not done yet, Una. Smile."

Watching his smiling face on the display, Dominique matched his expression. After snapping a few in quick succession, he slipped the phone into her pocket and closed the zipper.

"Now, don't forget to send those to me."

Snuggling into his embrace, Dominique nodded in agreement as she watched the skyline get smaller as Clarence changed the direction of the hot air balloon to take them back home.

A lone arm reached from under the covers to tap against the phone as Dominique blindly silenced the alarm. Waking in bed by herself the next morning made the previous night feel like a dream. However, when she cast her sleepy gaze around the room, evidence of the night she and Denzel spent together was everywhere her eyes landed. Shifting in the bed, her lips twisted at the aching reminder of the acrobatic ways her body was bent in pursuit of commemorating their Valentine's Day together.

Haltingly stepping down out of the bed, she walked gingerly to the bathroom. She was never more thankful she'd rescheduled her workout with Kam than she was when she lowered herself onto the toilet to take care of her morning needs. The way her thighs screamed, Dominique might've fought her trainer if she'd been asked to do even one squat during their workout.

The sauna feature of Denzel's shower was definitely on her agenda. Dominique wished she had time for a quick soak, but she had to get to the studio. They were in heavy pre-production in preparation for actual shooting to start next week. Some of her excitement surrounding being the title character for a much-anticipated series had waned. Nothing overt had occurred, but Dominique remained on guard—especially after her conversation with Jerricka.

Last week

Leaning into the smooth bench seat of the booth, Dominique quirked an eyebrow at Jerricka. They were in a relatively private area of the restaurant, and the head stylist was giving her all the tea on their new cast addition. Dominique refused to refer to her as a co-star. Call it instinct, but she felt even referring to Bliss as a co-anything in her mind was an invitation for the other woman to gain a foothold.

"That little trick is trouble on two legs. I was hoping they weren't going to cast her after Holly did such a good job in the pilot episode."

Dominique nodded. She'd fully expected Holly Claire to be a part of the cast. They'd shot the pilot episode together, and from her perspective, they had great chemistry. There were only a couple of scenes, but she thought Holly had done really well. Apparently, talent wasn't top priority for the role.

Stirring her drink with the straw, Jerricka continued, "it's not that Bliss doesn't have talent. She does. She's no Holly Claire, but she can cry on cue and emote when required. But, for lack of a better way to say it, she's a backstabbing bitch. I've had to soothe too many ruffled feathers behind her and the way she treats anyone she deems unnecessary in furthering her career."

Dominique shook her head. Bliss wasn't the first young actress she'd met with a similar mindset, and she wasn't looking forward to having to share space with someone like that.

"So, what seems to be her goal? Get to the top no matter what? Does she not realize she won't always be twenty-something with a tight little body and a pretty face?"

Using the straw to stab at the ice floating in her drink, Jerricka replied, "I don't talk to her more than I have to, but making it big seems to be her primary goal. And she doesn't give a shit who she steps on to get there."

Lowering her voice and leaning closer, Dominique lifted an eyebrow as she stared at Jerricka knowingly.

"Apparently, it doesn't matter who she has to fuck either. We probably both know people who were forced to do things, but it doesn't look like the deal between her and Douglas."

"I'm sure we weren't the only ones who saw the way he was fawning over her." Jerricka bobbed her head in agreement.

Dominique hated having to think of another woman that way. And she was more than aware of the quid pro quo many studio execs operated under for nearly a century. You want the role, gotta fuck someone. However, it was completely possible to make it without trading sexual favors.

If it wasn't, then it was likely she would never see herself as a household name. Because, sacrificing her dignity was one bridge she never intended to cross. The offers had been there, especially when she was struggling to even get a call back, but it wasn't the way Dominique wanted to build her name.

As they were wrapping up with lunch, Jerricka snapped her fingers as if she'd just remembered something.

"Hey, did you get in touch with Candy about doing your make-up already? I reached out to her booking agent to see if she would contract with the show, and I was told she was already booked for a gig."

"I did. We got it squared away a few weeks ago."

Jerricka's expression was hard to read as Dominique watched her. "Is my booking her a problem? I wasn't sure who the show would hire, and I *know Candy can work with my skin tone as well as do some of the special effects makeup when needed."*

"She can. No. It's not a problem. We just need to let it be known that she's only there for you. When we worked together a while back, there was an issue with Bliss and Candy refuses to work with her again."

Dominique's brow lifted in understanding. She didn't care if she had to pay Candy out of her own pocket. There was no way Dominique was going to subject her to anyone she'd expressly refused to work with. She wasn't losing her makeup artist over someone else's bullshit.

Present

By the time Dominique was dressed and had dragged herself downstairs, Haley was sitting at the kitchen island chatting with Silvia. She didn't ask where Erik was. He'd show up when it was time to go.

"Buenos Dias, Dom. Do you want breakfast this morning?"

Silvia asked the question with a glint in her eyes. She'd never said a word, but it was as if she knew Dominique turning down breakfast would be a problem when and if Denzel found out.

"Good morning, Silvia. Don't go to any trouble. I can just have some fruit and oats."

"You let me worry about what's trouble. Haley was just telling me the traffic report looks good. So, you have time for more than a little bowl of instant oats."

"Silvia, between you and Chef, Kam is going to have to add reps to my routine to help me stay in shape for this role."

Flipping her hand, Silvia brushed Dominique off. "Pssh! You don't have to worry about that."

Arguing wouldn't make Silvia *not* fix a full breakfast. So, Dominique simply slid onto the seat next to Haley and accepted the small mug of coffee placed in front of her. The travel tumbler containing her peppermint tea and honey was next to appear. Even though her role as Marissa Clarke didn't require Dominique to sing, she liked to keep up the regimen, because she'd learned it helped her speaking voice as well.

Ever efficient, Silvia presented Dominique with a steaming plate of food minutes later. Despite her objection to a full meal, Dominique ate it all. Thanking the house manager, Dominique and Haley left the kitchen. Erik met them at the door as they were exiting the house.

Depending on the day, sometimes the three of them chatted on the way in to the studio. Other times it was just Haley and Dominique. Then there were days like this one where they were quietly commuting. A buzzing drew Dominique's attention to her phone.

She didn't expect it to be Denzel as he'd left her a message before he'd flown out to let her know his day was going to be pretty packed. They'd established a decent routine of checking in throughout the day, but it would likely be lunchtime before they touched base. Per her expectation it wasn't him. It was Zaria.

Grinning, she popped her earbud into her ear and answered the video call.

"Hey, Zee! What has you up this early in the morning? It's not even seven a.m. in Vegas."

"I have a job too, ma'am. And, I do stuff before seven a.m."

Suppressing a snort, Dominique sat silent following Zaria's blatant lie. Her gaze flicked over Zaria's still bonnet covered head and her obvious position still in bed.

"Okay fine. I don't do much of anything before seven a.m. But I'm up, and I wanted to ask you a favor."

"You know if I can, I will. So, what do you need?"

Zaria rarely asked for anything. So when she did, Dominique bent over backwards to try to make it happen. Her big sister-cousin was always there for her. The least she could do was return the support.

"Will you sing at my wedding?"

Dominique's smile was so wide, it felt like she was showing all thirty-two teeth. Andrei had proposed in January, but no one had mentioned a date being set for an actual wedding.

"Of course! When is it? I need to let the studio know so we can work it into my schedule."

"That's the thing. We know we want to do it next month, but we can't set a formal date until we decide on the venue. I'm trying to pick between using the grand ballroom at Anton's or using a place near the beach in L.A. since it's only a short trip. Alyssa can't fly and I'm getting close to not being able to do much long-distance travel myself."

"Okay. Well, as soon as you know an exact date, you know I'll do what's necessary to be there for you."

"Good, because I also want you to be my Maid of Honor. Alyssa has already agreed to be Matron of Honor."

Dominique hugged herself since she wasn't close enough to Zaria to hug her. Zaria grinned in response as if she knew exactly what Dom was thinking.

"That's not a problem either. Send me the deets, and I'll get it worked out."

"Great! Andrei, she said yes."

Dominique heard Andrei's gruff voice and realized he must have entered the room during their conversation.

"Of course she did, Svet." His face appeared on screen next to Zaria's wearing his version of a smile. "Thank you, Dom. See you soon."

With his curt dismissal, the call ended. Before the video cut away, she did see him turn Zaria's face to his. Dominique had a pretty good idea how those two would spend the rest of the morning.

Chapter Eighteen
WHERE'S YOUR TEFLON?

Denzel swirled the liquid in the glass before tilting it up to his lips. The smoky notes in the flavor of the whiskey were perfect. Although he wasn't worried about the cost of the drink, at least it lived up to the promises made by its hefty price tag. But, it was the Rooftop Bar at Anton's, there was no such thing as a cheap drink in this place.

Glancing up when Carver slid onto the bar stool next to him, Denzel gave his friend a nod of acknowledgement. He knew the only reason he'd been able to get Carver away from Alyssa was his obligation to show his face at league functions in his city. Even if his team hadn't made it past the first round of the playoffs.

"What sorrows are you drowning in liquor? I thought you were living the high life."

Raising his elbow on the bar top, Denzel accepted the fist bump to the back of his hand.

"I *am* living a high life. I'm not drowning any sorrows. Just appreciating fine whiskey."

A lifted finger called the bartender over to them.

"I'll have one of those."

Nodding, the bartender grabbed a fresh glass. "Coming right up,

Coach." Once he'd placed the whiskey neat in front of Carver, he looked at Denzel. "Would you like another, Mr. Reyes?"

Shaking his head, Denzel declined. "I'm good. Maybe in a few."

Letting them know he was available whenever they were ready, the young man backed away to attend the others wandering up to the bar. Swiveling on his seat, Denzel put his back to the bar top, resting his elbows against the edge.

"How do you think Andrei managed to get the league to spring for this place for an official pre-game event?" Carver asked the question as he scanned the room filled with people associated with professional sports and entertainment in some form or the other.

Shrugging, Denzel perused their environment as well. Of course, along with the men and women who were actively associated with the industry, there were a few non-associated persons who'd managed to get an invitation. He was thankful for the location because no one wanted smoke with Andrei if they were caught taking or selling photos of anyone or anything on the premises without express consent.

The last people who'd risked it were lucky they were simply unemployable. The vloggers, paps, and influencers who profited from it felt the pain as well. It made Denzel chuckle to think how they probably got the shakes anytime someone brought up anything to do with Andrei Antonov or his establishment.

Hell, Denzel kind of wished he'd been as vicious when he was under social media attack because of Melody. Instead, he'd gone the non-volatile route and hired a social media manager. Urena was amazing. Excellent at spin. But, it had still taken a few months for things to die down. In the meantime, he'd continued to try to live his life amidst being called a man whore and emotionally abusive.

Although he never claimed to not enjoy good pussy as much as the next pussy loving man, he didn't step out when he was in a committed relationship. He damn sure didn't abuse anyone. If he couldn't say anything civil, he simply didn't talk. Words mean things, and even at his most idiotic, he didn't sling them around carelessly in anger or with ill intent.

So, the times he'd gone on rants in locker rooms and ripped a teammate a new one, he meant all that shit. He'd said it with a hot head, then again once he'd cooled down.

Movement caught his attention and he looked to his left. Shifting to face Carver, he caught his gaze.

"Where is your Teflon? I need to borrow some."

Despite the oddness of what he'd said, Carver knew exactly what Denzel was talking about. With a quick glance over Denzel's shoulder, he met his gaze again.

"She's definitely coming over here." Holding up his left hand, the ring on his finger caught the light. "This thing doesn't repel worth a shit. I have to be blunt as fuck. That's all I can offer. But I don't think it's your body she's after. She's more interested in wallets and portfolios."

Denzel always appeared approachable, which helped in his career interviewing athletes and working on panels with other sports analysts. It worked against him in times when he really would rather not be bothered, and especially when he wasn't interested in conversation.

"Denzel Reyes and Carver Jamieson. Have I stepped back in time? I don't often get to see the Dynamic Duo in the same place at the same time. Reminds me of all the money I made when you two were on the field winning championships."

Marjorie Tenor smiled widely showing off her expensive dental work. Either her original teeth resembled a horse, and she didn't want them cut down, or they'd oversized the veneers, but it was off-putting when she exposed so many of them that way. Besides, the smile didn't reach her eyes.

"Marjorie." The lack of enthusiasm either of them displayed would've been a hint for a normal person. However, Marjorie took the mere mention of her name as an invitation to keep talking.

"I was just speaking with a few people about what the game is missing. The kind of power the two of you brought to the field when you played is almost non-existent."

Flattery was the way to many a human's heart, but when it came from Marjorie Tenor, it simply made Denzel suspicious. He'd never worked with her directly, but he'd observed enough to know she wasn't the kind of person he wanted to do business with. It didn't stop her from pitching one idea or another whenever she saw him.

He never bit. He lacked one specific characteristic which prevented him from failing up the way some people did. Although it depended on what one considered lack. He had too much melanin inherited from his Black mother. Whichever way old money elitists sliced it, he didn't meet the bill. Too Black. Too Mexican. Not enough European DNA to make up for either.

So, he didn't get involved in Marjorie's poorly researched financial escapades. The great friend Carver was, he looked off as if Marjorie wasn't even standing there allowing the full brunt of her attention to be focused on him. Just when he thought he'd have to gnaw off a limb to get out of the trap, Andrei walked over.

"Excuse us. I need to speak with these two gentlemen."

Pressing a hand to her throat, Marjorie hopped a little when she looked up to see Andrei standing there.

"Oh! Hello there. Good to see you, Andrei."

Denzel had to bite the inside of his lip to keep from laughing at the pointed look Andrei gave the woman. He never returned her greeting. He simply stood there. After a few awkward moments, Marjorie slid away, but not before promising to be in touch with Denzel about a lead she had on a company.

Once she was a safe distance away, Andrei looked at Carver and began to speak as if she'd never been there.

"I assume your wife has spoken with you."

"About?"

"The wedding."

Interrupting at the 'W' word, Denzel put his hands up with one flat on top of the other pointing up. "Time out. What wedding? Your wedding? You and Zaria set a date?"

Glancing at Denzel, Andrei seemed to consider whether he wanted to answer or not.

"Don't give me that face. You're the one who said you wanted to talk to *us*. The only way *we* can talk is if *all of us* know what we're talking about."

Huffing, Andrei folded his arms across his chest and came as close as he would to conceding Denzel was correct.

"Yes, my wedding to Zaria. She has agreed to a date next month, but we have to decide the venue."

Smiling, Denzel leaned against the bar top again. "Which tropical island are we going to this time?"

"My wife can't fly right now." Carver answered before Andrei could respond.

As strange as it was to hear Carver refer to someone as his wife, Denzel was surprised at himself for not remembering how far along Alyssa was in her pregnancy. Although he was nowhere near an expert to know when it was not recommended for a pregnant woman to travel, he didn't think they were in that range. He wisely kept his thought to himself. His friend got a little unhinged when it came to keeping his woman safe.

"Da, and I do not want my Svet on a plane right now either. However, she asks for so little, it is hard for me to tell her no."

As much as he wanted to, Denzel didn't check his own body to make sure he was still there, or pinch himself to assure he wasn't dreaming. His friend was having an adult conversation and expressing an emotion. He could be mature for at least five seconds.

"Do you have a compromise?" Denzel probed, sincerely making the effort to meet Andrei where he was. "You have a beautiful ballroom here and you could assure the privacy of the event. There's also the possibility of a short flight. Or car ride." He added quickly, "to the beaches of California. If she wants a beach, it doesn't have to be an exclusive island."

Andrei lifted one eyebrow as he stared at Denzel. "Have you spoken with Dominique about this?"

"No." Surprised he'd asked, Denzel returned the expression. "Why do you ask?"

"Because Zaria spoke with her this morning to ask her to be in the wedding. She mentioned to her that we were trying to decide between using the casino ballroom and a property in Los Angeles."

Until Andrei answered him, Denzel hadn't thought about who in their intersecting lives knew of their relationship. While his friends were aware he intended to make moves. They hadn't gotten on the phone like teenagers to trade secrets once he and Dominique finally connected. Making a mental note to discuss the unintended secrecy surrounding their relationship, Denzel refocused on the conversation at hand.

"Okay. So, what do you need from us?"

"Groomsmen. Zaria will have...bridesmaids." Andrei said the word as if it were a curse. That time Denzel couldn't contain his laughter at his friend's discomfort.

Resting a hand on his shoulder, Denzel gave Andrei a reassuring tap. "Don't worry, big guy. We got you covered."

Entering the house in the wee hours of the morning, Denzel hoped there wouldn't be a repeat of the last time he'd left Dominique in his bed, only to have her return to her rooms while he was away. As he crossed the threshold into the bedroom, the sliver of light filtering through a gap in the curtains displayed the outline of her voluptuous body beneath the covers.

The feeling rolling around inside him couldn't adequately be described as relief. But, it was somewhere in the same vein. He really wasn't sure how he would've responded if she hadn't been there. With his internal question answered, Denzel continued on to his closet to drop his clothes before hopping into the shower.

After sliding into bed and curving his body around Dominique's, the exercise of getting on a plane after putting in a grueling day of play-by-play analysis and post-game activities was all worth it. Every second of pushing himself to be able to get home was absolutely worth it to hold her close to him. Feel her softness pressed against him.

It was a non-sexual move. Although he couldn't tell his dick that. It was already hardening from having her lush bottom cradled against him. More than he wanted to be inside her, he craved being near her, holding her in his arms and listening to her even breathing.

The way she snuggled against him was the best reward—if there ever was one given for choosing a late-night flight over an early morning option. A soft sigh preceded her sleep laden voice murmuring nonsense before she became coherent.

"Den..."

"I'm here, Una. Go back to sleep."

"What time is it?"

"Too early, baby. Three-thirty. We'll talk in a few hours."

Another sigh was followed by Dominique's breathing returning to the even pattern, letting him know she'd drifted back off. He didn't have a session with his trainer until Tuesday. So, he planned to sleep in for a change.

When Dominique's alarm sounded less than three hours later, Denzel grumbled before tightening his hold. Squirming in his embrace, she tapped his forearm in a silent request to be released. Letting go enough for her to shut off the noisemaker, he re-established his position once she'd completed the task.

Rotating, Dominique tucked her head beneath his chin. Warm puffs of air brushed his skin prior to her soft lips making contact with his clavicle.

"Hey..."

Her sleep filled voice was slightly scratchy as she resettled her softness against him. He didn't particularly care for the nightgown hindering him from fully feeling her silky skin, but he wouldn't complain. Even partially clothed, she felt amazing.

"Hey yourself. Why is your alarm set for before six a.m.? Do you have an early day on set?"

Shaking her head, Dominique slid one leg between his and tightened the arm she draped across his torso.

"No. I forgot to delete the alarm. I was supposed to work out with Kam, but we changed it to Wednesday."

After a few seconds of silence, she sighed again. "I wasn't expecting you until later today."

Trailing his fingers up her arm, Denzel relished having her curled against his body.

"Yeah, I decided I didn't want to spend another night away when I had a beautiful woman at home in my bed."

"Mmm...Is that so?"

Capturing her fingers, Denzel stopped Dominique's walking digits from tickling along the side of his ribcage.

"Yes, that's so."

She flipped her hand in his, tangling their fingers together. They lay there silently, simply enjoying one another in the quiet of the morning. After a moment, she turned her head, placing her chin on his chest.

"So, what's your plan today? Meetings, post-game stuff at the network?"

Shifting slightly, he relocated her to lying on him fully. He damn near moaned at how amazing it felt being even partially surrounded by her soft curves.

"No plan. Other than stay in this bed with you as long as humanly possible, eat, get re-acquainted with Her Highness..." He trailed off.

Her eyes sparkled at the suggestion before dimming slightly.

"That would be really nice, but I have the first day of shooting today. We're doing it in studio and not on location. So, we don't have to worry about the time of day for lighting. But I still have to be there by eight a.m. for makeup and hair."

Because of how closely he watched her, she wasn't able to mask the light grimace which flitted across her expression before she tried to wipe it from her face. Immediately suspicious, Denzel's brow creased.

"What's wrong?"

Shifting under his gaze, Dominique attempted to look away, but Denzel wouldn't allow it.

"Hey, look at me. What's wrong?"

Why was he immediately ready to burn shit to the ground because she looked slightly uncomfortable? Denzel didn't take time to mentally assess his position. Cupping the back of her head, he stroked his thumb along her jaw. Her soft digits felt warm against his wrist when she placed her hand on him.

"Nothing's wrong. It's just..." Dominique's eyes darted away as her sentence trailed off.

"It's just what?"

Sighing, she brought her gaze back to his. "I was super excited about this role. It has the potential to be something really great, and show that I have what it takes to carry a series. The original script was compelling and showed a character with layers and nuances. I couldn't wait to dig my teeth into Marissa Clarke. But I noticed a trend in table reads..."

Her bottom lip disappeared between her teeth for a second as she seemed to consider her next words. As much as he wanted to know the rest, Denzel didn't rush her. He wanted to. Badly. But he didn't. He simply waited for her to gather her thoughts to continue.

"My series is based on the books and in the books, Marissa is pretty much a loner with a few friends, a lot of resources from favors she's done over the years, but not much family to speak of. Why does she now have two little sisters? It didn't seem like a huge departure because in the pilot episodes, there were two short scenes with one sister, but the other wasn't even mentioned.

Now there is a story line I can see developing about one of the sisters getting into a situation. This series is a crime drama with super hero comic book elements. Marissa is a detective looking to solve crimes, not a harried older sibling trying to keep her younger sisters from doing stupid shit every episode."

With a creased brow, Denzel continued in his attempt to soothe her as he digested her words. It sounded fishy as hell. Although his experience in movies and television was limited on the side Dominique was familiar with, he was able to detect something was potentially going on in the background.

"Have you spoken to anyone about this new direction?"

"I talked to Adam, the director, and we had a conversation with the writing team. Let's just say they hinted at being instructed to veer more from the books based on feedback from the pilot episode."

Not liking the implication, Denzel's frown deepened.

"What kind of feedback?"

"Something about humanizing the character more by not having her appear to be such a loner. My stance is, that's how the character is written in the books and every installation in the series has hit the top ten on the bestseller's list according to the news outlet considered the holy grail of literary accomplishment. Why would they want to mess with a working formula?"

Denzel wondered the same thing. It didn't sit well with him to hear it. The part of him that said he should back off and just be the kind of supportive partner who simply listens was shoved to the recesses of his mind. He was already considering which of his contacts could find out what was really happening. Movie making may have become more spread out away from Hollywood, but some of the same narrow-minded thinking had transferred with it.

Bankability was tied to some of the most random shit. For people of color and Black women in particular, he'd seen the bar moved so much it was worse than a roller coaster. Despite the verified success of movies and shows with them as the lead characters, there was always someone stuck in the past who wanted to steer the ship back toward days gone by or at least a contrived market which edges out people who didn't conform to their narrow view of what was acceptable or marketable.

Keeping himself tethered to the moment while he searched his mental Rolodex was a skill he'd perfected when he'd begun his life as a professional athlete. Denzel could work out a plan, lob questions, and actively listen to the answer simultaneously.

"I can see you aren't buying what they're selling. What about Adam or the producers?"

Dominique's twisted lips answered before she could say a word. "Adam is fighting as much as he can, and one of the other producers is on our side, but the main executive producer has assumed the role of showrunner. He's the main one touting this feedback that no one else seems to know anything about."

"Oh yeah? Caplan Moore is the head producer, right?" Denzel probed.

With a brief shake of her head, Dominique corrected him. "No. It's Douglas Fowler."

"Oh. Ok. I've heard of him." Denzel didn't comment as to how he'd heard of Fowler. Instead, he concentrated on spending the next few moments encouraging Dominique and giving her something else to focus on to get her day off to a good start.

Chapter Nineteen

IT WON'T BE THAT KIND OF PARTY

Dominique walked into her trailer to the sound of her ringing cellphone. Quickening her step, she wondered who it could be. No one called her during the day by design. Besides, she thought she'd turned her ringer off. They weren't shooting close enough to the trailers for it to matter. It was simply something she'd gotten into the habit of doing on set.

Reaching for the device, tucked into the side of her messenger bag, Dominique saw her mother's image on the display. The smile on her face was in her voice when she answered the call.

"Hey, Mama."

"Hey, my baby." Her mother practically sang the words. "I'm sorry to call while you're working, but we haven't really talked lately and we gotta start coordinating for Zee Baby's wedding."

"It's fine, Mama. I have some time."

Dominique settled onto the couch, tucking one foot beneath her thigh. They were taking a lunch break, so she wouldn't be needed for at least an hour. Other than anticipating Haley coming back at any moment with food, she wasn't expecting anyone.

"I thought she had a wedding planner."

"She does, but wedding planners don't handle every single detail."

Lifting one eyebrow, Dominique stared at the phone as if her mother could see her. "Mama, I'd bet my signing bonus whoever Andrei hired to plan this wedding is most definitely handling every single detail. So, whatever it is you're trying to do is off script."

"I don't like the way you said that, Dominique. It makes it seem like I'm up to something nefarious."

Biting the inside of her cheek, Dominique contained the bark of laughter threatening to spill out. Being called by her actual name instead of one of the many nicknames her mother dispensed, meant her mama was serious. Belinda Truman wouldn't take kindly to being laughed at while she was in business mode.

"I didn't mean anything by it, Mama. But if the wedding planner doesn't have it on their list, it sounds like you haven't mentioned it."

"I may or may not have mentioned it, because it may or may not be any of that woman's business."

Looking up when Haley entered carrying a paper bag, Dominique waved as she continued talking to her mother.

"Mama, why are you referring to the wedding planner as *that woman?* I'm sure Zaria and Andrei didn't hire a disagreeable person. What's really going on?"

"Dominique Latoya Truman. Don't be getting fresh with me and insinuating I've done something to the wedding planner."

Accepting the covered container from Haley, Dominique mouthed her thanks. She was now more certain than ever her mother had done or said something and bumped heads with the person hired to plan the wedding. Given the limited timeframe, Dominique was certain the person had to be extremely busy taking care of all the moving pieces for the day.

"I'm not getting fresh, Mama. I was just asking a question. If you don't want to tell me, it's fine."

The aroma of the warm Cuban sandwich hit her the moment she lifted the lid on the container. Her mouth watered in anticipation of the first bite. Seeing where the cheese had melted, and some had escaped the pieces of toasted bread to drip along the edge, made her want it even more. For a brief moment, her mother's voiced faded into the background.

"All I asked for was to be included on the conference calls. I know Zaria has her own mind and ideas. And she and Dray are aware of what they want. But, she's my eldest child. I thought I'd be a little more involved in the process, is all. So, if I can't be, then we can plan our girls' day stuff. You know how we used to when your daddy would take Cisco off on one of their trips with his brothers?"

Dominique was glad she'd tuned back into the conversation to hear what was really bothering her mother. She wondered if her mother had said anything to Zaria. Belinda Truman could be a conundrum. Sometimes, she was outspoken to a fault. At others, she held things close, and didn't speak on them. All the while, she was prodding others to tell her everything going on with them.

"Mama, did you tell Zee any of this?"

The other end of the call went silent for so long, Dominique looked at the phone to make certain the call was still connected.

"Mama?"

Her prodding was rewarded with the easily recognizable sound of her mother sucking her teeth. Dominique had struck a nerve.

"I never pressed you girls about getting married and having babies, but I've made no secret about wanting to be involved if you ever decided it was something you wanted. Why do I have to tell her that I wanna do more than just show up and look pretty on the front row with the other parents?"

"Because...Mama, she can't read your mind." When her mother huffed, Dominique hurried to add, "Zee has a lot she's trying to get done in a short amount of time. Even with help, I'm sure she's being pulled in a few directions, especially with her managing her own law firm and trying to prepare to be a first-time mom."

Mumbling filtered through the phone before her mother's voice came through clearly again. "Maybe you have a point, but it doesn't let you off the hook to help me with our pre-wedding girls' day."

"Would it take the place of a bachelorette party? Because, we should probably talk to Alyssa too. She's her Matron of Honor."

"It's not bachelorette stuff. I don't need to see any of my kids drooling over half-naked men. And, I'm not spending a perfectly good

DRAFT PICK SEASON 3: DENZEL

night looking at somebody's son swing his peter around like a windmill."

Dominique shoved her food away as she bent over, laughing at her mother's description of male exotic dancers. She should have, but she didn't expect her mama's level of candor. It took her a few moments to get the giggles under control before she spoke again.

"Mama, it won't be that kind of party. Zee's closest friends live in Vegas. They can see a male revue whenever they want. Strippers wouldn't excite them. Besides, more than a couple of them have husbands or fiancés who might make those dudes go missing if they danced around their woman half naked."

Tucking the phone between her ear and shoulder, Dominique picked up her discarded lunch and bit into the succulent pork, topped with pickles and cheese on grilled toasted bread. The dill flavor from the pickle paired perfectly with the smoky flavor of the sliced pork. Chewing, she nearly choked on the bite when her mother shifted gears mid conversation.

"Speaking of men, how are things going for you since you've been in Atlanta?"

Coughing into her napkin, Dominique struggled to regain her composure. As if Dominique wasn't presently grappling with gaining access to much needed oxygen, her mother continued.

"Don't think I missed the way Denzel Reyes was eating you up with his eyes. He didn't fool me for a second with his lil offer to help you find a place to live. That man is interested in you. Has he called since you've been there?"

Clearing her throat, Dominique accepted the bottle of water Haley pressed into her hand. Nodding her thanks, Dominique took a long draw on the liquid while she tried to get her thoughts together. In the month since her relocation to Atlanta, her conversations with her mother had been sparse, with Dominique directing the discussions by asking about her father and brother or prodding her mother about the most recent family gossip. She wasn't necessarily trying to hide her relationship with Denzel, but she wasn't ready to share it with her mother.

Especially not since Zaria's whirlwind courtship with Andrei. It would just give her mother ideas. She was right earlier when she said she hadn't pressured Dominique and Zaria about getting married and having babies. Not pressuring them didn't mean she didn't ask questions if there was even a whiff of a man being in either of their lives.

"Yes, ma'am. I've talked to him since I've been here."

Dominique wouldn't mention them having said conversations face to face. It was enough to have the immediate image conjured be of him saying nasty shit in her ear as he took her from behind in the shower just this morning. There was no reason for her mother to be updated on any of those things.

"Okay...Why did you say it so dry? Are you not feeling him?"

"Feeling him, Mama?" Dominique's brow dipped at her mother's attempt to use current slang.

"What? Y'all young folks still say it like that, right? When you're interested in a man?"

Plucking at the material of her jeans, Dominique stared at the rip near the knee.

"Yeah, mama. I guess they still use the phrase. I just didn't expect to hear it from you."

Dominique closed her eyes when her mother huffed and put the conversation back on the track she really wanted to get away from.

"So...answer my question. Are you not feeling him? Or was he just being a player?"

Releasing the inside of her lip before she drew blood, Dominique scrambled for a way to be honest with her mother, but also keep Belinda Truman out of things for the time being. Her acting classes paid off when she was able to keep her breathing even. Once she responded, her voice didn't have even a hint of deception.

"I didn't say I wasn't interested. He's a very attractive man. Who wouldn't be interested? Or at least curious?"

"So...? What's the deal-ee-o?"

"Mama..." Dominique put her free hand to her forehead. "Mama, what have you been watching on TV?"

"Pfft. I can't get hip from a TV show. I watch videos on the internet. Zaria showed me how to get to Messytok." Her mother's voice lowered conspiratorially. "Gurl...it gets juicy on there. But of course, I only started looking to make sure they weren't talking stuff about my babies."

Simply from the change in her mother's tone, Dominique could visualize her sitting up straighter and smoothing her skirt out as she delivered her last statement.

"Of course, Mama. I understand how it is. That's why I watch them too."

A rush of relief flooded Dominique's body when there were three sharp raps to her trailer door. They were loud enough for her mother to hear and question her about them.

"I hear someone knocking. Does that mean you have to go?"

Trying to infuse regret she didn't feel into her words, Dominique responded, "yes, Mama. I'm so sorry. I'll call you when I'm free."

"Okay then. Have a good day."

"You too, Mama."

Ending the call as Haley answered the door, Dominique swung her gaze to the person stepping over the threshold. Erik was hanging around outside the trailer, so she didn't worry that it would be someone she wouldn't want to see. He'd check first before letting anyone not on the approved list get past him.

"Hey, Adam. What's up?"

Dominique closed the lid on her food, giving the director her full attention. An uneasy feeling settled in her stomach as she studied his face. He looked from her to Haley, then back to her.

"Could I speak with you privately?"

While her trailer was nice, it *was* small. Simply being across the room from Haley wouldn't afford them a private conversation. Dominique honestly felt no hostility from Adam. A hint of sadness maybe, but not hostility.

"Haley, could you give us a minute?"

Nodding, Haley walked into the rear of the trailer containing the small sleeping compartment. That was as good as it would get with them being away from home. They had a strict policy to be no more than a room away unless they were dismissed for the day.

Once Haley was gone, Adam took the seat Dominique offered him on the nearby chair. His hair was disheveled, and from the hand he ran through it when he sat, Dominique didn't have to wonder why.

"What's going on, Adam? You look stressed." Cutting through any potential hedging, Dominique jumped right into the discussion.

Tugging on the cuffs of his cardigan, Adam settled into the seat. "Stressed? Nah... This is actually par for the course. I just don't like it."

"You don't like what?" Sitting up taller, Dominique tried not to read too much into what he hadn't said.

"I was going over the plan for the rest of the week with Violet. We should be able to wrap up this episode today and start the next one by Wednesday. But she had some changes we'll need to go over before we begin shooting."

With her hackles now completely up, Dominique lifted one eyebrow. Folding her arms across her middle, she pressed her back into the firm cushion of the sofa.

"Changes like what?"

Not mincing words, Adam launched into what the writer was calling tweaks at the behest of the showrunner. While it wasn't major, it was part of the emerging pattern she'd mentioned to Denzel a couple of weeks ago. Because she'd seen it coming, she wasn't even angry. Just frustrated. A call with her agent and attorney was in her near future. They needed to discuss the terms of her contract.

It was the frustration driving when she pinned Adam with a direct stare. "Adam, how far away from the original series format are they willing to go? Do they even have Leona Jiles' permission to change the premise this much?"

Holding up his hands in conciliation, Adam shook his head. "You know how these things go, Dom. The studio bought the rights. Unless there were specific terms spelled out, they can change it as much as they want. We both know the television or movie versions are rarely exactly like the book."

Sucking her teeth, Dominique peered at him. "Not being exact and being a hack job are two different things."

"Come on, Dom. It's not a hack job."

Her pointed look had him breaking eye contact before turning back. "Okay... maybe it *is* turning into a hack job."

"So, how far are you willing to let them go?"

Dominique knew she wasn't quite at A-lister status, but she wasn't without pull in the industry, and she'd had about enough of Fowler's manipulations. Her question made Adam sit back in his seat. It was as if it reminded him of who he was in this equation. Just like this wasn't her first job, he wasn't fresh out of film school. They'd both been nominated for and won numerous industry awards.

"You know what? I think I need to have a few discussions. Take some extra time for your lunch break. We'll start back up in a couple of hours."

Tapping his hands on his thighs, Adam lurched to his feet. His cardigan swayed around his slim frame as he strode toward the trailer door. His movements were purposeful as he swung the door open and stepped out. From the glint of determination in his eyes, Dominique knew whatever ensued would be a show she'd regret missing.

However, the extra time wouldn't be squandered. Picking up her phone again, she shot Candy and Peaches text messages letting them know about the delay after lunch. Dominique had been unable to secure Stephanie Barker personally—at least not full time—as her hair stylist. But she did set up a contract for her to provide someone. Peaches had been highly recommended and had done a great job so far.

Calling Haley back into the room, Dominique picked up her lunch and resumed eating. While she wasn't as eager to finish the meal as before, she ate it since she didn't know when she'd get another break to have anything. Passing along to Haley what Adam said about the delay, Dominique grabbed the folder containing the daily to review it for the afternoon.

Before she dove into it, she shot off another message. This time, it was to her agent. She'd been keeping Tammy abreast of the happenings on the set. It was time to apply pressure. She couldn't allow her potential breakout role to be co-opted without a fight.

Instead of staying in her trailer the entirety of the extended lunch, Dominique ventured out after she was done eating and reviewing her lines for the next couple of scenes they were scheduled to shoot. She ran into Jerricka as she walked around, watching the people scurrying about, despite the extended break. With a nod to Haley, Jerricka stepped closer to Dominique.

"Hey, do you know anything about what's going on today?"

Keeping her expression neutral, Dominique considered how to respond. "What's going on with what?"

"First, we get extra time for lunch. That's not suspicious alone since it sometimes takes longer than planned for the next set up to be ready." Taking another step closer, she leaned in. "But I heard through the grapevine, Adam and Douglas were going at it in the production trailer. I didn't personally hear what they were into it about, but I *did* see Violet coming out of there a few minutes ago looking shook."

Dominique and Jerricka had always had a great working relationship. Which was why she didn't hesitate to tell her things directly affecting her. But this wasn't one of those things. It went without saying that Adam approached her in confidence earlier. She wouldn't break it. What she *could* do was speculate right along with Jerricka.

"If Violet was there, it was probably something to do with the script. You know they've been making changes since we started table reads."

Jerricka turned up her red-tinted lips and sucked her teeth. The changes meant more screen time for Bliss, which translated to more wardrobe changes and interactions between the two women. While she remained professional, Jerricka's disdain for Bliss wasn't a closely held secret.

"Ugh! I hope they aren't giving the lil' heifah more screen time. If I have to explain one more time that her character isn't a femme fatale and shouldn't be dressed like a high-end prostitute, I'm gonna put her in a burlap bag."

Biting her lip to hold in her laughter, Dominique maintained her composure. With Bliss, less wasn't more. More was more, and she always wanted it. It was tiring, to say the least. Since Dominique couldn't guarantee the outcome Jerricka wanted, she placed a hand on the other woman's shoulder in commiseration.

"I guess we'll find out when things start back up. If a new script is shoved into our hands, we'll have our answer."

Chapter Twenty
TRIPLE THREAT

Subtly, without drawing attention to what he was doing, Denzel checked the time on his watch. Now that the regular football season was over, his television schedule had been drastically reduced. But, it didn't mean he didn't have to sit in on the occasional program planning meeting. And as scintillating as they were, he was bored out of his mind. The top of the hour couldn't come fast enough.

The moment the timer went off, he sat up straighter. Yes, he'd set a timer. He didn't give a shit if they had more to say. They weren't getting another second of his time. He already wanted to revoke the hour he'd given them. At least they knew not to fuck around and wrapped up the conference call less than a minute later.

As soon as it was over, he got a notification from Tiffany. His personal assistant had his next meeting already on the line. Selecting the link, he replaced the previous meeting box with a new one. Once again, sitting at his desk with the ocean at his back, Cristiano stared into the camera.

"Beunas tardes, amigo." Denzel tossed out the greeting as he slid his laptop closer to him.

"Beunas tardes." Cristiano's reply wasn't exuberant, but he sounded friendly enough.

Still, both of Denzel's eyebrows lifted, creasing his forehead. "What's up with the dry good afternoon?"

"Eh. I didn't think it was dry, but why don't we get down to the reason for this meeting?"

"Fine with me."

Denzel was happy to oblige. The sooner they talked, the sooner he could call it a day. He'd spent the morning in meetings with his business manager and reviewing the most current reports from his latest acquisition.

"Your hunch was correct. Douglas Fowler has been making discreet inquiries about what would happen if the show only ran for one season before going into a spin off. Their contract with Leona Jiles for the rights to the story had some pretty impressive riders in it.

Usually, an author doesn't get the kind of say she has in the finished product. Not without being an executive producer. I know she's big time, but I know some really big names who don't have the leeway to have their rights reverted back to them."

Nodding as he listened, Denzel pulled his notepad closer, scribbling a few notes on the page. He didn't let it show, but his blood was boiling. Who the fuck did Fowler think he was to push Dominique to the side? Even with his complete bias when it came to his Una, Denzel wasn't exaggerating Dominique's talents.

In the industry, she was a true triple threat. She could act, sing, and dance and had done all three on Broadway and in film. Hell, he knew for a fact she could write as well. He'd seen her working on a screenplay she'd called a passion project and read a few pages before she hid it away.

"I haven't heard anything about Leona Jiles having direct involvement in the show." Denzel tapped his pen against the pad lightly.

"To my knowledge, she doesn't. Other than the statement her camp released when Dominique was named as the lead actress for the series, she hasn't said anything."

Denzel recalled the snippet of an article released the previous month. Dominique's excitement was contagious as she read Jiles' words stating how pleased she was to have Dominique bring her character to life. There was also a buzz amongst the Blerds and other fans of the book series.

As far as talent and physical appearance went, many of them lauded Dominique as the best actress for the role, and they were naming The Clarke Files was one of the most anticipated series set for Fall release. Apparently, none of that meant anything to Fowler.

"Are there any takers for his idea?"

Tilting one hand left to right, Cristiano's expression matched the motion. "It depends on who you talk to. A lot of the industry operates by going straight to streaming or the big screen. Since this series straddles two lines without being firmly one or the other, the audience could be very wide or very niche.

There's just enough of the crime drama stuff to keep some of the older demographic interested. The superhero slant will attract some of the younger crowd and possibly the comic book audience. At this point, he has no firm takers since her pilot episode tested so well with the viewers."

"No firm takers, but he still has his ass out there shopping the idea and pressuring the writers to change the script to feature characters who weren't even in the books to begin with. What part of that sounds like a good option?"

"None of it." Cristiano shook his head. "So, what do you want to do?"

Staring at him blankly, Denzel tilted his head to one side. "I asked you for information, because I know you play in that sandbox way more than me. I never said I wanted you to *do* anything."

Smirking, Cristiano returned his blank stare with an expression of disbelief. "Please... You can't sell innocence to me. I know you don't have any."

Denzel sat back in his seat, crossing his arms over his chest. "I take offense."

A wry chuckle escaped Cristiano. "For what? Hearing the truth. You and I both know you didn't ask me to look into this just so you'd have the information. Or did you forget who you were talking to? I know you're more than just an avid fan and *friend of the family*."

Cristiano placed air quotes around friend of the family and a smile took over his face. "So, I'll ask again. What do you want to do?"

Shaking his head, Denzel leaned forward, placing his forearms on the dark mahogany conference table.

"If I plan to *do* something, are you offering to help?"

Cristiano's grin stretched wider. "You know me. Nothing I love better than crushing idiots hanging on to stereotypes. Besides, I know the people you want to know."

Shooting his friend a glare, Denzel groused, "Fuck you. I know people."

"Calm down. No reason to go all Diesel on me."

"Don't act like you want me to run straight over you and there won't be a need."

Cristiano's reference to his nickname from his days playing professional football drew a grunting chuckle before Denzel fixed his face.

"And don't tell me to calm down. I am calm."

And he was. Mostly. He was still mentally scrolling through his contacts. He knew Dominique didn't confide in him to get him to fix her situation. Hell, she'd probably be angry if she found out he'd been poking around. Those two things wouldn't stop him from using his influence to keep anyone from negatively impacting her career. She would just have to be mad.

Wearing a lopsided grin, Cristiano leaned forward with his elbows on his desk, mimicking Denzel's previous posture.

"Yeah... You're calm alright. So, am I calling my cousins, or are you calling yours?"

An uncontrollable tug lifted one side of Denzel's lips at Cristiano's question. "Hell, why not both?"

At Denzel's response, Cristiano's eyes lit up. "Which set of your cousins? Reyes or Colliers?"

While Cristiano had some interesting ties, Denzel's cousins on his dad's side had their fingers in several different legal-adjacent activities. His mama's folks, the Colliers, were more academics. They could get grimy, though. None of them were in the film industry, but they knew people with influence in certain circles.

He'd only been partially joking about calling his Reyes cousins. Pablo was likely to suggest Fowler take a cruise down the San Antonio River. Knowing the river poured into the Gulf of Mexico was particularly appealing to his younger cousin. At the moment, making the executive producer disappear wasn't on the table. Fucking up his name in the industry was a whole other ball game. So, the Collier cousins it was.

"The Colliers. I'll keep the Reyes option in my pocket for now."

At his statement, Cristiano's smile grew even brighter. The next half hour passed quickly as the two put their heads together and discussed resources. Although the other man couldn't seem to resist floating the Reyes option again before they hung up. Waving him off, Denzel flipped his leather binder closed.

"You're awfully blood thirsty, Ortiz."

"Who said anything about un-aliving someone?" Cristiano shot back.

"You, when you suggested I call Pablo. You know his ass ain't wrapped too tight."

Cristiano's only response was laughter as they ended the video call. Mirth hovered at the edges, as Denzel straightened his office, before calling it a day. He shot off a few text messages, but didn't expect to hear anything immediately. Certain pieces of his plan would have to be handled delicately.

Opting to use the back stairs instead of the elevator, he avoided contact with any of the household staff on his way up to his suite. The sight which greeted him when he crossed the threshold into his bedroom was unexpected but pleasing nonetheless. Dominique was home from the studio early.

Standing near the window overlooking the pool, she had her messenger bag in her hand like she'd just taken it off of her shoulder. When she noticed him, her face lit up with a smile, but he caught the hint of fatigue before she wiped it away. He wondered if she knew how transparent she was with him.

"Hey, Baby." Wrapping his arms around her waist he tugged her body to his, before kissing her upturned lips.

"Mmm. Hey, yourself." Her fingertips traced random patterns on his back as she returned his hug.

Soaking in the moment, he simply held her for a few minutes. Instances like this were quickly becoming his favorite part of the day. Why in the world had he waited so long to make his move? While he knew the answer, it seemed trite now that he was aware of how great the two of them were together.

After another minute, he nuzzled the side of her neck. "How was your day? Everything go okay? Another episode wrapped?"

Her head shake was slight and her words were muffled against his chest. Pulling back, he put a finger beneath her chin to tilt her face up toward his.

"What was that?"

Releasing a sigh, she laid her head on his chest again. "I said it was a day. We did get done with the episode, but not without a little drama."

Denzel was proud of himself for keeping his immediate tension from being noticeable. His voice was light when he asked a follow-up question.

"Drama? What drama? It's been a while since I was on a set not directly related to football, but isn't there always drama?"

Nodding, she replied, "no set, movie, television, or otherwise doesn't have a little drama. But I can't say I've had a director threaten to quit, and mean it, over the executive producer being too heavy-handed with the writers and the script."

Backing them up until he could sit in the chair near the window, Denzel arranged Dominique on his lap with her legs draped over his.

"Damn, Adam was big mad, huh?"

"Oh yeah."

The fatigue she'd tried to cover up had returned, and she melted into him, tucking her head beneath his chin.

"Well, you said he *threatened* to quit, not that he actually *did*. So... did he win the disagreement?"

Her response was given with a sigh. "For the time being. I'm not holding out hope he'll win the war just because he won this battle."

His mumble was noncommittal as he held her in his arms. His recent conversation with Cristiano floated to the surface, but he didn't think mentioning it now would help her. It felt like piling on to him. So, he went to the next thing he *could* do. Which was finding a way to bring her a little joy. Even for a moment.

"Hey, Baby. You know what always makes me feel better after a trying day?"

Tightening her arm around his middle, she snuggled against him. "What's that?"

"My abuela's tamales."

Dominique tipped her face up, wearing a slight frown. "Your abuela is here? To make tamales?"

Her confusion was so cute, he couldn't resist tasting her lips again. Releasing her from his kiss, he smiled down at her.

"No, smartass. My abuela was still home in San Antonio the last I checked, but that doesn't mean we can't have some tamale therapy."

Tapping her on the hip, he encouraged her to stand. Instead of moving, she snuggled deeper into his embrace.

"If your abuela isn't here to make me tamales for my therapy, why do I have to move?" Her mumbled grousing was once again muffled against his chest.

"Because." Denzel lifted her from his lap, holding on to her until she was steady on her feet. "My abuela might not be here, but I found a place near Piedmont that comes close. I'm gonna take you there."

She let him lead her to the closet for him to make a quick wardrobe change, but her facial expression said she wasn't convinced.

"Chef was prepping when I came home. Why don't we eat whatever he's cooking?"

Since she was dragging her feet, he grabbed her sneakers, then picked her up.

"We're going out for tamale therapy, woman. You'll thank me later."

Her giggles were music to his ears, and she squirmed to be let down. He finally obliged once they were in the elevator when he placed Dominique on her feet so she could put on her shoes. Walking through the house, he sent a quick message to Juan, who met them next to the car in the garage.

"Where to?" Juan opened the back passenger door of the SUV, and Denzel helped Dominique inside.

Sliding in behind her, he gave Juan the name of the restaurant. "El Rincón Mexicano."

Nodding, Juan closed the door and they were off, driving in the direction of the setting sun. When Dominique continued to look from him to Juan, Denzel finally asked her what was going on.

"I just find it interesting that when I leave the house alone, I'm required to have a whole team. But we're going into the city with only Juan accompanying us."

Smirking, Denzel took her hand in his. "What's your point? You don't think Juan is enough security? We're still close to the house. We can get one of the other guys."

Shaking her head, she squeezed his hand. "I'm not doubting Juan's protection abilities. I'm simply pointing out a discrepancy."

Denzel lifted their joined hands and kissed the back of hers. "Juan protects me and I protect you. We'll be fine. Besides, we're going on a weekday before peak hours. It shouldn't be too crowded."

As he predicted, when Juan parked the vehicle in front of the restaurant, there were very few cars in the parking lot. He smiled at the expression on Dominique's face. She wasn't a snob, but he knew how the establishment appeared at first glance. While brightly colored and displaying the care the owners had taken to make it nice, it still looked like exactly what it was—a hole in the wall.

Holding her hand in his, he assisted her out of the back seat. He planted a kiss on her cheek as he whispered in her ear.

"Come on, Mississippi girl. We both know you've eaten at more than one hole in the wall in your lifetime. Don't be extra bougie. Trust me."

One perfectly arched eyebrow shot up her forehead. "Excuse you. I'm not being bougie. I was just looking around. I've visited Atlanta too many times over the years and even been on this street, but I don't remember this place."

"That's just because you didn't have me to show you around." Tugging her to come with him, they walked toward the door where Juan stood. Having already visually swept the inside of the restaurant, he held it for them.

The moment they stepped inside, a heavily accented male voice called out to him.

"Denzel!"

With his thick accent and José's attention to pronouncing his name correctly, it came out more like *Din-sul* than *Den-zul*. Which Denzel's mother was adamant was the correct pronunciation.

"José, como éstas?"

"Muy bien. Muy bien."

José's eyes left Denzel. He stared at Dominique with a lifted brow, projecting his surprise at the way Denzel had her tucked into his side. Continuing their conversation in Spanish, he asked Denzel who the beautiful lady was. Before Denzel could reply, Dominique responded.

"Soy Dominique. Encantado de conocerte."

Her accents and inflections were perfect. Too perfect. Denzel's initial prideful smile was quickly replaced when an even larger grin stretched across José's face and he reached out a hand to take hers. He complimented her as if she'd just sang the Mexican national anthem in perfect pitch instead of introducing herself and saying it was nice to meet him.

"Hey, hey. Enough of that. We came for tamales, not for you to flirt with my woman. Does Ana know this is how you act when she's not around?"

At the mention of his wife, José stood up straight and looked over his shoulder. When he didn't see her standing there, he brushed Denzel off.

"Don't be jealous, Denzel. I was just being friendly, welcoming the beautiful lady to my restaurant."

"*Your* restaurant?"

It was seriously scary the way Ana seemed to appear out of thin air. While Denzel managed not to flinch at her sudden appearance, José was unable to disguise his surprise. In a quick hop-step, he moved to the side with a hand on his chest.

"Mi amor." Dipping his head slightly, José went to relieve her of the tray she held. "Let me take that while you speak to Denzel and his guest."

Denzel smiled as Ana gave José the stink eye before she turned her attention to Dominique, transforming her face with her bright smile. As if she hadn't just non-verbally threatened her husband, she launched into her greetings before leading them to a table. The place was small, with few options. However, there were only a couple of other patrons. So, they didn't have to sit close to anyone else.

"You two have a seat and we'll get your tamales out to you in a few minutes."

With a tap on his shoulder, she went back toward the kitchen. Dominique stared at Denzel with a smile in her eyes. There was also a hint of humor, prompting him to ask.

"What?"

"We didn't even tell her what we wanted."

"Ana always knows when it's a tamales kind of day." Sitting back in his seat, he waved a hand. "Don't worry. You'll love them."

Chapter Twenty-One

ABSOLUTELY THE FUCK NOT

It only took Dominique a few minutes and one bite of Ana's signature tamales to understand why Denzel considered this a form of therapy. The spicy flavors burst on her tongue. The corn dough, filled with a blend of meat, beans and cheese, seemed to melt in her mouth. Very little chewing was required.

Eating them took her back to the days when her mother would pile them into the car and drive to the Mississippi Delta, specifically to buy tamales. Dominique had nearly forgotten about those times until the memory resurfaced with the first taste of her therapy meal. Or was this a snack? Either way. Her insides were warmed by more than the heat from the chile peppers used in the sauce.

Moaning around a bite of her second helping, Dominique looked up to see Denzel simply staring at her. Her raised eyebrows asked the question for her.

"Nothing, Una. I'm just enjoying watching you enjoy your food. I knew you would love them."

Nodding, she swallowed, then took a sip of her drink before speaking. "They're delicious. As good as these are, they make me wonder about the ones your abuela makes. If these are *almost* as good, how do you stop yourself from flying home every time you want a batch?"

Warmth enveloped her hand when Denzel reached across the small table and covered it with his. His fingers tangled with hers as he rubbed his thumb on the back of her hand.

"When I first moved away from home, that's exactly what I wanted to do. It's actually how I found this place one weekend. I was missing home. Honestly, my dad might've caved and sent a plane ticket for me, but I stuck it out.

As delicious as they are, it's not about the tamales. It's about what they remind me of when I eat them. So, I found a place that helped me connect with those feelings.

I will admit though...Sometimes, abuela makes tamales and freezes them for me. My supply at home has been depleted. And, although she taught me how to make them, it's a process, and I wanted you to have more immediate results than having to wait until tomorrow."

"Wait...Back that sentence up." Dominique twirled her finger in reverse. "You can make these?" She pointed to the half-eaten deliciousness on her plate.

"Of course. I told you my pops owns restaurants back home. He started the first one with my abuela, Rosa. They both taught me to cook and put me to work in the kitchen when I was a teenager."

Dominique had recognized that he seemed comfortable in the kitchen, but she hadn't realized just how comfortable. Although she'd never actually seen him cook, she suspected he'd prepared some of the things he'd brought her while she was soaking in the bath or when he delivered breakfast in bed.

"So, you're a man of many talents."

Smiling broadly, Denzel ran his other hand down his chest to his stomach. "I'm glad you recognize that I've got skills, Baby."

Tugging her hand from beneath his, she gave it a swat. Muttering about him being cocky, she went back to eating her food. True to Denzel's prediction, she loved it. Also, in keeping with his statement in the car, there wasn't a crowd while they were there. So, no one bothered them.

Things were beginning to pick up as they were leaving. But Juan was leading them to the vehicle to go home before there were ten other customers in the establishment. Dominique did notice a few curious stares as they were saying their goodbyes to Ana and José, but no one approached them.

With a lighter mood settled around them, they went home, diving into what had become a regular routine for them of spending quiet time together. Dominique was getting comfortable in the media room when Denzel entered, followed by Raffi, each carrying a tray with snacks and drinks.

"I found the stray scrounging around in the kitchen like Silvia didn't buy him groceries." Denzel passed Dominique her fruit blend before sitting next to her.

"I keep telling you I'm a growing boy, Jandro. What do you want me to do? Starve?"

The side-eye glance Denzel shot his cousin would've sliced Raffi in two if it was possible for a gaze to have such an effect. Dominique bit her lip to keep from laughing at their banter. It was nice to see. Like her brother, Denzel didn't have any brothers of his own. But his relationship with his cousin strongly resembled a sibling bond.

Once they were done trading barbs, she started the movie. It wasn't a long one, and it held her attention. Yet, sleep still claimed her less than thirty minutes into the film. Denzel nudged her awake enough for her to get ready for bed.

The next couple of weeks went along the same pattern. Dominique had been in contact with Zaria and her mother the closer they came to the actual wedding. She'd also arranged the time off from shooting to attend. Although she still hadn't spoken to her mother about her relationship with Denzel, Dominique was confident she'd be able to navigate it, considering the focus would be on Zaria and Andrei the entire weekend.

The morning before she and Denzel were scheduled to fly to Las Vegas, Dominique awoke in bed alone. Assuming he was downstairs working out, she went about her morning routine. She was seated on the tufted settee in the closet applying moisturizer when she heard the notification chime on her cellphone. Tying her robe, she strode into the bedroom and picked it up.

Tammy had sent her a message containing a link. Checking the time, Dominique frowned. It was early for her, but it was really early for

Tammy, who was on west coast time. Slowly walking back into the closet, Dominique looked at her phone, noticing the link was one for the tabloid news outlet, GMZ. Once she realized it, she was even more curious as to what her agent was sending her.

The website populated with the video paused. The image displayed on the screen between the two hosts was of Douglas Fowler. Plopping back down on the settee, Dominique put in her earbuds and selected the play option and adjusted the volume.

"GMZ sources have confirmed that Executive Producer and long-time showrunner, Douglas Fowler may be in hot water amid allegations of misuse of authority."

Crispin Fells turned toward his female counterpart as if they were in conversation instead of reporting the news.

"Have you heard about this?"

Missy Rothschild shook her blond head, affecting an expression of shock. Ignoring her poor acting, Dominique focused on what was being said.

"I haven't. Not until this news came across our desk."

Crispin swiped on his tablet like he was sifting through a large volume of information.

"Well, according to our insider, there have been reports of him being improper with young actors and actresses either working on television series he produces or looking to work on those series."

Missy held up one hand. "Wait. Did you say *young* actors and actresses? How young? Underaged?"

Putting the device on the news desk, Crispin held up both hands. "I can't confirm they're underaged. The only info I have is that they are young, which could be anything from three to thirty. But as of now, we can only report on what we've actually been told."

Nodding as if they hadn't discussed the segment before it aired, Missy looked down at her own device before looking back up at Crispin.

"Well, it's no secret he's been in short-lived relationships with up-and-coming actresses over the years."

"Yes, but while he's aged, the actresses have typically been in the same age range."

Proving they'd pre-planned the discussion, the viewscreen behind them was populated with images of Fowler with the various actresses he'd been seen with over the years. Curiously absent were any images more current than the past twelve months.

"Well, that sounds familiar," Missy quipped.

"Hey, let's not go there."

Crispin's attempt to back away from the implication of Fowler having a similar M.O. to a very popular, aging actor, was transparent. Dominique's lips tipped up into a wry grin; because she knew the actor. He'd sued GMZ and won in the past.

Holding her hands, palm out, Missy made a pushing motion. "You're right. You're right. Let's stick to the subject at hand. So what, if anything, does this mean for the series he's the showrunner for right now? Aren't they in full production for the series adaptation of The Clarke Files? I have to think Leona Jiles wouldn't want her good work associated with any potential scandal."

Crispin held one hand out toward his co-host. "That is an excellent question. GMZ has reached out to the series, but hasn't received any comments on the topic."

"So, I guess we'll have to keep our eye on this to see how it develops."

Sliding his tablet closer to himself, Crispin held it up while wearing a sly grin. "We will have to wait on that one, but not on the rest of what our source had to say."

Missy leaned over with her chin propped on her hand. "Oh, this sounds juicy. Do tell."

Dominique watched the remaining video as Crispin Fells listed some of the shady, over-reaching things Fowler had done on the set so far. Sadly, every word he said was true. So, even if Douglas threatened to sue, he wouldn't have a leg to stand on. As soon as she was done watching the segment, she called Tammy.

Her agent answered almost immediately. Not giving Dominique a chance to even say hello, Tammy answered the phone with a question.

"So, did you notice who was missing from the little photo array they put on the screen?"

"Yes, ma'am. I did. I also caught that there was no clarification on which actors he'd been inappropriate with."

"Dom, you'd tell me if that asshole tried anything with you, right?"

Looking down at the phone with a frown, Dominique stared at Tammy. "First of all, yes. Second, we don't have to worry about Douglas coming on to me. I'm not his type."

Before Tammy could gear up to correct her, Dominique continued, "His track record speaks for him. He preys on those who really are willing to do anything to make it. Also, I'm not the physical body type he goes for. If the woman is taller than him, which I am, he likes them rail thin—which I'm not. Even when she's not taller than him, she can't have close to my kind of curves."

From the way Tammy replied, Dominique knew her lips were pursed in disbelief, but she'd decided not to argue the point.

"Well, if his sights change, you let me know. I won't have him pulling his bullshit on you. It's bad enough I had to get DJ involved to remind them of your contract."

Dominique didn't add on to Tammy's statement because that had been a tense week. Fowler had given her a wide berth since the blow up with Adam and the studio becoming more interested in what was happening on set following DJ's calls. More than one person wasn't happy with the increased involvement, but Dominique couldn't be bothered to care about Bliss being upset.

"You know I'd tell you. I really want this project to be great, but I'm not playing this particular game. I'm not trading my body for a chance in the spotlight."

"Absolutely the fuck not." Denzel's declaration startled Dominique, causing her to nearly drop the phone.

With a sheen of sweat on his torso, he stood framed in the doorway between the bedroom and the closet, glaring at her.

"Hey, Tammy. Let me call you back." Dominique tapped the earbud to end the call before her agent could respond. Setting the phone to the side, she stared at the man who'd entered the room seizing her full attention.

Using the towel clutched in one hand, Denzel dabbed at his sweaty body as he closed the distance between them. When he was near enough to touch her, he stopped.

"Why is there even a suggestion of you using your body for a chance in the spotlight?" His expression matched his dark eyes, probing hers for answers.

"There isn't."

Tilting her head back, Dominique stared up at him and tried to ignore how delectable he looked with his chest bare, wearing only his exercise shorts. The rest of his clothing was mysteriously absent.

"I was telling Tammy it wasn't an option unlike some people we'd been discussing."

Dropping the towel, Denzel captured her face between his large hands. The tips grazed the bonnet still covering her hair. When he licked his lips, Dominique began shaking her head.

"Den, I *just* got out of the shower."

Ignoring her paltry excuse, Denzel planted his lips on hers, swallowing anything else she might say. Once he'd scrambled her brain to mush with his kiss, he pulled back.

"Get wet with me."

It wasn't a request. It wasn't even an offer to actually bathe together, because they both knew getting clean wouldn't be the first or second thing on the agenda when they stepped into the spray of water. And Dominique couldn't think of one good reason to deny him.

Her robe and his pants lay in a heap on the floor and they were inside the tile and glass shower with their bodies mashed together as their tongues danced. Dominique's hands roamed Denzel's hard body, appreciating the work he put into sculpting his frame. When he walked her backwards toward the bench they loved to use, she sat immediately.

However, instead of allowing him to lower himself to his knees to worship her, she closed her fingers around his shaft as far as she could reach, leaned forward and swiped the droplet of pre-cum pearling at the tip of his dick.

"Mmm." She moaned at the flavor.

"Una..." The single word sounded as if Denzel was warning her and being tortured all at once.

"You said you wanted me to get wet with you." Taking another swipe at the bulbous head of his length, she looked up at him. "This makes me wet."

Following her statement by taking him into her mouth, Dominique hummed around the thickness stretching her lips.

"Fuuuck... Una."

Denzel's hands landed on her shoulders, squeezing, then releasing. She knew he was battling with allowing her to continue or pulling her away to plant himself inside her. Her core clenched with the anticipation of being filled. She hadn't lied or exaggerated. Pleasing him this way excited her. He normally didn't give her the chance. So, she had to wrest the opportunity from him whenever she could.

Two seconds after she cupped his balls and licked down the side of his shaft, he jerked back.

"That's enough."

Before the pout could fully form on Dominique's lips, he'd tugged her to her feet, turned her toward the bench and bent her over. Her walls stretched to accommodate his thickness as he fed his length into her channel until his pelvis was resting against her upturned ass.

"Oh... Den..." Dominique's head dropped forward, hanging between her shoulders.

"That's it, Una. Take it. Take it all."

With a swivel to his hips, Denzel used his knowledge of her pleasure points to drive her up to and over the edge. His campaign to deplete her body of its juices wasn't complete without him peppering it with his nasty words of encouragement.

Telling her how good she was at taking his dick and how beautiful she looked swallowing him. About the many ways he planned to fuck her—ways they hadn't tried yet. His words combined with him ending each promise by asking her if she wanted it was usually enough to have her gushing. Him applying the correct amount of pressure to her clit while he pinched her nipples was the sensory overload which had her drowning his cock with her essence.

Denzel used her hips to push and pull her on and off his length while he thrusted. The sensation of having his tunneling shaft plumbing her depths turned Dominique's limbs to jelly. Her man didn't care about her limp body. He simply arranged her the way he wanted on the bench and continued to drive them both to completion.

The final time she was catapulted into nirvana, he joined her. His dick thumped against her walls as he released his cum. *Damn...* They really needed to be more careful. As soon as the thought flitted across Dominique's mind, it was shoved aside. Her contraceptive was doing its job, and she loved feeling his veiny thickness inside her bare.

"Mmmm..." The reluctant moan came when Denzel removed his softening length from her channel.

Delivering a light tap to her ass, Denzel maneuvered her to a seated position. His lips were soft against hers, and his facial hair tickled her skin when he kissed her.

"You rest here a minute. I'll take care of you."

Nodding and staring from beneath half-lowered lids, Dominique watched him. He stepped beneath the spray of water on the opposite side of the shower and began cleansing his body. Although, she was thoroughly satisfied from their round of lovemaking, watching him stirred her once again.

Knowing she was observing him, Denzel turned under the spray. His formerly softened dick was once again erect in his hand as he lathered it with body wash. The towel in his other hand may as well have been the flag used to start a race. Her sexual engine revved to life as if she hadn't just been fucked to within an inch of her sanity.

Turning under the cascading water, he removed her visual treat. Her disappointment barely had time to set in before he was facing her again. The towel had been discarded and his hand was no longer on his thickness. Instead, his fingers curled, beckoning her to come to him.

Dominique's uncertainty of whether she was capable of walking didn't stop her from trying and succeeding to reach Denzel to let him use his beautiful cock to send her into ecstasy one more time.

Chapter Twenty-Two

NOT ACCEPTABLE

The humming of the plane shifted as they began their descent to the private airstrip just outside of Las Vegas. With Dominique's hand clasped in his, Denzel looked past her at the approaching landscape. They'd already been given their schedules and knew they'd have to part ways at the airport.

Dominique was going off to do things with her cousin and the rest of the ladies, while Denzel planned to swing by CleanSun. His pop in was unscheduled. Not even the acting CEO was aware of his plans. He wouldn't be there long, as he'd received a message about them meeting at Anton's for a final fitting of their tuxedos.

After that, there was supposed to be some kind of guy's night. Andrei refused to call it a bachelor party since there was a joint event immediately following the rehearsal dinner the next night. Denzel and Dominique were cutting it close coming in three days before the wedding, but there would still be plenty of time for her to hang out with Zaria, their mother, and the other ladies.

Denzel wasn't one hundred percent sure what Vitaly had planned. He was a little light on the details. However, since he was the Best Man, the responsibility fell to him. Denzel could've offered him a little advice having just been in the seat with Carver. But he didn't.

Little Antonov was still on his shit list for being a little too touchy feely friendly with Dominique. Even though Denzel knew Vitaly did it to push his buttons, it didn't matter. Andrei's little brother took too much pleasure in making Dominique laugh. It grated on Denzel's nerves.

There was the lightest of bounces when the wheels of the plane touched down on the runway. The jostling was minimal as the aircraft slowed before taxiing toward the designated drop location. From his vantage point, Denzel saw the two vehicles waiting for them on the tarmac.

Although members of his and Dominique's detail traveled with them, he noticed the drivers standing beside the SUVs looked suspiciously like the kind of people Andrei used at Anton's. Denzel wouldn't complain. Especially not since he'd had to explain to Dominique that Andrei having tight security didn't mean they wouldn't travel without their own.

Denzel had no plans of staying with Andrei nor did he have a suite at Anton's. When he'd purchased CleanSun, he'd also secured two new units in the building where the company had already established corporate housing. The penthouse unit stayed empty for him at all times, while he planned to use the other as part of the enticement to the new CEO of CleanSun—whenever they secured one permanently.

While Clarkson was doing an adequate job, he was much better equipped for the CFO role he was promoted to when Denzel became majority owner. He'd been thoroughly investigated and was one of the few executives who made the cut as he'd been actively working to do things correctly—against the wishes of the then CEO Hiriam Baxter.

"This is your captain speaking. We've landed safely at our destination. It's now safe to remove your seatbelts."

The moment the pilot said the words, Denzel flicked the latch on the belt to release it. He freed Dominique's hand so she could do the same. Averting his eyes so as not to look like a total creeper staring at her while she stretched to loosen her limbs after the long flight, Denzel stepped into the aisle.

Unlatching the drawer on the custom console, he slid it open to retrieve Dominique's messenger bag, along with his own. As they left the plane, Denzel had a thought concerning the variance in their schedules. Once they reached the bottom of the stairs, he slipped an arm around her waist to lead her to her transportation.

"Since Andrei isn't having a formal bachelor party, I'll likely be back at the penthouse no later than ten p.m. tonight. If things change, I'll shoot you a message."

Denzel couldn't miss the way Dominique's body stiffened slightly before she looked up at him.

"Okay, well, I don't know what time I'll be done with what Mama has planned for us. So, I was thinking I'd just stay with them at the house tonight."

Her momentary stiffness was multiplied by ten when it transferred to his body once he heard her insane plan. A plan she hadn't mentioned to him before then.

"Uh-uh. That's not going to work for me, Una."

"Well, this trip isn't about you, Den. We're here for Zaria and Andrei, remember?"

Turning her to face him, he caged her between him and the vehicle with the rear passenger door at her back. His jaw ticked as he attempted to keep his knee jerk response from flying from his mouth.

"I know why we're here. What I don't understand is why us being here has to be different from when we're home."

He didn't like the first place his mind went when there was the slightest hesitation before she answered.

"I just thought it would be easier for the things Mama and Alyssa planned for us to do with Zaria if I was already there at the house."

Before she even finished her little speech, he was already shaking his head. The two of them sleeping apart was unacceptable, and he told her so.

"No. Not acceptable. We both know your mother isn't going to be up all night and neither will the very pregnant bride and her even more pregnant Matron of Honor."

"Den, I'm her Maid of Honor. I can't bail on her."

Although he should have, Denzel didn't anticipate this particular complication. Even when Dominique informed him that Zaria didn't just want her to sing at the wedding, but also be Maid of Honor, he didn't foresee them having to sleep separately. They only slept apart when he was out of town. Since the very first night, they hadn't done so when they were both in the same city.

"How are you bailing on her by not sleeping under the same roof? Will Alyssa be staying overnight with y'all? Or the rest of the bridesmaids?"

Dominique's head rocked back, and a line appeared between her eyebrows, as if he'd said something completely insane. But they both knew there was no way Alyssa was spending the night away from her husband. Nor would the other married or engaged members of the wedding party—aside from their mother.

"Den, what Alyssa or the other ladies decide to do is on them. Zee is my big sister. As far as I know, she's only getting married once and I'm not going to do anything to make her think I'm not supporting her."

Logically, Denzel could concede her point. But logic wasn't ruling his actions at the moment. Knowing the ladies had already planned to stay together in a suite of rooms at Anton's the night before the wedding, what she proposed would mean he wouldn't see her except during pre-ceremony events. And neither of those times would they be alone.

As the thought occurred to him, he wondered if she'd even considered it. He wasn't the only one addicted. She'd let it slip that she slept better when they were together and how it took her longer to doze off when he was away. So, the possibility of going consecutive nights apart, when they were within miles of one another, couldn't possibly have crossed her mind.

Settling his body close to hers, he allowed her to feel his hardness against her soft curves.

"I'm not asking you not to support Zaria. But what I'm hearing is that you're perfectly okay with us essentially being in the same city but not having any time together or alone for the next couple of days."

Dominique's lashes lifted and her eyebrows shot up her forehead before dipping into a different furrow than before. When she spoke, her speech was slower. Measured.

"If that's what you heard, I don't think you were listening, Den."

"I'm positive I was listening. I don't believe you've taken the next few days into consideration."

Using one hand, he cradled the base of her head, tilting her chin upwards with his thumb.

"Today, you have things planned with the ladies and you don't know when y'all will be done. And that's cool. I have stuff with the guys."

As he caressed her, he reminded her of the long list of joint and separate activities planned over the next three days. Once he was done, her eyes were wider, but she still had a hint of stubbornness in the set of her jaw.

"So, you see. If we do things the way you suggested, this..." He pressed his lips to hers, swiping his tongue along the seam, requesting entrance. "Will be the last time we have where it's just the two of us."

Putting all of his desires into the kiss, he didn't stop until Dominique's hands were fisted, holding on to his shirt. Only then did he pull back to look into her face.

"Like I said before. Not acceptable."

Standing up straight, he tugged her away from the door to allow him to open it and help her inside. Once she was seated with the seatbelt clicked into place, he leaned in, snagging one final kiss. Smiling when she followed his lips after ending the smooch, he pierced her with his direct stare.

"Una, don't make me come looking for you."

Denzel didn't care how unhinged he sounded, as long as the end result was the two of them sleeping under the same roof and in the same bed. Not giving her a chance to reply, he stood up straight and closed the door. Tapping the roof of the vehicle, he gave the driver the signal to leave. Their luggage was being loaded into a third vehicle that would take it directly to the penthouse.

It only took him a few moments to settle into the blacked-out SUV waiting a few feet away. Soon, they were following the other one, leaving the airstrip. Their paths separated after they reached the main road, with Denzel heading right and Dominique heading left going toward Andrei and Zaria's place outside the city.

The moment he couldn't see Dominique any longer, Denzel

switched his mind over to the business at hand. While his quick visit to CleanSun was unannounced, it wasn't without an agenda. Tiffany had blocked time on the calendars of some the executives and department heads, but he'd allowed them all to believe it was going to be another video conference.

With his first step onto the tiled floor of the lobby, a buzz swept through the building. By the time he stepped off the elevator on the executive floor, Vernon was standing there waiting for him.

"Good morning, Mr. Reyes. This is a surprise."

"It is, isn't it?"

Denzel didn't say more to explain his sudden appearance. Instead, he strode through the office in the direction of the conference room. Vernon quick stepped at his side to keep up with Denzel's long gait. He didn't try to fill in the silence, even though Denzel could practically see the questions bouncing around inside the other man's head.

Making it to the conference room, Denzel decided to finally give Vernon some relief. Tapping his shoulder lightly, Denzel pasted a smile on his face.

"Relax, Vern. No one's being fired today. I'm just looking around, talking to a few people. That's it."

With that little taste of reassurance, Denzel walked into the conference room filled with nervous executives and department heads. Walking around the long table, he greeted them as he made his way to the center seat on the side opposite the door. Once he was seated, he placed his folio pad on the table and swept his gaze around the room.

"Okay people. Talk to me. I've seen the reports and projections, but I want to hear it from you. What's the good word?"

Everyone didn't immediately start speaking at once, but Denzel made note of the brave souls who ventured into the fray first. It took them until the third person spoke to realize he wasn't there to hand anyone their ass. The meeting was exactly what he said it was, an opportunity for them to relay their progress—even the small wins.

CleanSun had operated under terrible leadership for so long, Denzel knew it would take them a while to shift the culture. Getting rid of some of the main culprits had been a start, but until they found someone with vision and the right attitude to fill the CEO's role, they would flounder. So, they were getting more of his individual attention than his other acquisitions.

An hour later, he was once again in the back of the SUV, being taken to the next stop on this trip. He was looking forward to spending a little time with his friends—even if it did mean he'd have to endure Little Antonov.

When they arrived at the casino, the driver stopped the vehicle at Andrei's private entrance. As Denzel stepped out of the vehicle, another drove to a stop behind him. Two seconds later, the rear door opened and Carver stepped out. Like Denzel, he hadn't given his security detail the opportunity to open the door.

Although the difference was, Carver's detail was one guy who was also driving. Nodding toward Michael, Denzel lifted a fist toward Carver, who bumped it when he was within reach. Pulling him into a half hug, Denzel tapped his friend on the back a couple of times before releasing him.

"How long have you been in town?" Carver started walking toward the opaque glass doors leading into the building.

"Not long. I did a pop in at CleanSun before I came here."

Nodding, Carver went silent. Once Andrei's security opened the outer door, they stepped inside. The cool air whooshed past them in stark contrast to the dry heat in the parking area. It wasn't even the hottest part of the year, and it was already hot enough for those few seconds to cause a slight sheen of sweat to dot Denzel's brow.

"Mr. Reyes, Mr. Jamieson." A youngish man roughly the same height as Denzel and Carver nodded and held out a hand. "I'm Trevor. Mr. Antonov asked me to escort you to Savile."

Shaking Trevor's hand in turn, Denzel and Carver fell into step shoulder to shoulder as they followed him to the elevator. Once Trevor placed his thumb on the biometric scanner, the doors slid open and their group stepped inside.

Leaning against the back of the car, Carver looked over at Denzel. "So, how'd it go? Your surprise visit?"

"Not bad. It's gonna take a while for the culture to fully shift, but they're off to a good start. I just need the team to pick up the search for CEO. Clarkson is good, but he's not the guy for the role."

"It's only been a few months. But they haven't come up with anything?"

Denzel shook his head as the doors parted once again. "They've presented a few people, but they were the same kind of cookie cutter CEO to the one I kicked out. I'm not interested in someone who's resistant to change while operating in an industry that needs to stay on the cutting edge of technology and development. They don't have to be technically proficient in regard to the product, but they can't be a hindrance to growth."

"That's understandable."

Carver's agreement was the end of their discussion. The moment they stepped off the elevator onto the promenade of the exclusive shopping level at Anton's, their focus shifted to their reason for being there.

Trevor led them to Savile, the exclusive haberdasher catering to clientele who preferred the custom fit and quality they provided. Once they were inside, there was an attendant present to immediately offer them beverages and anything else they might desire while they were there to see the tailor.

"It took you two long enough to get here." Vitaly strode from the back of the boutique with a low-ball tumbler in one hand. Spinning on his heel, he went in the direction he'd come from, lifting his other hand to beckon them to follow him.

"If you wanted us here earlier, maybe you should've been a little clearer about the time." Denzel shot back, watching Vitaly's retreating back until Andrei came into view.

Andrei was standing on a low platform while another man appeared to be taking measurements and placing colorful pins in various places.

Vitaly took a sip of whatever was in the glass before he responded.

"What do you mean? I said eleven a.m. It's noon. I've been here for an hour. It's a good thing me and my brother gave Regis plenty to do while we waited for you two to show up."

Looking from his watch to Carver, then to Vitaly, Denzel shook his head.

"It *is* eleven a.m. Little Antonov. Actually, it's ten fifty." Ignoring Vitaly's frown at being called Little Antonov, he continued.

"Either your smartwatch is dumb or you don't have it synced to switch time zones. You're still an hour ahead." Looking past Vitaly to Andrei standing silently on the platform, Denzel pierced him with a knowing glare.

"You didn't tell him on purpose, did you? You were going to let him keep showing up to places early until he figured it out."

Shrugging one thick shoulder, Andrei looked straight ahead. "He was here, and no one was forced to wait for him. I consider this a win."

"Your big ass would." Denzel muttered as he accepted the glass bottle of PureGlacial water from the attendant.

Vitaly cursed under his breath, then pulled out his cellphone. The death glare he shot his older brother didn't faze Andrei in the slightest. If Denzel wasn't mistaken, he could've sworn he saw a ghost of a smile before Andrei shuttered his expression.

While Vitaly was fiddling with the application on his phone, to get his watch configured correctly, Carver and Denzel moved to the oversized chairs placed strategically around the seating area.

"So, what's on the agenda today? Besides me reliving my modeling days with this fitting?" Denzel took a deep draw on his water, waiting for someone to clue him in on the plan.

Plopping into the seat on the other side of Carver, Vitaly assumed a similar posture crossing his legs, with one ankle resting on the knee of his opposite leg.

"Well, since party pooper over there doesn't want a bachelor party, I had to get creative."

"Creative?" Ryker Stephen's question caused their small group to turn as he approached. "Why are you guys so comfortable? Am I late? I thought you said eleven?" The big Texan shot Vitaly a questioning glare.

"You're not late. CJ and I just got here. The little guy forgot to sync his watch, and the big guy thought it was funny not to tell him he was still on mountain time."

"I'm not going to be too many more littles." Vitaly narrowed his eyes as he stared at Denzel.

The look would probably scare someone else shitless, but Denzel wasn't bothered in the least.

"It's technically true though. Of the five of us, you're the little guy."

"Yeah..." Carver chimed in on the game. "This is probably one of the few times someone your height *could* legitimately be considered the little guy. You're shorter than all of us."

"By what? A half an inch? Fuck off. Just because I'm the youngest, doesn't mean I'm putting up with your bullshit."

"Gentlemen...Language please."

Regis's admonishment was issued in a mellow, sing-song voice as he ran one hand along the back of Andrei's suit as if he hadn't said a word.

Denzel had to avoid looking at Carver in order to contain the laughter threatening to bubble over. Vitaly flipped Denzel the bird before turning to talk exclusively to Ryker. A moment later, Gregor and Yeva entered and Regis was forced to get his assistant in to begin working with the group.

Chapter Twenty-Three
YOU PUT THE DE-LU-LU IN DELUSIONAL

The SUV had barely driven off the tarmac before Dominique pulled her phone out, tapping at the screen. The ringing sounded extra loud in her ear as she drummed her fingers on her thigh, waiting for Syd to answer. After what felt like forever, her best friend's voice came through the earpiece.

"You know I have a job, right?" Sydney asked the question in lieu of a greeting.

"Of course, I know you have a job. But aren't you supposed to be getting ready to come here for the wedding?"

A thought occurred to Dominique, causing her to sit up taller in the seat, her posture stiffening.

"You aren't backing out, are you? You better not be backing out, Syd."

"Whoa, Miss Ma'am! I'm not backing out. I'm just wrapping something up before I go home and finish getting my house in order. You know I can't leave my house looking any kind of way when I go out of town."

"So, you're still flying here in the morning?" With her friend's reassurance, some of the tension drained from Dominique's shoulders.

"Yes. My flight leaves entirely too early in the morning, but I'll be there before brunch. Now...tell me why you're in a panic about me possibly not showing up? It's not like you're getting married instead of Zaria."

After a pause barely long enough for Dominique to take a breath, Sydney squawked her name. "Dominique! You *aren't* getting married, are you?"

"What?! No! Why would you ask that? I'm not even close to marriage."

Dominique didn't care for the turn this conversation was taking. This wasn't the reason she'd called. However, they were now on a tangent, and she had to figure out a way to get them back on track. Syd wouldn't make it easy.

"What do you mean, why would I ask that? You're *living* with Denzel Reyes."

"Shh!" Dominique put her finger to her lips despite being separated from the others by the privacy partition in the vehicle.

"Why are you shushing me? Unless you have me on speaker, no one can hear me but you. I'm in my office alone. Wait... Do your folks not know?"

As her best friend, Sydney knew far more about her living situation than anyone else. The two talked so regularly, it was inevitable she'd hear Denzel in the background. Also, once Dominique spilled the beans about Vic and the security detail, Syd had gone on a deep dive into Dominique's business.

Since things were so new between Dominique and Denzel, she'd sworn her bestie to secrecy. She wanted to tell her family in her own time and in her own way. However, Denzel's recent demands, and the circumstances of the wedding, were swiftly taking the decision out of her hands. And, she was regretting skirting the topic every time she spoke with her mother.

"Dominique...Please tell me you've told them, or at least Zee by now. It's been months."

"It hasn't been months."

"Dom...It's almost April. You've been in Atlanta since the end of January. You two have essentially been together from the moment you crossed the threshold in his big ass house. That equates to months."

Pursing her lips, Dominique looked out of the window, refusing to acknowledge the truth of Sydney's statement. But her friend knew her too well to be ignored.

"You can pretend you don't hear me all you want. But, I'm telling you what God loves, and that's the truth."

Folding one arm across her middle, Dominique released a huffing breath.

"Okay. Fine. It's been months, and I know I've missed opportunities to let them know before now. But there's nothing I can do about the past. I'm trying to figure out what to do about the present."

"Uh-oh. That doesn't sound good."

Biting her bottom lip, Dominique transferred her gaze to the passing landscape again.

"It's not awful, but it's most definitely going to take some emotional navigation skills, I'm not sure I have, to solve it."

"Okay, other than them not knowing, what else is there? Is he huge on PDA and won't keep his hands and other body parts to himself? What is it?"

Even though they weren't speaking via video chat, and Syd couldn't see her, Dominique closed her eyes, bracing herself.

"I'm positive Mama and Zee will expect me to stay with them at Zee's this weekend, with the exception of the night the ladies in the wedding party are staying together in a suite at Anton's."

"And I take it Mr. Reyes isn't on board with that plan."

"Not even a little bit."

Instead of the sage advice Dominique expected. Or even more reprimands. What she received from Sydney was an earful of laughter. Loud. Belly deep laughter. A furrow creased Dominique's brow. Staring at the cellphone screen as if the device itself had delivered a great insult, she huffed.

"I don't see anything funny, Syd."

"You don't? Because I find this completely hilarious. Friend... You put the de-lu-lu in delusional."

Releasing another peal of laughter, Sydney offered Dominique zero solace in her situation.

"Syd...you're supposed to help me. This isn't funny."

"What is it you southerners are always saying? Bless your sweet lil' heart."

Sydney's fake southern accent was terrible, but Dominique grudgingly admitted she had the inflections right for the circumstances. Sulking silently, Dominique waited for Sydney to get herself under control. When the giggles tapered off to intermittent sighs, she tried again.

"Den bought a place here, and he expects me to stay with him when I'm not with the wedding party."

Clearing her throat, the next time Sydney spoke, there wasn't a hint of amusement in her voice.

"That's to be expected, Dom. The two of you are together every night, with the exception of when he goes out of town. Why would he assume things to be different? You have family in the city, but not your own place. You live with him in Atlanta, so..."

"Technically, he lives outside of Atlanta in Logan City."

"Tomato, to-mah-to. The bottom line is you're cohabitating, and for most couples who cohabitate, it extends to wherever they sleep when they travel."

Dominique couldn't believe Sydney didn't see her side of things. While the logical part of her knew her friend was simply stating facts, it felt like she was taking Denzel's side. But, taking sides implied she and Denzel were fighting.

They weren't. She was simply looking for an option to help him see reason. Although, she in no way looked forward to not sleeping next to him, absorbing his body heat, and feeling his solid form wrapped around hers. It was addictive as hell to be cocooned by all of that maleness every night.

"Syd, I get your point, but I'm here to support Zaria. What would it look like for me to bail on her when I came specifically for *her* wedding?"

"It would look like you have a man the same as she does."

Rolling her eyes, Dominique prayed for strength. Apparently sky daddy wasn't in the mood to listen to her, because Sydney kept talking, reminding her it was impossible for her, Zaria, their mother, and the other ladies to spend every moment together. Especially if it wasn't planned in advance and announced to all participants.

She didn't want to hear Dominique's interjections about her being the Maid of Honor or Zaria being her older sister. Sydney held firm to her assessment.

"Girl, unless you plan to work in your sleep, there's no reason for you to spend all day and all night there. But here's an idea. From what you said, the house is huge. Why doesn't he simply come stay there?"

Dominique gasped so deeply, she was certain all the oxygen in the space should've been depleted.

"Have you been snorting California fairy dust? Or is it smoking? You went to a dispensary with strains that put rappers on their ass."

"Ma'am. I'm trying to help you. There's no call for you accusing me of partaking in party drugs."

"I'm not. What you had must be stronger than the party variety."

As if they were in the same room, Dominique flipped her hand. "Anyway, this isn't about semantics. Did you forget who my mother is? Two unmarried people sharing a bed under her roof will send her into palpitations."

"It's not her roof, though. It's Zee and Andrei's place."

Dominique snorted. "You say that as if it matters. No. Him staying over there isn't an option."

"Then, it sounds like you have the answer to your dilemma."

Dominique noticed the area changing and realized they were less than five minutes away from their destination. She and Syd would have to wrap up this call. But she still didn't know how she was going to handle things.

"If you say so." She murmured quietly.

Dominique released a sigh before wrapping up the call with her friend. Promising to contact them as soon as she landed, Sydney once again encouraged Dominique to come clean before saying goodbye.

The vehicle rolled to a stop underneath the canopied driveway in front of the mansion. Taking a deep, fortifying breath, Dominique stepped out of the SUV when the door was opened.

She didn't get the opportunity to ring the bell, because the heavy wooden door was flung open to her mother standing on the other side.

"I told Zee Baby that was you! Hey, my baby!"

Not giving her the opportunity to do more than brace herself, Dominique's mother pulled her into a hug. Sound effects accompanied the squeezing, along with a little side-to-side rocking as if they hadn't just seen one another the first week in January.

"Hey, Mama. Good to see you too."

Pulling away, her mother kept her hands on Dominique's shoulders as she swept her gaze over her. Used to the visual inspection, Dominique didn't have to wait long for her mother to speak again.

"You look good! Atlanta must be treating you well. I know you've been too busy with the show for visitors, but I wouldn't mind seeing you more, since you're closer."

Patting her hands, Dominique nodded. "I know, Mama. But remember, this isn't a permanent move. Just while I'm working on the show."

"Mhm." Her mother's lips twisted, displaying her displeasure at Dominique's reminder.

"And who is this?"

Dominique looked over her right shoulder to see Haley standing there, slightly behind her.

"This is Haley. Remember I told you Denzel helped me find a security service that wouldn't be intrusive? Haley is a part of the team."

Beckoning Haley closer, Dominique introduced the other woman to her mother.

"Mhmmm... Denzel Reyes has been *very* helpful, hasn't he? First he helped you find a place to live, then he helped with hired security—which I think you should've had a long time ago."

Not wanting to get off on a tangent, but also not wanting to respond to her mother's dig about Denzel's helpfulness, Dominique chose to remain silent. Especially since she hadn't completely clarified her living situation with her parents.

Her reprieve was short-lived when her mother looked around Dominique and Haley as if she'd lost something. Glancing around, Dominique gave her a quizzical expression.

"Where's your luggage?" Her mother's question sent a jolt through her.

Shit! Dominique barely managed to keep the expletive from flying from her mouth. She was certain her eyes would pop from their sockets if she stretched her eyelids any wider.

"Umm..."

"Hey, Dom!" Zaria's cheerful greeting sent a wave of gratitude washing over Dominique. Without thought, Dominique's feet moved her closer to her sister-cousin.

Wearing a flowing dress which skimmed her hips and showed off her baby bump, Zaria approached in sure strides. Her smile reached her sparkling eyes and preceded the hug she wrapped Dominique in once they were close enough to embrace.

"Hey, Zee baby!"

Dominique was genuinely happy to see Zaria, but she was also elated to not have to address her lack of luggage. She knew she'd have to tell them something, but she needed a minute. When they pulled away, Zaria's gaze swept over Dominique in a manner similar to their mother's.

"Looking good, Dom. I swear you're practically glowing. And listen... Is it me being envious because my waistline is expanding or is your waist looking snatched? Do you have on ammunition?"

Laughing at Zaria's statement, Dominique shook her head. Ammunition is the nickname their granny gave body shapers—or girdles, as they were called in her day.

"No. No ammunition. Just a devil trainer by the name of Kam, who works me out like I'm going to be doing my own stunts."

Running a hand down her midsection, Dominique smiled.

"I won't complain, though. I didn't set out to lose weight, and I haven't. But I'm seeing the slight changes. I wish I could pack her into my suitcase and take her with me when I go back to Cali."

"Speaking of suitcases. Where did you say your luggage was?"

*Damn...*Dominique thought she'd gotten away from her mama's question.

"I'm sure it's in the car. Someone will bring it in."

Zaria to the rescue again. Looping her arm through Dominique's, she led her toward the stairs.

"Come on, Dom. We turned one of the suites into our own private dress shop slash all things wedding spot. Everybody else is already upstairs."

"Who is everybody?"

"Alyssa, Ensley, Carmen, Deirdre, and Autumn."

Her cousins, Alyssa and Zaria's legal friend Ensley she expected, but... "Autumn?"

When Dominique's face scrunched in confusion, Zaria tapped her arm.

"You remember Autumn. You've met her a couple of times. She's in my Black Lady Lawyer group."

The name and face dropped into Dominique's mind as they walked up the stairs toward the suite. No matter how many times Zaria said it, Dominique remained amused by her calling the African American Women's Association for Nevada attorneys, her Black Lady Lawyer group.

With their mother and Haley trailing behind them, the two kept up a steady stream of catch-up conversation until they reached the suite. Once inside, Dominique saw for herself that Zaria wasn't exaggerating.

The area had been transformed into a wedding everything boutique. Dresses hung on clothing racks in an organized corner of the room. A small platform had been placed nearby. Ensley currently stood in the center wearing a formfitting, off the shoulder dress in a beautiful lilac color which bordered on being a soft pink.

In another section, there were two massaging spa pedicure chairs, both of which were occupied. Alyssa was in one, while the other was taken by Autumn. In front of them, on the same low stools she recognized from the nail salon, were two technicians giving them both pedicures.

Dominique's gaze swept around the rest of the space. There was a lounging area near the wall mounted television and something of a buffet of snacks and beverages were nearby completing the setup. That's where her cousins were posted, nibbling. Dominique didn't know whose idea it was, but they'd seemingly thought of everything.

It almost made her feel some type of way. When she and Alyssa had talked about pre-wedding things, this setup hadn't been a part of the discussion. Dominique thought they were going to the bridal boutique.

However, it appeared the boutique had come to them. A tailor was actively checking the fit of Ensley's bridesmaid dress while her assistant was flitting about doing what, Dominique wasn't sure. But, she looked busy.

"I know that look." Her mother looped her arm through Dominique's on the other side. "You're forgetting the man Zee-Baby is marrying. Between him and Alyssa's husband, things had to be rearranged for minimal running around. Everything we want and need is coming to us."

Dominique's mind whirled with possibilities and the implications of the changes. If all of their activities had been rearranged so the services would happen at the mansion, it was really going to be difficult if she decided to spend the night away from her family. Many thoughts rolled around in her head.

"Does that mean we aren't staying in the suite of rooms at Anton's after the rehearsal dinner tomorrow?"

"Oh, we're definitely still having our sleep over," Zaria replied. "Everything is already arranged. Margarite is going to have the dresses delivered there first thing in the morning, and we've got our girls' night stuff all planned out."

"Girls' night? I thought you and Andrei decided against bachelor and bachelorette parties. You said the rehearsal dinner was enough."

"Dom. Look at me." Zaria gestured to her body. "Now look at Lyssa. Do you think either of us will be getting up to shenanigans? I mean, I'm not as far along. So, I might be able to shake a tail feather. But I'm just lucky Lyssa is staying awake and is still willing to stand up with me."

Alyssa piped up from her reclining position. "I can hear you, Zee. I don't sleep all the time. It's this little girl. She keeps me up at night. She's already got her hours mixed up."

Zaria didn't refute Alyssa's assertion, but her facial expression told Dominique that Alyssa's explanation wasn't one hundred percent accurate. There was no way she was getting between the besties. So, she changed the subject.

Briefly introducing Haley to the ladies, Dominique slipped into her Maid of Honor role and started feeling out the plan for the next couple of days. It was only once their mother drifted away to speak to the tailor that Zaria tugged Dominique into the adjoining room.

"Where the hell is your luggage? If Auntie asks again, I might not be able to save you."

Caught off guard, Dominique was struck mute.

"Don't play crazy. The few times we've talked since you moved to Atlanta for the show, Denzel's name has been sprinkled into the conversation like paprika on potato salad.

I don't need to know all your business to know the two of you have gotten close since you've been there. What I don't know for sure is, is it sleepover close or occasional dinner close?"

Well...shit. Zaria had just disabused Dominique of the notion Belinda Truman would be the only one trying to get all up in her business. Apparently, Zee wasn't so embroiled in wedding activities she wouldn't create time to get answers.

With a tentative look over her shoulder to make certain they were still alone, Dominique licked her suddenly dry lips.

"I don't know where my luggage is." Despite them being far enough away from the door to prevent being overheard, she spoke lowly.

"How do you not know where your luggage is? You didn't fly commercial. It's not like you had to wait by a carousel for your stuff."

Baring her teeth in a light grimace, Dominique avoided Zaria's direct stare.

"Because I flew in with Den, and he took care of everything. I'm guessing my luggage is either on its way to or already inside his penthouse."

"Wait...Uh-uh, back that shit up. You aren't gonna just plop that down like you don't realize what you're implying. Your luggage is on its way to where?"

Flicking her eyes to the closed door, Zaria got closer to the silent Dominique. Pulling her to a couch on the other side of the room, Zee encouraged her to sit.

"So you and Denzel are definitely in sleep over phase, but this sounds like more than you packing a spinnanight bag."

Dominique's shoulders dropped, and she leaned over until she could lay her head on Zaria's shoulder. The whole story spilled forth in a jumble of words.

"It is. So much more. And I haven't said anything to anyone other than Syd. Now Den wants me to stay with him at his place while we're here, because it's what we're used to at home. He's not listening when I tell him I'm here for you, and it would be messed up for me to dip on you like that.

Then, as soon as I set foot in this place, mama is on me asking questions. She has no idea the place Denzel helped me find in Atlanta is actually *his* place—as in the house he lives in. I can't tell her that. She'll burst a blood vessel if she finds out."

The warmth of Zaria's arms around her drained some of Dominique's tension. She didn't feel judged, only supported.

"First of all, Dom. You're an adult. You don't have to hide a relationship, or your living situation. It doesn't matter what anyone else thinks about you living with Denzel. Not even Auntie."

"But—"

"No buts, Dom." Pulling back, Zaria peered into her eyes. "Are you ashamed of your relationship?"

Dominique's frown was immediate. "Absolutely not."

"Then, don't worry about what Auntie will say. I know it's easier said than done. But trust me. She's more interested in whether he treats you well than if you two are living under the same roof."

Both of them jumped when the door burst open and Belinda Truman came strutting inside.

"There you two are. What are y'all doing huddled up in here?" Her shrewd stare raked over them. "What's wrong? Why do you look upset, Dominique?"

Double shit. Her mama had used her real name, not a nickname. It was time to put up or shut up.

Chapter Twenty-Four

SHE'S GONNA SHIT A BRICK

After spending the latter part of the morning doing their best imitations of mannequins and male models, they went up to The Rooftop for a light lunch. Sitting in a reserved area outside, they had an excellent view of the Las Vegas Strip. From their vantage point, they could see the city bustling with tourists.

It wasn't the most popular time of year for visitors, but Las Vegas was nearly immune to slow tourism periods. Things may get slower, but they never came to a complete halt.

Servers brought out drinks while the group sat around the table chatting amiably. Of course, not everyone could abstain from discussing business in some form, but no huge debates broke out amongst them.

"So, tell me again why I have to eat bird food instead of ordering what I want?" Carver stared at Vitaly, looking as if he was on the edge of being hangry.

"Because, Uncle Neal said not to get too full. He's making barbeque."

Denzel sat up straighter in his seat with Vitaly's statement. "Just for clarification. Did he say he was making barbeque? Or. Did he say he was putting some meat on the grill?"

Texas born, and having spent some of his summers with his mother's parents, Denzel knew there was a difference between the two. Especially when it was a Southern Black man making the statement. Having immigrated to America as a teen, he wasn't sure if Vitaly was aware.

"Isn't it the same thing?" Gregor surprised him by asking.

"No!" Denzel, Ryker, and Carver answered simultaneously.

Their response tipped off a twenty-minute discussion where Denzel and the other two southerners had to explain the subtle differences. The other transplants not only listened raptly, but asked questions. Yeva was particularly interested in the differences between sauces from state to state and even regions within the same state.

"Will you require time off to investigate the differences?" Andrei asked his head of security, who was obviously also considered a friend.

Yeva appeared to think on it before he gave a curt head shake. "Nyet."

Denzel doubted the other man ever took time off. If Yeva followed his boss's example, he likely worked every day ending in 'y'. Not that Denzel had room to judge, but he did manage to carve out days here and there. He couldn't effectively woo his woman if he was always working.

But, it did help that Dominique had her own things going on. So, she didn't complain about the hours he put in working one of his many endeavors. Never far from his thoughts, when he considered their situation, it brought their parting interaction to the forefront of his mind.

He knew it was a dick move to have her luggage loaded with his and taken to the penthouse. He really couldn't bring himself to care. Having her next to him when they were in the same geographical area was non-negotiable.

However, her response made him wonder about some things. Like if her family was aware of their relationship. Also, did they know she'd been living with him since she relocated in January? His gut said the answer to both was no.

Denzel didn't like thinking it. He liked knowing the truth of it even less. On one hand, he could understand her not broadcasting it publicly. Despite their living situation, their relationship was still in its infancy. Yet, what did she assume would happen with the two of them around her family for at least three consecutive days?

Did she expect them to pretend to be friends or close acquaintances? Because that shit definitely wasn't gonna fly. He wasn't likely to tongue her down in front of her parents. But, he couldn't see himself *not* touching her in some way. It was impossible for him to be in her orbit and hold himself apart from her.

The two of them would simply have to figure something out. And to keep things even, they'd need to set aside a weekend for her to meet his parents. Denzel was convinced his mother, Tia Isabel, and Silvia had a group chat going. Although, all three denied it when he asked.

He couldn't blame her for the phone call he received from his mama, though. Raffi, with his mooching big mouth, got all the credit for Denzel's mama calling him.

Three weeks ago

"So, I have to hear from your Tia that you're not just seeing someone, but said someone has been living with you for over a month."

Denzel looked at the device in his hand, trying to squelch the urge to toss it against the wall. He stopped himself, because it would be a waste of his money and not nearly as satisfying as inflicting bodily harm on the person who'd decided to run their mouth to Diana Reyes.

"Hey, Mama. How are you today?"

"Don't get cute with me, little boy." His mother's sharp comeback following his attempt to remind her of phone etiquette was filled with her thoughts on the matter.

"I'm not being cute, Mama." Lie. Total Lie. "I genuinely would like to know how you're doing today." Only partially true.

"I would say don't lie to me; lie to your mama. But since I am your mama, I'll just remind you that I didn't raise you to lie to me, Denzel Alejandro Reyes."

Releasing a huffing breath, Denzel leaned back into the chair. He was seated at the conference table in his home office, having just completed a video call with an associate.

"Yes, ma'am."

Denzel agreed, because the last thing he wanted was smoke from his mama. She'd whipped out the full government on him. So, he cleaned up his act and reserved his ire for whoever sent her his way. There were only two possibilities. However, since he'd had a conversation with Silvia regarding his boundaries, there was really only one option. Raffi.

"Now. Back to what I was saying. What is this I hear about you having a woman and moving her into your house? And not just any woman. Dominique Truman. With her pretty self."

The muscle in Denzel's jaw jumped in response to his clenched teeth. He was going to have a serious talk with his cousin about telling other people's business. Raffi was super smart, but he let his mother, Tia Isabel, play him like a violin, skillfully picking him for information.

"Mama...it's true. I wasn't hiding it from you or anyone else. You know how I roll. I don't go around flapping my gums about my personal life. And I don't appreciate people in this household doing it on my behalf."

His irritation with being caught off guard, and wondering who else in the family his Tia decided to share his personal business with, had him building up a head of steam. While he was confident in how he felt about Dominique, and he was pretty certain of her feelings for him, he wasn't keen on having people in their business. Even family.

It didn't bother him for his parents to know they were together, but he wanted to be the one to tell them. He also didn't want family members outside his immediate family to be in the loop until he was ready. They were used to him, but Dominique was a movie star.

Some of them wouldn't be able to help themselves from putting her name in their mouth. What he wouldn't have, is anything resembling the Melody debacle. And, there was bound to be at least one of them to compare the two women.

"Don't you go blaming Raffi. If you had told me yourself, Isabel wouldn't have been able to run tell me anything."

Because you would have told her... The thought was in Denzel's mind, but he didn't dare voice it. Those two were thick as thieves. He had no doubt the second his Tia weaseled the information out of her son, she immediately got on the phone with her sister-in-law. He also knew his mother was looking for an apology to go along with her quest for information she hadn't gotten from Raffi via Tia Isabel.

"Lo siento, Mamá. Like I said, I wasn't hiding my relationship. We

haven't gone public. But, yes, Dominique and I are together. She moved in with me when she came to the Atlanta area to work on her new series. She's only been here since January."

Denzel pulled the phone away from his ear to keep his eardrums intact after his mother's squeal. Once he heard her voice return to a normal level, he put it back.

"I knew you had it in you. You had to kiss a few frogs, but you finally got it together and got a real one."

Denzel's brow creased, and he wasn't sure if he was frowning because it sounded as if she was comparing him to the princess in The Princess and The Frog story or because she'd insinuated he'd taken longer than she deemed necessary to 'get a real one'.

"Um... Thank you?"

"I haven't told your daddy, but you know his sister probably called him the second we hung up the phone anyway. I'm so excited! My baby boy got himself a nice southern girl who's beautiful, talented, and has some home training."

Denzel listened for a while as his mother let him know just how closely she'd been watching Dominique over the years. If he wasn't head over heels for his Una, he would almost say his mother had a bigger crush on his woman than he did. She knew things about Dominique's upbringing and her early days in the theater.

"Not that we base our lives on what other people think, but I would love to be a fly on the wall when the lil' tramp finds out who you're with now."

His mother's cackle was reminiscent of a villainous witch from the cartoons, drawing a smile from Denzel despite him not giving two shits what Melody thought of his current relationship.

"That little heifer thought she was going to ruin you, and she hasn't been able to do more than sing at lounges and get bit parts in low budget movies since y'all broke up.

When she finds out you're with an award-winning actress and singer, who's starring as the title character of her own TV series, she's gonna shit a brick."

He didn't want to encourage his mama's rant, but her glee did make him chuckle. She wasn't normally a vindictive or petty person, but Melody was on her forever shit list. Still, he did what he could to rein her in. Until he and Dominique decided to publicly put their relationship out there, he didn't want anyone else putting them on blast.

"If you say so, Mama. But, I'm not worried about Melody. How she will feel about it or what she'll think, isn't in my realm of concern."

Denzel steered the conversation to discussing his parents and other current family events before he ended the call to go on with his day.

Present

Denzel tuned back into the conversation the others were having regarding the rest of their day, just in time to hear about the party moving to Andrei's place. His rise from his seat was done quickly, but not noticeable, because more than half of the men had women at Andrei's. It really didn't matter what anyone said about the events not being joint until the rehearsal dinner, they were obvious in their quest to get inside the same building with the ladies.

Not uttering a word, Denzel fell into step with the group as they walked through the restaurant to the private elevator. Once he was in the back seat of the vehicle, he considered sending Dominique a text to warn her about the men converging on them. However, he changed his mind. She was likely busy doing bridesmaid things. He could go more than a few hours without blowing her phone up.

Their caravan of SUVs pulled into the long circular driveway in front of Andrei's place and they converged on the front entrance together. Once Andrei opened the door, everyone followed him inside, in no particular order. A feminine voice drew Denzel's attention to the curved stairway leading to the second floor.

"Hot damn...Was there some kind of extra big and super fine contest and no one told me about it?"

Looking in the direction of the voice, Denzel noticed the women lined along the railing at the top of the stairs. Dominique was standing next to the woman, who was still speaking, but Denzel had tuned her out. His Una was his primary focus.

Although his steps didn't falter and he never stopped moving forward, he kept his gaze firmly on his woman. His lips tilted into a crooked smile from knowing she was staring him down with the same level of intensity.

"Ladies." Finally breaking eye contact with Dominique, Denzel nodded to the other women.

"Imma need a drink." The woman to Dominique's right spoke again. The resulting giggles made Denzel smile a little brighter as he followed along with the group to the adjoining hallway.

When he finally put his attention on the man walking in front of him, he saw the tail end of Carver doing the same as him, watching his woman. A broad smile was on his friend's face. Denzel couldn't blame him. After fifteen years, Carver had managed to connect with the woman he'd been in love with since college, then proceed to court, marry, and impregnate her all within a year's time. No. Denzel didn't blame him at all.

"Hey, Pop. They're here." Cisco's voice called out the moment Andrei pushed open the garden doors leading to the poolside patio.

Standing under a pergola next to a smoker and a combination gas and charcoal barbeque grill was Neal Truman. Turning, his wide smile brightened his expression as he waved the group over.

"Hey, fellas. Y'all are just in time. Dray's chef finished the sides and I'm about to pull the butt out of the smoker. Another ten minutes and the last of the ribs will be ready."

Mr. Truman reminded Denzel of his mother's brothers and uncles. Except he didn't have anyone battling with him for the position of barbeque king. The Colliers liked to compete to see who could grill the best. They had serious competitions for the title. Today, Neal Truman had no opponent. So, he claimed an outright victory.

Once he lifted the lid on the smoker and cracked open the foil wrapping, Denzel conceded that Dominique's father might know what he was doing. The pulled pork was so tender, it fell apart with the slightest touch from a fork.

Their light snack at The Rooftop was a distant memory as each of the guys was given a task before filing into the sunroom where the rest of the fare had been laid out. Although Andrei's chef specialized in Italian cuisine, he appeared to have done an excellent job on the side dishes.

"Have the ladies been taken care of?" Andrei's question was directed to Cisco, who was carrying a pan of meat.

"Yeah, they have a whole buffet laid out upstairs. Pops and Chef sent up the first batch of everything to them so they wouldn't have to wait."

Denzel had assumed the ladies were on their way down the stairs when he'd seen them earlier. But, when they didn't join them, he began to wonder. Andrei's query got him the answer he needed.

Dominique tended to get absorbed in tasks and skip meals. She had a hearty appetite when she did eat. There was just the matter of getting her to do it on a consistent schedule. At least one he considered consistent. She joked about him always trying to feed her to keep her at the level of plump he liked, but that wasn't it.

Whether she lost weight or gained it, had no bearing on how attractive he found her. It wasn't about her size. It was about making sure all of her needs were met. Even the ones she didn't think were a big deal—like having three solid meals a day.

Denzel was piling food onto a plate when Carver lightly bumped his shoulder, getting his attention.

"Do you think you stared at her hard enough for her to get the point?"

Flicking a glance at his friend, Denzel cocked an eyebrow. "First of all, I don't know what you're talking about. Secondly, how would you know what I was doing? You were too busy staring at your wife."

While he'd made no attempt to be subtle in his continued study of his favorite subject—Dominique Truman, Denzel didn't consider him looking at her to be him attempting to make a point.

"I see having her under your roof hasn't stopped you from being delusional as fuck."

It wasn't long after Dominique moved in and their relationship took a turn, that Carver was in the loop on their updated status. Denzel didn't exactly run to tell his friend, but knowing him the way he did, Carver picked up on Denzel's response after he asked if Denzel had kept his promise to help Dominique find a place in Atlanta.

If they weren't such good friends, Denzel would've been offended by Carver's bluntness. But, since the guy knew him better than most, he let it slide. Putting his plate down at the first empty table he came to, Denzel pulled out a chair.

"And just what am I being delusional about? I wasn't making a point. I was simply enjoying the view."

As he took the seat to Denzel's right, Carver stared at him. "So, that's what we're calling it when we strip someone naked with a look? Got it."

Pointing at him with his fork, Denzel shot him a mild glare. "You were watching me awfully close for a man with his own woman to worry about."

A piece of pulled pork disappeared into Carver's mouth before he gifted Denzel with a grin. "Don't worry about me. I can multi-task. Besides, you should be wondering what else I saw while you were fixated on Miss Truman."

Denzel had looked down at his own plate of food. However, when Carver called Dominique, Miss Truman, his gaze flew to his friend's face. Something about hearing her called *Miss Truman* grated on his nerves. But, he wasn't so sidetracked by it that he missed Carver's implication.

"What do you mean, what else you saw?"

"Oh... Nothing.... Except, while you were staring a hole through Dom, her mother was giving you a Black mama once and twice over."

Putting his fork down, Denzel gave Carver his full attention. "Just what do you know about a Black mama once over?"

Lowering his own fork, Carver returned Denzel's stare. "I know more than you think. I got the same look from your mama the first time you introduced me as your friend and a similar one from Bit's mama when I took her home right before we got engaged."

"Ok. So, since you brought it up, do you want to tell me what you think it means?"

Spearing a forkful of potato salad, Carver popped it into his mouth. He didn't speak again until he was done chewing. By then, Andrei was seated on the other side of Denzel, bringing his little brother along for the ride.

"It means she has her eye on you. You're also on borrowed time before she talks to her husband."

Denzel wasn't afraid of talking to anyone's parents, but he wouldn't lie and say it didn't make him even a little anxious at the thought of having a *talk* with the Trumans regarding his intentions toward Dominique. It wasn't because he wasn't serious about her. It was the exact opposite. He was very serious about her.

But, they were also a tight-knit family. Her parent's impression of him would matter a great deal to Dominique. So, the stakes were high. Very high.

Chapter Twenty-Five
EVERY DAY AND TWICE ON SUNDAY

Earlier

Dominique pulled away from Zaria, staring at her mother with wide eyes. A nudge to her side was Zaria's form of encouragement, but before Dominique could get her words together, her mother strode into the room, filling in the blanks with her own thoughts.

"Is this about that Douglas man? The producer on your show? Eugenia sent me a link to the GMZ report about him." Her steps faltered as she got closer.

"Did he try something with you?" The two octave drop in her mother's voice made Dominique jump to her feet.

"No! No, Mama. He hasn't tried anything with me. Also...I'm not upset. Not really. I was just trying to work out the logistics of something, and Zee was being a listening ear."

Dominique struggled not to fidget under her mother's scrutiny. It was like the woman had X-ray eyes and could peer directly into whatever secret her children were trying to keep from her. The only way not to spill the beans was to stay away from her.

Staying away wasn't an option this weekend. Besides, as Zee would say, it was time to put her big girl panties on—take control of the situation like an adult. Although, truth be told, Dominique wanted to call in an adultier adult to do the talking for her.

"Dominique..." Just the way her mama enunciated each syllable of Dominique's name let her know her time was well and truly up.

"You were right earlier, when you said Denzel has been really helpful. He's been more than helpful." Biting her lower lip, then releasing it, Dominique straightened her shoulders and met her mother's gaze.

"We've been seeing each other, exclusively, since I've been there."

Her mother's eyes narrowed. Glancing between Dominique and Zaria, she dragged out her next word.

"And...?"

"And the place he found for me there is actually his place."

"So, you've been living with Denzel Reyes since you moved to Atlanta...He got you personal security and flew you here on a private plane... Let me guess. You don't know where your luggage is because he's had it taken to wherever he stays when he's in the city."

Dominique wasn't sure how she felt after hearing it laid out in such plain speech. A hint of guilt for the secrecy, keeping it from her parents, and for *living in sin*, as the old folks used to say. Toss in her avoidance of the subject anytime they spoke, and the shame intensified.

Along with the guilt was a contrasting sense of relief. She no longer had to worry what her mother would think when she found out, because everything was out in the open. Well, almost everything.

"Yes. He really does have rental properties around the city, but he said the ones he had available wouldn't be good locations for me. So, he was going to let me use his pool house—which is *really* nice, by the way. But, his aunt asked him to let his cousin stay there.

So, he ended up setting me up with a suite of rooms in the main house. They're bigger than the apartment I had when I lived in New York. He really did think of everything."

"Uh-huh... I just bet he did."

Walking around her to the sofa, her mama sat next to Zaria, then patted the empty space to her right. Obeying the unspoken command, Dominique lowered herself onto the plush cushion.

"I know you're expecting me to go off. I have no intention of doing that. But we are going to talk, Miss Ma'am. Right now."

Opening and closing her mouth, Dominique composed her next words. Then, she looked into her mother's eyes and let it spill out. When she was done, her mother stared at her for a solid minute.

"I have smart children. Actually. Brilliant. All three of you. Y'all are so intelligent it makes me send up prayers of thanks for my blessings. But... Sometimes...Sometimes common sense and deductive reasoning just leaves y'all. The trip is, you don't even realize it's gone."

Dominique's brows drew together as she tried to figure out what her mama meant. She'd said she wasn't going to go off. However, to Dominique it sounded a lot like her mama had just called her dumb. After praising her intelligence seconds before.

"Ma'am?"

Glancing at Zaria, her mother looked at her cousin before pinning Dominique again with her too-knowing stare.

"You don't even see it, do you? Not that I wanna know, but the man must have some kind of magic in his pants or...somewhere. Because you don't seem to see everyone else can see. He never intended for you to be anywhere else except with him."

Holding up a hand when Dominique opened her mouth to refute her mother's statement, she continued, "Nope. Don't try to fix it up. I really don't want to know what he told you. What matters is how you feel. Other than stressing about what me or your daddy would say when we learned you were shacking, how do you feel?

Are you happy? Do you feel prioritized in your relationship? I can tell he's as heavy-handed as his friend."

Pausing, she gifted Zaria with a knowing expression. In turn, Zaria hunched her shoulders, giving a quizzical look.

"How did I get in this? I was just a listening ear."

Twisted lips were her mama's response. Turning back to Dominique, she shook her head.

"See what I mean? Brilliant and oblivious."

Having Zaria catch a stray didn't make Dominique feel any less like she was in the hot seat. Also, her mother's probing stare was a clear indicator she expected an answer. Ignoring the jab about her and Denzel shacking, Dominique returned her mother's stare when she responded.

"Yes, Mama. Despite him being heavy-handed with a few things, he does make me, and our relationship, a priority. I'm very happy."

"That's all I need to know. Come here."

Pulling her into a hug, her mama helped most of the tension drain away. There was still the issue of her daddy, but with her mother on her side, Dominique thought it would go infinitely better. *For her.* She really couldn't predict how he'd respond to Denzel. They'd seemed cordial enough during the Novy God celebration, but she and Den hadn't been living together then.

Now

"Hot damn...Was there some kind of extra big and super fine contest and no one told me about it?"

Dominique barely contained the giggle behind her smile at Carmen's outburst when Denzel and the rest of the guys in the wedding party strolled through Zaria's foyer. Her words were funny, but it didn't mean they lacked the ring of truth.

The collection of men sauntering past them were all large, very handsome men. The testosterone levels shot up astronomically when they crossed the threshold. Despite the visual buffet parading before her, Dominique's focus was completely consumed by Denzel. It had only been a matter of hours since they'd last seen each other, but she couldn't stop herself from devouring him with her gaze.

It was only after she couldn't see him anymore that she realized more than one pair of eyes was on her. Looking around, she stared back at the inquisitive faces regarding her.

"What?"

Dominique didn't see the big deal. She was aware of her actions, but she wasn't the only one ogling the big and tall male model revue.

"Is there something you wanna share with the class?" Her cousin Dierdre slid in next to her and bumped her hip.

Recalling Carmen's giggle-inducing statement, she nodded.

"Since you mention it, I do. It's okay to enjoy the view, but don't get any ideas about Denzel Reyes."

Dierdre's jaw dropped and her eyes rounded. "Oh. So it's like that, Cuz?"

Nodding in the affirmative, Dominique was unrepentant.

"Every day and twice on Sunday."

Carmen's laughter entered the conversation. Bumping Dominique's other hip, she slipped an arm around her waist.

"Come on back into the Bridal everything suite and talk to me. Reyes is fine and all, but he wasn't the only member of the too tall, too fine brigade."

At Carmen's remark, Ensley interjected. "Cowboy boots is mine." Holding up her left hand, she pointed to the massive jewel on her ring finger.

While she was sure Zaria had given their cousins the rundown on everyone in the wedding, Dominique couldn't be mad at Ensley for making it known. Hell, she'd just done the same thing. So she didn't consider it insecurity at all. It was making it plain for everyone involved.

Carmen didn't appear offended in the least. She actually lifted her hand to give Ensley a high five.

"Go head, girl!"

Blushing under the attention, Ensley slapped her palm against Carmen's before they all turned in the direction of the rooms they'd been in and out of for most of the morning. Dominique didn't even remember what drew them from the rooms in the first place until her full belly reminded her.

Chef and her father had sent food for them. They'd taken a little walk afterwards to ward off the *itis*, but she could still go for a quick nap.

Once they were back in the suite, they fell into talking and laughing again while they switched places, enjoying the services of the nail and spa technicians. They were done with their final fittings. So, the tailor and her assistant had left, taking the dresses with them.

The remainder of the day was uneventful. At least it was for Dominique—right up to the moment someone suggested they go downstairs to see what the guys were up to. The knot in her stomach, she thought she'd gotten rid of when she'd spoken to her mother, returned with a vengeance. She couldn't pick out who said it because she was too busy trying not to mentally spiral from the suggestion.

She'd seen her mother whispering to her father when he'd come up briefly while they were eating lunch. Although he hadn't said a word to her beyond his initial greeting, Dominique couldn't be certain if her mother had given him the quick version of what she'd said earlier.

Her parents didn't keep secrets from each other. So, telling one was akin to telling both. The source of her angst was in not knowing what he knew at the same time as realizing she couldn't be in the same room with Den without them gravitating toward one another. Even before they'd begun seeing each other, it seemed he was never too far away from her.

However, she couldn't come up with a plausible reason not to go down to where the men were gathered. More than a couple of hours had passed since their arrival. But they were still on the premises. That tidbit of information was courtesy of Carmen. How she knew was a mystery. As far as Dominique was aware, her cousin hadn't left the suite since they'd return from having lunch.

"Why are you looking like someone directed you to stand in front of a firing squad?"

Dominique shot her sister-cousin what she hoped was a confused expression. Zaria's smirk said she wasn't buying it. Instead, she looped her arm through Dominique's and tugged her toward the door where the rest of the ladies were filing out. While Dierdre, Carmen, Ensley and Autumn went left, Dominique, Alyssa, Zaria and their mother went right.

Dominique partially understood where they were going when they stopped in front of the elevator she'd never noticed. Looking toward the other ladies going down the winding staircase, she wondered why they weren't joining them in the elevator. It was spacious enough.

"Why aren't they coming this way?"

"They didn't want to crowd me and Lyssa. I told them there was plenty of room, but they were fine taking the long way." Zaria's response was accompanied by a shrug as she pressed the button to take them down to the lower level where Andrei's man cave was located.

Dominique heard the men before they reached the room. Various deep timbre voices, at different volumes, were talking excitedly before reaching a peak just as Zaria pushed the door open.

"Aw, man! You were so close." Cisco slapped Vitaly on the back. It was interesting to see how her brother had transitioned from being star struck to treating Vitaly like the older brother he'd never had.

The scene they walked in on was surprising—especially considering the normally stoic man her cousin was set to marry. On previous visits, Andrei had referred to his man cave as the media room. Since that time, someone had transformed it into a true man cave—similar to her father's, but with a few additions. One of which was the ping-pong table where Vitaly stood facing off with Andrei and had apparently just lost the matchup.

"I thought goalies were supposed to have quick hands." Denzel quipped, earning a glare from Vitaly.

Dominique recognized the exact moment Denzel realized she was in the room. He dismissed whatever Vitaly mumbled in reply to his jibe to cross the room.

"Ladies, to what do we owe the pleasure?" Stopping next to Dominique, he kissed her cheek before sliding an arm around her waist, tucking her into his side.

Instead of answering Denzel's question, Dominique's eyes immediately sought out her father. She quickly located him standing on the other side of the ping-pong table with a glass in one hand. The contents of the glass weren't her concern.

She was checking for his response to Denzel's familiar behavior. However, Neal Truman was revealing not one thing. As a matter of fact, he wasn't even looking in their direction.

"Una?"

Concern was evident in Denzel's tone when he used the pet name he'd given her. Up till now, he'd only called her Una when they were alone. His comfort level in showing that degree of affection in front of her family spoke volumes. It was far more intimate than the kiss he placed on her cheek. More than the arm he'd wrapped around her waist as he moved her farther into the space.

Tearing her gaze away from her father, Dominique looked up at

Denzel. She could only hope the expression she gave him appeared genuine and hid her anxiety.

"I'm fine. The ladies were wondering what you guys were up to. So, we decided to go on a little field trip."

As she mentioned their reason for being there, the rest of the ladies made an appearance in a flurry of giggles and activity. The laughter told Dominique one of her cousins likely made another colorful comment. If the Truman and Green women had a plethora of anything, it was sass and witty banter at the ready, inspiring giggles.

Apparently, Denzel wasn't completely sold by Dominique's response because his gaze remained trained on her face. Taking her hand in his, he led her to the door. He paused long enough to allow the other ladies to completely enter before he guided her into the hallway.

"Den, what are you doing? I said I'm fine."

"When did we start lying to each other?"

Denzel didn't stop walking until they were far enough away from the door to give a semblance of privacy. Dominique's stomach performed an uncomfortable flip from the intensity of his stare. He was right. She wasn't being truthful. She'd had pockets of normalcy all day, but the not knowing was getting to her.

"I'm sorry."

"Don't be sorry. Be honest. Tell me what's going on."

Dominique leaned into the comforting feeling inspired by the warmth from his hands rubbing her arms.

"I was just worried."

"About?"

"About what my daddy might have said to you, or vice versa."

The best description Dominique could come up with to describe Denzel's expression was indulgent. A rueful smile lifted one corner of his lips.

"Did you think your daddy was gonna take me out back and beat me with one of Andrei's hockey sticks or something?"

Rolling her eyes, Dominique's lips twisted. "Of course not. My daddy isn't a violent man. At least not normally. If he were to put hands on somebody, they earned it."

Crowding her against the wall, Denzel dropped his hands to her hips, giving her a squeeze.

"So you don't think he would feel some kind of way if he knew all the ways I have, and plan to continue, to defile his baby girl?"

"Den!"

Whipping her head in the direction of the door, Dominique checked to make certain they were still alone. Once she was positive the coast was clear, she looked back at the man smirking at her. The tap she delivered to his chest didn't hold any real venom, other than to display her annoyance at him being flip while she was on the verge of a freak out.

"What? It's a valid question."

Sucking her teeth, Dominique folded her arms across her middle, only to have Denzel tug them free before tangling his fingers with hers.

"Seriously, Una. What did you think would happen?"

"I wasn't sure. I saw Mama talking to him not long after I'd spoken to her about us, but he never said anything to me."

Dominique observed the shift in Denzel's expression and knew she'd jumped into the deep end without realizing it.

"Are you telling me your parents weren't aware until today that we're more than casual acquaintances?"

His voice was low. Steady. Too low. Too Steady. His neatly trimmed beard didn't hide the tick in his jaw from his clenched teeth. Dominique didn't want to argue. She wasn't a person who reveled in conflict. Which is why her stomach had alternately been in knots all day. However, she didn't allow her desire to keep the peace to lead her to sugarcoat her answer.

"No. They didn't. I wasn't ready to tell them yet."

"Why not?"

Denzel's short question was sharp. Biting.

"It's not unusual for me to not tell them about a relationship until it passes the three-month mark. At most, they might hear I went out on a date."

While her answer was truthful, she read his expression clearly. It hadn't simply been a surprise to him. It wasn't what he wanted to hear.

"So... What? You were waiting to see if we made it to your magical number of months before you said anything?" Denzel's dark eyes blazed. "We *live* together, Dominique. We sleep in the *same* bed nearly every night. And you thought it was a good idea for us to come into this weekend, surrounded by your family, without giving them even the slightest heads up?"

When he put it like that, Dominique felt like a complete ass. Even the part of her which wanted to turn the tables on him and ask if his parents knew about her was quieted. This wasn't a 'what about' contest. Finger pointing and blame had no place in the discussion.

Him calling her Dominique caused an unexpected ping to her heart. The only time he used her given name was when he introduced her to someone or was speaking to someone about her. Almost from the beginning, it was Una or some other sweet pet name. Never Dominique. That stung. More than a little.

Dominique guessed she'd earned it. Her omission was disrespectful to their relationship, as well as her cowering like a little girl. What he hadn't said hung between them. He didn't have to. Zaria had voiced it earlier. Her silence gave the impression she was ashamed of their relationship.

Turning her hands in his, Dominique squeezed Denzel's fingers. There was nothing she could do but fall on her sword. All the tension and anxiety she'd allowed to flourish could've easily been avoided if she hadn't been so determined to hide her head in the sand.

"I can't say what I was waiting on, because I really wasn't thinking the way I needed to be. I'm sorry if it put you in a bad spot with my father. The last thing I wanted was for anyone to be blindsided or there to be tension or animosity."

"Una..." Denzel released one of her hands to wrap his fingers around the back of her neck. Tilting her face upward with a thumb beneath her chin, he dropped his forehead to hers.

"It's a good thing for you that you're with a grown ass man. I know how to handle myself. And there's nothing your old man could've thrown at me to cause me to walk away from you. Not even a threat to bury me in the desert."

Gliding her fingertips along the buttons of his shirt, Dominique fell into his confident gaze. Her nod of understanding halted after the second dip. A frown drew her eyebrows together.

"Wait. Why did you mention the desert? That's oddly specific."

Chapter Twenty-Six

KEEPING PROMISES

Earlier

Either Carver had become even more perceptive than Denzel realized or he was clairvoyant. No more than five minutes passed before Neal Truman walked over to their table. As if they'd developed some sort of non-verbal shorthand, Andrei looked up at the older man, tapped Vitaly's arm, and gave him the barest of head tilts.

"Really? I wanna stay for this part." Vitaly groused, earning a glare from his brother.

"Brat..."

"Fine." Grabbing his plate and drink, Vitaly rose from the table to follow his brother.

Sitting in the seat Andrei vacated, Neal Truman looked at Denzel. Without turning his head, Denzel spoke to Carver.

"Hey, CJ. Can you give us a few minutes?"

Carver's response was to vacate his seat in a similar fashion to Andrei and Vitaly. Placing his napkin on the table, Denzel pushed his plate away, folding his hands atop the surface. Since Mr. Truman came to him, Denzel simply waited for the other man to speak.

"Reyes."

"Mr. Truman."

"What's this I hear about you shacking with my daughter?"

"Is that what she told you?"

If he hadn't been looking directly into Neal's eyes, Denzel would've missed the marginal widening of surprise at his quick return question. Respect for his elders had been drilled into Denzel's head from birth, but he was also taught to stand up for himself. It was extremely difficult for anyone to intimidate him.

While it might not have been Neal Truman's goal when he sat down, Denzel wanted to set the tone as far as what he was and wasn't willing to endure to get into the good graces of his woman's parents. He wouldn't instigate tension, but he wouldn't cower either.

"No. What she said was, you'd found her a place to stay. A place you were already living in. She also said you two started up a relationship not long afterwards. In my book, that's shacking."

Denzel knew the explanation he'd used with Dominique wouldn't hold up with her father. And kissing *him* into submission wasn't on the menu. So, regardless of if the other man thought he was full of shit with his answer, Denzel spilled his truth.

"I'm sure you view it that way because she's your daughter. So, I understand. To me, I'm living with the woman I want to share my life with. Providing for her using all the tools at my disposal. Protecting her to the best of my abilities and doing whatever's necessary to make her happy. If you call it shacking. Then, I *guess* that's what we're doing."

Neal Truman's expression remained hard and unreadable as he stared at Denzel.

"I should've known you'd have some slick response."

"No offense, sir. But what did you want me to say? That I'm playing with your daughter's emotions? That I'm using her while she's in the city because it's convenient? Or she's some notch on my bed post? None of those things are even close to the truth."

"I want you to be man enough to offer my daughter more than a new address and the chance to be your secret girlfriend. She deserves better than a man hiding his relationship with her. And if you can't give it to her, I'll tell you just like I'd tell any other—get the fuck away from her and stay away. If you can't leave on your own, there's plenty of empty desert between this place and the airport. They're always adding on, so construction equipment shouldn't be too hard to find."

In response to Dominique's father essentially threatening his life, Denzel simply stared at the man. For a solid ten seconds, he ingested Neal Truman's words, allowing them to roll around in his head. He couldn't be upset at Dominique's father loving her enough to care if she was being treated well by the man in her life.

He didn't fault the man at all for doing what he could to protect his little girl. The problem, as Denzel saw it, was that Dominique wasn't a little girl anymore. Her father was simply going to have to come to terms with the fact—sooner rather than later.

"Mr. Truman... Dominique is not, and never has been, my secret girlfriend. We're both private people. I don't have to parade her around in front of cameras for us to know what we have is real. Also, the only reason I haven't offered Dominique more than a *'new address'* is because she'd run. Immediately.

If she ran, I'd chase her. Because us not being together isn't something I can live with. Not after having her in my life the way I have for the past few months. So, our relationship might not be moving at the pace you want, or be as flashy as you think it should be. But, my goal is my Una's happiness. As far as I know, she's happy with the way things are between us."

"Your Una?"

"Yes. *My* Una."

After a beat, Mr. Truman gave the barest of nods, before he launched into his next question.

"Bee told me Dom has a personal security detail now. A whole team. Was that you?"

"Yes."

This time, his nod was more perceptible. "Good. She should've had one a long time ago. Pretty, single woman, living out there in L.A. alone. It didn't sit right with me for her to only use a service when she went to big events."

"Well, you don't have to worry about that now. Her team goes where she goes. They're highly trained. She'll always be protected."

Either Denzel had said the magic words, or Neal Truman had

reached the end of his interrogation. With another brief nod, he picked up his fork, stabbing the mountain of potato salad on his plate.

"Aren't you gonna eat? My wife made the potato salad, and I grilled the meat."

Knowing an olive branch when he saw one, Denzel pulled his plate closer and forked his own helping of potato salad, taking a bite. Closing his eyes as a taste of home danced on his tongue, Denzel attacked the rest of the food with gusto.

"Well, at least I know you won't starve my baby girl. Any man who enjoys good eats the way you do isn't the kind who expects a woman to only eat air sandwiches and salad."

Swallowing the remainder of his bite, Denzel shook his head. "Absolutely not. I have to remind her to eat. She gets busy and forgets sometimes. I keep telling her it's not good for her."

Moving to the pulled pork, Denzel had the sandwich halfway to his mouth when Mr. Truman slapped his shoulder.

"I might like you a little bit, after all." Adding a chuckle to his statement, he lifted a hand.

"Y'all can come back now. It's not like you weren't sitting over there ear hustling anyway."

Wagging his head, Denzel conceded the truth of the older man's statement. The conversation around the room had been essentially nonexistent while the two conversed. The second he gave them clearance, Carver, Andrei, and Vitaly returned to the table.

Now

"Wait. Why did you mention the desert? That's oddly specific."

Dominique's brow furrowed and her face scrunched in the cutest look of confusion Denzel had ever seen. Still, he had no intention of telling her the sweet, good-natured father she knew was dead ass serious. She didn't need to know her seemingly mild-mannered dad wouldn't hesitate to put anyone down if he saw them as a threat to his family.

She hadn't been in the room the night Andrei told them what happened when he flew off to Russia, chasing Vitaly on Christmas Eve. So, she didn't hear the steel in Neal Truman's voice when he extracted promises from the brothers regarding his expectations in the future. Dominique didn't know, and Denzel didn't plan to be the one to tell her.

Some things were better left unsaid. The details weren't important as long as the end result was their loved ones being safe and protected. So, instead of informing his Una about her father's undercover gangster behavior, Denzel smiled, tugging her closer into the cradle of his arms.

"It's not really that odd. It's Vegas. People joke about the things they can hide in the desert all the time."

Peering up at him with one eyebrow lifted, Dominique didn't seem to fully accept his answer.

"They say it because of the number of times people have gone missing and their bodies have been discovered years later—*in the desert.*"

"Baby, what did I tell you about watching those crime documentaries? They make you suspicious of everything and everybody."

Lightly sucking her teeth, Dominique smirked. "Some people and situations deserve my suspicion. It keeps me alive."

Their conversation was taking a turn Denzel didn't like. The mention of anything happening to her, whic was remotely close to the things in those shows, was enough to make him triple her security and not let her be anywhere that he wasn't—including their home. So, it was best to shift the discussion. Wrapping an arm around her shoulders, he steered her back toward the room with the rest of the party.

"You know what? Why don't we go back inside and see if Andrei's ping-pong winning streak will last?"

He was pleased when Dominique simply shrugged and allowed him to guide her. Her fingers tangled with his where they rested on her shoulder.

"You know, I'm not sure what I expected to find you guys doing when we came down, but it wasn't playing tabletop games."

"I know. This is by far the tamest bachelor party I've ever attended."

It took him all of zero point five seconds to realize what he'd said, so Denzel quickly filled in the next sentence before Dominique could latch onto it. Stopping, he stared into her face while trying to fix his gaff.

"Vitaly said he had to get creative because Andrei didn't want a traditional bachelor party. He told us he got the idea from something

Zaria did for Andrei at Christmas. You know the big guy didn't have much of a childhood. So, Vitaly figured, why stop at an adventure box?

I'll admit, his idea has merit. We're too old to be getting shitfaced drunk just for the fun of it. Besides, most of the guys I knew who got wasted right before their wedding did it because they didn't really want to get married. They just didn't want to lose their woman."

"That's messed up." Wearing a pitying expression, Dominique shook her head. "Not the part about the games. I think it's sweet. Vitaly looked for a different way to celebrate the event to be respectful of Andrei's wishes. I've heard a little about how differently they grew up. So, it was pretty cool of him."

"Yeah it was. Don't tell him I said that, though. His ego is big enough."

With laughter on his woman's lips, they returned to the rest of the group, where they proceeded to join in with the others. Denzel was surprised at the more straightlaced of guys being willing to participate, but it just went to show one could never be certain about another person by merely looking at them.

With food and drink flowing freely as they enjoyed the unpretentious simplicity of the activities, it was well past dark before people began to drift away. As far as the men went, their obligations for the next day would begin later, but Denzel wasn't sure about the women.

What he was certain about was his desire to be alone with Dominique. After his conversation with her father, he didn't anticipate any pushback from her regarding where she'd be sleeping the majority of their visit. He'd concede the bridesmaid sleepover. But it was the only night he was willing to allow them to be separated.

Neal Truman's joking statement about maybe liking Denzel a little didn't stop him from giving Denzel serious side eye when it became obvious Dominique wouldn't be staying over at the Antonov's. It wasn't until they were in the back seat of the vehicle, being driven to the penthouse, that Dominique said anything regarding her father's behavior.

"What did my daddy say to you earlier?"

Navigating the landmine of her question made him feel like he was back on the field using spin moves to dodge tackles.

"Earlier when?"

Leaning away, she met his gaze with raised brows and pursed lips.

"Don't play, Den. When the two of you talked, what did he say?"

Tugging her until she was once again tucked beneath his arm with her head on his chest, he shook his own.

"What me and your dad discussed is between us. All you need to know is we're good. How we got there isn't relevant."

"If you say so... I saw him staring a hole in the side of your head when you mentioned us leaving to go to your place."

Rubbing along her arm, Denzel released a little chuckle. "There's nothing for you to worry about. I don't blame him. You're his daughter. His *youngest* daughter at that. Knowing you're an adult and seeing you go off to do adult things with a man probably isn't high on his list of stuff he wanted to know first-hand."

Grabbing Dominique's fingers when she swatted his chest, Denzel brought them to his lips, kissing them before folding her hand in his.

"You're being mighty presumptuous. Just because I'm going to the penthouse with you, doesn't mean anything other than sleep will happen in your bed. Maybe I should've accepted Zaria's offer for us to stay over there."

"Aw hell naw." Every ounce of Texas twang coated each syllable of Denzel's response.

"What? It's not like they don't have the space."

Tipping her chin upward, until he was certain she could see his eyes, he shook his head.

"First of all, I'm not being presumptuous. We both know how you like to be put to sleep."

Running one hand down her side, he cupped her ass. Dipping closer, he ran the tip of his nose along the column of her neck, then placed a kiss on the underside of her jaw near her ear.

"And we also know how loud you get. Did you really want to risk your parents overhearing the nasty things you say right before you come?"

Pulling back, he stared into her face. When Dominique's expression took on a glazed over effect, Denzel knew the discussion was done.

Rational thought had flown completely out the window. Which was just the way he liked it.

Despite it being less than twenty-four hours since the last time they'd made love, he was anxious for them to get to the penthouse so he could get inside of her. The partition separating them from the others wasn't enough privacy for what Denzel had planned for Dominique. That was the only reason he didn't get things started right there.

Not being able to do everything he wanted didn't stop him from capturing her lips with drugging kisses and teasing the parts of her, which didn't require him to remove her clothes. It definitely wasn't his smartest move. It was absolute torture to hear her moans of encouragement and not be in a position to bring her to a climax. But, he also couldn't **not** kiss her and touch her—especially when he knew how much she wanted those things.

If Denzel did nothing else, he was serious about his mission to please his Una. So, heavy petting was all he allowed for the duration of the drive. When they arrived at the building, he wasted no time getting them from the car to the elevator, then into the penthouse.

Mumbling about giving her a tour later, he swept Dominique into his arms, striding directly into the bedroom. Knowing Juan would take care of the rest of the team, he didn't stop to give any instructions. The second he stepped over the threshold into the main suite, his lips were on hers again. This time, he could allow his hands to roam the way they weren't permitted earlier.

"Mmm... Den."

Dominique's moans of pleasure may as well have been her soft hand reaching into his pants and stroking his dick. They carried the same weight. His shaft hardened, straining against his zipper. Had his pants been any looser, there would've been a tent situation to contend with. However, since they were in the seclusion of their bedroom, he made quick work of ridding both of them of their clothing—removing the barriers separating them.

Once they were both naked, and Dominique was spread on the bed for him like a sumptuous buffet, Denzel crawled over her body, depositing kisses and touches, keeping her tethered to the moment. He bypassed Her Highness. *Her* deliciousness would have to wait for a moment.

Allowing Dominique to feel his weight pressing her into the mattress, he stared into her beautiful face. Her lashes partially hid her eyes from him. But, what he could see, was her desire for him in her every breath. Every movement. It turned him on even more. Gently biting her plump bottom lip, Denzel trailed kisses from her mouth to her ear.

"Hey, Baby. It's time for me to keep my promise." He nipped her earlobe after making his statement.

"Hm?" A sigh mingled with Dominique's semi-verbal response.

Having her so obviously caught up in the moment gave Denzel a jolt of pride, drawing a cocky smile. Continuing his nibbling kiss assault, he added nipple tweaking to his sensual arsenal. Dominique's hissing gasp went straight to his dick, taking it from merely hard to ramrod stiff.

"I'm positive I promised to defile you."

Kissing a trail down to the nipple between his thumb and forefinger, Denzel flicked it with his tongue.

"You know how I am about keeping promises."

Following his words by seizing the turgid peak between his teeth, he clamped them with more force than before. Not enough to truly hurt her, but enough to give her the sting he knew she liked.

"Ah shit! Den!"

Dominique's back arched, practically shoving her breast into his mouth. Her perfectly manicured fingernails bit into his shoulders before scraping across his scalp in an attempt to grab his hair. The scratching prompted Denzel to make some noises of his own. A growl rumbled from his throat. He loved the feeling of her nails on him, especially when she ran them across his scalp.

"Fuck, Una."

With parting kisses to her breasts, he gave himself permission to put his mouth where he'd wanted to be the second they were naked. Savoring her taste was an addiction he would never seek therapy to correct. Dipping between her folds, he hummed as her flavor coated his tongue.

His arms were wrapped around her thick thighs, holding them

open, but it didn't stop his Una from rocking her hips, tilting her pelvis to allow him better access.

"That's it. Feed my pussy to me just like that."

Even to his own ears, Denzel's voice was barely recognizable. It was so deep and gravel filled. This woman. She did things to him. Made him want things. His dick pulsed in anger at being denied his turn with Her Highness.

Her moaning sighs of appreciation and the increase in the flow of feminine juices made pulling away from her decadence nearly impossible. Yet, somehow, he managed. Dragging himself away, he kneeled on the bed. A tap to the outside of her thigh snapped Dominique's eyes open.

"Turn over. I want you on your knees."

Without an ounce of sass or pushback, she rolled over. Once she was on her knees, she rocked her hips back, snatching a groan from deep within Denzel's chest. She wasn't playing fair. Her ass was a thing of beauty, and she knew how much he liked touching and kissing it. Right below the generous globes was Her Highness. Glistening and earnestly vying for more of his attention.

Since he was a faithful attendant, he rubbed her ass while he dove face first back into her delectable pussy. Using the tip of his nose to massage the sensitive space between, he teased her star. He didn't stop until the ache of his own groin was unbearable.

The moment just happened to correspond to when Dominique's cries entered the higher end of her vocal range. The second he removed his mouth from her sweetness, her tune changed. Rubbing the cheeks of her ass before grasping her hips, he soothed her.

"Don't worry, Una. I've got you."

Following his assurances with a pelvic thrust, he buried his length in her heated core. The velvet walls hugged his shaft like she was custom made just for him. Dominique's keening wails ceased in a hitching gasp. Leaning over her back, Denzel kissed the spot below her ear.

"Breathe, Baby."

Apparently, his encouragement was what she needed to release the breath pent up in her lungs. Letting it go in a whoosh, she showed her thanks by rotating her hips in time with his thrusts. Her silky channel undulated along his length, nearly sucking the cum directly from his balls.

Gripping her hips, he halfheartedly attempted to prevent her from controlling the tempo, but his damn hands were as unruly as his dick and his own hips, which continued their quest to push his dick as far inside her honeyed walls as humanly possible.

However, at this point, he'd completely lost control. They were both too close to rein it in. Heavy breathing coalesced with their vocal appreciation. All the nasty things he'd teased Dominique of saying fell from both their lips as they encouraged each other.

When she commanded him to fuck her and paint her insides with his hot cum, it was all Denzel could take. With his hands at her hips, he tugged her into his firm strokes, burying his shaft inside her to the hilt. Her channel trembled around him, flooding him with her slick cream.

Wanting to hear the sound of her completion before he fell over into the abyss, Denzel reached around to stroke her clit. A pinch with the right amount of pressure catapulted her into her climax. A deep groan tore from his throat when he joined her. His essence shot into her depths, giving her exactly what she demanded. He painted her insides with his release.

Chapter Twenty-Seven
MY DATE WITH HER HIGHNESS

Dominique stood next to the gleaming white grand piano. Sweeping her gaze around the room, she stopped briefly when she reached Denzel. Standing in line with the other groomsmen, he was entirely too handsome. The suit was cut to perfection.

It was a testament to the tailor as well as to Denzel's gorgeous physique. Fine was an understatement, but it was the only word in Dominique's arsenal at the moment. Cisco's fingers tickled the piano keys with the opening strains of the Roberta Flack classic, prompting Dominique to tear her gaze away from Denzel to avoid missing her cue.

Instead, she focused on Zaria and Andrei as the words floated from her lips.

"The first time, ever I saw your face."

As she sang, she observed the love the two had for one another. It was a tangible thing hanging in the air. The lyrics fit them perfectly. Seemingly oblivious to everyone around them, they stared into one another's eyes. Andrei whispered words meant only for Zaria's ears before removing a handkerchief from his pocket and dabbing the wetness gliding down her cheeks.

It was a beautiful wedding. The grand ballroom of Anton's was decadent, without much need for extra fluff. However, the additional decorations were tastefully done, lending even more elegance to the affair.

The rest of the band came in, adding a fuller sound. Dominique couldn't stop her gaze from locating Denzel's striking form once again. Their eyes met, and only muscle memory allowed her to continue singing about the stars and the moon being a gift to the dark.

However, when she reached the lyric about laying together, her breath caught ever so slightly at the intensity of his stare. It made her feel as if they were the only two people in the room. Promises filled his dark gaze. Dominique wished she was able to tear her eyes away, because she felt infinitely exposed—even though there was nothing she needed to hide.

Finally, she had to close her eyelids, tip her head back, and allow the words of the song to flow through her. Once she released the last note, the music faded, and she lowered her head. When she lifted it and opened her eyes, Denzel's were there waiting for hers. The passionate heat of his expression rooted her feet to the floor until Cisco took her hand to escort her back to her position next to Alyssa.

The remainder of the wedding passed in a blur, with Dominique smiling while looking everywhere but at the man claiming her through his every glance. How was she supposed to remain poised when he reminded her of his promises with every glimpse?

Thankfully, neither Zaria nor Andrei wanted a long-drawn-out affair. So, soon after the officiant pronounced them husband and wife, the guests were ushered into the reception area. The bridal party took the remainder of the photos, which included the bride and groom, and Dominique was officially relieved of almost all of her Maid of Honor duties.

The second the camera flashed for the last photo, Denzel was at her side, wrapping an arm around her waist. Tugging her into his body, he nuzzled her neck while guiding her to a secluded area.

"You smell as delicious as you look, Una."

"So do you." Returning the compliment, Dominique concentrated on keeping her eyes open. They threatened to close from the feel of his short beard brushing against her skin.

"Mmm... I missed you last night."

Punctuating his statement with a kiss to her neck, he squeezed her a little tighter before he pulled back enough to look into her eyes. Instead of reminding him they'd been apart less than twenty-four hours, she rubbed his beard with her fingertips before trailing her hand down his neck to rest on his shoulder.

"I missed you too, Den."

Wrapping her in his arms completely, he turned her, placing the wall was to her back, blocking her view of anything else in the room. His intentions were clear in his expression, but his next words confirmed it.

"How long do we have to stay to still be considered supportive and polite? Please don't say until it's over."

With a wry grin, Dominique shook her head. "Den, you know I can't skip out on Zee any more than you can on Andrei. Besides, it's not that bad. I don't know how the Antonovs get down, but the Trumans know how to party."

"Oh yeah?"

If Dominique wasn't mistaken, Denzel's response held a hint of challenge.

"Absolutely." She had full confidence in her family's penchant for creating an atmosphere for people to have a good time.

"We'll see. But you should keep in mind, I got a double portion of festive party genes. Black and Mexican. Both families are large and love to throw parties for any reason under the sun. So, it's a high bar."

"It sounds like you're challenging us." Dominique quirked an eyebrow, tilting her head slightly as she stared up at him.

"Take it how you will. Just know that if this party isn't hitting on anything, you'll have to make up for it in other ways."

Dominique's jaw dropped when Denzel gave a slight hip thrust, pressing himself against her. Even flaccid, his dick was impressive. But, she couldn't let herself be distracted by potential orgasms—no matter how mind blowing.

"Denzel Reyes. You stop it. We have to get to the reception. Which I can guarantee will be fun. We can't—"

"We can't what, Una?"

Denzel cut her off, pressing his body closer to hers, then lowering his head until their lips were mere millimeters apart. His fingers flexed against her sides before slipping behind to her ass. The tips pressed into her flesh, allowing her to feel his hard body aligning with hers. *Why did it feel so good?* Knowing he could deliver on his silent promise made sticking to her guns even more difficult.

"Do you two plan to stay glued together in a corner all night, or are you coming to the reception?"

Vitaly's voice pierced their private bubble, drawing a grumble from Denzel. Delivering rubbing pats to Denzel's chest, Dominique leaned around him to see the smirking Vitaly standing a few feet away. Before she could say anything to him, Denzel answered.

"Why are you here, man? Isn't there some Best Man duty you're supposed to handle?"

Vitaly's smile widened. "That's exactly why I'm here. To perform my Best Man duties. Which is why I need the Maid of Honor."

Turning to the side, he offered Dominique his elbow. "Our public awaits, Starlet-mine."

"If you don't get the fuck on and quit calling my woman that. She's not your anything."

"Den!"

Dominique couldn't believe Denzel was letting Vitaly goad him. His only response to her admonishment was to look at her with a lifted eyebrow. He obviously had no intention of apologizing or backing down.

Vitaly didn't make things any better by smiling broadly while he smoothed a hand down the front of his suit. However, he finally, seriously, explained why he was there to find them.

"They're waiting to introduce the wedding party to officially start the reception. I was sent to find you two."

When he held out his elbow again, Denzel literally growled, prompting Dominique to slip her hand into his, instead of taking Vitaly's bait. Sending Vitaly a knowing expression along with a head tilt, she gestured for him to lead the way. Playing his annoying little brother role to the fullest, he held his cheeky grin, then spun on his heel.

The others were gathered outside the closed doors, waiting for the three of them to arrive. Ignoring her cousins' knowing glances,

Dominique turned her attention to the wedding planner, who was lining people up in the order they'd be introduced.

When the woman instructed Dominique to stand next to Vitaly, it took her a moment to separate herself from Denzel. He'd tightened his hold on her hand while staring daggers at Vitaly. Speaking softly, and for his ears only, Dominique attempted to smooth things over.

"Den, he's only acting that way because he knows it irritates you. He's not interested in me. Even if he was, I'm not interested in *him*."

That last part transformed Denzel's warning glare at Vitaly to a softer expression when he looked at her. She didn't begrudge him the cocky smile tilting his lips. The added height from her heels put her closer to his, but she still had to tug him down to plant a light kiss on his lips.

"It'll only be for a few minutes. Then, I'm all yours."

"You're all mine anyway. But, I'll let you walk next to him this time."

With a final peck, Denzel escorted her into position before taking his spot next to Autumn. Poking Vitaly in the side when he snickered, Dominique followed the wedding planner's instructions. Soon, they were being announced as they entered the ballroom to begin the reception.

As she'd promised Denzel, they were only separated for a few minutes. Someone had the presence of mind to rearrange the seating to put them beside one another, leaving Vitaly to sit next to Zaria's friend Autumn. It was enough to stop Denzel from glaring at anyone else—for the moment. Dominique didn't hold out hope Vitaly would be the only one to have the honor.

Once they were in the thick of the reception, Denzel didn't mention slipping away early again. With Dominique beside him, he mingled with the guests, discussing a variety of topics ranging from sports to business interests.

They were walking away from one such discussion when Cisco nearly tripped into Denzel trying to get to Dominique.

"Hey, Dom. Have you seen Mama and Pops?"

Looking around, Dominique frowned. She hadn't seen her parents in a while, but hadn't thought much of it.

"No. I haven't. What's up?" Immediately shifting into big sister mode, Dominique scanned Cisco's face.

"The agent. The one Zee and Dray said I should meet. She's here. I don't want to bother Zee, but they told me not to talk to anyone by myself."

Looking around, Dominique searched the small crowd again. Denzel's fingertips pressed into her lower back, getting her attention. But, when she looked up at him, his focus was on her brother.

"Which agent are you talking about?"

"Jamie Shannon."

Dominique watched as Denzel scanned the group gathered in the ballroom, nodding in understanding.

"Okay. I see her. Come on. I'll introduce you."

Not waiting for either of them to agree or disagree, Denzel applied pressure to Dominique's lower back, steering her to the opposite side of the room. By the time Dominique figured out where they were going, she'd noticed Vitaly standing near two women. One was about Dominique's height while the other was shorter—just below average height.

She also spotted the way Vitaly was looking at the shorter woman. The taller woman was speaking to him, but he was entirely engrossed in the other woman. His face wasn't set in his normal irreverent, on the verge of joking, fashion. He was focused. Similar to how he looked when he glided out onto the ice to take his position in front of the goal. He didn't look away until Dominique, Denzel, and Cisco were within speaking distance.

"Jamie, long time no see."

Denzel entered the conversation, stretching out a hand, offering to shake with the taller of the two women.

"Denzel Reyes, nice to see you again."

Jamie glanced at Dominique and Cisco, effectively prompting a formal introduction. Smiling, Dominique offered the other woman her hand. Jamie returned her smile, shooting one to Cisco as well.

"Nice to meet you, Francisco. I've heard good things." Turning to the woman on her right, Jamie introduced her. "This is my sister, Jacelyn."

Dominique got caught up in watching Denzel work, guiding the discussion after presenting Cisco to the agent. Although, she couldn't help but note the way Vitaly fell back during the conversation. Considering Jamie represented him, it would have been a good opportunity for him to set her and Cisco at ease. Instead, it was Denzel who asked Jamie questions, feeling her out as he coaxed Cisco into the exchange.

If she hadn't known he'd spent the start of his career as a professional football player, Dominique would've thought he'd spent it as a student of the game both Cisco and Vitaly loved. When Jamie began quizzing Cisco on where he saw his career going after college, Denzel tapered off his contributions, allowing the two of them to talk.

Seeing her man control the interaction without constantly inserting himself into it was sexy as hell. Dominique was so caught up she almost missed when Jacelyn slipped away and Vitaly quietly followed her.

Later, her parents joined them. Once they did, Denzel smoothly excused himself and Dominique from the group. She uttered not one word of protest because she was suddenly extremely horny and looking for opportunities for them to steal away unnoticed.

While in some ways, Andrei and Zaria held to tradition, they didn't perform every wedding custom. There were no speeches from the Best Man and Maid of Honor. However, when the two left the reception, the guests all gathered to send them off. As far as Dominique knew, they were heading to a mountain retreat within driving distance.

Andrei was serious about Zaria not getting on an airplane unless absolutely necessary. His protectiveness was one of the many reasons Dominique thought he was good for Zaria. Zee was always trying to protect someone else. Dominique was happy someone was protecting her for a change.

"They're gone. That means we can go too, right?"

Denzel's words glided across her eardrum on a path directly to her aching center. Goodness... The man's voice was lethal. He should come with a freaking warning label.

Looking up over her shoulder, Dominique nodded. He stood behind her with his arms wrapped around her. His large, warm hands rested on her belly. At her nod, his fingertips pressed against her lower abdomen before he released her, taking her hand in his.

"Don't look directly at anyone. They might try to stop us to talk. I can't promise I'll be polite if they hold me up from my date with Her Highness."

Dominique would've laughed, but the expression on his face said he was very serious. The power radiating from him sent an involuntary shiver down her spine. The ache in her center became more of a throb as she quickened her steps to keep up with his long strides. The area of the casino he guided her through wasn't familiar, but she didn't question him.

She didn't recognize anything until the elevator opened, and she saw the door leading to the private entrance/exit they'd used when they arrived at the building the night before for the rehearsal dinner. Once they were inside the vehicle, Dominique could barely sit still. Her skin felt like it was on fire. A single touch and she'd go up like kindling.

Apparently, Denzel didn't care if she was consumed by flames, because he fanned them. His fingers were as busy as his mouth. The kisses he rained on her shoulders and neck were accompanied by his digits sliding beneath the split in her dress. He didn't even slip them under the edge of her underwear. He simply rubbed on top of her panties with such precision Dominique nearly came.

Her cries were muffled against his shoulder. It was likely she would leave makeup stains on his shirt and suit, but she couldn't bring herself to care. For once, it didn't matter if the people on the other side of the partition knew what they were doing. Dominique's drive to connect with him was on overload.

Adding her own busy fingers into the mix, she trailed them down his body until she reached the bulge straining against his pants. His length pulsed under her touch, and her mind immediately went to how it felt when he drove into her. Unlike Denzel, she didn't restrain herself from touching him skin to skin.

The lowering of his zipper was quickly followed by her using the opening to bring his hardened shaft through the slit. Long and thick with a mushroom shaped tip, his dick begged for her touch. Considering the pleasure she received from it, Dominique couldn't deny the request.

Stroking him wasn't enough. When a pearlescent drop of pre-cum appeared at the tip, she leaned over to have a taste. If the sudden change of position surprised Denzel, he recovered quickly. Humming around the head, Dominique savored the tangy flavor of his essence. Widening her jaw, she swallowed more of him before drawing back and running her tongue along the underside.

"Fuck, Una."

Denzel's groan was strained, but his touch on her head was contrastingly gentle. Although, his fingers did tangle in her hair, giving it a tug. The pull was like a rip cord, causing the immediate descent of her juices. Her underwear was definitely ruined, but Dominique gave not one fuck.

All too soon, her prize was taken from her. Her pout was muted when she realized the SUV had come to a stop at their destination. Kissing her lips, Denzel promised a quick transition into the building, and he kept it.

The heat coursing through her didn't have a chance to cool. They were soon naked and tangled together atop the huge bed in the master bedroom. It was amazing they'd made it that far before Denzel was plunging his thickness into her blazing center.

"Ah, shit... Den."

Being stretched to the limit was an experience Dominique relished each and every time. How she had thought she could deny herself the feel of him at all was inconceivable. The years they'd danced around each other now seemed foolish and unnecessary.

With her face pressed into the mattress and two pillows wedged beneath her hips, Denzel blanketed her back as he plunged into her depths. Feeding her pussy every millimeter of his turgid length, his words were growled into her ear.

If quizzed, Dominique wouldn't be able to repeat not a single one of them. She was too enraptured. Too caught up in the things he made her feel. When she reached her climax, her scream into the soft sheets was accompanied by his shout of release as he joined her in nirvana.

Sleep sang a siren song Dominique wasn't able to resist, taking her under soon after. Their recent activities, along with the previous week, came down on her, making her descent to slumber swift.

Softness under her cheek, warmth at her back and a gentle rocking motion, were Dominique's introduction to the new day. Cracking open one eye, then the other, the startling brightness she expected didn't greet her. Instead, a muted glow welcomed her.

"Where the hell am I?" Her voice was a hoarse croak as she came to the realization the bed in which she'd awakened wasn't the one she'd fallen asleep in.

Chapter Twenty-Eight

BREATHE, BABY

Denzel realized he should've probably made sure Dominique was completely awake after he coaxed her into the leggings and loose-fitting top. It was hours after they'd initially fallen into bed following the wedding reception. In their time together, he'd learned her nightly routine. So, he removed her makeup while she remained sleeping, but the attire was for what he knew was coming. Their flight from Las Vegas to San Antonio.

It wasn't a long one, but he'd essentially transferred her from one bed to another. Deducing from her question, when she came awake, he realized she had no memory of even getting dressed—let alone him carrying her onto the plane. *This could go so many ways.*

"You're on my plane."

"Oh." Dominique's eyes drifted back closed, and she snuggled against him as if she was preparing to return to dreamland.

Rubbing her arm from shoulder to elbow, Denzel let her have a few moments. He'd received the message about them being less than an hour from landing. She would need time to get herself together before that happened.

Nudging her lower back, Denzel reluctantly interrupted her plans.

"We'll be landing soon. You might want to take a trip to the lavatory."

"Landing?" A line appeared between Dominique's eyebrows when she drew them together. "I slept through an almost four-hour flight? I must have been more tired than I thought."

Shifting in his embrace, she rubbed her eyes before covering her yawn with one hand.

"No. It's only been an hour and forty-five minutes."

Denzel loosened his hold to allow her to sit up. He watched the incremental changes in her demeanor as she seemed to fully process what he'd said.

"If it's only been an hour and forty-five minutes, how are we landing soon? Did your plane grow a faster engine, and you forgot to mention it?"

Sitting up next to her, Denzel took one of her hands in his. Rubbing his thumb along the silky smoothness of the back of it, he stared into her eyes.

"Because we aren't going home. At least not yet. We're making a pit stop."

Dominique's fingers tightened in his as confusion pinched her expression.

"A pit stop where?"

It felt like her dark gaze was stripping layers of his skin away until she could see everything which lay underneath. His idea had sounded great. In his head. Now. In practical application, he conceded he was quite likely dumber than a box of rocks.

"A pit stop to where, Den?"

"San Antonio. To visit my folks."

Dominique's eyelids slowly drifted closed. She pulled her hand from beneath his and her lips pinched together tightly. It felt like an eternity before she looked at him again.

"Denzel... When did we discuss visiting your folks? Are you getting back at me for not telling my parents about us?"

Taking her hand in his again, Denzel kept her from leaving the bed. Tilting his head to one side, he maintained eye contact.

"I'm not getting back at you for anything. There's nothing to get back at you for. I don't play those kinds of games. I know we haven't talked-talked about it, but I have mentioned us visiting.

You must not have thought I was serious. Since you have more time off before you get back to shooting, I shifted my schedule around to give us a few more days of vacation."

Dominique's bottom lip disappeared between her teeth before she released it. She shifted in the bed again as if she was preparing to stand, then looked at him through a narrowed gaze.

"You're calling this a vacation? For you maybe. Not for me. And you should've said something. I didn't pack enough to spend even two extra days away."

Denzel knew the rise and fall of Dominique's chest had nothing to do with arousal. She was building up to being big mad at him. Closing the distance she'd created between them, Denzel slid his arms around her.

"It *is* a vacation. Neither of us will be working. We'll just be hanging out together and occasionally with a few of my family members. And, you don't have to worry about not having enough clothes, or whatever. I've taken care of it."

Tilting her upper body away, she peered at him. "I'm sure you do see it as a vacation. You won't be under a microscope trying to make sure you don't say or do the wrong thing. I'm not even getting into how you've 'taken care' of my wardrobe concerns."

Pressing against his locked hands, she attempted to free herself. "Can you let me go, please? I need to use the bathroom and freshen up."

She didn't cuss him out, but Denzel almost wished she had. He had a feeling it would've been better than the disappointment and quiet resignation in her mannerisms. Instead of immediately releasing her, he tightened his embrace.

"Den..."

"I'm gonna let you up. But first, I need to talk to you for a minute—and know that you hear me."

Dominique looked everywhere but at him for a solid minute. Finally, her shoulders lowered, and she returned her gaze to his. A single eyebrow lifted as she stared at him.

"I'm listening."

"This is a vacation. Not a gig. No acting required. No one is expecting you to be anyone other than yourself."

Rubbing her back in slow gentle circles, he attempted to infuse in her a confidence he wasn't one hundred percent sure he felt himself. He was certain his family would fall head over heels for her. How long she'd be upset with him for springing it on her was up in the air.

"I promise; you'll have a good time. Everyone is going to love you, and my abuela will make you all the tamales you can eat. Then, she'll send a huge container home that's just for you."

"Tamales?"

Seeing an opening with her question, Denzel held her tighter, putting one hand on the back of her head to keep her face tilted upward toward his.

"Yeah, Baby. She's probably already sent my dad to get everything she needs to make them and has the first batch cooking."

Dominique's other brow joined the first in reaching toward her hair line.

"Oh. So, she got advanced warning I was coming, but I didn't get to know I was going?"

Shit. Denzel had made two strides forward, only to leap backwards.

"Not cool, Den. Not at all. Please let me go. I really do have to use the bathroom."

Feeling like he'd done enough damage and needed to regroup, Denzel released his hold. Silently, he watched as she located her cosmetic pouch and went into the lavatory. The covers lay in a jumbled heap when he left the bed as well. Unlike their normal routine, he didn't follow her into the bathroom.

Instead, he pulled a small roller bag from the luggage compartment located on the opposite side of the room. Unzipping it, he flipped it open on the bed. Inside were organization cubes containing a small selection of Dominique's clothing. Rather than ask Silvia to have someone handle it, he'd packed it himself.

Depending on how someone looked at it, what he'd done was either extremely sweet or extremely controlling. However, Denzel considered it a part of taking care of his woman and doing things to make her life easier. Usually, she appreciated it.

However, the way she'd stalked into the lavatory said this might not be one of those times. For him, it was no big deal. He was already packing for himself. After his years traveling so much playing football, then later with his business interests and sports analyst gigs, he'd developed an efficient system. Everything was visible and coordinated to make grabbing what was needed easy.

One of the many lessons he'd learned from his mother. She'd made it a point to teach him things to allow him to be truly self-sufficient. It still boggled his mind when he met a man who couldn't do something as simple as packing a bag for a weekend getaway. *How hard is it to pick out clothes and put them in a bag with toiletries?*

Granted, he'd done it for Dominique, but it wasn't because she didn't have a clue about how to do it for herself. He'd simply wanted to keep the surprise a surprise. The same surprise that might just bite him in the ass.

He was honest when he said he wasn't trying to get back at her. When he'd made the plans, he had no idea she hadn't told her folks about him. So, there was no retaliation involved. Besides, he'd never view introducing her to his family as a punishment. While some of them could be annoying as fuck, meeting them wasn't a form of torture.

The click of the door releasing drew Denzel's attention. Turning, he observed a more refreshed looking Dominique as she emerged. Her features were at a neutral setting. So, he had no idea what she was thinking. Stepping aside, he allowed her to see the open suitcase.

"You don't have to change, but if it will make you more comfortable..." He let the sentence trail off.

Watching her slowly approach the bed, he waited for her next move. When she just ran her fingers over the packing cubes without speaking, he stepped behind her and slipped his arms around her waist. Apparently, simply looking at her and remaining silent wasn't how he was built.

"This trip was supposed to be a good surprise, not a stressful situation. Yes, I told my parents and abuela in advance. It's close to the time of year when my abuela visits her sister in Mexico. I wanted to make sure she'd be there, because I really wanted her to meet you."

Dropping his chin to rest on her shoulder, he tilted his head until their faces were a hairsbreadth from being pressed together. She didn't push him away, but she didn't melt into his embrace like she normally did. That stung. When she finally spoke, she hit him right in the gut with her words.

"You didn't tell me. You didn't ask. Because you thought I'd say no. Didn't you?"

Dominique never turned her head to make eye contact with him, but it still felt like she was boring a hole into the side of his, even with her gaze focused on the open suitcase. Her question forced him to examine his reasoning, and he didn't want to think about it.

Also, he didn't want to admit, if he didn't take her to them, having them show up in Logan City was a distinct possibility—especially with his mother and Tia Isabel being in the know about their relationship. They weren't above hopping on a plane or using Raffi as their excuse for showing up unannounced.

As much as he didn't want to confirm her assertion, Denzel wouldn't lie to Dominique. Withhold things that might cause her distress? Maybe. But outright lie when she asked him a question? He couldn't and wouldn't do it.

"I thought there was a small chance you'd want to wait. Or you'd say it was too soon. After you told me why you hadn't spoken to your parents about us. I was certain I was right."

Her body stiffened, yet she remained tucked into his embrace. "It *is* too soon, Den. This whole thing between us is moving faster than a bullet train. I've never..."

When her sentence tapered off without an ending, he tightened, then relaxed his hold on her. Once he realized the action wasn't enough of a prompt, he turned her around to face him. Lifting her face with a finger beneath her chin, he searched her eyes.

"You've never what, Una?"

Silence. Then, the avoidance of eye contact were his answers. Denzel didn't like those responses. Shoving the suitcase out of the way, he sat on the bed and arranged Dominique on his lap.

"You've never what, Una? Never shared your life with someone the way we do? Never had a man put you first? Make you and your happiness his priority?"

Dominique's dark brown eyes peered into his, and her bottom lip disappeared between her teeth. As much as he wanted to press her further for answers, Denzel forced himself to wait. He remained focused and undistracted by the shiny wetness when she released her captive.

"I don't know how you manage to turn every conversation back around to a question I have to answer, or something I need to confront."

Clamping his mouth closed on his immediate inclination, Denzel delayed his response.

"I wanted to be mad at you. And I was. Right up until I looked at myself in the mirror. Then, I had to let it go. I also had to recognize my part in all this."

Her fingers tangled themselves into the loose material of his t-shirt right above his belly button. The material twisted under her manipulation, but didn't give.

"I've never gotten so deep, so fast. Not with anyone. Not to the point where we lived together and essentially blended our lives. We haven't even discussed our future after I'm done with the show—my whole reason for being in Atlanta—and we're meeting each other's parents. It's a lot, Den. And I can't even be mad at you because I keep folding like origami. Every. Single. Time."

"Una..."

Dominique's confession hit Denzel harder than he'd ever experienced. The emotional tug, seeing her processing her own angst, threw him into a different head space. *Was she saying what they had was a mistake? That she wished she didn't want to want him the way she did? More than those things, was she saying they were temporary?*

"Una, I need you to make plain what you're trying to say here."

Her eyes flashed to his. "I'm being as clear as I know how to be, Den. We've known *of* each other for years. But it's been a relatively short amount of time since we've really gotten to know one another. And it's been pedal to the metal from the first day."

Emotion filled her expression, causing him to tighten his hold on her. Logically, he knew she couldn't slip away. However, logic wasn't his strong suit when it came to Dominique. What he did know with certainty was he didn't like her beating herself up for giving their relationship a chance—in spite of the optics.

Gentling his hold, Denzel spread his fingers wide, cradling her back with his fingertips cresting the tops of her shoulders. Her bottom lip was being tortured by her teeth. With his thumb, he applied pressure to her chin, coaxing her to release her hostage.

"You're scared..." Spoken softly, just above a whisper, Denzel voiced what she'd admitted without using those exact words.

"I understand you being afraid. What scares you about us? How fast we made it to this point? That, like you said, you can't stay mad at me when you think you should? Or do you think you're in too deep and I'll hurt you? Make you look like a fool for trusting me?"

Dominique's gaze darted away from his face, but his hold on her chin kept her from turning her head. Her actions spoke volumes, but he still wanted the words. Stroking his fingertips along her jawline, Denzel hoped his touch conveyed the tenderness and support he wanted her to feel from him.

Tilting, he placed himself within her line of sight. "Hey, look at me. Is that it? Do you think something will happen and you'll look foolish?"

It was jerky. And, if he hadn't been studying her so intently, he would've missed it when she nodded. On one hand, he was relieved she trusted him enough to admit it. On the other, he was disheartened to know she was afraid she'd one day learn her trust in him was misplaced.

It hit him then...She didn't know. Dominique had no idea he was just as exposed and vulnerable as she was in their relationship. He didn't simply wear his feelings for her on his sleeve, they were tattooed across his forehead. They fell from his mouth with every word he uttered.

"Dominique."

Her eyes whipped to his when he spoke her given name instead of one of the many pet names he normally used. Her sharp inhale wasn't followed by an immediate release, which concerned him after a few seconds.

"Breathe, Baby."

Cradling her face with one hand, he rubbed between her shoulder blades with the other. When wetness began to form in her eyes, he rained kisses on her face in an attempt to reassure her.

"Una... I've been told most of my life not to make promises that I can't keep. It's a lesson I took to heart."

Peering into her misty eyes, Denzel stroked her cheek. "I could ask you not to worry about optics and what other people think, but I won't. I promise you. I will *never* do anything to make you look foolish. I won't betray your trust in me. I love you too much to risk losing you over dumb shit."

The wetness hovering in her eyes dripped off Dominique's lashes, followed by a new crop of wetness. Swiping at it, Denzel kissed her lips, cheeks and eyelids.

"Den..."

Tears clogged her speech. Denzel felt the tug of his shirt as her fingers fisted in the material as she clung to him. She stared at him, searching his face. He prayed she saw what was always there. His love for her.

She glanced away, but quickly brought her gaze back to his. Her hold on his shirt transferred to his chest, and she leaned in closer. Her expression still held a hint of uncertainty.

"You love me? How can you say that? It's too—"

"You don't get to put a time limit on my feelings, Una." Denzel's gritty rebuttal wasn't intentional, but he couldn't allow her to go another step down that road. "I'm a grown ass man, Una. I know the difference between love and infatuation. I love you. All of you. And you can be secure in that knowledge."

Denzel observed the play of emotions flitted across her face. Things she probably didn't realize she did when she was in deep thought. He tried not to dwell on the fact he'd declared his feelings, but she hadn't reciprocated. By her reaction, she hadn't considered this turn of events when she admitted her fears.

"Den... I..."

Kissing her when her sentence trailed off, Denzel tried to soothe them both.

"Don't feel like you have to say it back."

"But—"

"No, Una. I didn't tell you to apply pressure. I told you because you needed to know where I stand in this. I love you. We're together and I want the people who are important in my life to meet the woman I'm in love with. The rest, we can figure out."

Two soft fingers pinched his lips until his mouth was closed, stopping the flow of words. Holding them there, Dominique shifted until she was scant millimeters from his face.

"I love you, Denzel Alejandro Reyes." Her fingers kept him from immediately responding, which was good. Because it appeared his Una wasn't done.

"This is fast and scary as fuck, but I don't care. I love you."

With that, she replaced her fingers with her lips. She didn't have to probe him to open his mouth to invite her tongue inside. Denzel was already there. Crushing her to his chest, he poured every ounce of what he felt for her into the kiss.

A polite knock to the cabin door pulled them apart.

"Yes?" Denzel's voice conveyed his frustration with being interrupted.

"My apologies for disturbing you, sir. But the pilot asked me to inform you we'd be landing in twenty minutes."

"Thank you, Calvin. We'll be out shortly."

Pilfering one last kiss, Denzel tapped Dominique's thighs. "Come on, Una. You've got five minutes. I like to be strapped into a seat during take-off and landing."

When he lifted her from his lap, Dominique stood on sturdy legs. As she perused the clothing offering in the small suitcase, she shot him a glance.

"Fyi, you aren't off the hook for this stunt you pulled."

In spite of her attempt to look stern, Denzel smiled.

"I'm sure I can find some way to make it up to you."

"Hmph."

Grabbing two of the packing cubes, Dominique turned her back to him and strode into the lavatory. The sway of her hips belied her little show. However, if she was serious, Denzel would happily take his punishment—so long as it didn't include being away from her.

Chapter Twenty-Nine
SAY WHAT?

The meditation technique her acting coach taught her when she made her stage début didn't help Dominique as she sat in the back seat of yet another blacked out SUV. Watching the endless, lush green landscape passing by, she tried not to get worked up over the implications of Denzel taking her to meet his family. Especially after his declaration of love.

Syd was right. Dominique was delusional as hell. How had she not seen what was clearly in front of her? The answer to her internal question was a blaring neon sign she couldn't ignore. Even if she was too scared to acknowledge it. By admitting it was there, she'd also have to concede her feelings weren't simply intense lust.

She wouldn't be able to blame her behavior on being dickmatized. So, she'd acted like a puppy with a blanket thrown over its head, rendering it invisible. Only she wasn't a pup and no imaginary cloak could hide the truth she'd have to confront—sooner rather than later.

"We don't have to go directly to my parent's. We can stop at my place to drop off our things."

Denzel made the offer, with the unsaid portion hanging in the air between them. If she needed more time, he'd make an excuse to delay the meeting. *Fine time for him to give her options.* She kept her snarky remark to herself. Instead, she responded to his suggestion with a question.

"Are they expecting us?"

Texas was located in the southern part of the United States, but it wasn't The South as other southern states were called. It was Texas. A place unto itself. But some things still held true. Older people got up with the sun. And, when they knew company was coming, they prepared a meal.

In their case, it wasn't even nine a.m. So, said meal would be breakfast. Dominique wouldn't be the person who held up or skipped a gathering orchestrated specifically for her. Denzel's expression indicated what he was going to say before he said it.

"It doesn't matter. I can call and let them know we had to make a stop. It'll be fine."

With a firm shake, Dominique refused his offer. "No. I'm okay. We don't have to stop anywhere."

It was only after he nodded in response, squeezing her fingers clasped in his, that the second part of his sentence was translated by her brain.

"Did you say your place? As in, you have a house here too?"

"Yes. My place here was actually the first one I purchased. I leased while I was in San Diego. Even though I had a multi-year contract, there was no guarantee I'd make it home.

I knew, as long as my parents and abuela were here in Austin, this place would be home to me. So, I bought some acres not too far from them, and built a house."

Dominique stared at him for a beat. The man was full of surprises.

"Isn't it a little wasteful to have a home just sitting empty the majority of the time?"

"It would be if I didn't make it work when I'm not using it."

Turning to face him fully, Dominique asked her follow-up question with lifted eyebrows. After which, Denzel proceeded to tell her more about the property management portion of his business, which handled the exclusive events and celebrities he allowed to rent the home when he wasn't using it.

"You haven't considered doing something similar with your house in L.A.? You could generate passive income when you're on location for months at a time and it's simply sitting empty."

"I've thought of it in passing, but I usually get a house sitter. I've had a couple of gigs get cancelled midway through the contract period. If I'd rented my house, I would've had to find somewhere else to live until the end of the rental agreement."

Denzel's thumb stroked the back of her hand in the absent way he did when they rode together in any vehicle.

"I see your point, but I think it could be a viable option. It's all in the way the contracts are worded and how much they're willing to pay for the privilege. If it's turning enough profit, it could be worth the minor inconvenience of not being able to immediately return there once a project is over."

Dominique was perpetually in awe of the way Denzel was able to shift gears from a relaxed, personal state into business mode. It was impressive. And sexy as hell.

Murmuring a non-committal statement that she'd think about it, she returned to watching the gorgeous landscape. Soon after, dense foliage gave way to flat green fields and fences. They rounded a curve and a large estate came into view. If Dominique had to guess, it was almost as large as his home in Logan City, but it didn't appear to have more than two floors—unless there was a basement.

She didn't have to hear him tell her they'd reached their destination. The slowing of the SUV and the turn onto the long, paved road answered the unspoken question. The nervousness, which had subsided, came roaring back to life. Had Denzel not been holding her hand, she would've certainly had her fingers twisted together in her lap.

His reassuring squeeze to her digits offered a modicum of comfort. But even he wasn't able to alleviate the knot in her stomach. The scruff of his facial hair tickled the back of her hand when he brought it to his lips, placing kisses on it.

"Relax, Una. It'll be fine. My mama already has a girl crush on you. So, you have nothing to worry about."

"Is your mother the only person who'll be here?"

"Of course not. My dad should be home. And my abuela lives with them."

"So...your mother speaks for the three of them?"

Kissing her cheek, Denzel chuckled. "Don't be a smart ass. I'm just saying, having her in your corner makes the rest of them a piece of cake. Besides, you're not considering the most important thing."

"What's that?"

"I love you. So, what anyone else thinks doesn't really matter. Them liking you is simply a bonus."

Dominique stared at him, wishing what he said was how things really were. However, this was the real world. And in the real world, being disliked by your partner's family was a setup for a potentially miserable relationship or some awkward holidays.

Even having that thought ratcheted up her nerves. It implied they'd have a future together. Granted, they both admitted to wanting one. Desiring something and having it come to fruition were two different things.

It didn't help for her to see cars parked in the curved driveway. Attached to the house was a garage with what looked like two large doors. Quick math said it could hold at least four vehicles. So, who did the other three belong to? Turning an inquisitive stare to Denzel, Dominique pointed toward them.

"Is there something else you forgot to tell me?"

Cursing under his breath, Denzel shook his head.

"No. But, it looks like someone forgot to tell me something." His brows dropped lower over his eyes, giving him a fierce expression. "I have a good mind to turn this car around and take us home."

No sooner had the threat left his lips, than the front door swung open and a woman stepped out onto the wide porch. Walking to the top of the short flight of stairs, she waved vigorously. Even without being able to hear her, Dominique was certain of what she was saying.

She was announcing their arrival to God-knows-who inside the house. Her pretty face was stretched into a wide smile as she used her other hand to brush her long wavy hair out of her face. They weren't quite close enough to see her features clearly, but Dominique had a good idea who it was.

"It looks like it's too late." Dominique had become the comforter, patting Denzel's hand and squeezing his fingers as he'd done with hers moments before. "Let me guess. That's your Tia Isabel."

"Good guess."

"When you tell me things. I listen."

Dominique leaned into him, bumping his arm with her shoulder. Although, she was partially teasing, she knew he'd pick up on the inference in her statement as well. Proving that he had, Denzel shot her a rueful glance.

By the time the car rolled to a stop, there were three other people standing on the porch. Even if she hadn't seen pictures of them, she'd recognize the tall, fair complexion man with his arm around a shorter African American woman. She guessed the third person was one of the many cousins Denzel and Raffi spoke about.

Not waiting for their security, Denzel opened the rear passenger door and stepped out. Accepting the hand he extended to her, Dominique followed. His encouraging smile bolstered her courage. Just a little, but a little was more than nothing.

"I just knew tia was exaggerating..." The man Dominique didn't recognize was the first to speak.

Despite being almost covered in tattoos, and looking like the very definition of badass, he drew his arms close to his body and shrank away when his tia swatted at him. Rapid fire Spanish flew from her lips as she chastised him for calling her a liar.

"I didn't say you lied, Tia. I said exaggerate."

All Dominique had to do was close her eyes, and he'd turn into a little boy. This could be a scene out of her childhood with Auntie Em getting on to someone. She never actually spanked a soul, but she pretended to be tough. Dominique had the sneaking suspicion Tia Isabel was similar in that regard. Not a single swat she landed had any force behind it.

Chuckling, Denzel led Dominique to the stairs. Her fingers held his in a vice gripe. Despite the smiling faces of the people on the porch, she remained more than a little nervous. Of course, Den wasn't feeling the same trepidation as evidenced by his first remark after saying hello.

"Are we having a reunion no one told me about?"

"Don't be cute, Jandro." Having finished swatting at one nephew, Tia Isabel turned her sights to Denzel.

"It's impossible for me not to be cute, Tia Isabel."

"Ricky, get your son." With her bottom lip poked out, Denzel's aunt folded her arms across her middle, staring at her brother.

"Get him for what? It *is* impossible for him not to be cute. He takes after me."

Dodging a swat from his sister, Denzel's father stepped out of her reach, guiding his wife closer to the edge of the porch.

"Come on up here, hijo. You have that beautiful woman thinking we have no manners. Introduce us properly."

Contrary to his words, Dominique didn't think they lacked manners. Their antics actually had the effect of making her feel more at home than if they'd actually pulled her into a welcoming hug. Releasing her hand, Denzel applied pressure to her lower back, encouraging her to ascend the short flight of stairs.

"Everyone, this is Dominique Truman. Una, these are my parents, Diana and Ricardo Reyes." Raising his arm, he swept it around the porch to the others. "This is my tia Isabel and my cousin Pablo."

"Nice to meet you." Dominique's small wave and extended hand were swatted away before Denzel's mother swept her into a hug.

"We don't do handshakes around here. Not with family."

As comforting and familiar as the embrace felt, Dominique's heart rate kicked into high gear at Diana Reyes' statement. *Not with family? Say what?* She wasn't given time to fully process it before she was tugged into a similar embrace from Isabel, who promptly informed Dominique to call her Tia.

"Only if you feel comfortable. It's okay with me if you want to. But only if you feel comfortable."

Dominique's eyes searched for Denzel as she leaned over to accommodate the shorter Isabel in another hug before she was gently extricated by his father. While not as tight as the ones from Diana and Isabel, his father's hug was no less warm and welcoming.

"It is very nice to finally meet you, Reina."

Dominique's brow quirked, but she didn't correct the older man when he called her Queen. Some fans of the comic book character modeled after her tended to use the title when speaking to her. Unsure which context he meant it in, she let it slide.

"Pop, don't flirt with my woman in my face and in front of your wife."

Wrapping an arm around Dominique's waist, Denzel pulled her back to his front. The two had a silent conversation over Dominique's head, which lasted a few seconds before Pablo stepped forward with his arms out.

"Den!" Dominique's voice was no more than a squeak, when Denzel quickly swung her sideways, tucking her into his side, farthest from his cousin. Staring up at him in surprise, Dominique observed him staring at Pablo.

"Immediately no. Why do you have your arms out? A handshake. And not a long one."

"It's like that, primo?"

"I said what I said." Denzel's reply was met with snickers before Pablo lowered his arms and extended one hand toward Dominique.

"It is nice to meet you, *Miss* Truman."

Dominique accepted his handshake. Per Denzel's mandate, it was very brief. Without thinking, she rubbed the hand clamped around her waist. A small voice interrupted them.

"Abuela says to come inside now."

Everyone's gaze turned to the owner of the voice. A little girl with dark eyes and an abundance of even darker, curly hair piled atop of her head in a bouncy ponytail stood in the doorway. She was adorable, with her rounded cheeks and bright expression.

The second she saw Denzel, she appeared to forget about her assignment, racing forward to fling herself into his arms.

"Uncle Jandro!" Her already high-pitched voice entered the squeal level.

Obviously used to the treatment, he scooped her up into a hug. Dominique watched them with a soft smile. It was sweet and touching to see yet another side of Denzel. As did Raffi, she noticed many of his family members referred to him by a variation of his middle name. Including the little girl in his arms.

"How's my favorite niece?" Denzel held the child, who looked to be just out of toddler age. At his question, she burst into giggles.

"I'm your only niece, Uncle Jandro."

"That doesn't mean you can't be my favorite, Nanda."

Ever the charmer, Denzel shot his answer back before giving her another hug and setting her on her feet. She immediately latched onto his hand.

"If she's your favorite niece, then I guess you're the one who's gonna pay for the quinceanera she's planning." Pablo folded his arms across his chest. His lips quirked into a lopsided grin as he stared at Denzel.

"Quinceanera? She's five."

"Hasn't stopped her from picking out her dress and telling me who she wants to perform."

Dominique found the entire exchange fascinating. From his parents' and Tia's expression, they weren't surprised in the direction the conversation had taken.

When Nanda rattled off the name of a well-known pop artist, Dominique sincerely couldn't tell if Denzel was humoring the little princess when he told her he'd make it happen. A voice, muffled by the glass storm door, interrupted the rest of Nanda dutifully listing the other things she wanted for her milestone birthday party.

Although Dominique couldn't determine what was said, she was certain from everyone else's reaction, the voice belonged to Denzel's beloved abuela. His father immediately turned on his heels, opening the door and guiding Mrs. Reyes inside.

Lifting Nanda again with one arm, Denzel slipped the other around Dominique's back. As she yielded to the directional pressure of his arm, she didn't miss the curious stare from the little girl. Dominique simply smiled and continued into the house.

When they were on the porch, she could faintly smell the savory scents. However, when she crossed the threshold, the aroma hit her full force. The nervous knot in her stomach from earlier became a persistent gnaw of hunger in reaction to the smell.

Standing in the center of the corridor with arched ceilings, Denzel's abuela looked like she'd stepped right out of a painting. The vibrant multicolored floral apron she wore partially covered her ankle length bright pink dress. Only the streaks of gray hair fanning out from her temples into her otherwise dark hair gave a clue to her age.

Her face appeared to decline the aging process and sported very few lines. While her eyes were a soft brown, her expression hinted at her annoyance with being forced to come out of the kitchen. Dominique wondered if the long wooden spoon in her hand was used for the food she was preparing or served a similar purpose as when her Granny Truman pulled out a comparable one when she and Zaria were children.

Her question was answered after the older woman waved the spoon then pointed at a young man sitting on the sofa with his face glued to a cellphone screen.

"Tonio! What did I ask you to do?"

Dominique was barely able to keep up with the woman's rapid-fire Spanish, but the lanky teen seemed to catch every word. Dropping the phone on the sofa cushion, he shot to his feet. While he appeared to understand her clearly, his response was in English.

"I'm sorry, abuela. I'll do it right now."

He'd taken two steps before coming to an abrupt halt in front of Denzel's parents, at which point he turned back to his great-grandmother.

"They're inside already."

"No thanks to you."

Giving the spoon one more warning shake, she tucked into the pocket of her apron. The softness in her eyes transferred to the rest of her face when her gaze landed on them. Dominique hoped she was included in the warm smile spreading across the older woman's face.

"Nieto!"

Setting Nanda on her feet, Denzel strode toward his abuela, tugging Dominique with him. He only released her hand for a few seconds to accept a hug. Once his grandmother let him go, he recaptured Dominique's hand.

"Abuela, I'd like you to meet Dominique Truman. Una, meet my abuela, Rosa."

The nervous butterflies in Dominique's stomach calmed more when Rosa Reyes smiled at her. They completely disappeared when the other woman snatched her hand away from Denzel's, pulling

Dominique into a tight hug, then releasing her, still wearing a broad smile.

"Ella es mas hermosa en persona, nieto."

Although Denzel's abuela was looking at Dominique, her comment was directed toward Denzel. She wondered in what universe she was more beautiful in person than when she was glammed up in movies and in photos at industry events. However, she wouldn't argue the point. Evidently, Denzel wouldn't either.

"She is beautiful, isn't she?"

After years in an industry where her looks were often the topic of discussion, Dominique still blushed when given direct compliments. She had no idea what to do with herself after people gushed about her while she stood right in front of them. If it was on television or online, she could turn away or mute the sound. It wasn't an option for live, in person, situations.

Releasing Dominique, his abuela placed one hand on his low beard. Making a comment about him being just like his father, she dismissed him, giving Dominique her full attention.

Speaking in heavily accented English, she looped one arm through Dominique's as they walked farther down the hallway.

"So, my Diana and I watched you on the television. In the movie where you were a lawyer. You are magnificent. Mira, I do think you should have had the part they gave to the other woman. You acted circles around her. I do not know what those Hollywood people were thinking. How did they not see it? But what do I know? I'm just an abuela."

Not sure what to say in response, Dominique put together a sentence she prayed was diplomatic. She agreed with the older woman, but it wasn't something she could go around saying.

Dominique looked over her shoulder to see Denzel following closely behind them with a wide grin on his face. Blowing her a kiss, he winked at her. Smiling back at him, she returned her attention to his grandmother, who led her into the spacious kitchen overflowing with the tantalizing scent of a freshly cooked meal.

Chapter Thirty

IS HE TROUBLE?

Denzel watched the play of emotions flitted across Dominique's face. Anyone who hadn't studied her the way he had wouldn't have picked up on even half of them. When his abuela linked her and Dominique's arms, essentially hauling her in the direction of the kitchen, he gave her a smile and wink of assurance.

He'd never been worried his family wouldn't accept Dominique. His mother's reaction after learning of their relationship was enough of an indicator. Besides, he rarely brought women home to meet his family. Even when he'd dated Melody, she'd met his parents after they'd come into town for one of his football games. There was no special trip made to introduce them.

Even though his parents, especially his mother, didn't care much for Melody, they never let on to her. To this day, she probably thought they loved her. However, Denzel could tell the difference. Their reception of Dominique was genuine.

The only person likely not to receive her well was his abuela's mother. She wasn't likely to ever meet Dominique, anyway. He'd only seen her a handful of times in his life because his abuela had gone no contact with her before doing such was even a thing. It happened before he was even born, but his abuela made sure he understood why, when he was old enough to ask.

Many would say it's a blessing to still have a living great-grand, but after learning the reason why they no longer spoke to her, Denzel stopped asking about her. Guadalupe Perez had an issue with his mother. Not because Diana wasn't a great choice for her grandson to marry.

She was educated, hardworking, kind and beautiful. None of it mattered. Her skin was too dark. It wasn't her being African American. It was her being a dark-skinned African American who might give Ricardo even darker children. His abuela had been furious. She not only made sure his mother knew she didn't share her mother's concerns or beliefs, but she told her mother the same.

It caused a rift between them, but his abuela said she never looked back. A few of her siblings didn't agree with her harsh stance, so their contact was limited as well. She had her children and two of her siblings on her side. His abuela's mother was near the century mark now.

And, despite him being significantly lighter skinned and more Mexican presenting than Black, her stance remained the same. Thankfully, he had family on both sides who didn't allow colorism to dominate their life choices.

As he rounded the corner into the eat-in kitchen, he saw who the third vehicle in the driveway belonged to. His uncle Raymond, his mother's older brother, entered from the side door carrying a large aluminum pan. He placed it on the island where his wife, Penny, stood. Then, he turned toward their approaching group wearing a wide smile.

His gaze easily met Denzel's over the heads of Dominique and his abuela.

"Nephew! It's about time you got here. I thought we were gonna have to eat this fatty without you."

His uncle's bright smile reached his eyes as he transferred it to Dominique. Before he could start flirting, Denzel prepared to hop in to make the introductions. However, his abuela beat him too it.

"Raymond..." Rolling the R in his uncle's name; she shook her finger. "No one will eat before my nieto and his beautiful lady."

She hadn't switched back to speaking Spanish, even though his uncle was fluent. It was likely for Dominique's benefit. After their tamale date at El Rincon, Denzel began feeling out just how much of the language Dominique understood. While there were some regional things she didn't know, she was pretty fluent.

However, he didn't point it out to his abuela. He'd let his family find out the same way he did. He could've told them, but he was looking forward to their surprised expressions when they learned. Denzel smiled as his abuela began bossing his uncle around in the same manner she did with his father and her other children. The entire time, she kept Dominique close to her.

"If you're gonna fuss at me, do I at least get a formal introduction?"

Stopping in her tracks, his abuela shot his uncle an astonished glare.

"You do not recognize her? How is that possible? She is very famous, you know."

The pride in her voice would lead one to think Dominique was a blood offspring and not someone she'd met less than ten minutes prior.

"Of course I recognize her, Mamá Rosa, but she doesn't know me from a hole in the wall."

Denzel had a hard time containing his laughter as he observed his abuela cycle through her decisions. The woman behaved as if Dominique was there specifically for her. Finally, she turned, tugging her new best friend until they both faced the other occupants of the room.

"Everyone, this is Dominique."

In a sweeping arc, she waved her arm around the room, pointing to his uncle, aunt, and cousin, naming them. When she was done, Denzel's father stepped around him and attempted to extricate Dominique from his abuela. It wasn't a smart move, but Denzel nor his mother attempted to stop his dad.

"Mamá, don't be rude. Come with me, Reina. I'll introduce you."

The wooden spoon magically appeared, and Denzel's father hopped back with his hand cradled to his chest.

"Mamá! You hit me."

"Do not cry, hijo. I did not hurt you."

Denzel knew he wasn't being subtle when he clamped his hand over his mouth, hiding a smile and attempting to hold back laughter. The swat he received from his own mother was worth it when his father stared in disbelief. Tugging her husband out of the way, Denzel's mother shooed the people standing around the room.

Soon they were all behaving as if it were a normal Sunday morning. Denzel had his usual Nanda sized shadow, and he put her to work, helping him set the table as she continued her quinceanera planning list. Dominique fit right in with the rest of the family.

Once they were all seated around the large, oblong table and the food had been properly blessed, his abuela finally allowed someone else to talk to Dominique. Denzel thought maybe she'd realized how she was monopolizing his Una, but the idea was quickly squashed.

Having seated Dominique on her right, it was easy for her to lean over and speak to her. The hand she placed alongside her mouth did nothing to disguise what she said.

"Mira, sweetheart. I was watching the GMZ with my Diana. The blonde one said something about the man—the producer. She said he is on the show, the one where you are the star. They say he is trouble. Is he trouble, mija?"

Denzel was certain the hand his abuela used to shield her words had done nothing, because all other chatter at the table came to a halt. Every eye and ear were attuned to their little area. Dominique sat ramrod straight in her seat. Her fingers held her fork in a death grip, but she didn't lift the bite of the breakfast sausage to her lips. Instead, she stared at his abuela with wide eyes.

He was positive the question caught her off-guard. And while he was well versed in exactly which producer his abuela mentioned, he wouldn't dare fill in the blanks. Pablo caught his eye and lifted one eyebrow. Being as inconspicuous as he could manage, Denzel shook his head.

When he looked back at Dominique, she was staring at her plate. Placing a hand on her thigh, he gave it a gentle squeeze and a rub. It probably wasn't longer than a couple of seconds before she replied, but the air was so thick with anticipation, it felt like it was longer.

He would've attempted to rescue her, but his thoughts on Douglas Fowler would come flying out instead of the diplomatic answer Dominique gave.

"Well, ma'am. He's obviously done some things many of us weren't aware of. So, I can't say he isn't in trouble, but I can't say that he is either."

"No, mija. Not is he *in* trouble. Is *he* trouble? Is he a bad man like the blonde one on GMZ said? In the pictures, he looks like one of *those* men."

She lowered her voice when she said *those,* as if the designation alone should be enough. However, it was also the moment she realized their conversation wasn't private. Everyone, including the children, was attuned to the discussion. Tapping the back of Dominique's hand, she encouraged her to eat.

"We will talk about it later. Eat your breakfast before it is cold."

Denzel felt the tension drain from Dominique when she was granted the short reprieve. His abuela was relentless in her pursuit of information, and she was fiercely loyal. Everything about her acceptance of Dominique said she considered his Una part of the family—which meant she would be concerned about anyone in Dominique's sphere who might cause her harm.

Of course, Denzel knew part of her question stemmed from shear nosiness. But that wasn't the whole of it. With his abuela making it clear the discussion was over for the moment, the tinkling sounds of utensils hitting plates resumed. Soon, conversation started back up.

Dominique relaxed even further after she was asked more general, expected, questions about herself and how she liked being an actress. Although she was obviously more comfortable, Denzel kept one hand on her thigh throughout the meal. He didn't lie to himself that it was for her comfort and reassurance. He still couldn't seem to be next to her without touching her in some way.

Once the meal was done, the women dragged Dominique off while the men were assigned clean up duty. It took a promise to take her to Jumptastic, the trampoline play center, to get Nanda to leave and not remain glued to Denzel's side.

Saying the men were assigned to clean up duty was a relatively blanket statement. It was more like the youngest men were assigned clean-up. Denzel's father and uncle remained in their seats at the table, giving instructions.

His father's primary offer of help was to remind them of the potential wrath of abuela if they were to mistreat any of her precious cookware. Not really wanting to be on the receiving end of his abuela's wooden spoon, Denzel handled the cast iron.

The group effort cut the job time significantly. Not long after the women left them in the kitchen, the men were sitting outside in the shade of the patio. The water cascaded over the small, manmade waterfall at one end of the pool. Crashing against the smooth stones at the bottom, it flowed until it joined the rest of the crystal-clear water in the pool.

The area was designed for peace and relaxation. However, the low conversation of their group couldn't exactly be considered peaceful. They weren't loud. They couldn't be, considering where they were.

Having sent a grateful Tonio back into the house to connect with his electronic best friend, they spoke freely.

"So, what's up with the producer guy?"

Pablo's gaze was trained on one set of doors leading into the house as he asked his question. Not looking directly at his cousin, Denzel watched another set of doors, covering any potential avenues for someone to approach them.

"He's going down."

Denzel didn't feel an ounce of guilt for the ball he'd set in motion with Douglas Fowler. The guy was scum. It's possible he could've made it a while longer, but he fucked with Dominique, which earned him Denzel's attention.

"How much longer before he knows he's cooked?"

"Not much. I don't like my baby being stressed about someone else's fuck shit." As an afterthought, he glanced at his father and uncle. "Sorry, Pops. Unc."

Both men waved him off. Although they'd lifted the no-cursing edict decades ago, Denzel still tried to keep the harder words to a minimum around his elders.

"What about the other thing?" His uncle leaned forward, bracing his elbow on the arm of his chair.

"I wanted to talk to you about that. You're still in touch with Professor Jiles, right?"

"Yep. I just saw him at a symposium last month."

Denzel's Uncle Raymond had spent more than twenty years as a history professor. He was tenured now, but had spent some time at other universities before coming back to Texas. So, he had connections in the academic community.

Breaking from his door watching vigil, Denzel made eye contact with his uncle. "Do you think he'll give you his daughter's direct contact information?"

"Hijo?..." His father's warning tone had Denzel shaking his head.

"Come on, Pops."

He didn't have to finish the sentence. Besides his father knowing him better, Denzel made no secret of how he felt about Dominique. He wouldn't risk their relationship trying to hook up with another woman. His question had a completely different purpose.

"So, there is more to your plan?" Denzel's father read into what he hadn't said.

"There's always more, Pops. You and Mama taught me that."

Returning to his uncle, he posed his question again. Shrugging, his uncle pulled his cellphone from his pocket.

"Let's find out."

Once again placing his gaze on the set of doors behind Pablo, Denzel wore a slight smile as he listened to his uncle chat up a colleague. Even though he hadn't given out all the details, his uncle Raymond simply went with Denzel's request. It was one of the things he loved about his mother's sibling.

Family was everything. And, if you're in a position to help and it's requested, you help. Period. No one abused the relationship—well, almost no one. So, it worked. In less than ten minutes, his uncle had obtained a direct email address.

Sure, Denzel could've gotten an investigator to get the information, but he didn't want to make contact out of the blue. He actually already had something he could work with, but he wanted her to be aware and expect it. He also didn't want to come off as a creeper. So, this way was better.

Of course, his dad wasn't going to let him get away without giving up more details. Denzel relented, letting him in—a little. He pushed away his conscious, nudging him, pointing out the reasons he was with-holding information. He wasn't five. He didn't need his daddy's approval for everything he did.

As their group was breaking up, Denzel and Pablo walked shoulder to shoulder back toward the patio doors. Denzel shot his cousin a glance when Pablo performed a quick check over his shoulder.

"You know my offer is always open, right? I can arrange a cruise down the San Antonio River any time."

Denzel was sure his grin projected what he thought of the sugges-tion, but he shook his head to decline.

"Let's try my plan first. If we do it right, he'll take care of it himself, and save the world the trouble."

In no way was Denzel making light of suicide, but Douglas Fowler doing the deed was a likely outcome of him being exposed and facing real consequences for his actions. Many in his position chose that route because accepting responsibility wasn't something they ever considered.

"If you say so, Primo. You know where to find me."

With a fist bump, Pablo veered off once they entered the house. Calling out Nanda's name, he went in search of his daughter. It wasn't long after Pablo found her that the two located Denzel in the family room, so she could remind him of his promise to take her to Jumptastic.

Giving her his finger, he made the unbreakable pinky swear to take her and a few of the other cousins before he left town. Once they were gone, he sat with Tonio for a while, but the teen wasn't interested in anything not associated with the game he was playing on his phone.

Denzel finally gave up and went in search of his woman. He discov-ered her in his abuela's sitting room. In order to give his grandmother a sense of independence, she had her own suite of rooms, which was more of a small apartment. Situated in the rear of the house, it even had its own entrance and exit other than the one directly attached to the house.

Giggles were his first clue that he was in the right place. His uncle Raymond and aunt Penny were gone. So, it was just his abuela, mother, tia Isabel, and Dominique in the room. The four of them were lounging comfortably on the overstuffed sofa, chaise longue and chair with a coordinating ottoman. All they needed were muscle bound men fanning them with large feather fans on poles.

"Excuse me, ladies." Denzel was forced to speak when clearing his throat didn't get their attention.

"No."

His abuela's sharp response was immediate. And, just in case there was any confusion as to which unasked question she was answering, she clasped one of Dominique's hands in hers.

"Abuela..."

"I said no. You just got here, and you are already trying to take her away."

Slowly approaching, Denzel looked toward his mother for help and received nothing.

"Abuela, we've been here for hours. We're just going to get a little rest. We're not leaving town. We'll be here all week."

While Denzel was happy the women in his life had taken an immediate liking to Dominique, he wanted to laugh. The idea had occurred to him before, that his abuela was behaving as if Dominique was there specifically for her. Now, he was starting to believe he wasn't too far off the mark of what she actually thought.

They had a short stand off before she relented, tapping Dominique's hand.

"You go on. He always did have a problem with sharing. I don't know where he gets it from."

Suppressing the eye roll and look of astonishment, Denzel went around the room saying goodbye. Saving his abuela for last, he kissed her cheek and accepted the sharp pats she put on his.

"You aren't fooling me, nieto. I know you just want to be alone with her. But you go on. Be sure to come back for dinner."

With permission granted, Denzel didn't squander the opportunity to escape. The little woman was exactly right. Denzel had missed his alone time with Dominique. He hadn't intended for them to spend every waking moment with his family.

He'd made plans to show her around the city, since she'd never visited. The city had many hidden gems, and he was eager to introduce her to them. Taking her hand in his, they made their getaway while the getting was good.

He wasn't going to risk his abuela realizing they'd technically been there long enough for it to be lunch time. If she noticed, they'd have to stay to let her feed them again.

In the short drive to his place, he watched Dominique as she stared at the passing landscape. She appeared so content. Relaxed.

"Did you enjoy yourself this morning, Una?"

Chapter Thirty-One

I TRIED TO BE GOOD

Dominique looked around the dressing closet located right off the main ensuite in Denzel's Texas home. She'd only had so much packed for Vegas, and Denzel had taken it upon himself to supplement those selections with an additional suitcase he didn't tell her about until they were in the air.

On top of that, he'd managed to have some outfit options, including purses and shoes, available in the closet. The man was entirely too much and not in the least bit ashamed of himself. They'd been in Austin for a few days. While a great deal of time was spent with his family, he'd taken her to different places around the city.

Tonight, they were going to hear a live band. And thanks to his over planning (very heavy-handed) foresight, she had options on what to wear on their date. She was torn between a light sweater dress and a Maxi. It was warmer during the day, but she'd been informed the temperature could drop significantly at night.

Her decision was made when she considered the amount of moving around potential there was with the possibility of them not just listening to the music, but dancing as well. Besides, Denzel couldn't take his eyes off of her when she wore Maxi dresses. Dominique suppressed a shudder at the memory of what happened to one of her favorites the last time she put it on.

The poor thing became a casualty of his sensual onslaught. At the time, she'd been more focused on the amazing backshots he delivered and not the fistful of material in his hand as he jerked her backwards to meet his thrusts. Her dress was being ripped apart didn't compute until he fell over her back and his sweaty chest made contact with skin in a place which should've still been covered.

She'd really liked that dress. However, it was irreparably damaged. So, into the trash it went. The one in her hand wasn't identical. But it was made on a very similar style. The ombre effect created by the golden yellow graduating to flame red at the bottom brought out the different undertones in her dark skin.

Slipping it over her head, she selected the matching strappy sandals and two potentially coordinating shawls. Dominique was still standing in the closet trying to pick between the two wraps when Denzel strolled in.

"If you changed your mind about going out, you should've just said so, Baby."

Strong hands tugged her into Denzel's hard body, drawing a gasp from Dominique when she felt his hardening length against the rise of her ass. The gentle scrape of his facial hair against the bare skin of her shoulder sent a shiver skateboarding down her spine. The wraps dropped to the floor, forgotten as her fingers delved into his hair, with her fingernails lightly scratching his scalp before gripping the strands.

It was entirely too easy to get swept away in the sensual wave rocking against her whenever Denzel was nearby. But, Dominique managed to pull herself together—mostly.

"Den...I didn't change my mind about going out."

"Then why are you wearing this fuck-me dress?"

A giggle flew from her smiling lips. Releasing his hair, she tapped his hand at her waist.

"If I let you tell it, every dress I own is a fuck me dress."

Gripping his fingers, she tried to peel them away from her body and place a little distance between them.

"You shouldn't be so sexy, and we wouldn't have this problem."

Re-asserting his grip, he eliminated the space she tried to create. Once his fingers curled as if he were about to fist the material, Dominique grabbed his wrists.

"Den, no. Don't rip my dress. I really like this one."

"I do too." Trailing kisses up the side of her neck, his deep voice wasn't making it any easier for her to focus on their original goal.

"I think I'll like it even better when I use it to hold you in place while giving you exactly what you asked for when you put it on."

Her eyes fluttered closed for the briefest of moments before she stiffened her resolve. Staring at their reflection in the mirror. She ignored the beautiful contrast of their skin tones and the smolder in his gaze. Grasping at something, anything, to derail the fuck train pulling into the station, she met his gaze.

"Do I need to pull a Nanda on you?"

The little girl had video called Denzel early Monday morning to remind him of his promise to take her to Jumptastic. Before the call was over, she'd extracted a commitment from him to pick her up from school that day to fulfill it. Apparently, bringing up the little girl was enough to douse the flame attempting to blaze between them.

"Wow, Una... I think I might've let you hang around my family a little too much this week."

His grip loosened, but he didn't completely release her. Gifting him with a dimpled grin, Dominique blew a kiss at him in the mirror, rubbing salt in the wound.

"I had to do what I had to do. You promised me live music and dancing." Sweeping a hand from her head downward, she gave him a lifted eyebrow stare. "I didn't do all of this just to end up bent over in the closet."

Denzel tightened his hold, pulling her back flush to his front again. His voice in her ear was laced with grit.

"See... I was willing to let it go, but you had to keep talking. Watch yourself or you'll end up kissing the mirror, changing outfits, and redoing your hair."

Punctuating his threat with a hip tilt and a squeeze of her breast, his eyes promised an inferno guaranteed to consume her. While her mind was being logical and reminding her of their plans, her lady bits were perking up and preparing to surrender to every lusty vow he made.

"Umm..." Clearing her throat, Dominique tried again. "Compromise?"

Turning in his embrace, she lifted on her tip toes delivering a peck to his lips, then his chin as she lowered herself. By the time she was on her knees, she had his pants unzipped as his hardened length was in her hands. Licking the drop of pre-cum from the tip, she glanced up at him.

"I can take the edge off for you. Then, when we get back, you can do whatever you want to this pretty dress."

Not waiting for his agreement, she engulfed the head of his shaft. Humming around the thickness, Dominique glided her palm up and down the base to meet her descending lips. Denzel's guttural moans of appreciation sounded far away as she threw herself into the act of pleasing her man. The sexy sounds he emitted made her increase her efforts.

The moisture gathering in her core had nothing to do with the temperature outside. Giving him oral pleasure always stimulated her as well. Denzel's hands in her hair and his muttered curse were the only warnings she received before she was hauled up from the floor. Whipping her around to face the mirror, cool air hit her heated core at the same time a ripping noise reached her ears.

Dominique barely had time to process the position change before she was filled to the brim with Denzel's hardness.

"Ah! Shit! Den!" Her head rocked back, colliding with his hard chest.

Gripping her hair in one hand with the other fisting what was left of her beautiful dress, Denzel growled heated promises in her ear. Telling her how it was all her fault her pretty dress was ruined.

"I tried, Una. I tried to be good. But you had to go and put your beautiful mouth on me."

A swiveling thrust. "Then you had the nerve to look at me while you swallowed my dick. What did you expect me to do? Huh?"

It was a good thing Denzel didn't really want an answer, because Dominique couldn't form coherent words. All she could muster were mono-syllabic moans and gasps.

With the pace he set and the angle he held her body while shuttling his long girth into her channel, it didn't take long for her to slide over the edge into her release. Her entire body went rigid while her walls pulsed around his tunneling thickness.

"Fuck! That's it, Baby. Let Her Highness show me her gratitude. Drown my dick in her sticky goodness."

Adding action to his words, Denzel continued to glide inside her until he joined her, pumping his seed inside her. His arm was a steel bar around her, keeping her plastered to him.

It was just as well. Slumped against him, Dominique didn't have the strength to hold herself up. She offered no complaint when he sat on the built-in bench and arranged her on his lap. After a few moments of nothing but their synchronized breathing, he plucked at the tattered dress hanging off her body.

"I guess you're gonna need a new dress."

"I can't stand you."

"Sure, Baby. Whatever you say."

One hour, a shower and an outfit change later, Dominique sat beside Denzel in a private booth at the high-end bar, Crescendo, listening to a well-known band. He hadn't told her Tremor was the group they were coming to see. All he'd said was Austin had a great music scene. He'd hinted at famous artists doing impromptu performances at Crescendo, but wouldn't give anything away.

Despite his antics earlier, they'd only missed the opening act. Of course, he hadn't been worried because their table was reserved. Since this wasn't a regular concert, there wasn't a pit of screaming fans in front of the stage. Instead, some people were actually dancing, while others swayed in their seats.

The lead singer, Zane Rivers, had them eating out the palm of his hand. Having discarded his guitar, he held the microphone like a lover caressing the favorite part of their sweetheart's body. The man had a gift. Leaning into Denzel's side, Dominique impulsively reached up to kiss him on the cheek.

Serendipitously, he picked the same moment to rotate toward her and her lips landed on his. Going with it. She delivered a couple of lingering pecks before pulling back. One of Denzel's devastating smiles took over his face.

"I'm not complaining, but what was that for?"

Returning his grin, she swiped her finger across his lips, although very little of her lipstick had transferred to him.

"Thank you for this. I love Tremor. I haven't seen them perform live in years."

"You're welcome." After Denzel pilfered a more thorough kiss, they turned their attention back to the stage.

Zane was entering the last run of the upbeat tune, which was a mashup of rock and the soul music he'd grown up listening to. When he held the last note, the crowd went crazy clapping and stomping their feet in appreciation. The music stopped with his arm drop and the room exploded once again.

The spotlight, which had been on Zane during his solo, widened, showing the rest of the band more clearly. All wore smiles, basking in the audience's response. Once the applause started tapering off, Zane placed the mic on the stand, pulling it to the center of the stage. Pushing his long hair out of his face, he gripped the stand waving his arm in the universal signal for everyone to lower the volume.

"Thank you for the love, Austin. It's great to be here tonight. We don't do as many of these more intimate performances anymore, but we always have a great time at Crescendo."

Dominique's smile widened as she watched Zane in his element. They'd attended the same performing arts high school in Tennessee. He was a senior when she was a freshman. They'd hit it off when they were chosen for the starring roles in one of the big musicals during her first semester there.

Over the years, they'd worked together sporadically before Tremor took off and she landed her first big role on *She's It Girl.* She'd even done background vocals on a few of their tracks. Because of the agreement Zane had insisted on, she still received royalties for those songs. Although small, those checks helped to keep her fed during some lean times.

"Can we turn the lights up just a little? I want to get a look at this amazing crowd tonight."

Working the audience, Zane talked to people in a seemingly random selection process. People loved it when he interacted that way, and it served a dual purpose. It gave the band a chance to rest before continuing the set and it gave the fans the opportunity to talk one-on-one with him or one of the other guys.

Wait...What had he just said? Dominique's fear was realized when a bright light swung to the booth where she and Denzel sat.

"Dom! I thought my eyes were playing tricks on me, but it's really you. The fabulous Dominique Truman, everybody!"

Dominique fought against the urge to shake her head vigorously when Zane smiled widely at her. In lieu of giving in to her desire, she waved and returned his smile. When he grabbed the mic and hopped off the stage, she wondered if it would be too obvious if she crawled under a table.

She was a performer of stage and screen, but she still didn't like being put on the spot. The look on Zane's face projected his intentions, and there wasn't much she could do about what was coming towards her. As he strolled in her direction, he informed everyone of how they'd met in high school.

By the time he reached their table, he was lamenting about them never officially laying down the vocals for a yet to be recorded duet he'd written years ago. Zane was busy working the crowd. Everyone was hanging on his every word. Including Denzel.

However, from his posture, Dominique was certain her man was hearing something completely different from the rest of the audience. With her hand wrapped around his arm, she rubbed his bicep and leaned into him a little more. He wasn't insecure, but he didn't mind letting any man know she wasn't even remotely on the market.

"So, Miss Truman. How about it? Will you grace us with your beautiful voice?" Leaning one arm and a hip against the table, he looked between the two of them.

"Come on... Help me out, Reyes." Zane turned his full attention to Denzel, who simply shrugged.

"It's up to her."

"He said yes, Dom."

That absolutely was *not* what Denzel said, but it was apparently what Zane heard. Standing up straight, he held out his hand. Dominique wasn't crazy enough to actually take it. Instead, she nudged Denzel and whispered in his ear.

"This is your fault. So, you have to go up there with me."

Smirking, he stood from the booth before helping her out. Showing he was only concerned with the results, Zane's grin grew blindingly bright.

"Yeah!" With a fist pump, he bounded up the stairs, going straight to his band mates.

In less than five minutes, she was standing beside him in front of her own microphone. A table had miraculously become available for Denzel, who was seated close to the stage adjacent to the small dance floor.

Although the night took an unexpected turn, Dominique had a great time. It felt amazing to be on stage again, and it was fun singing with Zane. It was similar to old times—only she got to be out front with him instead of standing between the bass guitarist and the drummer with the other two backup singers.

They were near the end of their set when she joined them, so she stayed through the final few songs, finishing the night with the duet Zane mentioned earlier. When he escorted her back to Denzel, he brought up the idea of them recording together again.

"I'm serious, Dom. I'm going to have my agent reach out to yours. I know you're doing the acting thing primarily, but it's a shame to confine a voice like yours to limited performances."

Leaning into Denzel when he slipped his arm around her waist, Dominique smiled at Zane.

"You do understand the 'acting thing' is my career, right?"

"Your career is entertainment. Why not make use of all your gifts? I bet your fans would gobble up an EP if you put one out."

Holding his hand up when she shook her head again, Zane continued, "You don't have to decide anything tonight. I'm just saying. Think about it."

Looking at Denzel, he tilted his head toward Dominique. "Try to talk some sense into her, Reyes. You saw her up there."

Denzel didn't respond, he simply squeezed Dominique closer. When Zane said his final goodbyes and walked away, Denzel escorted her out to their waiting vehicle. When Haley appeared next to the door, Dominique was momentarily startled. She'd actually forgotten their security detail was even around. Denzel was right about GPS. They blended in so well, no one would realize they had bodyguards.

Later, despite their interlude in the closet, Denzel was insistent on her keeping the promise she'd made for him to do whatever he wanted to her pretty dress. It didn't matter that he'd already destroyed the dress in question. Besides, it wasn't as if Dominique wasn't enthusiastically in agreement with his proposal.

Sunlight tinted the backs of her eyelids red, causing Dominique to squint and roll away from the brightness. She rolled into a wall of man. Cracking one eye open slightly, she was met with the golden tan, lightly hairy chest belonging to her man. Tilting her head back, she met his gaze.

Lying on his side with his head propped on his fist, he gave her a lazy smile. Dominique's internal monologue dripped with saltiness. *It was entirely too early in the morning for him to be so damn sexy. Smiling at her and shit. Who wakes up looking that perfect?*

Closing her eyes again, she twisted her lips and grabbed the pillow, trying to bury her head beneath it. Her temporary protection was plucked from her fingers. She was unceremoniously hauled closer to Denzel's warm, hard body.

"What do you think you're doing, Una? Hiding from me?"

Since her pillow option was taken away, Dominique burrowed closer, pressing her face into his chest, beneath his chin.

"I'm hiding from the sun. Not you. But it is too early for you to be so cheerful."

"Baby, it's ten o'clock."

A frown marred Dominique's brow as she attempted to reconcile what she'd just heard with how tired she still felt. That couldn't be right.

"Ten o'clock? In the morning?"

Of course it was in the morning. Hadn't she just been trying to run from the sun? Denzel's sarcasm button must have been broken, because he didn't point out the obvious with his normal witty comeback. Instead, he rubbed her shoulders. Then she felt him press a kiss to the top of her satin bonnet.

"I let you sleep, since we were pretty... active last night. But, breakfast is ready when you are. Although, it's more like brunch now."

On cue, her stomach grumbled its objection at not being filled. Dominique didn't want to move. Being cuddled against Denzel felt too good.

"Come on, Baby. Shower or bath? Which one do you want?"

Dominique considered the bath, but when another protest issued from her belly, she opted for the shower. Denzel left her beneath the hot spray, since he'd been awake for hours. He'd worked out, showered and cooked breakfast for the two of them.

It was just as well. If he'd joined her, there wouldn't have been much cleaning involved—at least not at first. Once she was dressed in a comfortable lounging outfit, she walked into the bedroom to the sound of her cellphone vibrating against the nightstand. Lifting it, she checked the display before answering.

"Hey, Tammy. What's up? Did we have a meeting this morning?"

"Hey, Dom. No, we didn't have a meeting. I know you're taking a little time off, but I was wondering if there was something you wanted to tell me."

Dominique perched on the side of the bed. Grabbing the case for her earbuds, she pushed one into her right ear, switching the call to hands free.

"Something I want to tell you like what?" Dominique wracked her brain. It took her a minute, but she remembered what Zane said the previous night about having his agent reach out to hers.

"Is this about Zane Rivers? I thought he was just talking when he said he was going to have his agent reach out to you."

"No, this isn't about Zane. Although thanks for the heads up. I'll be on the lookout for correspondence from his people."

Dominique frowned. If it wasn't about Zane, what could it be? She hadn't discussed any career related items she'd not already mentioned to Tammy.

"If it's not about Zane, I don't know what you mean, Tammy. You know I don't like guessing games. So, give it to me straight. What's going on?"

"What's going on? You mean you don't know? Did you just wake up or something? Has your phone been dead?"

"Not dead, but it has been on vibrate. I haven't been awake for very long. Like you said, I'm on vacation. What do *you* mean? What is it I'm supposed to know?"

Chapter Thirty-Two
DENZEL MUTHAFUCKING REYES

"What is it I'm supposed to know?"

Denzel strolled into the bedroom to those words. Finding Dominique sitting on the side of the bed with her cellphone in her hand, he realized she wasn't speaking to him nor herself. She was quiet for a long period after her statement. Her brow creased. Then, her fingers were suddenly flying across the cellphone screen, swiping as if looking through multiple images.

"There's something else? Another link? Hold on a sec. I'm looking."

That sentence had him advancing farther into the room. He didn't stop until he was standing close enough to see what had put a frown on his Una's pretty face. Should he have respected her privacy and waited for her to show it to him? Possibly. Did he? No. No, he didn't. Denzel scanned the upside-down image displayed.

It was a video of them at the Crescendo the previous night. Their date was apparently captured and uploaded to the internet. He couldn't hear what was being said, but the inference was clear: people were speculating about them and their relationship. When their voyeur captured the moment when Dominique spontaneously kissed him, a woman's head popped onto the screen, temporarily obscuring the video.

Her hand was clamped over her mouth and her eyes were rounded, as if in excitement or shock. Since he had no audio, he couldn't be sure of which it was. However, seeing that there was a video made him consider why he hadn't received a call himself from his social media manager. Since he hadn't, it was likely Urena already had someone working on any negative spin coming from the internet gossips.

Finally, Dominique looked up at him. He couldn't entirely read her expression to know if their moment being captured bothered her. She looked caught off guard, but that was to be expected. At least in part. Being a celebrity, this wasn't the first and probably wouldn't be the last time someone recorded footage of her in public and posted it online. It was simply the first time for them together.

"Hey, Tammy. Let me call you back." Dominique shook her head in response to something her manager said. "No. I'm good. I'll touch base with you later."

Another nod, then she tapped the earbud in her ear. Removing it, she placed it into the case. Denzel took a seat next to her on the bed. He didn't have a long wait for Dominique to shift the phone. Swiping her finger down the screen, she disconnected the device from the earpiece, allowing him to hear the audio on the video she was watching.

It had rolled back to the beginning, and the excited voice of the woman who posted it came through the speakers.

"OMG! Y'all! It's true. I saw a post a few weeks ago about Denzel Reyes and Dominique Truman being seen together at a small hole in the wall restaurant in Atlanta, and I brushed it off. Because... Pics or it didn't happen and they didn't put up any pics.

Anyway, So what you're seeing here is from last night at this bar in Austin, Texas named Crescendo. The band Tremor was doing a surprise performance there. And who is that? Right there, hugged up in a booth smooching? Denzel Muthafucking Reyes and Dominique Muthafucking Truman."

Now Denzel had context for the woman's head popping onto the screen with her hand over her mouth. She disappeared again, and the video continued with her voice-over commentary.

"I know y'all are probably thinking, so what? Celebrities hook up all the time. What's the big deal?"

The video of the two of them paused, and the woman was fully in the frame again as she spoke.

*"The big deal is Dominique Truman is **never,** and I say again, **never** photographed with her love interests. We know she's dated. The only time we knew she was with anyone was after it was done. She keeps her shit on lock. And for her to be seen with not just any old body, but fine ass Denzel Reyes. The Denzel Reyes, who has been rumored to be **for the streets** for years now. But look at them y'all! Have you ever seen either of them look at another human like this? I think they're in love. For real, for real. But wait! There's more!"*

The woman continued to talk, and the video behind her started back up showing Zane coming off the stage, leaning over their table. It was sped up in places and spliced in others, but they did capture the moment when Dominique was singing while making eye contact with Denzel. The woman's reaction was the actual embodiment of the giggling and kicking their feet that Denzel had heard about.

While the video was a little invasive, he wasn't sure it was enough for the frown he'd seen creasing Dominique's brow. The woman did speculate about a potential love triangle or tension based on Zane's posture and positioning before and after Dominique performed. She made certain to point out how Zane never stood too close to Dominique and never actually touched her—even while escorting her to the table where Denzel was seated.

Once the video ended, Denzel searched Dominique's face. Her expression was still somewhat shuttered and unreadable. He didn't like it.

"Una, does this bother you? I'm sure my social media manager is working on it. Anything painting us in a negative light will get handled."

Finally, her gaze met his. He was able to release some of the tension he held in his shoulders when she shook her head.

"No. This video doesn't bother me. I didn't know people were paying such close attention to us last night. Usually at higher end places, the patrons aren't impressed by people like me. I might be Queen Neferata to the comic heads, but I'm not Queen Mother Angela or some other big name. So, I typically don't have to worry about stuff like this."

Denzel nodded, waited a beat, then rephrased his question. "So, does it bother you now, since it seems more people *are* paying attention to you like this? Is that why you were frowning when I first walked in?"

As he waited for her response, Denzel landed on why the thought of her being bothered about the video didn't sit right with him. It was their first public appearance in an unguarded environment. Most of their time together had been spent at his place, with them only venturing out once. The outing was during a really slow time of the day and not many people saw them.

Since Andrei and Zaria's wedding was held inside Anton's, none of the moments they shared there would've been documented. However, Crescendo was very public. And, they hadn't made any secret about being together. Did Dominique now have buyer's remorse?

"I wasn't frowning about the video." Dominique met his gaze with a steady stare. "She's really cute and seems genuinely happy for us—even if she did throw in some speculation about Zane. And while I didn't particularly care for her describing you as being for the streets, I don't sense any malice on her part. Gotta keep the views up."

There was very little space between them, but Denzel edged closer anyway. "So...if it wasn't the video, what was it?"

It was obvious Dominique was skirting around the point, and he wasn't about to have it. How could he fix something if he didn't know what it was?

"It was the stuff Tammy sent before the video."

When she went silent again after her statement, Denzel gave her a few seconds before prompting her again.

"Stuff like what?"

"Here. It's better just to show you."

Making a few swipes and taps on the cellphone screen, Dominique passed it to him. Accepting the device as if it was likely to spill or explode, Denzel pulled it closer to him. Almost identical frown lines appeared between his brows when he saw the Rumor Mill article on the screen. The heading for the gossip blog caught his eye immediately. *Denzel Reyes: Dipping into the movie business?*

Fuck. Since when did those assholes start printing the truth? They phrased it as speculation and unverified, but it appeared there was a leak in someone's camp. Since his people were trustworthy, he'd guess it was the studio. He scanned the article without reading every word, then swiped to the next image which turned out to be the rest of the same article, followed by some still images of him and Dominique together the previous night—arriving at Crescendo, inside and leaving.

This wasn't the same as the video loaded onto social media. It appeared someone was actively watching them. Making a mental note to speak with Nikki about it, he passed the phone back to Dominique, who mutely accepted it. Her hopeful expression was tinged with disappointment.

"Is it true? The Rumor Mill isn't big on being sued, so they try to keep their stories as close to the truth as they can get and still be salacious. But if you tell me it's not true, I'll believe you."

"Una..."

Denzel searched for the right words. He wouldn't lie, but he wasn't ready to tell it all. Things between them were going well. This week, visiting his family had been amazing. He didn't want anything to mar it.

"Just tell me, Den. Is it true? Have you been making backdoor deals to buy Radiant? Is this because of me? Or..."

Fire blazed to life inside Denzel and he was certain it was evident in the fierce look he gave her.

"Don't. Don't for a second think it." Skipping past her other questions, he jumped to the sentence she didn't finish. He wouldn't let the thought fester even for a second that he was using her to get the inside track on purchasing the studio.

Dominique shook her head. "What am I supposed to think, Denzel? That you just so happened to start looking at going into film production after I came to Atlanta?"

Her using his full name instead of the shortened version was jarring, but Denzel pushed past it.

"You're supposed to think you're worth far more than being used to close a deal. That I meant it when I said I love you. And I wouldn't do such a thing to the woman I love."

Dominique's lips twisted. The hurt he hadn't wanted to cause her was written clearly in her expression.

"So, you wouldn't use me. You'd just lie to me while you went behind my back."

"I didn't lie to you. I just hadn't told you yet. I was waiting until things were done. It was supposed to be a surprise."

"A surprise?" Dominique shook her head in obvious disbelief. "You don't surprise your significant other by letting them know they work for *you* now."

"That's how you see it?"

Denzel wasn't intentionally trying to turn this on her, but it felt like she was lobbing verbal bombs at him and they had timers set to explode at any moment.

"How else am I supposed to see it?" Dominique's chest rose and fell with her deep breathing, and Denzel knew he needed to de-escalate this situation—quickly. As much as he wanted to continue to hold things close to the vest, he couldn't do it.

"Baby, please stop to think. When have I ever surprised you with anything that wasn't a gift? For you."

After his question, Denzel waited, watching the play of emotions cross Dominique's face as she processed what he said. He didn't mark time, but he was certain the eternity it felt like was actually less than a full minute.

"What the hell? Denzel...Are you sitting in my face telling me you're buying a studio—a movie production company—for me? Are you out of your mind?"

"Yes, I am. And no, I'm not. It's a sound investment that will give you the creative freedom to move behind the camera the way you've been wanting. Put some of your own ideas out into the world. Support other women of color by giving them the chances they aren't getting."

Slowly, almost in micro-motions, her head began to shake back and forth. Denzel mirrored the action, while giving into the desire to pull her into his arms.

"No. No, Den. It's too much. You can't do this."

Tilting her chin until their gazes were locked on one another, Denzel gave her a resolute stare.

"I can and I am. There is no such thing as too much when it comes to you, Una. And like I said. It's a sound investment. You'll have majority control, and I'll be a silent partner."

Dominique's penetrating stare was so compelling, he'd swear she was reading everything written in his brain patterns.

"Can you *be* silent?" Dominique's quirked eyebrow seemed slightly whimsical, but the rest of her face was set to serious.

"Of course I can. Given the right motivation."

Feeling as if they may have turned the corner, the tension in Denzel's body faded. Kissing her forehead, then the tip of her nose before capturing her lips, he was buoyed by her acceptance of his affection. When the kiss ended, she pulled back far enough to make eye contact with him again.

"I don't know if I can accept your *gift*. But, I'll think about it."

"You'll do more than think about it, Una. You'll let me do this and take advantage of the opportunity to secure your future by seizing the reins."

Dominique's slow head shaking started again. Denzel once again mimicked the motion before capturing her face in both of his hands. His fingers extended into her hair, but he didn't wrap them around the strands.

"What else is there to say, Una? Why are you shaking your head?"

"Because, you buying the studio behind my back isn't all of it. I know it's a gossip blog, but they seem to have enough of the story right to make me wonder how close they came when they speculated on if Douglas Fowler's problems are linked to why you're looking into buying Radiant."

Dropping his hands from her face, he kept her loosely encircled in his arms. The tension in his body returned with a new friend. *Shit... Fucking nosey gossip reporters.* He'd hoped she wouldn't latch onto that piece of the article. After all, she hadn't looked at it for long enough to see everything. Denzel glazed over the fact he'd seen it when he'd essentially skimmed the article as well.

"I won't say the thought of you being forced to work with a potentially habitual predator sat right with me. He seemed to work almost exclusively with Radiant. So, I can't say he *wasn't* a factor. I don't like the idea of anyone playing in your face and fucking with you."

This was the perfect moment for Denzel to tell her everything, but they'd just crossed a pretty big hurdle. *How* Douglas Fowler's issues became public wasn't her question anyway. Her question was if it played a part. He stomped his foot on the part of himself which wanted to confess it all and ground it beneath his heel. If he played this right, she'd never have to know, and this discussion would never be had again.

"Den, this isn't elementary school. You can't beat up someone because they don't like me."

"I know it's not. And it isn't just that he doesn't like you. From my viewpoint, he seems to be actively trying to sabotage you. Nah... I can't have it."

"So, basically, you're buying a studio to give to me so I can fire Douglas? That's totally normal."

Squeezing her in his embrace, Denzel gave her a crooked grin. "Who told you I was normal, Baby? Who said either of us was? Because we aren't. We're all the extras, and it's perfectly fine."

"If you say so." This time, Dominique's head shake didn't come across as a denial or rejection. Denzel took it as a concession to his point.

"I do say so. Now, are we done with this? Can we go downstairs so I can feed my baby?"

"Excuse me? What baby?" Dominique's whole body went rigid against him.

"You, Una. You're my baby." Denzel watched the stiffness retreat before Dominique released the breath she held. "You are my baby, aren't you?"

Tapping her chin with her forefinger, Dominique pretended to consider his question. "I don't know..."

"What do you mean you don't know, woman? Do I need to show you again?"

His question prompted Dominique to attempt to wiggle out of his embrace. She dissolved into a fit of giggles when he resorted to tickling her sensitive ribcage. The entire time, he was peppering her with the question of who was his baby. When Dominique finally conceded with a screaming, *me,* he relented. Standing, he tugged her to her feet.

"Come on, let's get you fed."

This time, there wasn't any hesitation on her part. She allowed him to pull her to her feet and guide her to the kitchen, where he reheated their meal. As he went about the process, he allowed his mind to wander back to her response to his comment about feeding his baby.

The more he thought about it, the more his mind wouldn't let it go. Was she keeping her own secrets and thought he'd discovered them? They hadn't ever used protection. After a brief discussion early on, they'd decided they didn't want to use condoms.

As much as he enjoyed releasing inside her, he didn't do it every time. He did it a lot. But not every time. And, Dominique was on birth control. Denzel couldn't claim to be anywhere near an expert on female birth control, but he knew some things. The interaction made him wonder if his carelessness was more than the simple desire to be as close to her as possible. It wasn't like him to be so reckless.

Now that the thought was there, he couldn't let it go. He had to catch himself because he kept staring at her, imagining how she'd look growing round with his child in her belly. Once the thought took root, he was fixated. It made him more determined to carve out a future where she didn't have to worry about the impact on her career if she became a mother. She would be the true master of her fate and could make sure she still had opportunities to work on quality projects.

"Why are you staring at me like that?" Dominique's question yanked Denzel from his thoughts.

"Staring at you like what? You'll have to be more specific. I spend a lot of time looking at you, because I enjoy it."

"No... The expression on your face didn't look like enjoyment. I can't explain it. I just know it's not the normal way you look at me."

Stretching his lips into a wide smile, Denzel began the dance he was used to when he wanted to keep his thoughts to himself.

"If you can't describe it, how am I supposed to answer? I don't know what you saw when you were looking at me. I only know what I saw when I was looking at you."

Taking a bite of his frittata, he chewed the fluffy egg, cheese and meat mixture, savoring the flavors before swallowing.

"Now, I'm more than happy to tell you what I see in your beautiful face, but you're the shyest actress I've ever met. It still boggles my mind for a person who transforms themselves on stage and in front of the camera to be so averse to one-on-one compliments. How did that happen?"

Successfully putting Dominique on the ropes. Denzel kept the focus on her and didn't allow his mind to take him down baby road again during their meal. The rest of their day was booked. So, Dominique would need to the fuel to make it through.

Chapter Thirty-Three

KICK ROCKS

Being back at the studio after more than a week away was a slight system shock, but dealing with the curious stares and whispering was worse. It had only been a few days, but it was starting to be really annoying. Dominique had no proof the hushed conversations were about her, but the accompanying sideways glances were pretty solid indicators. She still couldn't believe Denzel was doing something so outrageous.

Who actually does things like this? She was around the rich and mega rich all the time. Not once had she heard anything of the sort. Well... except for when Andrei bought the building housing Zaria's law offices and gifted it to her for Christmas. With real estate prices in Vegas, it was no small gesture.

Dominique had also heard rumors that Carver bought the company Alyssa worked for and gave it to her as a wedding present. So, the men in Denzel's circle seemed to make this kind of stuff a habit. But still... A movie studio? Seriously?

"Hey, Dom. How's it going?"

Jerricka's normal cheerful greeting caught Dominique unawares. She was so wrapped up in her thoughts, she hadn't seen the woman approach as she and Haley walked toward her trailer.

"Hey, Jerricka. It's going okay. Just getting back into the swing of things."

Jerricka nodded. "Totally understand." Lowering her voice, Jerricka tilted her head. "Can we talk? In your trailer?"

"Sure. I was on my way there anyway."

When she returned, Dominique learned about additional scenes that were being added into a couple of the episodes. They weren't being given very long to learn their lines, and there was some choreography she'd have to learn for a fight scene. It meant an earlier start for at least a week to get familiar before they could begin shooting.

Douglas Fowler had been suspiciously absent from the set, and no one had mentioned his whereabouts. Dominique wanted to ask Adam about it, but she kept her mouth closed and focused on the work. One upside to Douglas's absence and potential legal issues was Bliss Meadows was blissfully silent. Her normally smug demeanor was markedly subdued. It was yet another thing Dominique decided not to dwell on.

Once she and Jerricka entered the trailer behind Haley, it wasn't long before Haley let Dominique know she'd be right outside. The sweeps she did were now so normal Dominique didn't blink at them. Offering Jerricka a seat on the sofa, Dominique sat on the other end.

"So, what's up?"

Dominique waited semi-patiently for a response. She had a decent idea of the potential subject, but she didn't jump to conclusions. It was probably a good thing she hadn't, because Jerricka said something she couldn't have predicted.

Placing her hands out with her palms facing Dominique, Jerricka spoke softly, as if they weren't in Dominique's trailer alone.

"I'm not going to ask about your business. You know I'm not like that. I don't go digging for things. Now, if people volunteer stuff... totally different topic of discussion."

Dominique nodded, waiting for Jerricka to either get to her question or ramble into whatever she wanted to tell her.

"I was discussing wardrobe with another costume designer and happened to overhear a conversation I'm sure neither of us was supposed to be privy to."

Clasping her hands together, Dominique fought against twirling her finger to encourage Jerricka to move a little more quickly with dispensing the information.

"Of course, since they were talking about The Clarke Files, I tuned in to what they were saying." Leaning closer to Dominique, she dropped her voice even more. "Did you know Leona Jiles didn't completely sell her rights when the studio optioned her book?"

Dominique shook her head. "No. I just figured it was the normal selling of rights." Matching Jerricka's posture, she couldn't seem to stop herself from lowering her volume as well. "What do you think it means? Why were they talking about it?"

Thoughts whirled in Dominique's mind about the potential implications. They'd filmed a little over half the episodes. With the exception of the added scenes, they had a maximum of three months of work ahead of them before everything went to post.

"I'm not exactly sure what it means, but the two people talking said she'd been in touch with the studio about being more hands on with the series. She's listed as an executive producer, but you and I both know not all executive producers are hands on. Sometimes, it's just a title without any real responsibilities to make sure they get a cut of the royalties."

At Dominique's nod, Jerricka continued, "Well, they were saying she wants to see scripts and footage. They're trying to hold her off, saying nothing has been edited beyond the pilot, but I don't think she's having it."

At this point, the tops of their heads were nearly pressed together. They'd scooted closer on the sofa. Unless there was a listening device in her trailer, there was zero chance of them being overheard, but that fact didn't seem to matter.

"They're worried she's going to pull her rights back and they'll have to eat the money they've already put into the show. I don't know who she knows or how she negotiated such a deal, but I need to be her friend. Because she has them shook. Shook!"

Dominique kept her breaths measured, but she was shaken as well. If what Jerricka overheard was true, what would it mean for her? The Clarke Files was supposed to be her breakout role. It was her first chance to prove she had the star power to lead a cast. What Jerricka had just told her put a potentially dark cloud over everything.

Before her thoughts could send her into a complete spiral, Dominique pondered what Denzel confirmed regarding purchasing Radiant Reels. What she'd considered outrageous was quickly becoming a career lifeline. If he really did buy the studio, maybe they could find a way to restore Leona's confidence in the production and keep her from pulling out.

"Wait, wait, wait." Dominique was talking as much to herself as she was to Jerricka. "Did they actually say she was going to pull out, or are they just speculating?"

"They don't know anything for certain. So, I guess it's speculation. But the way they were talking, it sounds like a viable option if she doesn't like what she sees with the script and in the episodes. They brought up Douglas and the changes he'd asked for trying to expand Bliss's role."

Dominique listened closely as Jerricka relayed the rest of what she'd overheard. Every word was catalogued for her to think about later when she was alone. Because, if Leona Jiles was as bent out of shape as *she* was about the direction Douglas seemed to be trying to take the series, things would get pretty ugly. What it would mean for her, Dominique couldn't be certain.

However, she wasn't simply concerned for herself. Other cast members had a stake in things as well. Not to mention the implications to the people hired to support the series from craft services to the production crew. Things could get really bad for a lot of people.

"I didn't want to upset you, Dom. But, I thought you should know —especially if no one from the studio has said anything about what's going on."

"Thank you. They probably won't say a word to me unless I push the issue." Dominique gently tapped Jerricka's knee. "I'm sure you saw the article in the Rumor Mill last week."

In the mark of a true friend, Jerricka waved her off. "Girl, nobody really believes the stuff they run on gossip blogs."

"Oh yeah? Tell that to the people who've been whispering behind their hands and staring at me all week."

Dominique hadn't mentioned any of it to Denzel. He'd kept up his normal routine of asking her about her day each evening over dinner, but she simply discussed the changes regarding the added scenes. When he asked directly about anyone mistreating her or making remarks, she could honestly tell him no. She really didn't feel it was necessary to give him a blow by blow of the awkwardness following the gossip piece.

"Well, until I see something from a legitimate news outlet or you tell me to my face, The Rumor Mill can kick rocks." Jerricka patted the back of Dominique's hand and bobbed her head in a nod, which sent her pretty braids swinging.

"Thanks. I appreciate the support."

"You're welcome..." Jerricka's sentence was complete, but the way her voice changed indicated there was something she hadn't said or asked.

Quirking an eyebrow, Dominique sat up straighter. "What? Is there something else?"

"Nope." Jerricka shook her head. "It's against my policy."

Smiling, Dominique decided to put her out of her misery. They weren't as close as Dominique and Sydney were, but she trusted Jerricka.

"Yes, Denzel Reyes and I *are* seeing each other. We have been for a while now."

Jerricka's face split into a wide smile. "That's great, Dom! I'm really happy for you. Denzel is a cool guy."

Dominique leaned away from Jerricka slightly. She wasn't aware the two were acquainted. It was curiosity, not jealousy, which made her ask, "You two have met?"

"You know I'm local, right? I live in Logan City too." Jerricka waved her hand. "Besides, I met Denzel years ago when he had a walk-on role for a series I worked on for a little while. He was still playing football then. He was super cool. Totally different from the way they talked about him in the media."

He was on maybe four episodes of the show. The whole time, he was friendly, but never said or did anything out of the way. It was messed up the way some paps, trying to get a payday, took pictures of him with one of the women from the show and tried to blow it up into something it wasn't."

Dominique remembered exactly what Jerricka was talking about. It wasn't long after that when he experienced a very public and ugly break up with the R&B singer, Melody. Dominique never truly bought into everything they said about him—especially the things Melody tried to insinuate about him being abusive. She'd only admit to herself, she'd been far too easily persuaded of his fuckboy ways by the images on social media.

Knowing him as she did now, she understood. He was a person who drew people to him. Men and women. It was his energy and personality. Some people read too much into any time he was within five feet of a pretty woman. She felt a twinge of guilt for giving him so much hell and dodging him for so long based on that perception. Well...The perception and the gut feeling she had about the potential for how emotionally attached she could be to him, if she gave him a chance to be more than a casual acquaintance.

Her hunch had been one thousand percent correct. She was so far gone with him, there was very little she could deny him. It was scary as hell if she thought about it for too long.

After talking with Jerricka for a little while longer, Dominique had a quick lunch and went about the rest of her day. She was looking forward to getting home, but not the empty house. Technically, the house wouldn't be empty. Raffi, along with a few staff, would still be there. But Denzel wouldn't. He had a business trip and wouldn't be back until late Friday night.

It was less than forty-eight hours, but to Dominique, it felt like forever. She'd well and truly become addicted to going to sleep next to Denzel's warm body. The body pillow he'd gotten for her to use when he wasn't there was simultaneously sweet and insulting. As comfortable as it was, it didn't compare to having him wrap his arm around her, pulling her close to him each night.

When Dominique walked into the front door and closed it behind her, she was deep in thought about how to manage her time for the rest of the evening. So, she didn't hear the footsteps until they were within a few feet of her.

Strong arms. The same strong arms she'd been thinking about on the drive home gathered her close to a warm hard body. *Denzel*. Melting into his embrace, Dominique tipped her head to one side to give him better access as he nuzzled her neck. His deep voice sent tingles down her spine.

"Mmmm... I missed you, Baby."

Turning, she rested her hands on his chest, peering into his eyes.

"I missed you too. I thought you wouldn't be home until tomorrow night."

They'd barely been separated for thirty-six hours, but it felt like longer. Dominique was happy he was back.

"I was able to get things wrapped up more quickly than I thought."

His big hands caressed her back, keeping her firmly tucked into his large frame. Beneath her fingers, his heartbeat was strong and steady. Going up on her tiptoes, she puckered her lips for the kiss she knew was coming.

Since Denzel did nothing half-assed, it wasn't a simple *hello* peck. No, he kissed her as if they'd been separated for years instead of hours. The hands on her back migrated to her ass, squeezing, then cradling as he lifted her off her feet. Being lifted as if she was tiny would never get old. Her legs automatically went around his waist and she gave no care as to where he was taking her when he started walking.

Loud throat clearing penetrated their fog and Denzel pulled away with a groan.

"Shit. I forgot."

"I can see you did."

That voice sounded familiar. Dominique frowned, then looked over Denzel's shoulder. Standing in the foyer was Cristiano Ortiz.

"Cris? What in the world?"

Her gaze pinged between the two men for a moment before she realized she was still being held in Denzel's arms, with her legs wrapped wantonly around his waist. Cristiano wore a knowing smile as he nodded in response to her confused query.

"Den, let me down, please."

With obvious reluctance, Denzel placed her on her feet, but he didn't completely let go. He kept an arm around her waist as he turned so they both faced their...guest? Dominique wasn't sure what to call him, since she had no idea why he was there, nor how long he'd be staying.

"Does someone want to tell me what's going on?" Dominique looked up at Denzel for answers despite asking the question generally.

Denzel's fingertips against her back applied pressure, guiding Dominique toward the front sitting room. Cristiano followed behind them silently. Him not immediately saying Cristiano was a guest who simply stopped by was a huge clue that she'd been on target with her suspicions about his presence. Once she was seated, she stared at them expectantly. Just when she was about to remind them of her question, Denzel spoke.

"You remember last week when we talked about Radiant?"

Dominique decided not to bring up the detail of them only talking about it because of the article. She was looking for answers, not another argument.

"Yes..."

Dominique dragged the word out as she attempted to connect the dots before Denzel filled in the blanks. What did their discussion about Radiant have to do with Cristiano? He was mainly a producer these days. His time being a gopher was long behind him. He didn't work as much in the United States since he started making films in South America, where he was originally from.

"This week, since you've been back, you said Fowler hasn't been there and they haven't said anything about it."

"True." Dominique didn't know what the deal was today with people hedging and not getting to the point, but it was about to make her scream.

"Well, I ran into Cristiano at the airstrip. It seems Radiant flew him in to try to woo him into taking over Fowler's place. Fowler doesn't have a stake in Radiant, but as Executive Producer, he has a financial stake in The Clarke Files."

Understanding dawned on Dominique. If Radiant was serious about replacing Douglas Fowler, they'd need someone to take up the financial slack. Of course, they may have to give up a larger percentage of the royalties to get it, but if Radiant operated like many production companies, they secured loans to fund their films and paid them back when they sold their distribution rights.

"So, what? Cris, are you seriously thinking of signing on to the show?"

Dominique didn't want to get her hopes up. Things sounded far too good to be true. Working with Cristiano would be miles better than dealing with Douglas. Cristiano could be a demanding taskmaster, but he didn't play favorites. It was about the work and putting out the best product possible.

"I'm considering it. Reyes and I were talking about what it would look like, especially when the deal is finalized and you become my boss."

Flames engulfed her face. Dominique felt like one of those cartoons where literal fire was surrounding the character's head. She couldn't categorize her emotion as embarrassment, but it was surreal listening to him discuss her becoming majority owner in a production studio. To have him mention it as if they were discussing what to have for dinner just intensified her feelings.

Denzel squeezing her thigh offered some comfort, but it also served as a reminder of how all of it would come to pass. Once reminded, her brain was bound to go down a path keeping her from being in the moment.

Dominique hadn't spoken to anyone about Denzel's plans. Of course, Zaria was still on her honeymoon. So, talking to her was out. Syd had messaged as soon as she saw the article, as did Dominique's mother. However, she hadn't spoken at length with either of them. They were both champing at the bit for details, but she was keeping things as much between her and Denzel as was possible. Considering the reporters and social media personalities latching onto the story, it was a battle she was certain she couldn't win. It didn't mean she wouldn't fight.

Chapter Thirty-Four

TEAM REYES

Denzel observed the play of emotions on Dominique's face. His Una was a phenomenal actress, but when she was with him, her expressions told all. She didn't have to tell him her mind was overflowing with scenarios and possibilities. He saw it in the set of her lips and the change in her breathing.

He'd managed to get his business taken care of much quicker, because the person he was meeting with was far more receptive than he'd imagined. He thought he might have to work harder to convince them. So, he was able to move to the next item on the list and get it done in time to make it home a day early.

Glazing over might be a kind description of what he'd told Dominique about the purpose of his trip. While she listened attentively when he spoke about his work, she didn't probe into specifics unless he'd displayed a desire to go deeper. She let him talk and occasionally interjected with clarifying questions. He had to admit his favorite part of those conversations was when she complimented his abilities as if it were a foregone conclusion he would succeed at any task he undertook.

"Y'all are talking about the studio sale as if it's a done deal." Dominique finally climbed out of her internal thoughts to speak. "I didn't think they were even looking to sell it. So, wouldn't something like that take a long time?"

Denzel didn't suppress the damn near cocky smile stretching his lips wide.

"You're right. They weren't looking to sell, but this stuff with Fowler has people nervous. They're being watched and reported on, and not in the best light. Also, we're not going for one hundred percent ownership right off—only controlling majority. We'll leave a little in the pool for other investors. But if anyone looks squirrelly, we'll scoop those shares up as well."

One of the things Denzel loved about Dominique was her intelligence. Unlike some beautiful people, she didn't rest on her attractiveness. She worked on not just her craft, but other aspects of life in the industry. So, when she nodded while he explained, he knew she wasn't simply doing it to show him she was listening.

But, he did wonder if she was picking up on his purposeful use of the word 'we'. Although she'd outright asked him if he was out of his mind, he was buying Radiant for her. However, he knew she hadn't been working toward business ownership outside of her personal branding. So, he would be there beside her to guide her through it. Like a team. Team Reyes. Once he took care of officially making her a part of the family.

"You're awfully confident, Mr. Reyes. What if someone else sees what you see? If the sharks are circling, Radiant might decide to grab onto a different lifebuoy."

Rubbing her leg, Denzel kept his smile. "I'm loving the nautical references, Baby. Remind me to take you sailing soon. But, to your point, no one else has positioned themselves to be able to act as quickly as we can."

"Who is this we?"

Dominique's gaze pinged to Cristiano, who was sitting back in a chair in a very relaxed posture. When he noticed her stare, he threw up his hands.

"Nope. I'm not the 'we' in this scenario. I'm not looking to own part of another studio at the moment. I'm just entertaining a new job.

That's it. I don't have another film on my schedule until the end of the year. So, I have the time."

Shrugging, he lowered his hands. Using his eyes instead of his finger, Cristiano pointed at the two of them. His gaze pinged between Denzel and Dominique. It was almost comical watching Dominique connect the dots, but Denzel wouldn't dare laugh. He didn't want her thinking he was poking fun at her.

Swiveling to face Denzel, she lifted an eyebrow. "You mean us? Now you want to include me in the process?"

"That was always the plan, Una. Paperwork will have to be signed. I can't just march into the headquarters with my arm around you and tell everyone you're their new boss. They won't simply take my word for it."

Dominique's demeanor had shifted from the happy greeting he'd received moments before. Now, scrutiny coated her expression.

"I still don't know about all this. I'm an actress. Maybe one day a screenwriter and a producer. I know nothing about running a studio. And if I accept, yeah, I'll be able to green light some movies, but when will I actually have time to be in one? I don't know about this."

Denzel flicked his gaze to Cristiano. "Can you give us a minute?"

With a nod, Cristiano left the room. The pointed look he gave Denzel on his way out was mentally brushed off. It was obvious what he was silently saying, but Denzel wasn't trying to hear it. Dominique just needed to see the whole picture, and she'd be on board one hundred percent.

Gathering Dominique's hands in his, Denzel stared into her eyes. "Talk to me. I thought we had this worked out. What changed?"

"Nothing has changed. I've just had some more time to really think about it and process what it could mean. It didn't help for me to hear about Leona Jiles possibly pulling out and revoking the rights to her books."

Denzel's brow dipped so low, his eyes almost closed. "What do you mean? Who told you Leona was pulling out?"

Dominique's shrug was likely intended to be nonchalant, but Denzel wasn't fooled. He stared at her until she gave a verbal answer.

"I heard it on set today. They didn't say it was a definite. They just said she was asking questions, and someone was trying to stall her. I've never even heard of an author having that kind of creative control after optioning their book."

Nodding, Denzel patted the backs of her hands before giving them a squeeze.

"I don't want you to worry about it. I'm positive it will work in our favor."

Her raised eyebrow sort of reminded him of the wrestler turned actor, but she was way cuter.

"And how are you positive it will work in our favor?"

"Because, Baby." Bringing the palm of her hand to his lips, he kissed it. "I talked to Leona less than an hour ago when I dropped her off at her hotel room at The Fountaine."

Dominique's eyes rounded and her mouth dropped open. As tempted as he was to use his own to close it, Denzel managed to maintain control. It only took her a few seconds to gather herself and be able to form words again.

"What do you mean you talked to Leona when you dropped her off at her hotel? She's here?" Denzel could practically see the light bulb going off in her mind. "She's the business you went to take care of."

"Partially. My trip to New York was primarily to get a meeting with her. But, I did meet with some people about other interests. You know I like to multi-task."

Denzel was becoming well versed in Dominique's silent conversational skills. Her slow head shake clearly projected her disbelief in his brazenness.

"How did you even manage to get her to see you? Let alone come down here? She's so private she makes Andrei look like Chatty Cathy in the media."

The reference to the talking doll elicited a chuckle. Her mention of Andrei was hilarious in its accuracy. But, she was far too young to have been exposed to the doll. Hell, the only reason he knew about it was because his Tia Isabel still had one. It was a collector's item she kept on a shelf high and away from little hands.

However, Dominique was spot on about Leona Jiles. When her first book hit the bestseller list nationally and her international sales went through the roof, she became a household name overnight. To do it as an Independent Author was an anomaly millions of others were probably trying to duplicate. She wisely shut down her social media and moved. Her relative isolation doesn't keep people from speculating, but no one really believes them when they do.

"I know people."

Denzel smiled in response to Dominique's pout when he answered her question. He could be confident about it now, but he got lucky when she actually replied to his email. Having an uncle in the academic community helped. Especially when that uncle was friendly with her father. Leona was a daddy's girl. So, dropping Professor Anderson Jiles' name didn't hurt.

"I know people too, but the most I got was to talk to her on the phone for a few minutes when I landed the role."

If Denzel didn't know any better, he'd swear Dominique was pouting because he'd gotten actual face time with Leona when she hadn't. She appeared to feel some type of way about it.

"What can I say? I guess I know better people."

"Den!" Dominique swatted at him, but there was no real heat behind her swing.

"Okay, okay. Uncle Raymond is cool with her dad. He got me her email address, and I contacted her."

Her serious face returned before she asked her next question. "So, how did an email end with her coming down here? And why *is* she down here?"

They were fair questions, and Denzel spent the next fifteen minutes giving Dominique the background on how he approached Leona Jiles, the way he'd learned she wasn't aware of Douglas Fowler's shenanigans when it came to story changes, and how she'd decided a trip to Radiant was in order after she did a little digging of her own.

"So, she's here to do what?" Dominique probed him with her steady gaze.

"She's here to give them a chance to make it right before she exercises the pull-out clause of her contract. Since Radiant was banking on this show more than they let on, it would be a huge blow to lose her."

Dominique nodded. "If they were smart, they already had plans to acquire the rights to her sci-fi series as well. It's a fantastic space opera."

"In order to do that, they'd have to make good on the loans they took out to keep this and their other projects going. There was a bidding war for The Clarke Files. They leveraged themselves pretty heavily."

Dominique's eyes widened again. "So...no pressure on me or the show to be successful."

Noting her sarcasm, Denzel stroked her hands. "Between the Dominique Truman fans and the fans of Leona's books, the show is bankable as a success. All Radiant had to do was not fuck it up."

Dominique turned her hands in his, tangling their fingers together. She added her opinion in an even tone.

"I want to say they shouldn't have hired Douglas Fowler. But, he's had *some* hits in the past. It's probably why they let him get away with the bullshit he's been accused of. However, he has also fumbled. Now that I think of it, his fumbles happened when he worked with women led casts. Why would they pick a showrunner with a history of not doing well with female actresses in the leading role?"

"Maybe they felt like it was a sure thing, and he was fresh off a win on the last movie they produced."

With a pensive expression, Dominique dropped into silence. Their voices no longer filled the space, so it was easy to hear the grumble coming from her stomach. His chuckle mingled with her giggles at the rumbling intrusion.

Flipping his wrist over, Denzel looked at the display screen on his watch.

"Your stomach is right on schedule, Una. Let's go see what Chef Bo has for dinner."

While he was gone, the only way Denzel could be certain Dominique was eating on a regular schedule was to arrange for meals at designated times of the day. Silvia was more than happy to help him with it, since he didn't want to ask Dominique's security to do anything beyond seeing to her safety. If they were running food errands, they weren't watching her back. And that's where he wanted them.

Draping an arm across her shoulders, he tucked her into his side as they left the sitting room.

"Hey, Baby. Quick question."

"Shoot." Dominique's expression was far too serious when she glanced up at him.

"How do you know anything about Chatty Cathy? They had to be out of production more than twenty years before you were born."

"Do you understand that means you shouldn't know either? You're two years older than me. Not twenty."

Tipping his head toward her, he smiled. "Touché, my sweet. But I thought a lady was never supposed to tell her age."

"That's for people who are aging like spoiled milk. I have good genes."

Dominique's quip was so matter-of-fact Denzel almost choked on his own spit laughing. He was still chuckling when they rounded the corner into the kitchen. The aroma of perfectly seasoned meat and veggies was thick as they entered the space. Chef Bo was standing in front of the stove with a large wok in one hand and a long wooden spatula in the other.

He flicked his wrist and the contents of the wok were tossed into the air before landing back inside with a sizzle. Cristiano and Silvia were seated at the island watching. They appeared to be in the midst of an animated chat as well.

As he grew closer, Denzel caught a snatch of their conversation. Silvia was expressing her discontent with one of the current storylines in her favorite Telenovela. It was one produced under the umbrella of Cristiano's South American studio. Denzel was still curious about how the acquisition came to pass.

"To have Marisol pursuing her madre's school crush..." Silvia made a clicking sound with her teeth. "It is too far. Her mother is still in love with him. It will devastate her."

If Denzel didn't already know the people Silvia spoke of weren't real, he would've immediately gone to her side to comfort her. That's how distraught she looked while speaking to Cristiano. To his credit, Cristiano nodded and gave her a similarly pained expression.

"I understand, senõra. But what can I do? The writers come up with these things."

"Don't you own the place? Tell them to do better."

Denzel was certain Dominique was suppressing giggles when she covered her mouth. Taking pity on Cristiano, Denzel jumped into the conversation when Silvia paused to take a breath.

"Ortiz, I see you've gotten re-acquainted with my house manager."

This wasn't Cristiano's first visit to Denzel's Logan City home. He'd been there previously when Denzel threw a party not long after he bought the place. Several people from the film industry were invited, as well as those he associated with in the sports world. Cristiano had been one of the few who'd stayed over rather than leave after the party ended.

"Yes. I was just chatting with Miss Silvia while Chef Bo worked his magic over there."

Gesturing to the sushi platter in front of him, his grin broadened. Denzel flicked his gaze toward the chef, who was astutely ignoring them while engrossed in his task. The saiku-maki resembled a floral arrangement on the platter.

"I see someone was in the mood to show off tonight."

Denzel hadn't alerted Silvia that he'd be home a day earlier than planned. So, who was Chef Bo planning to feed with such a spread? There were more sushi rolls than Dominique would ever attempt alone. Although, if Raffi stopped in, he'd devour the majority by himself.

Looking over his shoulder, the chef grinned at Denzel. "You don't pay me to be ordinary."

Since Denzel couldn't fault his logic, he guided Dominique to the in island sink for them to wash their hands before helping her into a chair. Soon, they both had small plates containing their selected sushi, with a dab of wasabi and a small ramakin of soy sauce to dip. When Dominique moaned around her first bite, Denzel shoved a piece in his mouth and kept his gaze trained on his plate.

He had to. If he'd looked in her general direction, he would very likely drag her from the kitchen and not give a fuck what anyone had to say. He was trying to decide how he should feel about another man being able to elicit that response from her when his phone rang. Checking the display, he excused himself from the group.

"Yeah, Tiff. What's up?"

His assistant rarely called him outside of regular business hours, So Denzel was on alert when he answered the phone.

"Sorry to bother you, but something just hit my inbox, and I thought you'd want to know sooner rather than later."

Striding down the hall to his office, Denzel entered, closing the door firmly behind him. With a tap to the cellphone screen, he placed the call on speaker and moved the mouse to wake up his computer.

"Hit me with it."

"It's about CleanSun. I set up a few alerts on the stocks and some other things like I normally do with new acquisitions, and I'm noticing a trend. I just placed a document on the shared drive."

Going to the secure folder, Denzel immediately noticed the new file. Opening it, he listened to Tiffany as he perused the spreadsheet and accompanying report. Someone using multiple shell companies was buying up available shares. The move was similar to what he'd done, but with a difference.

Since Denzel was holding onto his shares, no matter what whoever was behind the curtain did, they wouldn't get the majority. However, they could acquire enough to be a nuisance.

"Any thoughts on who it is?" Denzel knew Tiffany wouldn't call him without having options and solutions in mind. She wasn't the run-of-the-mill assistant.

"I know exactly who it is. Hiriam Baxter and Marjorie Tenor. Under the umbrella of a newly formed LLC. If I had to guess, I'd say Marjorie put up most of the capital to get them started. Baxter doesn't have pockets deep enough to make such large purchases—not at the current price per share. But, if the market value takes a hit..."

Denzel immediately saw where Tiffany was going. In the short time after his takeover of CleanSun, the solar energy company had experienced a resurgence. However, the charts in the report from Tiffany displayed a decline in market value.

The stock market ebbed and flowed, but the graphics showed a definite trend. Denzel wondered if their leadership issues were the source. They still hadn't selected a CEO to replace Hiriam Baxter. Not having a designated person at the helm could create market uncertainty.

"Get with the guys and get them to dig around. Let's make sure we don't have someone poisoning the water trying to help Baxter get back in the door."

Denzel issued his directive as he went through the motions of locking his computer once more.

"Sure thing. I'll let you know when I have something."

Chapter Thirty-Five

DOES IT TASTE GOOD?

Dominique leaned against the buttery soft leather in the back seat of the SUV transporting her to the studio. Beside her, Denzel's gaze was trained on the electronic device in one hand. The other was on her thigh. He flexed his fingers, giving her leg a reassuring squeeze. It was as if he knew, without her voicing it, how nervous she was about the pending activities of the day.

After dinner the previous night, she and Denzel had left Cristiano to get settled in one of the guest suites. Silvia retired to her little cottage on the property, and Chef had long since gone home. While she was eager to be alone with him, she had things on her mind. Denzel had given her a lot to process. It would take more than his confident smile to reassure her.

Although him being along for her ride to the studio wasn't their norm, she was happy he was there. His comforting touch helped ease her anxiety somewhat. Her electronic tablet lay in her lap untouched, not quite mocking her, but reminding her she hadn't given the latest script updates her full attention. She wasn't worried about it though. The lines were so close to the books she'd devoured, Dominique was sure she wouldn't have a problem keeping up.

Thinking of the changes took her mind to Leona Jiles and what

Denzel told her about the author being in town and potentially making an appearance at the studio. While Dominique was somewhat bolstered by Denzel's confidence there would be no pulling the plug, she remained cautiously optimistic. There were no true guarantees in this business.

Wherever Douglas Fowler was, she was certain he was having a conniption fit. The other executive producers had the writers adding scenes he'd removed—scenes which didn't include his little playmate. Bliss shouldn't even need to be on set for at least a week—which suited Dominique just fine. The less she had to put up with her pouting and posturing, the better.

Dominique had dealt with difficult personalities over the years. For the most part, she remained unbothered. In some ways, she even felt sorry for Bliss. The young actress didn't seem to have a clue who she was as a person and who she wanted to be. It was actually rather sad.

"You okay over there?" Denzel's question pulled Dominique from her thoughts.

"I'm good." Placing her hand on top of his, she wrapped her fingers around his fore and pointer fingers, giving them a squeeze.

"You're awfully quiet. What's on your mind?"

One side of Dominique's lips lifted in a half smile. "You know I'm not a huge talker in the mornings. So, me not talking doesn't mean there's something on my mind."

Denzel's lips twisted in an expression clearly projecting his disbelief in her denial.

"Come on, Una. Anyone able to use their brain would have *something* on their mind—especially after the talk we had last night. Not to mention knowing Leona will likely be on the set today."

Biting her bottom lip, Dominique finally acquiesced. "Okay, fine. I was thinking about everything that's happened. And yes, possibly seeing or interacting with Leona Jiles is high on the list of thoughts in my head."

"I know asking you not to worry is an exercise in futility, but I'm going to do it anyway."

Lifting her fingers to his lips, he kissed the back of her hand. "Can you try not to worry? It's going to be fine."

Tightening her fingers within his, Dominique really wanted to believe it. Holding onto that belief was difficult once she exited the car at the studio. She didn't bother to ask Denzel when he'd acquired clearance to be on the grounds as he sailed past security with her, before leaving her at her trailer. The man had a way of gaining access to wherever he wanted to be. Seeing it in action let her know the only reason she'd evaded him as long as she did was because he allowed it.

The kiss he placed on her lips prior to leaving her at her trailer was a heady reminder of what she had waiting for her at the end of this uncertain day. It also gave her something else to focus on besides her nerves. The next time she stepped out of the door, her concerns made a resurgence.

The set was normally busy. But today, there was definitely more of a buzz. People were moving at a clipped pace. The whispers behind hands she'd witnessed earlier in the week, were replaced by extra-wide, overly friendly smiles and greetings. *That's not creepy at all.* Dominique returned them with her normal level of enthusiasm.

If she didn't have forewarning and already suspected something was amiss, Dominique would've been completely on alert when she encountered Adam. The man was so giddy, he practically danced toward her.

"Hey hey, Dom! Beautiful day, isn't it?"

Slowing her steps, Dominique raised an eyebrow. Her response was slow and measured.

"Yes, Adam. It is a beautiful day."

A smile hovered at the corners of her mouth as she watched the formerly haggard looking director nearly skip to the booth he used when they were shooting. Other cast members and extras were milling around. Once again, Dominique was met with the too large smiles and eager greetings.

The only thing she could potentially attribute to their behavior was them taking the Rumor Mill article much more seriously than they had been. That had to be it. Because even if Leona Jiles was already on site, Dominique couldn't see where the author's appearance would cause anyone to be over-the-top friendly towards her. *Had she mentioned how creepy their behavior was?*

The cast members were gathered around the director's booth

getting final instructions on the upcoming scene when a murmur started from the back of the group, quickly making it to the front. Dominique looked over her shoulder to see none other than Leona Jiles strolling onto the set—wearing her signature red-framed glasses. Today, they were large and square, with the tops reaching above her eyebrows and the bottoms resting on her high cheekbones.

Oxygen was in short supply with the collective inhale. In many venues, it was possible for a person to walk right past the author and not know who she was. But on this show, there wasn't a person breathing who didn't recognize her on sight. Dominique was as star struck as everyone else. She had to gather herself when the shorter woman stopped in front of her, looking up to make direct eye-contact.

"Good morning, Miss Truman. It's great to finally meet you in person."

Dominique didn't bother to mention the only reason it hadn't happened was because Leona was essentially a recluse. Nope. It was completely unnecessary to bring it up. Instead, she extended her hand with a smile.

"Good morning, Miss Jiles. It's great to finally meet you as well. I've been looking forward to it."

Leona's smooth sable cheeks lifted her glasses higher on her face when she grinned.

"You have no idea how much that makes my heart smile."

From the way her eyes twinkled, Dominique believed Leona was being sincere. However, they didn't get to speak any further as the producers hovering nearby ushered her into the booth where Adam and a few others were gathered.

"Holy shit." Dominique wasn't sure which of the supporting cast members whispered the words, but she had to concur. *Holy shit.*

No pressure. No pressure at all. Just a normal day on the set of the show they were all hoping would be the beginning of a multi-season streaming contract with a major service. Knowing others were looking to her to lead, Dominique kept her demeanor the same, as if it was any other day. After a while, the rest of the cast calmed down enough that they were ready to go when the call came from the booth.

Dominique soon immersed herself in the work, blocking out

anything which didn't add to her being able to give her best performance on each take. Mid-way through the morning, Adam's voice came over the PA system.

"Cut. This one's a wrap. We'll move on to the next shortly. First, I need everyone to come to the booth."

Taking the hand one of the actors offered her, Dominique stood from where she was seated on the floor to end the scene. By the time she was completely vertical and dusting off her clothing, a crowd had assembled at the director's booth. They'd obviously made contact with the entire cast and crew, because some folks who weren't scheduled for the day were amongst those gathered.

In silent assent, bodies parted to allow Dominique to reach the front of the cluster. Although Adam made the announcement for everyone to assemble, he didn't speak once the group was there. One of the studio executives, whom she'd only met a few times, stood next to Adam and Leona. On Leona's right was Cristiano. Making eye contact with Dominique, he tilted his head in her direction in an almost imperceptible nod. Smiling in return, she gave the studio exec her attention.

"I'm sure many of you have been wondering and have seen some things in the media regarding the showrunner for the series. I just want to put your minds at ease. Radiant is committed to the success of The Clarke Files. As such, you're hearing from us, first, that we're happy to welcome Cristiano Ortiz to the TCF family as the new showrunner and executive producer."

Murmurs and clapping swept through the set following the announcement. Dominique couldn't describe the relief she felt knowing for certain Douglas Fowler would cease to have a hand in the show. It didn't escape her notice that, while the executive swept his gaze over the group, he kept coming back to her. She wanted to chalk it up to her being the title character and lead, but Dominique wasn't so naïve.

"Cristiano has graciously agreed to take over. He's already been reviewing dailies and talking with writers and producers to get up to speed as quickly as possible. We are lucky to have him." Gesturing toward Cristiano, he offered him the opportunity to speak.

"First, thank you all. From what I've seen, the cast and crew of this show are top-notch. I look forward to working with each of you. I welcome the challenge of helping translate Miss Jiles' work onto the screen and gaining millions more Marissa Clarke fans."

The rest of Cristiano's statement was perfunctory, but he had everyone's rapt attention. Dominique had to give it to the guy. He was magnetic. It was great to see him fully come into his own after meeting him as a production assistant on her first sitcom. At the time, she had no idea of his family ties in the industry. Now, he had the reputation and clout to take over a series from a prominent showrunner like Douglas Fowler.

Once Cristiano was done, they were given an early lunch to allow the team time to set up the next scene. Dominique ventured forward, offering Cristiano a handshake and taking a few moments to speak with him and Leona. The chat was brief, as both were being shepherded away by the studio executive. Promising to touch base later, Cristiano fell into step with the group.

Dominique wasn't very hungry, but she still stopped by the craft services table to grab a salad before heading to her trailer. The set was still abuzz with chatter about Leona's sudden appearance and the hiring of Cristiano. She answered a few questions along the way, but was soon free and clear. They'd been filming at a sound stage. So, there was a golf cart waiting outside the door. Erik slid behind the wheel and Haley took the rear-facing seat, leaving the one next to Erik free for Dominique.

She'd just settled her food in the convenient little nook in the dash area of the cart when a voice garnered her attention. Normally, it wouldn't have been something she noticed. Film sets were busy. There was usually all types of chatter. But this chatter had her name in it. Coming from the mouth of a person she was hoping not to see any time soon. Bliss Meadows stood a short distance away with a phone held up to her face on an obvious video call.

"You should have seen her. Dominique Truman was walking her oversized ass around like she already owned the whole fucking place. Grinning, showing those fake dimples, and acting like she'd won when the suits introduced Cristiano Ortiz."

There was a beat of silence, as if Bliss was listening to the person on the other end.

"But why should I play nice? I'm the one they came looking for. I didn't audition for this part. And now, they are adding scenes and cutting me out of stuff. It's not fair."

The whining tone of Bliss's voice scrapped across Dominique's eardrums. Normally, she would let petty grievances and personal opinions roll off her back. However, it was different actually hearing someone admit their disdain after she'd been nothing but cordial—cooperating with changes against her better instinct.

Before Erik could set the golf cart into motion, Dominique hopped out, reaching Bliss in a few long strides. While she didn't call out to her, Bliss must have caught the movement in her periphery. Her normally light golden complexion seemed to pale as she connected the dots and realized Dominique had heard at least part of her little tirade.

She lowered the phone without saying anything to the person on the screen. Dominique couldn't see who the other person was, but it didn't matter.

"Does it taste good?" Dominique tilted her head to one side as she stared at Bliss from a safe distance. Safe being more than an arm's length to avoid the appearance of her looming over the shorter, slenderer woman.

Bliss blinked and tilted her chin defiantly. "What?"

So, she wanted to play deaf and dumb? Dominique wasn't in the mood to let Bliss continue to pretend. "My name. Does it taste good? Because you seem to love having it in your mouth."

Flipping her hair over one shoulder, Bliss sniffed. "I don't know what you're talking about. Contrary to popular opinion, everything isn't about you. Just because people are writing gossip blogs about you now, doesn't mean anything. You're still B-list at best."

It was good she'd purposely maintained distance between them because she wanted to shake that little heifer when she turned her nose up.

"Trick, I've been in this game since before you had one knot on your chest and were trying to figure out why it was sore. Don't play with me. I'm sure you've pulled this little act with people in the past and gotten away with it.

I'm not them, and this ain't that. The mean girl shit may be what you need to make you feel better about yourself, but I suggest you find another way to deal with your insecurities. Seek therapy. This is your one and only chance. Come at me sideways again, you're gonna get your little feelings hurt and it won't matter who you're fucking."

Dominique wasn't moved by the tears welling in Bliss's eyes. It was a common mean girl tactic used when they were called out on their bullshit. Try to play the victim. Giving her a disdainful up and down look, Dominique turned on her heel and walked away. She was determined not to give Bliss Meadows another second of her time.

Astutely ignoring the smirk on Haley's face, she climbed into the golf cart again. Erik didn't offer so much as a glance before putting the vehicle into gear and continuing to her trailer.

Thankfully, the rest of her day was devoid of any additional drama. They managed to get a few more scenes wrapped before calling it. Yet another thing which didn't escape Dominique's notice since Douglas wasn't around. The interference with Adam and the other directors wasn't occurring. The vibe was lighter and more conducive to the atmosphere she'd been working to establish without him being there to undermine it.

Although Denzel escorted her to the studio lot at the start of the day, it was her normal security team who took her home. *Home*. She'd truly begun to think of the Logan City mansion she shared with Denzel as her home. She hadn't given a thought to the much smaller property she owned in Los Angeles. She currently had a house sitter, but had considered what Denzel mentioned about allowing it to work for her when she wasn't using it.

As she stared out the window mulling over the possibilities, her cellphone vibrated. If she hadn't been holding her bag in her lap, she might've missed it. Reaching into the inner pocket, she pulled it out. After seeing Syd's name on the screen, she quickly answered while rooting around for her earbuds.

"Hey, Syd! Give me just a second to get a bud in my ear."

"Get both of them. I want to make sure you're paying attention."

Sydney's reply put Dominique on alert. Despite Sydney not initiating a video call, Dominique still stared at the display as if she could see her friend's face. She didn't say another word until she had the devices properly inserted.

"So... you want to make sure I hear you. There must be something juicy you want to tell me."

"It depends on how you look at it."

Dominique's brow furrowed. She was thinking Syd had a bit of spicy gossip, but her response made it seem far more personal for Dominique.

"That doesn't sound ominous at all." Sarcasm dripped from Dominique's words.

"I wasn't trying to be gloomy. I just didn't want to send you down the wrong thought path."

"So, what path should I be on?" Dominique returned her gaze to the passing landscape and saw they were nearing the highway turn off. There were less than ten minutes of their commute remaining.

There wasn't a trace of humor in Sydney's voice when she spoke.

"So, you know how I told you the owner of the company was trying to get more of a foothold in film and print, instead of focusing on the plethora of advertising and social media money there is to make in this business?"

"Uh-huh." Dominique's stare remained glued to the landscape as she listened to her friend. It wasn't like Sydney to bury the lead. But, Dominique waited patiently for her to dispense the information.

"Well, we had a meeting at Celestial a few hours ago."

Dominique's brow lifted at the mention of the well-known studio. She'd worked on more than a few projects under their umbrella. Sydney's bosses were really shooting their shot in a major way if they approached Celestial.

"Oh yeah? How'd it go?"

"About as well as I expected, considering they have a whole division dedicated to the services Vivid is offering."

"Which was?"

"They humored us, but I doubt if they send any business our way. But, I didn't call you about Jude's film aspirations."

Dominique knew Sydney so well, in her mind's eyes, she could see her friend flipping her hand dismissively.

"Ok. What's up, then?"

"I was ear hustling while Jude was chatting up another executive and I heard some stuff about your showrunner, his career and now legal issues."

Dominique considered switching the call to video when she held up her finger to interject, once Syd mentioned Douglas.

"He's not the showrunner anymore. As of today, he's been replaced."

"What?! Okay, we'll cover that shortly. First, let me finish telling you."

"Yeah, sorry. I was just so happy to be rid of his ass, I couldn't wait to disown him."

"After what you told me about working with him, I understand." Following a short beat of silence, Syd continued. "I don't know-know the people who were talking, but I recognized them from my research on Celestial's executive staff. One of them brought up Douglas's name, mentioning him trying to get in the door to pitch a series.

The other guy shut him down so fast, I caught secondhand embarrassment for the first guy. Even though I've heard the things GMZ and other media have reported about him, I was surprised he barely let old boy get Douglas's name out before he went in on the damage and bad press which could come from them working with him."

As Dominique listened to Syd recount the conversation she'd overheard, she wondered why Syd would think anything said about Douglas suffering the consequences of his actions was something which would upset her. Just as the car rounded the curve and the gate at the end of the drive came into view, she jerked upright in her seat.

"Run that by me again."

"I know you heard me the first time, but I feel your need to hear it again to be sure. Dude said Celestial didn't want any problems with Denzel Reyes and his powerful friends. So, there was no way in hell they were touching Douglas with a fifty-foot pole. They might be able to navigate it if it was just some old allegations—just let the heat die down. But, between your man and the people he's connected to, Douglas Fowler's name is less than garbage. He's done-done."

Heat flooded Dominique's face. They'd talked. She and Denzel had what she thought was an extensive conversation when she'd learned about him buying the studio. And, while he hadn't told her immediately, they also spoke about him contacting Leona Jiles. But not once did he mention he was involved in anything related to Douglas and his woes. Not once.

Dominique barely heard anything else Syd had to say. She was fuming. ·What was he thinking? What all had he done? Hell, what *hadn't* he done? And if he was being so blatant with his maneuverings, why had it taken her friend randomly being in a position to overhear for it to get back to her? She had industry friends. At least she thought she did. Why hadn't any of them told her—especially once their relationship became public knowledge?

Not all of her questions could be answered any time soon. However, the minute Denzel Reyes stepped foot across the threshold, he had some explaining to do.

Chapter Thirty-Six

I STAY READY

Denzel kept one ear on the discussion in the room and his eyes on the occupants. He'd spent too much of his morning in meetings after taking Dominique to the studio. He wouldn't deny he was flexing just a little with the move. His Una needed his support. No matter how much he told her not to worry, she would anyway. She'd soon understand it wasn't necessary.

But he knew it might take some time for her to get there. Dominique had been raised to be independent and self-sufficient. Waiting for or expecting someone else to look out for her and her best interests wasn't her first inclination. However, she had him now. It was his job to make sure she was cared for in all the ways she needed. And he took it very seriously.

When he couldn't stop himself from glancing at his watch again, he knew it was time to wrap the meeting up. Thankfully, the person speaking was on the last slide in their deck. A few moments later, he was back in his car, leaving. The chances were slim he'd invest in the venture, but he'd wanted to see things for himself before making a decision. Virtual meetings were great for many things, but sometimes, he liked to meet face-to-face to get a feel for other people.

The buzz in his pocket had him pulling his phone out. Seeing Carver's name on the display simultaneously made him smile and raised his suspicions. Carver didn't do middle of Friday afternoon calls. Settling into the back seat of the SUV while Juan drove, Denzel adjusted the earbud and answered his friend.

"What's up, CJ?"

"So, I hear you're about to be the proud new owner of a film studio."

Grinning, Denzel considered denying it. Then he decided against playing cat and mouse.

"You heard right, even if the word on the street doesn't have it entirely correct."

"Oh yeah? What'd they get wrong?"

Denzel could tell from Carver's voice and the background noise he was home. Since it was the off-season, that tracked.

"The studio is Dominique's. Or at least it will be by this time next week."

"You're shittin' me."

"Nope."

Denzel's grin broadened at Carver's slip into his South Georgia accent. It seemed, since he had reconnected with Alyssa, that side of him came out more and more. Which meant Carver was very comfortable. Denzel remembered him working to scrub the twang from his speech his first few years in the league.

Carver's background noise changed and Denzel heard the distinct sound of a door closing, letting him know Carver had moved to another room to give them more privacy. The action put him on alert.

"You know, I can recall us having a conversation when Bit and I first got together last year. You were giving me shit, saying something about me plotting on people. I get the feeling you've been doing some plotting of your own. What the fuck happened? And does she know your game?"

"My game? Why did that sound like you think I'm playing around with her?"

"Don't give me shit, Den. You know what I'm saying. You're generous, but you aren't buy-a-fucking-studio-and-hand-it-over generous. So...does she know?"

Tapping the fingers of his opposite hand against his knee, Denzel considered what Carver was asking him. It was a loaded question. He wasn't just inquiring if Dominique knew what he planned regarding Radiant. The silence was thick between them before he answered.

"She knows I love her and that I'll protect her."

"No matter what it takes?" Carver's prompt made Denzel smirk as he let his gaze drift over the passing city scape.

"No matter what it takes."

The half grin slid from Denzel's face. It was the last part he couldn't be certain Dominique truly understood. He'd told her in so many ways, but it was possible she still didn't get how few limits there were to what he'd do for her.

Through the earpiece, Denzel heard the puff of air Carver released before his friend spoke again. Although he was certain Carver had moved to a more private space, his voice was lower when he next spoke.

"Listen, Den. I know you didn't ask me for advice, but I'm your friend. So, I'm gonna give it anyway. Whatever it is you're up to, she's gonna figure it out. If she doesn't, some little shit is gonna spill the beans and it'll get back to her.

Either way, keeping secrets from your woman can bite you in the ass. The only way to keep from getting caught is to not leave witnesses."

Nothing Carver said was funny, but Denzel suppressed a chuckle at the irony of Carver Wyatt Jamieson giving him advice that wasn't unhinged. Especially considering how far off the rails he was willing to go for his wife.

"What are you trying to say, CJ?"

"I'm not *trying* to say anything. I'm sayin' it. If you're up to something and you're keeping her in the dark, it's probably gonna come back on you. So, be ready."

"I stay ready," Denzel immediately shot back. As confident as he was when he said it, there was a miniscule kernel of doubt creeping into the back of his mind.

"Yeah, tell me whatever. Just know, if you don't have your shit wrapped up tight, it could cost you your relationship while you're doing your puppet master act and saying it's all for her—when you and I both know she would never ask you to do half of the shit you've done."

A line appeared between Denzel's eyebrows and his gaze went from the passing buildings to the phone in his hand.

"Did you call me to be nosey or be on some Mr. Miyagi bullshit?"

"Both."

If Carver was nothing else, he was blunt. Usually, Denzel appreciated his friend's ability to cut through the crap and get right to the point. In this instance, he wasn't sure he wanted to hear it. He and Dominique were in a good place. They'd parted ways that morning with kisses and 'I love yous'. Why would he want to think about anything which might fuck up those good feelings?

Regardless of if Denzel wanted to hear it or not, the seed had been firmly planted. Without his consent, his brain started considering the possibilities of anything he'd set into motion being linked to him. Even more, which of those things could find their way to someone who'd be happy to enlighten Dominique of what was happening right under her nose.

Not enjoying the thought or potential outcome, Denzel forcibly pushed it away, pointing the conversation in a different direction.

"Since when do you have time to dip your nose into my business, anyway? Aren't you on baby watch?"

Denzel knew the question was guaranteed to get Carver riled up. He'd been hypervigilant when it came to the birth of their first child. The due date technically wasn't until the end of April, but they'd been advised the baby could come early. Thanks to her oversized daddy and tall mother, their little girl was already well over eight pounds. Carver had proudly reported that in a text following Alyssa's most recent appointment. So, they could welcome the newest member of their family any day now.

"I'm quite capable of being in your business while simultaneously keeping an eye on my pregnant wife. Who is just fine, by the way. She was sleeping when I decided to call you. So, you can just calm—"

Carver's sentence cut off with a start. "Fuck! I gotta go!"

"CJ?"

Denzel's brow furrowed in concern. As much as he liked giving his friend shit, Carver's voice went from cocky to alarmed.

"CJ! What's going on, man? Talk to me."

Denzel received silence as Carver disconnected the call without responding. His background noise hadn't changed enough to give Denzel a clue, either. Whatever happened was important enough for Carver to hang up without an explanation.

While he wondered what it was, Denzel simply sent him a quick text about calling later and slipped his phone back into his pocket. By that time, the SUV was rounding the curve approaching the gate at the edge of his property. It was early afternoon, so Denzel didn't expect to encounter anyone but staff and he didn't. After a quick stop in the kitchen to grab a prepped meal, he went to his office to attack the remaining items on his schedule.

He didn't look up again until it was well after five p.m. Denzel only knew the time because of the chime from his watch. Carver had finally responded to his text. A smile split his face when he saw the contents of the message. It was a picture of Carver holding a little bundle wrapped in pink. The little knit skullie on the baby's head was a combination of light pink, blue and yellow.

The newest Jamieson made her debut a few weeks early, but according to her daddy, was healthy. And from her eyes being open in the picture, Denzel could see she was alert as well. With a few clicks of his mouse, he locked his computer and stood from the desk. Dominique would be home any moment. He couldn't wait to tell her about the baby. They'd have to check her schedule so they could visit once Alyssa was up to having company.

He'd already sent a joint gift on their behalf when he received the invitation to the Baby Brunch being thrown for them. It was actually scheduled for next week. But, it looked like baby Jamieson couldn't wait that long.

Denzel was still smiling when he walked out of the hallway into the foyer. The front door swung open and his Una stepped over the threshold. The moment he made eye contact with her, he knew something was wrong. Ignoring the feeling in the pit of his stomach of Carver's prediction coming to pass, he quickened his step, approaching where she stood just inside the entry.

"Hey, Baby. What's wrong?"

"Why would something be wrong, Denzel?"

Denzel came to an abrupt stop less than a foot away from Dominique. The hands, which had been reaching out to touch her, dropped to his sides. She'd called him Denzel. She rarely called him by anything other than the shortened version of his name or some other endearment. Denzel wasn't what he'd become accustomed to hearing from her sweet lips.

Scanning her face, he took in the set of her jaw and the single lifted eyebrow. *Shit...* Fucking CJ was right. Something was about to bite him square in the ass. But he still clung to hope like a teenager with a crush on a movie star.

"I don't know, Una. But, the look on your face isn't a happy one. So...at a minimum, something is bothering you."

"Bothering me? Something is bothering me?"

Denzel wasn't sure if he was projecting or if Dominique really appeared to be vibrating. It was no longer simply a facial expression giving him pause. Her entire body was coiled with what could only be anger. *Double Fuck.* There was no way in hell he was jumping blindly into anything, so he didn't respond. He took her question as rhetorical and waited for what she'd say next. The wait was short.

"I'm going to ask you a question. And this time. I'd appreciate it if you were completely honest with me."

"I'm always honest with you, Una."

Dominique's eyes slammed closed with a hiss. Her head jerked to the side as if he'd hit her, but he hadn't moved. Slowly, her lids lifted, and she stared up at him. Her gaze was clouded with what he could only describe as supreme disappointment.

"Don't. Don't say that. You may think it's true, but it's not. If it were, I wouldn't have had to hear about your name being batted around by studio executives in California from someone who wasn't you."

Denzel fought against closing his own eyes in response to Dominique's revelation. It would make him look guilty—ashamed. And while he might be guilty of withholding information, he wasn't ashamed of anything he'd done to protect her. None of it.

"Una—"

"No." Dominique took a step back and held up her hands like she was trying to keep him at bay. "Don't start with any sweet talk. I don't want that. I don't need it. What I need is for the man who says he loves me to be straight up. If you can't be, we don't have anything to say to each other."

Wait. What the fuck was that supposed to mean? Denzel was positive his facial expression matched his internal thought. A thought which soon came flying from his mouth.

"What is that supposed to mean? If I don't say what you want to hear, you're going to what? Leave me?"

Denzel didn't like the way the words sounded to his ears, nor the way they tasted on his tongue. Because what wasn't going to happen was Dominique leaving him. Her going anywhere wasn't an option, and he didn't care how crazy it sounded when he even said it to himself.

Watching as emotions flitted across Dominique's face, he had to tamp down the urge to get closer to her—to physically hold her so she couldn't do something as unthinkable as walking away from him. A line appeared between her eyebrows and her lashes lowered as she stared at him.

"I'm not under the impression I'll *want* to hear any of what you say. Regardless, I still want the truth. Not half of it. Not what you're okay telling me. All of it."

"All of the truth about what, Una? You haven't asked anything. All you've done is accuse me of not being honest with you."

Dominique's abundant curls shook when she tilted her head to one side.

"It wasn't an accusation. It was a statement. But, if you feel like I'm accusing you, it must mean I'm not too far off base. And that…"

Dominique's eyes slid closed before she opened them. The hurt in their depths punched Denzel in the gut, nearly stealing his breath.

"That hurts. Thinking you've been lying to me or telling me half of the truth, because what? You don't think I can handle it, or I don't need to know everything? I don't know. Either way, it hurts, Den."

Anger he could deal with. If she cursed him out or railed at him, he knew how to handle it. It was likely the anger would still come, but right now, what she was showing him was raw vulnerability and it was like he'd been hit in the back of the knees by a determined cornerback. It took everything in him to remain upright when he saw the pain in her eyes. Tears gathered, but didn't fall onto her cheeks.

"Baby, can you tell me what it is you think I'm keeping from you?"

It wasn't smart, but he still couldn't bring himself to jump in or fill in the blanks. He needed her to say it first. The way Dominique shook her head told him she had him figured out before she actually spoke.

"You're going to hold on until the last second, aren't you? Damn...I have no idea who you are. I thought I knew, but I don't, do I?"

"Of course you do, Baby. You know me; just like I know you."

A tear finally tumbled over her lashes and onto her cheek. Swiping it away, she shook her head again.

"I wanted to think you respected me enough, cared for me enough to be straight. But you can't do it."

"I can if you just tell me what the hell we're talking about here." As much as he tried, Denzel couldn't stop the volume of his voice from rising. He wasn't yelling, but he was coming damn close.

"You haven't actually asked me anything, but you've already assumed I'm going to lie to you."

"Because you are!" The words carried a cracked plaintive note as Dominique took a step backwards—away from him.

Taking a deep breath, Denzel steeled himself against doing something dumb, like grabbing her to keep her near him. It was hard as fuck not to touch her though.

"What is it, Baby? I can't address it, if you don't tell me."

Using the back of her hand to clean the tears streaking her cheeks, Dominique stared at him silently for a few seconds before she muttered, "Fuck it."

Once she started talking, Denzel knew she wouldn't be able to hear him if he tried to explain anything. Could he explain? Yes. Would it make perfect sense to him? Absolutely. It didn't mean Dominique would feel the same.

What she'd heard (from whom she wouldn't say) didn't have enough context for her to get a true understanding of the entire situation. But she'd connected the dots pretty accurately without having a whole picture. The question now was, what did she plan to do with her new knowledge?

When Dominique was done, she was no longer ripping his heart out with her tears, but Denzel couldn't say if she wouldn't just switch to using her words. Her chest rose and fell with her deep inhales and exhales. She appeared to be waiting for him to deny it. To say her informant had given her incorrect information. He wouldn't. At this point, he couldn't. The shit was definitely hitting the fan. How much of it splattered on the walls depended on what he did next.

"Can we sit?" Denzel didn't want to continue this discussion in the foyer. He wasn't stalling, but it was likely their conversation was carrying all over the house with them standing there in the doorway.

His hands ached to touch her. Soothe her. Instead, he held his arm out in the direction of the closest sitting room. Jerkily, Dominique acquiesced, walking ahead of him. She opted for the armchair instead of the sofa, not giving him the opportunity to sit beside her. Taking the seat as close to hers as he could get on the couch, Denzel clasped his hands together, letting them hang between his knees.

"If you haven't figured it out by now, I don't like when anyone tries to fuck with you or fuck you over. I noticed the change in your enthusiasm for your work and this role in the series long before I asked you about it. I was waiting for you to tell me. When I realized you wouldn't say anything unless I did—I asked.

Once you told me about Fowler, I had him investigated. I liked him even less once I heard what he was into. So, I dropped bugs in the right ears."

"What else?" Dominique hadn't jumped up in disbelief and cussed him out yet, but her question made him even more hyperaware of their current position. He still wasn't ashamed of protecting her, but...

"I've made some connections and investments over the years. So, when he kept up his bullshit, I called in a few favors to make certain he felt the consequences of his actions. I also made sure no one would be willing to stick their neck out for him."

"What else?"

Fuck! At this point, Denzel wasn't trying to keep anything back, but her repeating the same question said she knew there was more.

"I told the investigator to send what they'd found to the feds and local police in each of the states and cities where he owns property. It's only a matter of time before he's arrested."

"The feds? You put the feds on him?"

"He took minors across state lines for sexual purposes. Damn right I put the feds on him."

"Anything else?"

Dominique's posture said she was steeling herself for more. Her arms were folded across her middle and her legs were crossed. However, there wasn't anything related to Douglas Fowler that he hadn't told her. Everything else he'd done, he'd pretty much aired out previously.

"There's nothing else. That's all."

After his last word, Dominique popped up from the chair like a jack-in-the-box. She moved so quickly, she was halfway to the door before he grasped what was going on. Scrambling, he went after her. Catching up to her in the foyer, he clasped her hand in his.

"Hey! Where are you going? I thought we were talking."

"We were. I'm done."

"You're done?" Denzel's brows lowered as he calculated the different ways he could take those words. "What do you mean, you're done?"

"I'm done talking. I can't. If I say anything to you right now..." Her words trailed off, but he was able to fill in the blank from the expression on her face. Looking down at his hand around hers, she turned her gaze to his. "Please let go of me."

When she tugged at her limb, Denzel tightened his hold. But only for a second. Reluctantly, he relaxed his digits, allowing her to pull away.

"Don't do this, Una. We need to talk this out."

"Talk?" Shaking her head, she took another step away from him. "I can't do this. Not right now."

Without another word, Dominique turned on her heel and walked away. The only reason he didn't follow was because she was walking up the stairs—which meant she wasn't leaving him. Just not staying where he was at the moment. He'd give her a few minutes, then he'd try again.

When he could no longer see her, he lowered his gaze. Raffi was standing in the hallway with a drink tumbler in one hand and a plate of food in the other.

"Abuela's gonna kick your ass if you've fucked this up. You'd better fix it."

"Did I ask for your input?" Denzel pierced his cousin with a don't-fuck-with-me expression.

Raffi hunched his shoulders and backed away. "I'm just saying, primo. She's gonna be mad enough to make me her favorite grandson."

Ignoring his cousin, Denzel placed one foot in front of the other, going up the stairs. He'd been fooling himself when he said he'd give Dominique a few minutes. There was no way he could let the rift between them fester.

Chapter Thirty-Seven
WHAT IS WRONG WITH YOU?

Taking long strides, Dominique paced from one side of the sitting room to the other. When she'd walked away from Denzel, she'd felt his gaze burning her back the entire way up the stairs, but she didn't give in to the urge to look back. Instead, she kept her stare trained on the floor in front of her.

Before she realized where she was going, she was standing outside the door of the suite of rooms she hadn't set foot inside in months. Not since she and Denzel's relationship became an actual relationship had she spent even one night in the rooms she'd originally been given when she moved in. Without thinking about it too hard, she pushed the door open and stepped inside.

A quick flick of her wrist resulted in the satisfying click of the lock sliding into place. Neither the door nor the flimsy lock would stop Denzel if he was determined to get inside, however it made her feel better to have the barriers between them.

She ignored the niggling voice inside her saying she was doing the exact opposite of what she should be doing. Dominique was aware nothing would be solved between her and Denzel without communication. But she couldn't. At the moment, she didn't trust herself to talk to him like she had any sense. Worse, she didn't have faith in her being able to withstand the hurt expression on his face again.

It was the main reason she didn't look back when she ascended the stairs. If she had, the chances of her folding were high. Despite everything he'd revealed and knowing how he'd purposely told her half-truths and kept her in the dark, she wasn't positive she could've held firm. No matter how hurt and angry she was. Because, she was indeed very angry and hurt.

"But why are you mad, for real, Dom? You can't stand Douglas. He's always creeped you out. Even before the rumors about him being a predator."

The question from her internal monologue halted her campaign to wear a hole in the carpet, leaving her standing at the center of the room. It was the introspection prompted by years of regular therapy sessions to keep her head on straight. If she called her therapist, it would be the first question the woman would ask once Dom aired her grievances.

So... Why was she angry? Wasn't his protectiveness part of what made Denzel so attractive? That he listened and didn't just let her talk until it was his turn to say something. It didn't take but a few seconds for the answer to appear. Trust. He'd violated it.

Being raised by parents who told one another everything and supported each other fiercely, Dominique wasn't willing to accept a relationship where she didn't feel like an equal partner. Finding out from someone else, things Denzel should have told her himself, hurt. Deeply. It made her wonder what else he had or could keep from her. If he was so comfortable deceiving her, how could she ever trust him?

Her last thought put her feet back in motion, and she reversed course to the other side of the room again. With only her thoughts and muted footfalls making noise in the room, the sound of the doorknob being unsuccessfully twisted wasn't hard to detect. Dominique's stare snapped to the heavy wooden door as her steps slowed to a stop once more. She didn't say anything.

Without conscious thought, she held her breath. Waiting. Another thwarted twist of the doorknob was accompanied by two firm knocks.

"Dominique, open the door."

There was no 'please'. It wasn't even implied in his tone. It was a command, and it immediately got her back up. Because, who was he trying to order around? Not her. She wasn't his child. Reversing course, Dominique turned to move farther into the suite. Maybe if she couldn't hear him, it would be easier to ignore the fact that he was out there.

"Dominique... Come on, Una. We need to talk. We can't do it if you're hiding from me and locking doors."

Whirling around, Dominique glared at the closed door. How dare he accuse her of hiding! She wasn't hiding. She simply needed some time alone in a room he didn't occupy and hadn't bothered to tell him where she was. That's all.

Denzel's voice came through their wooden barrier again. This time, there was less command and accusation, but it wasn't completely void of either.

"Baby, open the door. We *need* to discuss this. I'm not leaving."

Knowing how stubborn he was, Dominique took hesitant steps toward the door. She'd rather have more time to get her shit together, but it appeared time was a luxury she didn't have. When she was within arm's reach, Denzel spoke again.

"Una, I'd rather not damage this door, but if you don't open it soon, that's exactly what will happen."

Anger flared and Dominique didn't consider her actions fed into what Denzel wanted when she flicked the lock and flung the door open.

"What is wrong with you?!"

She pierced him with a fierce expression of disbelief. Ignoring her heated glare, Denzel stepped over the threshold, lightly brushing past her to enter.

"I went to our bedroom, and you weren't there. I finally track you here and you won't talk to me. You have me standing outside begging instead of letting me in so we can work past this. That's what's wrong with me."

Following him with her gaze, Dominique folded her arms across her middle. *The nerve of this man.*

"I told you I was done talking, Den. I can't do this right now. I need space to think."

"No, you don't. You just want time to toss up barriers between us instead of facing it and navigating our way through this."

"You don't tell me what I'm thinking and feeling, Denzel Reyes." Dominique's response was sharp. Pressing a hand to her chest, she pointed at herself. "I'm the one living in this skin. *I* know what I need and what I need is for you to leave me alone, until I'm ready to talk."

"No."

Denzel's rebuttal was immediate and firm. Standing close enough to touch her if he chose, but far enough away for her not to feel the heat wafting off his big body, he simply stared at her. Under any other circumstance, she'd tuck herself into his side and absorb his warmth. But, not now.

"What do you mean, no?"

"Exactly what I said. No. *We* are an '*us*' now, Baby. That means, when we have a problem, we work through it together. We don't separate from each other. Why are you down here and not upstairs in our rooms?"

"They're not *our* rooms. They're yours. Just like this is *your* house."

The second Dominique said the words, she wanted to take them back. The immediate shift in Denzel's facial expression said she'd pressed a button she shouldn't have.

"Do you think one argument means you're not mine and I'm not yours? That you can just toss out shit like this isn't *our* house? Like you don't live here and I don't lie down next to you every fucking night? Is that what you think, Dominique?"

Every question he tossed out at her made her vacillate between wanting to apologize and throw back her own verbal bombs. But fighting fire with fire wouldn't help. It would only escalate things. Making this moment more emotional wasn't helpful to either of them. Still, he didn't get to try to turn the situation around on her as if her actions had brought them to this point. Logically, she agreed with those sentiments, but her mouth didn't consult the playbook before her next words spilled out.

"I didn't say any of that, but facts are facts. No matter how much I lie beside you, the name on the deed is yours. Not mine. My name is on 1582 Palm Vista in Los Angeles. Not Logan City, Georgia."

"Woman—" Denzel cut his sentence off and his face closed up with his lips pressed into a grim line.

His shoulders rose and fell with his deep breaths and Dominique was certain he had a similar view of her, since she was breathing heavily as well. Anger had taken over from hurt and they were careening down a road she didn't really want to be on, but couldn't seem to get off.

"I didn't come up here to argue with you. I'd hoped we could talk things out. Like adults."

"Oh, so I'm being childish now?"

"Fuck." Denzel grimaced around the expletive. "I didn't say that."

"Don't act like the implication wasn't there. What was I supposed to think you meant when you tossed in that last part? If we aren't talking like adults, there's only one other option."

"You're determined to twist everything I say, aren't you?"

"I don't have to. You're doing a bang-up job all by yourself."

Dominique really wished she could stop popping off at the mouth. It was only making things worse, but her impulse control had ghosted her. Trading barbs wasn't what she wanted. It was a fast track to people saying things they couldn't take back. Not a good end.

"Are you trying to hurt me, Baby? Is that what's going on here? You want me to feel what you're feeling? So, instead of talking to me and expressing yourself, you're lashing out. Is your goal to see how much I can take before I walk away?"

Fuck him for being so observant. Dominique managed not to blurt out her internal thought, but the look she shot him likely expressed it clearly. He'd nailed what she'd been trying to put her finger on when her mouth started running without her permission. Except the last part. She wasn't seeing how long it took him to walk away.

He wasn't going anywhere. Just like she wasn't. Even if she thought he wouldn't physically stand in front of the door if she tried, Dominique didn't want to leave him. It was never a thought in her mind.

"I've got news for you, Una. If that's what you're waiting for, you might want to pack a lunch, dinner and plenty of snacks. Because it's not happening. I'll never walk away from you."

Denzel took a step to close the distance between them and she matched it with a step back. His actions said what he hadn't with words. The only direction he'd walk was toward her. Never away.

Stretching her arm between them with her palm outwards, Dominique tried to protect her senses from the onslaught projected in his dark eyes.

"Stop, Den."

Wrapping his fingers around her entire hand, he tugged her to him as he eliminated the gap between them. His body heat immediately permeated the thin barrier of her clothing, causing Dominique's eyelids to lower briefly. Looking up at him, she tried to read his expression—to find a way to navigate this new situation.

"No. I won't stop. Not until we air this out."

Dominique didn't get excited when he released her hand, because she was quickly swept into his full embrace with his chest beneath her fingertips. He was too close. She couldn't think straight when he held her close like this. Denzel knew it, and it was probably why he did it.

She couldn't even turn her head to avoid his gaze, because he held her to him with one arm while delving his fingers into the hair at her nape to control her movements. Her eyes were locked onto his as he leaned down, entering her space completely.

"Now... Talk to me. I've done what you asked. I left nothing out. It's your turn."

Despite knowing it was futile to attempt it, Dominique tried to turn away from his penetrating stare.

"Nope. No avoiding it. No shutting down and locking me out. Talk."

The hard edge of the single word command loosened Dominique's resolve. She was positive being held in the circle of his arms had something to do with it as well.

"I'm not saying I don't appreciate your desire to protect me and give me the things you think I deserve. I do. But..."

Dominique's long pause elicited another prompt from Denzel. "But, what?"

Saying her internal thoughts aloud, to someone else, was scary. However, she knew it was necessary. "But it felt like you weren't treating me like a full partner in this relationship. Do you think I'm fragile, and I'll fold under a little pressure? Or did you think I'd try to convince you to stop?"

Denzel's piercing gaze swept over her face for countless moments before he responded.

"I never considered you so fragile that you couldn't handle knowing I'm willing to lay waste to muthafuckas to protect you. But, you're always taking the high road. So, I did consider that you might not want me to go too far. Not to protect him, but to protect me. You seem to think it's your responsibility."

"Because it is. Didn't you just say *we* are an *us*? Being a team means we're responsible for protecting each other."

The only reason Dominique detected the marginal widening of Denzel's eyes was due to them being so close together and her attention being laser focused on him. He looked surprised by her assertion.

What? The big strong man truly never expected his woman to want to protect him as well? Didn't he just say that though? She thought it, but Dominique didn't say it aloud. Him hearing her perspective and appearing to be taking it seriously was enough. His chin dipped in a slight bob, giving his acknowledgement of the veracity of her statement.

The arm around her back loosened as he transferred his hold. The slightly roughened pads of Denzel's thumbs brushed against her cheeks. His fingernails gently scraped her scalp when he slid them into her hair. His expression softened as he seemed to search her face.

"There's something you need to understand, Dominique. I love you. I also love that you want to share the load and look out for me just as fiercely as I look out for you." His gaze held her captive as he continued.

"No. I don't think you'll fold under pressure. But, my job as your man is to do whatever is within my means to make sure there is no pressure for you to concern yourself with. I'm your soft place to land, Baby."

His fingers in her hair gently rubbed against the strands, soothing her.

"When I call you *Una*, I'm not just saying you're *the* one. I'm not simply saying you are *my one*. Because, it's not all that you are. You're *first*. In *everything*. *Always*. Whether I'm cheering you on while you work toward your goals, or I'm being the muscle pushing the door open so you can step inside, I'll do what it takes. For you."

The surge of emotion swelling inside Dominique brought different tears welling in her eyes. Hearing him not simply declare his love, but what she meant to him, was damn near overwhelming. It was a depth of caring she'd never experienced from a man. One she wasn't sure she'd ever feel.

The fabric of Denzel's finely tailored suit was slick beneath her hands as she smoothed them over his chest before reaching up to clasp them at his nape. The close-cropped strands of his hair tickled her palms. Pushing past the lump of emotions attempting to clog her throat, she responded.

"I love you too, Den."

Dominique basked in the way his eyes openly shined with the depth of his affection for her.

"The way you take care of me and look forward to my happiness steals my breath. But, if you're doing all that for me, why can't I do it for you? When do *you* get to be happy? Why can't I be *your* soft place? The person you can tell anything—even if you don't think I want to hear it. Then...Maybe...we can kick in doors together."

A slow smile stretched Denzel's lips. "I didn't say we were kicking in the doors, but if kicking is what you want. Kicking is what we'll do."

Swiping at the wetness on her cheeks, he lightly kissed her lips. "Baby, taking care of you makes me happy. Knowing that I'm providing a space with me, where you can be your authentic self, brings me joy. You being in my life is a constant source of happiness."

Words failed her. Dominique genuinely couldn't formulate a sentence which could adequately convey how much what he'd said affected her. So, she lifted onto her toes, connecting their lips in a deeper kiss than the peck he'd given her before.

Initially, Denzel's lips softened against hers. His tongue delved into her mouth, tangling with hers while his hands gravitated from her hair to grasp the rounded globes of her ass. However, just as Dominique's core clenched in desire for him, he ended the kiss. Her pout was immediate.

Kissing it away, Denzel squeezed, then patted her on the ass. "We'll get back to that. But first, we need to make sure we're on the same page."

His countenance shifted to serious once more. "I won't apologize for doing what I thought was necessary to remove a barrier from your career and your life."

Dominique stiffened. She could've sworn they were turning a corner. Denzel obviously picked up on the shift in her body, because his fingertips pressed against her scalp gently as he shook his head.

"Hear me out. I can't sit idly by why someone tries to damage what you've built and cause you stress. Not gonna happen while I'm breathing.

I'm not saying I'd do it all again the same way. I'd definitely do it again. But you're right. If we're gonna be truly partners, we should be able to talk about the moves before they get made. So, I'll work on it. Don't expect changes overnight, but I'll work on it."

When he brushed his knuckles along her cheek, Dominique nodded, knowing his promise was all she could ask. After all, they had to start somewhere.

"But, Baby. If I'm working on bringing you into the plan before you hear it in the street, you have to do something for me too."

She couldn't pretend she didn't know what he was referencing, because it would be a bold face lie. However, in the interest of full cooperation, she asked him.

"What's that?"

Grasping the backs of her legs, just beneath her ass, Denzel lifted her in his arms and walked the short distance to the sofa. Once there, he arranged her on his lap with her legs straddling his.

"No closing me out. This, going to a separate room and locking the door. You can't do that, Una. No shutting down."

Although gentleness was in his eyes and the way he held her, his words were firm. Dominique was embarrassed it even had to be said. But everything surrounding her relationship with Denzel was so big...the feelings...it was so overwhelming all she wanted to do was pull away to gather herself. That's not the teamwork she claimed she wanted though.

So, she met his gaze with a nod. When he lifted a single eyebrow, Dominique gave in to his silent demand.

"No shutting down and closing you out. We talk. Even if it's hard. I won't go silent on you."

The scorching kiss Denzel placed on her lips felt like a reward for pulling up her big girl panties. When it took a carnal turn, Dominique was certain those panties would be somewhere on the floor in a matter of minutes. And she was right. Not having used the rooms for months didn't stop them from having make-up sex from the couch to the bedroom before ending in the shower with her riding him on the built-in bench.

Chapter Thirty-Eight

I'M A PRO

Denzel leaned back in his seat. The executive conference room wasn't filled to capacity, but the relevant parties were present. His personal life was on a path to perfection in the weeks following the argument between him and Dominique. They were still a work in progress, but their relationship was on solid ground.

With Cristiano as the showrunner for The Clarke Files, they'd managed to wrap up the primary filming and were now in post. So, Dominique wasn't required to be on set each day. Which was good because it gave her time to learn the ins and outs of owning a film studio. There were definitely some changes required at Radiant. So far, she'd taken to her role like a fish to water.

He couldn't be prouder of her if he tried. She'd been worried it would interfere. It hadn't. Denzel nearly broke into a smile at the memory of her face when she realized she could seriously look into the viability of the stack of screenplays she'd been secretly working on over the years. The resources to turn them into actual productions were now at her fingertips.

Having his personal life going well, made him want the rest of his ducks lined up. Which was why he was seated in a room with a select group of CleanSun executives. The investigators had been successful in ferreting out the evidence he'd wanted, along with some bonus information.

The posture of the majority of the room's occupants was semi-relaxed. Since he'd officially taken over the company at the start of the year, he'd ventured to improve the culture to where people didn't live in fear of being fired for having an original thought. So, many of the CleanSun employees appeared to flourish. Many, but not all. Those who'd missed the first sweep of him weeding out Hiriam Baxter's acolytes weren't happy they couldn't bully their way through, pushing their work onto others and fudging quarterly results to cover up their incompetence.

Leaning forward slightly, Denzel rapped his knuckles against the table to get everyone's attention.

"Thank you all for being here. This will be a brief meeting."

Scanning the room, he made certain to lock eyes with each person seated around the table. Not lingering on anyone in particular, he continued his short speech.

"As many of you know, we've been going through some realignment and growth here at CleanSun. I appreciate the efforts of everyone who saw the vision and worked within their teams to help us accomplish our goals as a company. It hasn't gone unnoticed."

Denzel observed as a few of the executives sat up a little straighter in their seats. They probably didn't even realize they'd done it, but the small morsel of praise seemed to bolster them.

"I'd like to publicly thank Vernon for temporarily shouldering the CEO role while maintaining his duties as CFO. I know it was difficult, but he managed it well."

Vernon Clarkson's face flushed lightly. Sitting up as tall as his small frame allowed, he nodded at Denzel.

Returning the gesture, Denzel resumed scanning the faces in the room.

"Today, I'm pleased to announce we've narrowed the search for a permanent CEO down to one candidate, and he has accepted the position."

Denzel tapped the intercom button on the console in front of him. "Sofie, can you ask Mr. Miller to join us?"

"Yes, sir." Sofie's efficient reply preceded the opening of the door connecting the conference room to the CEO's office.

Once Wilson Miller stepped over the threshold into the room, there were a few murmurs letting Denzel know the man's reputation preceded him. Standing, Denzel offered him a handshake before gesturing to the empty seat on his right.

"I'm sure many of you are familiar with Wilson Miller. He's worked in renewable energy for many years and was recently head of the EcoFusion Research group, where they've been doing groundbreaking work. We were fortunate to be able to woo him to CleanSun. So, let's give him a warm welcome."

As Denzel expected, the levels of enthusiasm were varying, but most of the executives managed to put on a good show. Or at least the semblance of one. The expression on Wilson's face couldn't be called a smile, but it wasn't an outright scowl, as he nodded while making eye contact with the occupants of the room.

Lifting one hand, he accepted their welcome. "Thank you."

Once the room quieted again, Denzel flipped open the folio in front of him before he spoke.

"Wilson, thank you for joining us as a part of the CleanSun family. I'm sure you'll want to set up your own meetings with the staff. So, I'll move to the next item on the agenda."

The two of them had already discussed the remaining item on Denzel's agenda. So, Wilson wasn't surprised by what he said next.

"While we have shown steady improvement, there have been some unexplainable dips in our stock. Knowing how diligently our teams have been working to make this company successful, I asked my assistant to put together a task force to get to the bottom of things. After all, you can't fix an issue, if you don't get to the root cause."

In his time straddling worlds, Denzel had come to realize different situations required different approaches. Dealing with athletes, he would've just ripped the band aid off and called out the person undermining the team structure. But, corporate environments were gigantic mindfucks. He wouldn't draw it out, but he wanted to see who squirmed, besides the person he knew was putting their thumb on the scale to help Baxter.

Other than the individual he knew of, only one other person looked uncomfortable with hearing about Tiffany's task force, which was really a team of investigators. Denzel made a mental note to look into the young executive, if he wasn't implicated in the scheme to get Baxter back into the CEO seat.

"Mrs. Brown, would you care to tell us why you misrepresented the revenue for the last two quarters?"

At the mention of her name, Jessica Brown's already pained expression became stricken. Her attempts to mask it were futile as guilt was plastered onto her every movement.

"Excuse me, sir?"

Denzel exchanged a sideways glance with Wilson, who tilted his ever so slightly. Returning the gesture, Denzel leaned back in his seat to let Wilson perform his first official act as CEO of CleanSun.

Flipping open his own folio, the glance Wilson took of the papers in front of him couldn't have been long enough to read anything—not even for a speed reader.

"Mrs. Brown, please don't bore us with pretense. You had a quick rise to the executive floor, but you've been here long enough to know accusations aren't tossed around lightly."

As Denzel listened to Wilson rip away the veil of subterfuge, he watched the room. He already knew the information Wilson was revealing. He'd seen the report first. So, he was well aware of her connection to Marjorie Tenor, who was her cousin. What Denzel didn't have the answer to was how much pressure was applied for Jessica to join in with Tenor and Baxter's plan. From the report he'd seen, it didn't appear much was required to get her on board.

The two had every eye in the room on them as Jessica Brown squirmed and attempted to sidestep the issue one more time. Holding up a hand, Wilson cut her off.

"Since it's obvious, you have no intention of being honest, we're done here."

After his statement, he tapped the intercom, but didn't speak. The buzzing sound was immediately followed by the doors to the outer office swinging open and security stepping into the room.

"We've collected your personal items from your office. You will surrender your badge and credentials to security on your way out."

"Excuse me, but what the hell is going on? Are you seriously saying I'm fired right now?" Jessica's frantic gaze flitted between Wilson and Denzel before landing on Vernon.

"Vernon, is this for real? After I filled in for you for months, while I was overseeing my own department, this is how I'm repaid?"

Vernon remained silent. In Denzel's estimation, it was in his best interest. The CFO had been on Denzel's radar when he was considering who would have the means and access to do what had occurred. But, learning Jessica had temporarily taken over some of his duties, and her association with Marjorie Tenor, allowed the pieces to fall into place.

Not only did Vernon not come to Jessica's aid, Wilson motioned to the head of security, who placed his hand on the back of her seat.

"Mrs. Brown, please come with us."

With a flushed face and her hands balled into fists on the tabletop, Jessica refused. "I'm not going anywhere until I get answers."

Denzel's urge to take control only lasted a split second. He was certain Wilson could handle the situation without his interference.

"Mrs. Brown, you are now officially trespassing on CleanSun property. You can either go quietly with security, or we can get Las Vegas Police involved, and you can be escorted out in handcuffs. The choice is yours."

The woman's flushed face gave way to heaving sobs. Denzel found it interesting that not one person in the room came to her aid or defense. It spoke to her relationship with her colleagues for none of them to be moved by her apparent distress. When the head of security rolled her chair away from the table, Jessica finally understood the game was over. And she'd lost.

Despite her attempt to hold her head high, her shoulders carried a slumped appearance as she was escorted from the room. Silence reigned until Wilson commandeered everyone's attention with a short speech regarding company unity and efforts to achieve their goals of bringing CleanSun to the forefront of their industry.

When the last person had filed out of the room, Denzel walked with Wilson into the CEO's office. The man hadn't even been there a full day, and Denzel could already see the changes in the room. There were no plaques or other accolades on the shelves. Missing from the walls were personal photos of him with celebrities and society elite.

Instead, the shelves were lined with industry texts and the pictures on the wall were nature photos from various places around the world. Denzel had no doubt, even if Wilson purchased the images from a professional, he'd actually visited each place.

"Well, that went over like a ton of bricks." Wilson dropped into the chair next to the sofa on the far side of the office space.

"Don't worry about them. They'll be okay."

Waving a hand, Denzel walked over to the console, pulling a bottle of water from the refrigerator hidden inside the well-crafted cabinet. He offered it to Wilson before grabbing another for himself. When he'd first taken over CleanSun, he'd found the refrigerator stocked with wine and craft beer while the console was bursting with overpriced liquor.

Denzel had all of it removed. He knew how things worked in the business world, but he didn't see a reason for any executive to require enough liquor to throw a frat party in their office.

By the time he settled into another chair, Wilson had opened his water and drained almost half the bottle. Denzel followed suit, then looked at his watch. *Still on schedule.* He'd allotted a certain amount of time to work, since this trip was primarily for pleasure. He and Dominique had plans to visit their friends and family before continuing on to Los Angeles.

"Do you think she was the last of them? Something tells me I need to keep my eyes open and an ear to the ground."

His shrug was non-committal, but Denzel let Wilson in on his gut feeling about one of the other execs.

"I don't think he and Jessica were working together, but he's guilty of something. So, yeah... Keep an eye on that one."

"What about Mrs. Brown's other friends?"

Denzel's cheeks should've ached from the wide smile stretching across his face.

"Oh, you definitely don't have to worry about them. While you were giving Jessica Brown her walking papers, the feds were knocking on both of their doors. As a matter of fact..."

Grabbing the remote from the side table, he aimed it first at the window, darkening it to block out the sunlight. Then he pointed it to the wall, revealing a television. A few clicks later and they were watching breaking news.

"If you're just joining us, we're watching as the situation unfolds. But it appears heiress, Marjorie Tenor, has been detained. Federal agents are at her home in the posh Las Vegas suburb, Majestic Ridge.

Our sources tell us this unexpected visit is a result of some questionable business practices by Miss Tenor and her associate Hiriam Baxter. Many may know Baxter as the former CEO of the solar energy company CleanSun, which was folded into the Reyes Group several months ago."

As the footage of Marjorie being escorted from her property in handcuffs played behind her, the journalist detailed the information Denzel's connection provided. When the live footage shifted from Marjorie Tenor, Denzel's impossibly wide smile got even bigger.

"Now, let's go to Chazz, who's on location at Sierra Heights, the luxury condominiums just off the southern end of the Las Vegas Strip, where federal agents are on the scene. We're told they are here to serve a warrant for the arrest of Hiriam Baxter..."

The young woman's words tapered off as she put one hand to her ear in the telltale sign of a person listening to someone else via an earpiece. Her expression, which had been professional, but eager in her reporting of developing events, shifted before she adjusted it back to a mask of professionalism. But the slip was long enough for both Denzel and Wilson to catch it. Exchanging a glance, they both leaned forward.

The live feed behind her showed emergency vehicles pulling in next to the government SUVs before paramedics exited the back of the ambulance with a gurney.

"Folks, it appears there's an injury of some kind. Chazz, can you tell us what's happening?"

The lanky young man held the slender neck of the microphone in a death grip as he looked from the camera to the activities just behind him.

"I don't have anything concrete yet. What I can tell you is that federal agents arrived on scene approximately an hour ago to serve a warrant on Mr. Hiriam Baxter. They gained access to the building, but I have no confirmation if they entered Mr. Baxter's residence. As you saw a few moments ago, emergency services arrived, and they've gone inside. At this time, there is no official word as to why they are here and if Mr. Baxter or one of the agents has been injured."

Denzel reduced the volume before placing the remote on the coffee table.

"Should I be worried about any of this coming back on CleanSun?"

Giving Wilson a rueful glance, Denzel sighed.

"I would suggest you get the PR team to craft a statement distancing the company from Hiriam. I already had my assistant draw something up to get you guys started. I'm sure, as things come out, there will be speculation as to if any of it was the reason he was fired. We'll want to get ahead of that."

Nodding, Wilson returned his gaze to the television. His next words were low and measured, but he didn't look at Denzel when he spoke.

"Is there anything *else* I should be concerned about?"

What he hadn't said hung in the air between them, but Denzel knew what he was getting at.

"Underhanded things have a way of coming to light. People who seek to hurt me and mine haven't been very lucky in keeping those things hidden."

It was as close as he'd get to acknowledging any personal involvement in Hiriam's and Marjorie's demises. If Hiriam's situation was what he thought it was, Denzel couldn't take full credit. Maybe some, but not all. The consequences of Hiriam's years of involvement in questionable business tactics were apparently more than he could handle. If Denzel was a betting man, he'd put money on Hiriam eating a lead and copper vitamin to avoid facing them.

Denzel had very little doubt he'd win, and he had no remorse for that potential outcome. The buzz on his wrist got him moving. Tapping the arm of his seat, he glanced at Wilson.

"I'm out of here. You have my info if you need something. Since you're here now, I won't be dropping in as frequently. But, if you need me, you know where I am."

Wilson stood with him and extended his hand.

"I won't need anything, but thanks for the offer."

With a nod, Denzel picked up his leather folio and left. He had a goddaughter in need of cuddles from her favorite uncle.

The scene Denzel walked in on when he arrived at Carver's was enough to make him forget to breathe. As a matter of fact, he did until his friend hit him square between the shoulder blades, restarting his exchange of oxygen for carbon dioxide.

Dominique was on the opposite side of the room. She was holding baby Ripley in her arms, singing softly to her. Officially named Brielle Ripley Jamieson, everyone had settled on calling her Ripley for the most part.

The little girl's eyes were open and one pudgy arm had escaped her swaddle. She was waving in the air almost to the tune of the song. Denzel was struck by the vision of his future. One he'd give both arms, legs and anything else he had to, to see come to pass. A future which was well within his reach, if everything worked out to plan.

He was so caught up in watching Dominique, he didn't notice anyone else until Carver strolled past him, cutting off his line of sight on the way to where Alyssa was seated. Near her, on the same sofa, was a very pregnant Zaria. Behind Zaria, standing as if he were her personal protection instead of her husband, was Andrei.

The way he watched her almost made Denzel crack a joke. But, another glance at Dominique and his words dried up. If Andrei felt half of what he felt for his Una, his bodyguard routine was completely justified.

Once he remembered how to work his legs, Denzel strolled over to Dominique. Tossing a greeting to the others, he didn't stop until he was in front of her. Dominique's smile reached her eyes, putting a sparkle in their dark depths as she tipped her chin up to accept his kiss.

"Hey, Baby. How was your meeting?"

"It went as expected. The other part went a little sideways, but I'll tell you about it later."

They'd made a lot of ground in the past couple of months. So, she was well aware of his plans regarding Hiriam Baxter and his cohorts.

Although his business dealings didn't necessarily fall under the umbrella of their tell-me agreement, Denzel wasn't taking any chances. He was glad he'd clued her in when he saw the footage of EMTs showing up at Hiriam Baxter's building.

Looking down into the sweet face of his goddaughter, Denzel pushed anything ugly to the farthest part of his mind to focus on the here and now. The slight flush of her little cheeks was too adorable to ignore. But, when he went to touch her, he met with his Una's shoulder instead of Ripley's chubby cheeks.

"Wash your hands first."

He'd totally forgotten baby protocol in his excitement. Properly chastised, he quick stepped to the nearest restroom. He returned, drying his hands on a towel. Tossing it over his shoulder, he held his arms out.

"Okay, Una. It's my turn."

Eyeing him skeptically, Dominique looked at his hands as she held the baby away.

"I washed them. They're clean."

"Mhm. You might want to take the jacket off."

Making quick work of shucking off his blazer, Denzel looked at Dominique for the next instruction. He ignored the snickers from Carver at the hoops his woman was making him jump through just to hold his own goddaughter.

Following her inspection, Dominique finally handed the baby over. Shushing her when she went to tell him how to hold her head, he slipped his hand beneath hers, cradling Ripley. With the size of his hand, his fingers kept her little head from bobbing unsteadily while simultaneously bracing her back.

"Shh... I've got this, Una. I'm a pro." Staring into the baby's face, he continued. "Tell her, Lil' Bit. Uncle Den is the best. He knows all the tricks."

"Den, I told you to find another nickname."

Denzel flicked his gaze to Carver. Patently ignoring him, he looked back at the precious bundle in his arms.

"Don't listen to him, Lil' Bit. He thinks he's the only one who can call somebody Bit. You're okay with it. Aren't you, baby girl?"

"Keep jawing and I'm gonna come over there and take my child and you can argue with yourself."

"Carver."

Vaguely, Denzel heard Alyssa attempting to rein Carver in. She was one of the few people who could. So, he tuned them out, giving Ripley his attention. However, he wasn't so focused that he missed Dominique trying to step away. When he caught the movement in his periphery, he reached out to tug her into his side.

She didn't resist, and they stood there together in front of the window with a view of the pool and the expansive backyard. However, Denzel didn't concentrate on those things. After tugging her closer to him, he caught their reflection in the glass. If he didn't know the baby in his arms belonged to his friend, he would say they presented the perfect picture of a family. He wasn't ashamed to admit he wanted that image to be reality.

Chapter Thirty-Nine
EVERYTHING YOU WISHED FOR

The few days they spent in Las Vegas were a much-needed recharge for Dominique. Since the studio purchase was finalized and they'd wrapped up on The Clarke Files, she'd been hopping around more than a long-tailed cat in a room full of rocking chairs. Denzel had been great with helping her get acclimated. Cristiano had also been a good resource.

It turned out that Leona Jiles' pop-up appearance at Radiant not only helped the show, but also paved the way for the purchase when she expressed her lack of confidence in the way the leadership was handling the production and roll out of the series. The author's connections caused a few other notable associates to express the same sentiments, and from then on, the process proceeded quickly.

Dominique closed the lid on her laptop, arching her back in a deep stretch before standing from her desk. She'd spent part of the morning going over a project she was considering as her first official production since taking over. The house was quiet, as Denzel was out running errands.

Clearing away the wrinkle in her eyebrow, she attempted to brush off the turn of her thoughts when she considered what he was doing. He'd been acting strange. At least, in her opinion, he hadn't been totally himself for almost a week. Dominique couldn't put her finger on any one thing, but something was definitely up with him.

However, she wouldn't press him. They were doing really well after their blow up surrounding his behind-the-scenes machinations with Douglas Fowler. Following that incident, he'd included her on things she probably would've never asked about. But, he wanted her to be aware. He'd told her about the problems his assistant unearthed with CleanSun.

Dominique would never cease to be amazed at how the entitled responded to having to face the consequences of their actions. Not even an hour after Denzel told her about the former CEO, Hiriam Baxter, did the news come over that he'd ended his own life rather than be taken into custody for his illegal business dealings.

Apparently, whatever he'd done would not only come with a hefty prison sentence, but asset seizure. Denzel said it was the prospect of being treated like a regular person and not a member of society's elite that pushed him over the edge. After what he'd told her about Baxter, Dominique's empathy meter wouldn't allow her to be too upset for him. Her compassion was reserved for the people he'd harmed.

Wrapped in her thoughts as she stood at the window staring, without seeing the lovely landscaping she'd always been so proud to have in her backyard, she didn't hear Denzel's approaching footsteps. Jumping slightly at his first touch, she quickly leaned into the warmth of his embrace when he gathered her close, nuzzling the crook of her neck.

"Hey, Una. Whatcha doing? I thought you were reviewing pitches?"

Leaning her head to one side to give him better access, Dominique hummed. "Mmm... I was. I just closed my laptop a few minutes ago."

Turning in the circle of his arms, she slid her hands up his chest. She wondered, not for the first time, who made his suits. Not only did they always fit his frame perfectly, the material was durable while still being comfortably soft to the touch. Lacing her fingers together, Dominique stroked the hair at his nape.

"What about you? I thought you were running errands for most of the day."

"Nope. You misheard me. I said most of the morning. It's not quite lunchtime and I'm done. Which is a feat considering the monster that is L.A. traffic. It's a good thing Juan knows his way around and drives like a professional stunt car driver when necessary."

Dominique's brow knitted. She didn't like the idea of Juan driving around Los Angeles recklessly. No matter how skilled he was, it didn't sit right with her.

"You're thinking so loud, I can see the words scrolling across your forehead." Denzel's smile could only be described as indulgent when he squeezed her a little tighter. "He wasn't taking unnecessary risks and breaking traffic laws. He was simply using his skills and knowledge of side streets to get us where we needed to go without being stuck on the highway."

"Mhm..." A single lifted brow and her murmur conveyed her thoughts. She didn't doubt Denzel saw whatever Juan did as completely necessary. So, their idea of what's risky wasn't the same.

"Anyway, enough about Juan driving me around. I'm going to go change, then we can head out."

Dominique's eyebrow raise was questioning instead of the previous skepticism.

"You were serious?"

"Of course."

During one of their many talks, Dominique told Denzel about the creative ways she'd entertained herself when she first moved to Los Angeles on her limited funds. She refused to ask her parents or Zaria for money. Her father managed to disguise his periodic deposits as gifts. Dominique continued to assert that she didn't want to be a financial drain on them. And, while Zaria was still a relatively new attorney, she'd landed a very lucrative position following graduation.

Either would've given her assistance, but Dominique simply worked, budgeted, and eventually found a trustworthy roommate in Sydney, who became her best friend. Without cash for more than bus or train fare, she had to get creative when it came to entertaining herself. Denzel expressed an interest in being introduced to her struggling actress's guide to a good time in LA.

"Ok. If you're sure. You'll want to change into something lightweight and comfortable shoes that you can walk in. Because it involves a *lot* of walking."

"You're not scaring me, woman."

Snagging her around the waist when she went to walk away, Denzel planted a kiss on her lips. Once he pulled back, she delivered two light taps to his chest.

"No need to be scared. You're in good shape. We just need to make sure to use the heavy SPF sunscreen. You're not gonna have your mama and abuela trying to jump on me for letting you get sunburned."

Her comment inspired a chuckle from Denzel along with the assurances that he was indeed a grown man who was capable of knowing when he needed to apply skin protection. Nodding mutely in agreement, Dominique mentally catalogued what she had on hand before shooting her assistant a message to pick up a good quality spray and meet them at their first stop.

Despite Denzel's urging to show him all the places she'd gone when she and Sydney would get out and about, she'd narrowed it down to three. The first would be the Santa Monica pier. Although it was a tourist trap, Dominique loved walking the area, people watching, and grabbing something to nibble on from one of the street vendors. It had been years since she'd been there. So, she was actually looking forward to showing it to Denzel. In all the time he'd played and visited the city, he said he'd never managed to make it there.

Patently ignoring Denzel's accusatory stare, Dominique motioned for him to spread his arms to allow her to spray the sunscreen Madison handed her the moment the vehicle rolled to a stop. Despite his cocky assertion he was capable of doing it himself, he'd walked right past the selections she'd set out for him on the bathroom vanity. While none of them would protect for more than thirty minutes, at least it was better than nothing. What Maddy brought should last them at least an hour and a half before they needed to re-apply.

"I feel like a five-year-old."

"This wouldn't be necessary if you'd been as grown as you told me you were and used something before we left."

"I don't see you slathering any on."

Dominique shot him a side eye glance before walking around him to hit the back of his neck and legs.

"For your information, I put some on before we left."

Once he was covered to her satisfaction, she walked back around him and made a show of sticking out one arm and spraying it. Snagging the bottle from her fingers, Denzel took over the task. After she rotated for him to coat the exposed areas of her back and legs, she retrieved the bottle once more, eyeing the male members of their security detail.

Without having to be told, they stepped forward and accepted the bottle. She didn't go so far as to perform the task for them, but she watched until they'd all complied. Haley produced her own small bottle and shook it in Dominique's direction, exempting her from further scrutiny.

"I'm pretty sure you're giving me a glimpse of your mothering side, Una." Capturing her hand in his, Denzel kissed the back of it. "I kind of like it. A little bossy. But caring. I can get with it."

"Mhm..."

Dominique's response didn't match the flip her insides made when she looked up at him. His expression projected a great deal more than his words. Tugging on his hand, she led him toward the ramp leading to the pier. As she expected, there was a decent crowd going in the same direction. Some were obviously families, but there were also couples and individuals who appeared to be doing the same thing Dominique had done during her struggling artist days.

As they walked, she reminisced about the ways she and Syd would make a dollar stretch. Although it had been close to fifteen years, the memories were vivid. She was glad she'd made plans to hang out with her bestie before she and Denzel went back to Georgia. One of the other issues they were still working through as a couple was which city they'd claim as their permanent residence. The jury was still out, but leaning heavily toward Logan City.

They'd had an early lunch at her place, so they skipped the restaurants. Although, they did have to take a detour to the arcade. When he saw it, Dominique couldn't resist the light in Denzel's eyes.

"That's a real arcade. Those are hard to find now. I mean, not like the ones attached to the sports bar. A *true* arcade."

"Yep." Dominique nodded as she observed him. "When we were feeling especially nostalgic, and we had the extra thirty bucks to burn, which wasn't often, Syd and I would go inside. We'd escape the heat for a little while and shuck off our status as grown women to play children's games, challenging each other the entire time."

As if she'd uttered the magic word when she said challenge, the light in Denzel's eyes got brighter. So, they spent a little more than a half an hour in the arcade as they worked their way through the games. Dominique was certain he didn't realize she was nearly as competitive as he was until they squared off in a game of Ms. Pac-Man.

"Okay. Okay. I yield. You have the superior Ms. Pac-Man skills."

Pretending to pop her collar, Dominique gave him a sideways grin. "Thank you for recognizing my greatness. Having good football handles isn't the same as controlling the joystick."

His hands appeared on her hips, tugging her body flush to his. "I'm with you there. You have excellent joy...stick... control."

Fighting the twitch of her lips was futile as she released a giggle. The tap to his chest lacked any strength.

"You're so nasty."

"You love it."

"Doesn't mean it's not true."

Denzel nuzzled the side of her neck, lightly scratching the sensitive skin with his facial hair. "But you wouldn't want me to be any other way."

"Whatever, Den."

Pulling away from his sinfully addictive kisses, she stepped back before she stopped caring that they were in public. Because, even though no one had approached them, she hadn't missed some of the glances they'd garnered as they walked around or even while they were inside the arcade.

Dominique had to hand it to their security detail; they blended into the environment well, but the second anyone looked like they were about to approach them, they were quietly deterred. Mainly it was people who recognized Denzel. But, there were a few people who murmured her name speculatively as they passed by.

Following their abbreviated walking tour of the pier, they were back in the car heading to the Getty Center. Miraculously, despite them not making a reservation, they were still allowed entry. There was no fee, which was one of the reasons it was on the list of Dominique's favorite places to visit.

They were strolling past the artwork when Denzel slipped an arm around her. Conversation was minimal as the other patrons marveled at the newest exhibit. Everyone appeared to be in their own little bubbles, the same as Dominique and Denzel.

"I can see why you liked this place. You could completely immerse yourself in the art here."

"I love the art, but my favorite part is the garden outside. Being around the plants and the beautiful way they've sculpted it made me feel closer to home. Even though there is nothing similar to it where I'm from, it still made me feel closer."

Since she'd mentioned the garden, they took a short stroll there before leaving the Getty. Even though Dominique knew it was likely Denzel wasn't really interested in flora, she pointed out things, places she'd sit or displays which had changed since the last time she visited.

With her hand folded in his, Denzel led her to the SUV following their short tour of the grounds. In the relative quiet, it wasn't hard to miss her stomach announcing its current empty state. Her free hand flew to her abdomen as she giggled.

"Well, dang. It seems like we just ate, but I don't think my belly got the memo."

Joining in her laughter, Denzel squeezed her fingers, then helped her into the vehicle.

"It's actually been almost four hours, and we haven't really snacked. Why don't we grab a bite somewhere before we go to the observatory."

Sliding over to make room for him in the back seat, Dominique considered his suggestion.

"If we stop to eat, it's going to be dark by the time we make our way there. We could try to fit in a visit tomorrow after my appointment.

There will be plenty of time between then and our dinner date with Syd."

"Is that your way of saying you're tired and ready to go home, Una?"

Dominique lifted a single eyebrow at Denzel's question. "No. I'm not tired. It was just a suggestion."

Her response was truthful. Mostly. The way her personal trainer worked her out, she was in great shape. So, the light activity they'd done hadn't worn her out. However, she wouldn't turn down a power nap. When her stomach protested again, she didn't have to look at Denzel to know he was staring.

"Your mouth is making suggestions, and your stomach is making sure we set the appropriate priorities." Wrapping one arm around her shoulders, he continued, "how about this? We'll find a place between here and there to quiet the protests. Then, we'll hit up the observatory afterwards? I don't mind seeing it at night instead of the daytime. It might be even better."

"It's gorgeous both ways. But, I admit, there's something about seeing the city lit up at night. We won't see the Hollywood sign, since it's not lit, but it's kinda small from there anyway."

"You sound like an expert."

"I told you. It was one of my spots when I wanted to get out and about on my starving artist budget."

The conversation shifted to a potential dining location. Denzel pulled out his phone to search for options. After immediately dismissing a few places, they decided on a cozy Mediterranean restaurant on Western Avenue. They chatted about everything and nothing as Juan expertly navigated the traffic.

When the flavor of the tomato and mozzarella hit her tongue with her first bite of the appetizer, Dominique was certain they'd picked correctly. The restaurant was located in a boutique hotel in the foothills of Griffith Park. So, they were minutes away from the observatory by car.

"Is something wrong with your food?"

Dominique paused in her enjoyment of the appetizer. Denzel had ordered the crab cake, but hadn't taken more than a couple of bites.

Small bites. Considering the way he normally enjoyed his food, she was mildly concerned.

Picking up his fork and spearing a generous portion onto the tines, Denzel shook his head.

"No. Nothing's wrong. It's pretty good."

"Just pretty good?"

One side of Denzel's lips tipped up. "Well, it's actually very good. Want to taste?"

Dominique was all set to accept the bite until the scent of it hit her nose. Pulling back, she shook her head.

"No. I'm good thanks. I'm going to stick with my cheese and tomato."

"You sure? I thought you liked crab cake." Denzel kept the fork aloft between them.

"Normally I do. Something smelled different about those though. You know restaurants like to put their own spin on things."

With a shrug, Denzel tucked into his appetizer. The rest of the meal was just as delicious as the starters. By the time they were ready to go, Dominique was certain she could go for one of those naps toddlers fought tooth and nail not to take.

But, since Denzel seemed to be looking forward to visiting the observatory, she didn't say anything. Besides, the place was essentially right up the road. It wouldn't be fair to suggest they go home when they were so nearby.

As the dome shaped roof of the observatory came into view, Dominique was able to shake off her bout of drowsiness as the memories came flooding back. Contrary to what she'd stated earlier, the sun was just beginning to set as they reached the entrance. Denzel's fingers flexed around hers drawing Dominique's gaze to his face.

The way he observed his surroundings was normal, but his expression wasn't nearly as relaxed as it had been earlier in the day. But the moment he looked at her, it changed. Since the first time they'd exchanged I love yous, they'd given the words to one another freely. However, the way Denzel looked at her said it louder than his words ever had.

"Mr. Reyes. Miss Truman. Right this way."

Dominique broke eye contact with Denzel to observe the older gentlemen standing a short distance away. He smiled cordially and extended his hand toward the interior of the building. When he did, Dominique noticed the relatively emptiness of the area. Aside from their small entourage, the man was the only other person there. Looking back up at Denzel, she quirked an eyebrow.

"I don't recall setting up a private tour."

"I took the liberty."

With a hand at the small of her back, Denzel urged her forward. His wink was accompanied by a satisfied grin at having surprised her. Dominique thought to herself, his planning was the reason he didn't want to put it off to the next day, and wasn't worried about stopping for dinner first. A single eyebrow lifted as she studied him while allowing him to guide her.

As extensively traveled as he was, Dominique wasn't surprised this wasn't his first visit to an observatory, but it was interesting to watch him interact as if it was. He held her hand as he pointed things out or quizzed her on her favorite constellation.

When they reached the observation deck with what she considered the best view of the city, the sun had fully set. Below them, the city was a beautiful array of lights. Dominique walked closer to the railing. Memories washed over her of the first time she'd seen the view. The lights were almost as bright as the stars in her eyes.

"I had no idea what life had in store for me the first time I came here. But, I was determined to not let this place chew me up and spit me out the way it did so many artists hoping to make it."

Dominique made her confession without turning to look at Denzel. Her gaze remained focused on the distant lights. As he tended to do, he didn't prod her to go on. His silent support had its usual effect as she continued talking about what she'd hoped for when she first moved to Los Angeles.

"So, has it been everything you wished for, Una?"

"You know what? It—"

The rest of Dominique's sentence froze in her throat. When she'd turned to look at Denzel. Instead of him being next to her at the railing, he was behind her. Down on one knee, he held a distinctive navy blue box with silver trimming. Opening the box, he revealed a radiant cut diamond outlined in emeralds and set in a platinum band.

Her words were stuck in her throat, but the tears which sprang to her eyes flowed freely down her cheeks.

"Dominique Latoya Truman, will you do me the honor of being my wife?"

"Den..." Taking a halting step forward, Dominique stared into his eyes. Seeing her love reflected back from the dark brown depths was everything. Instinctively, she cradled his jaw, stroking his beard. There wasn't any doubt what her answer would be, but she didn't withhold the words.

"Yes."

The second her 'yes' hit the air, Denzel slid the ring onto her finger and sprang to his feet, capturing her lips in a celebratory kiss. Dominique wasn't sure how long they remained locked in their jubilant embrace. No one came to interrupt. When they finally pulled apart, they decided to take the celebration home.

As they left, Denzel couldn't seem to resist telling their tour guide and their security detail that Dominique said yes. It took considerable effort for her to keep the tears at bay. Him proudly announcing it to them filled her heart near to bursting. He just kept giving her reasons to love him even more.

Chapter Forty

ALL OF YOU

Denzel leaned back, settling into the soft leather of the chair in Dominique's home office. His thoughts drifted to the previous night. Following her acceptance of his proposal, Denzel couldn't get her back home fast enough. A proper celebration of their future was in order.

And celebrate they did. All over the bedroom, shower, and kitchen when they came out for a late-night snack. Then, again this morning before she left for her appointment. He wanted to ask her to reschedule, but he didn't dare. She was already not looking forward to finding a new primary care physician and gynecologist. Asking her to beg off from her last appointment with the people she was most comfortable with wouldn't be smart.

Part of him wanted to suggest she keep them, but knew it wasn't always feasible to travel across the country for a checkup. Besides, whenever they started a family, he knew they'd both want someone who was more accessible. So, he kept his mouth closed. He already had his assistant working up a list of potential replacements anyway.

His cellphone buzzed, pulling his attention away from the large windows overlooking the backyard. Checking the display, he saw his father's face.

"Hola, Pops."

"It is not your papá. It is me." His abuela's heavily accented voice corrected him.

"Hola, abuela. What's going on? Why are you calling me on Pops' phone?"

Although he asked, Denzel was certain of the answer. She'd probably misplaced hers and would need someone to dig it out of whatever cubby she'd stashed it in. It was always somewhere she was sure she wouldn't forget. But, his abuela regularly forgot. It never seemed to occur to her to put it in the pocket of the apron she wore religiously.

"It does not matter. No questions from you. Where is my Dominique?"

With an involuntary, laughing smile, Denzel shook his head. "She's out. She had a doctor's appointment this morning."

"Is she sick?"

"No, ma'am. It's a regular check-up. She's fine."

"So, it is not about the baby?"

"No, it's not about the baby—" Denzel shot straight up in his seat. "What baby, abuela?"

When his grandmother responded, she spoke slowly. It was almost as if she were afraid her accent was keeping him from understanding what she said.

"The baby in her belly. My little bisneita. Or bisneito. I will be happy either way."

Being hit full force by a linebacker couldn't have knocked the air out of Denzel's lungs faster than hearing his grandmother say Dominique was pregnant with his child—her great grandchild. It didn't occur to him to dispute her assertion. Whenever she'd declared a pregnancy, she'd never been wrong. Even if the expectant mother had no idea. The earliest she'd ever made the proclamation was when Pablo's girlfriend was less than a month along with Fernanda.

His abuela's voice was distant in his ears as Denzel replayed the last few months in his mind's eye. It had been slightly over two months since he introduced Dominique to his family. Which meant they'd conceived prior to that trip. While he was counting, part of his mind reminded him which doctor Dominique was seeing today. *Shit!*

Amid apologies and promises to call them back, Denzel rushed off the call. Immediately dialing Juan's number, he alerted him to the change of plan. He was going out after all.

Denzel arrived at his destination in less than thirty minutes. Double-checking the name on the placard beside the tempered glass doors, he pulled on the handle, stepping inside. Juan was parking the car, so Justin had to quick step to catch up with Denzel. While his security detail was visually sweeping the area for threats, Denzel was looking for Dominique.

She wasn't there. Neither was Haley. However, Erik was standing next to a door on the opposite side of the room, which presumably led to the examination rooms. Bypassing the reception desk, Denzel immediately approached him. He didn't stand on pleasantries when he spoke.

"Where is she?"

Tilting his head toward the door, Erik stood up straighter, his gaze sweeping past Denzel before coming back to his face. His stance indicating his readiness to get to Dominique.

"Is there a threat, sir? Miss Truman is with the doctor. Haley went back with her."

Denzel was happy to see Erik was prepared to kick in doors to get to Dominique. But, since it wasn't necessary, and Denzel told him so.

"No. No danger. I was hoping I'd get to her before she was called back. I wanted to speak to her."

He flicked his stare toward the door again. He was seriously contemplating getting the room number from Erik and simply going in search of her when he heard a voice from behind him. Apparently, bypassing the reception desk didn't mean he was exempt from speaking with the staff. The very business-like voice belonged to a petite young woman.

"Hello, welcome to Ray-Davis. Is there something I can help you with, sir?"

Not being able to see or get to Dominique irritated him, but Denzel tried not to take it out on the clinic staff. Pulling up his most charming smile, Denzel extended his hand.

"I'm not sure. I'm Denzel Reyes. My fiancé, Dominique Truman, is here to see Dr. Ray. I was hoping to have a word with her."

When the indulgent smile appeared on her face, Denzel knew he'd hit a HIPPA wall. And, his new acquaintance would not be of assistance in getting him into the exam room with his Una.

"I'm sorry, sir. I can't release the names of patients. So, I am unable to allow anyone to go back without express instructions."

Denzel couldn't be angry at her for following protocol. If she had been willing to accommodate him, he'd be the first one to encourage Dominique to find a new doctor's office. Still didn't make the situation less frustrating for him though. His abuela's confidence and track record said either Dominique was with her doctor having her own pregnancy suspicions confirmed.

Or... she was in the examination room, learning of her pregnancy. Alone. Without him being there to assure her it was okay. Everything was and would be okay.

Causing a scene wasn't an option, but Denzel was actively trying to come up with a way to get to Dominique when the door pushed open and she walked out.

"Den?"

Surprise was in Dominique's voice and expression. Before she'd realized it was him, she appeared dazed. Reaching for her, Denzel folded her hand in his as he pulled her closer to him. He was aware he probably looked unhinged raking his gaze over her as if he had X-Ray vision.

"Den, is everything okay? What are you doing here?"

Denzel opened, then closed his mouth. Normally a man with a plan, he didn't stop to work out what he'd say when he actually saw her. If she hadn't already been back with the doctor, he would've been similarly struck silent when he approached her in the waiting area. It took him a few seconds and some distance from the others to get his words together. Bypassing her questions, he asked one of his own.

"What did the doctor say, Una?"

Staring up at him with a furrowed brow, Dominique's face went through a short series of expressions before she answered in a low voice.

"Can we talk about this privately?"

She glanced around the lobby furtively after she posed the question. Following her gaze, Denzel saw the few people, who were present, were making no attempt to hide their interest in the two of them. Unlike the receptionist, none of them were bound by HIPPA. So, they wouldn't have any problem sharing what they'd seen and heard between him and Dominique.

"Sure. Do you need to speak to anyone before you leave?"

"No. Everything is taken care of."

With a hand at the small of her back, Denzel guided her from the office. As much as he wanted to press for answers, he wanted their privacy more. It took every ounce of control he possessed to walk moderately out of the building.

Either one of the team had alerted Juan, or he'd never left, because he was there when they stepped outside. Denzel had barely seated himself beside Dominique in the back seat before he turned to her with questions in his eyes.

One corner of Dominique's bottom lip disappeared between her teeth before she released it with a heaving sigh.

"I'm..."

Her gaze flitted away from his and she dropped into silence. Cupping her cheek, Denzel leaned in until they were nearly nose to nose.

"Are you pregnant, Una? Is that what the doctor told you?"

Dominique's eyes widened, giving him the answer she hadn't been able to form the words to say.

"How—" Clearing her throat, Dominique tried again. "How did you know? Is that why you came?"

Instead of responding immediately, Denzel closed the miniscule gap between them, capturing her lips. He attempted to pour everything he felt into the kiss. His love, joy, anticipation. It was all in there. When he finally pulled away, he hardly noticed the vehicle was in motion.

"You might not believe it, but my abuela called to check on you."

Dominique's expression would've made Denzel chuckle if he didn't know how strange it sounded for him to seek her out at her doctor's office because his grandmother called and asked about her.

"Check on me? Why?"

"You know what? I didn't get around to asking her. Once I told her you had a doctor's appointment, and she asked me if it was about the baby, I couldn't hear much else."

"But how did she know? I just found out myself today. Less than an hour ago."

Slipping an arm around her shoulders, Denzel snuggled his confused woman into his side.

"Baby, that's a question many in my family would love the answer to. We don't know how she does it. She can just look at someone and tell if they're pregnant. She's been doing it as long as I can remember."

"But I've only met her once."

"Once is all it takes."

He released a light laugh at his response, because the reply was one he'd overheard on more than one occasion when his abuela proclaimed a pregnancy. She'd always shot back that it only took once to plant the seed.

As many deposits as he'd made at Her Highness' altar, it wouldn't surprise him if there weren't twins or triplets nestled in Dominique's womb. Although his knowledge of human reproduction told him it wasn't how things worked, he smirked internally at the thought.

Lightly shoving against his side, Dominique sucked her teeth. "I know that, smarty pants. You know what I mean. The only time I was around your abuela was when we visited after the wedding. Since then, I've only seen her on the phone when your mom video called."

Hugging her to him, he ran one hand down her side, resting it on her belly.

"I have no answers as to how Abuela knows the things she knows. At this point, I just accept them. But how she knows isn't my focus at the moment."

Rubbing the curve of her stomach, he flexed his fingers. Dominique's hand joined his, and he tangled their digits together.

"We're having a baby."

"Yeah." Her agreement given softly with a nod which caused her hair to brush against his neck, tickling slightly.

"How do you feel about that, Una?"

Denzel knew how he felt. He was fucking ecstatic. But, he couldn't get a read on Dominique, beyond surprised shock.

When she tilted her head back to look up at him, he met her stare.

"Surprised...happy... a little scared." Tracing random patterns on his skin with her thumb, she continued, "I guess I thought we had a little time before we talked about starting a family. But, here we are. What about you? How do you feel?"

Cradling her face with his free hand, Denzel stroked her cheek. "I'm so fucking happy; I don't know what to do first." Admitting it opened the floodgates and his thoughts poured out.

"I don't even know how much time we have. But, I know we have a lot to do to prepare. People we need to let know. Can we tell people? Do we need to move up the wedding? Shit! We haven't even set a wedding date."

Pressure from Dominique squeezing his fingers and her hand on his cheek halted the stem of his expanding list.

"Den... Stop. We'll work it out. We have time. According to Dr. Ray, I'm in the first week of the second trimester. So, technically, it's safe to tell people. My first thought is I'd like some time to get used to the idea before we spread the news. But, it appears your family knew before we did. I guess that means we need to at least tell my parents and confirm with yours."

Pressing a kiss to her forehead, then the tip of her nose before capturing her lips, Denzel attempted to soothe both of their little flares of anxiety. He'd felt her tension when she mentioned telling her parents. He knew his parents were going to be borderline unbearable in their excitement once they found out. And while he was fairly certain Dominique's parents wouldn't be disappointed, he couldn't say how her father would react to finding out another of his daughters was pregnant before being walked down the aisle.

After Dominique filled him in on the details from Dr. Ray, the remainder of the ride back to the house was done in relative silence. Each of them seemed to be absorbed in their own thoughts. By the time they reached the house, Denzel's phone began to ding and ping with messages. Mainly from his mother and tia. But his dad's number was there for good measure. It appeared his abuela had relayed their conversation, and the rumor mill was actively churning.

"Are you going to get that?"

Dominique pointed to his pocket as she strolled into the house.

"No. I'll talk to them later."

She kept moving until she was in the bedroom. Denzel followed behind her, closing the door once they were both inside. His gaze devoured her as she stopped in front of the waist high dresser. Her reflection in the mirror mounted on the wall above it showed a pensive expression on her face.

Approaching her, Denzel slid his arms around her waist, interlocking his fingers on her stomach. Standing this way, with his front pressed to her back, had long been among his favorite positions in which to hold her. But knowing his child grew in the womb beneath his hands, made it his number one—by a long shot.

"What's the face about, Una?"

"Just thinking." Dominique's hands seemed to gravitate to his, stroking along the tops of his fingers up past his wrist before moving back toward his fingertips.

"About?..."

"There have been so many changes in my life in less than a year's time. It's *a lot* to take in. I landed the role projected to be the breakout of my career. We started seeing each other. Then, the stuff with the studio. Now, new productions are on the horizon. On top of all of that, we got engaged and found out we're going to be parents in less than a twenty-four-hour window. That is... A lot."

Nuzzling the crook of her neck, Denzel kissed the sensitive space before looking up at the two of them in the mirror. Tilting his head until their faces were side by side, pressed lightly together from temple to chin, he observed their reflections.

"I can see how it would be a little overwhelming. But, you've handled it all—with grace. Us. Our relationship. Getting married. Being parents. It's a team sport. We're in it together, baby. We got this."

His pep talk included another squeeze as he hugged her from behind. Dominique's expression shifted from pensive to a soft acceptance, letting him know he'd somehow managed to say exactly what she needed to hear. Turning in his embrace, she slipped her arms around his neck. The delicate touch of her fingertips at his nape, with her nails lightly scratching, made him close his eyes in appreciation of her petting strokes.

"I like the sound of that."

Dominique's stroking became more fingernails scraping his scalp than smoothing caresses, which was a pipeline directly to the hardening of his shaft. Lifting on her toes, she tugged him until he met her halfway. Delivering a sweet peck to his lips, she pulled back.

"Team Reyes does have a nice ring to it."

"Oh, it does?"

Denzel began a slow walk backwards, tugging her along with him.

"Mhm..."

Dominique's response was accompanied by more touches against his neck and shoulders. Touches which were becoming more sensual in nature.

When he felt the bed at the back of his legs, he sat, spread his legs and positioned her between them. His hands began a slow exploration, slipping beneath the edge of her shirt to feel her silky skin.

"What exactly are you up to, Mr. Reyes?"

Leaning slightly away, Dominique lifted a single eyebrow. The smile stretching her luscious lips said she already knew the answer to her question.

"What do you think I'm up to, Mrs. Reyes?"

Filling both hands with her abundant ass, he lifted, guiding her to straddle his lap.

"Aren't you a little premature with that? I mean... sure. You *technically* put a ring on it, but there's more to it than simply asking."

"You said the magic words, Una. I put a ring on it. The rest is just semantics and details."

Burying his face in the crook of her neck, he attacked the sweet spot guaranteed to make her wet for him. It didn't matter how many times they'd come together the previous night or in the morning before her appointment. His dick was throbbing, demanding to be reunited with Her Highness.

She was still talking though. *Why was she talking and not moaning his name?* He needed to remedy the situation. Flipping them over amid her squeals and giggles, Denzel stripped Dominique naked in record time. If undressing your woman was an Olympic sport, he was certain his performance would've earned him a gold medal. Before her last fake squeal of protest hit the air, he had her thighs resting on his shoulders and his face in position to worship at her delicious altar.

"Oh!... Den...!"

Dominique's breathy moan was accompanied by her fingers delving into his hair, tugging at the short strands. That was a start. Denzel smirked and redoubled his efforts. By now, he was an expert in pushing her pleasure buttons. Usually, he'd choose his moments to extend things or bring her to a quick release. This time, he chose to draw them out.

Coaxing her pearl from its hood, he flicked it with a precise amount of pressure. Only his grip on her hips kept her from splitting his lip when she bucked under his ministrations. Her appreciative cries reached the notes he was waiting for just before a gush of her sweet nectar landed on his tongue.

"Fuck, Una." Denzel's groan against her folds elicited a quiver from Dominique. The fingers gripping his hair tightened as she attempted to pull him away.

"What is it, baby? What do you want?"

"You, Den. All of you. Always."

If there were such a thing as magic words, his Una had spoken them. Shucking his clothes off more quickly than he dispensed with hers, he was on her in seconds. His lips captured hers, sharing her taste with her, while he sheathed himself in her velvet heat. Their coming together was a contradicting amalgamation of tenderness and explosiveness.

The intimacy of their position with his hips in the cradle of her legs and her plush thighs pressed against his sides while he stared into her eyes was a heady experience. Denzel poured every molecule of love he had for her into their joining. They reached their climax together, with Denzel fighting to keep his eyes open to watch his Una in all her glory. His length pulsed inside her as he emptied himself into her throbbing channel.

When he was finally able to separate from her, he rolled to the side. Unable to not touch her, he wrapped himself around her, resting one hand on her abdomen. As he considered getting up to run them a bath, his phone buzzed again from somewhere on the floor.

"Eventually, you're going to have to respond to one of those."

Nuzzling the back of Dominique's neck, Denzel placed a kiss on her shoulder.

"I will. But, not until I take care of you. You're first, Una. Always."

Chapter Forty-One

SHE DESERVES THE BEST

Frozen midway down the stairs to her father's man cave, Dominique could practically hear her grandmother's voice in her ear telling her that eavesdropping was a sure-fire way to get your feelings hurt. Because, you were bound to hear something you didn't want to and wish you hadn't heard. Despite the warning memory from the Truman matriarch, Dominique still hovered on the stairs, listening to her father and Denzel speaking.

After receiving the news of her pregnancy, they added a stop on their way back to Georgia. She called ahead to make sure her parents were home and let them know they were going to stop in. They didn't plan to stay overnight, since the flight time between Southhaven and the Logan City airfield was barely over an hour.

However, once they stepped over the threshold, Belinda Truman started her campaign, which resulted in them agreeing to stay a couple of days. You could've bought Dominique for a nickel when her mother instructed Denzel to put both of their bags in Dominique's room. Without any additional house guests, there was plenty of space for the two of them and their security detail. So, a hotel wasn't a viable option.

Holding onto the wooden rail, Dominique trained her ears to the conversation she wasn't supposed to be privy to, but couldn't seem to resist.

"Why is my daughter pregnant and unmarried, Reyes?"

"Mr. Truman...you do recall that I asked your daughter to marry me and she said 'yes'. Right?"

"Did you ask because she was pregnant? Dom deserves better."

Dominique tensed upon hearing the question. She knew Denzel was just as surprised as she was by the news from Dr. Ray. It never crossed her mind that he'd asked her to marry him because she was pregnant. Denzel's reply was immediate. The offense was clear in his tone. Dominique was impressed to hear him manage to still be respectful despite being offended.

"I know. She deserves the best. For the record, I asked her to marry me before I knew about the baby. Finding out was simply a reason for us not to have a long engagement. I don't want our child born before we all have the same last name."

Her father's response to Denzel's declaration was a grunt. Dominique wasn't shocked to hear her father asking Denzel about her being pregnant before officially being married. As much as he liked Andrei, he'd grumbled about Zaria being pregnant and Andrei not appearing to be in any hurry to marry her.

As progressive as her parents were, they were very much old school in many ways. Making babies should happen within the confines of a marriage. But, they didn't believe in getting married simply because of an unplanned pregnancy. They were walking contradictions Dominique had long stopped trying to figure out.

"And why does she have to change **her** name?"

When he asked, Dominique knew her dad was simply trying to stir up shit. It wasn't as if her mama had kept her maiden name. She'd been a Truman far longer than she'd been a Green.

"Professionally, I wouldn't ask her to change her name—unless it's what she wants. She's put a lot of blood, sweat, and tears into establishing herself. Legally, we're **all** going to carry the name Reyes. That's not up for debate."

"So, my daughter doesn't have a say?"

"Your daughter agreed to be my wife, Mr. Truman. I didn't just become Denzel Reyes today. I've been this way. She knows who I am. If she couldn't accept this package, trust me, she wouldn't have said yes."

"And if she'd said no?"

"I would've accepted it."

Dominique was so shocked at Denzel's reply she audibly gasped, then slapped her hand over her mouth to quiet the noise.

"Just like that? You would've accepted it and walked away?"

"I didn't say anything about walking away." Dominique smirked at Denzel's rapid-fire response.

"I would've accepted she wasn't ready to say yes. Then, I'd have worked to eliminate whatever was keeping her from saying yes."

"You're stubborn, and more than a little cocky. But my baby girl loves you. And now, you've made it so if I bury your ass in the desert, she might not ever get over it. Shit."

"Little girl, what is taking you so long?"

Releasing a startled squeak, Dominique turned wide eyes to her mother standing at the top of the stairs. With her heart racing from being discovered, she still managed to hear the scrape of movement against the tiled floor. Which meant, not only was she busted by her mother, her father and Denzel were now aware she was on the stairs.

"I'm sorry, Mama. I got lost in my thoughts."

Her mother folded her arms across her middle and twisted her lips in disbelief.

"My daughter, the award-winning actress, can't even muster up a good lie."

Her mother's assessment was entirely accurate. Her performance was severely less than stellar. Dominique didn't even have a chance to respond or recover from her embarrassment before her father appeared in the stairwell with Denzel on his heels. Her father's gaze looked between them before settling on her mother.

"Is everything okay, Bee?"

Dominique looked at her mother with pleading eyes. She knew there was zero chance Belinda Truman wouldn't tell her husband everything. Dominique was simply hoping for a short reprieve—maybe she would save the full story for when they were alone.

If hopes and dreams were little golden statues, she'd have a dozen. Because her mama immediately told her dad exactly what was going on.

"It didn't take me but a few minutes to get stuff ready. So, I sent Miss Lady here to get y'all. When she took too long coming back, I came looking."

Snitch. Dominique worked to keep her expression neutral when what she really wanted to do was mean mug her own mama. Since she was caught, all she could do was roll with it. Maybe turn the tables a little. Get an answer to a question Denzel refused to give her, but her father mentioned it when she was eavesdropping.

"Daddy, did you threaten to bury Denzel in the desert when we were in Vegas for the wedding?"

Dominique found it mildly amusing, watching her father's face transition as he started and stopped speaking a few times before finally settling into a stern expression.

"What I talk about with Reyes is between us. Mind your business."

Feeling good after successfully redirecting the conversation, Dominique didn't comment on her mother's normal words coming from her father's mouth. Instead, she turned and walked up the stairs, following her mother into the kitchen. Before they made it inside, Denzel fell into step beside her, wrapping his fingers around her hand.

"You might not be quick to lie, but you have deflection down to an art form."

His whispered statement was disguised in the kiss he placed on her cheek as they crossed the threshold into the kitchen.

"I have no idea what you mean." Dominique suppressed her grin, giving him a side eye glance.

Once they were all settled around the table, her mother restarted the conversation the two of them were having before she sent Dominique to get the men.

"So, have you two come up with any wedding plans? Or do you intend to do the same as Zaria and Andrei? Wait until you're about to damn near pop to have the wedding?"

"Mama!"

Dominique nearly dropped the forkful of salad she had halfway to her mouth before her mother surprised her with the question.

"What? It's a valid question." In true Belinda Truman fashion, she had the nerve to look at Dominique as if she was being obtuse.

"Yeah, but you didn't have to say it like that."

Flicking her fingers in a cross between a shooing and a get out of here motion, her mother blew a soft raspberry.

"Pfft. What other way is there to say it? You're pregnant. It won't be much longer before that fact is obvious. And, from what you told me, your due date is seven months or less away. Time is of the essence, miss ma'am."

While her mother's blunt honesty was needed, it wasn't initially appreciated. Dominique glanced at Denzel before placing her fork back onto the plate. They'd discussed how to move forward with wedding plans over the past couple of days, after learning of their impending parenthood.

Neither wanted a long engagement. And, despite how harsh it sounded when her mother said it, the reasoning Dominique had was similar—without mentioning Zaria and Andrei. Just as he'd told her father, Denzel made it clear to her he wanted them to be married well before the baby arrived.

Dominique wasn't averse to the idea. She wasn't a fan of long engagements. To her, the only reason to wait longer than six months was due to venue and other considerations with the arrangements. Since she and Denzel had decided to have the wedding at his place in Texas, venue availability wasn't an issue.

"I know...*we* know that, Mama. We've discussed it."

Denzel's warm hand on Dominique's thigh stilled the bouncing motion she hadn't even realized she was doing.

"If you are in agreement, Mrs. Truman, we'd like to set up a phone call with my parents. Since Dominique and I are having the wedding at my estate in Texas, and it's a Reyes tradition, they're anxious to start working on the details with you."

Dominique's hand landed on Denzel's, where it rested on her leg. She thought back to when Denzel finally answered the phone when they learned of her pregnancy. The outpouring of affection from his family warmed her heart. Then, after they told them of their engagement, everyone began excitedly discussing potential ideas for the wedding.

It hurt her to hear the story of Denzel's parents and how his great-grandmother and a few of his grandmother's siblings didn't approve of or accept his mother. So, the normal involvement from the groom's large Mexican family didn't happen for them. His abuela was determined to make sure things were different for Dominique and Denzel.

Her father's token grumbling about why they chose San Antonio, Texas was quickly squashed by her mother, reminding him that their family was now scattered. No matter where the wedding was held, most people they invited would have to travel to attend. Therefore, the location wasn't a big deal.

"How about we set something up when we're done eating? With y'all here, I didn't plan on doing anything else."

Her Mother's request was the seal of approval, releasing any remaining tension Dominique was holding on to. Other than settling on a date which wouldn't put her into her third trimester walking down the aisle, the remaining item weighing on her involved her big sister. Without her mentioning it, her mother zeroed in on it.

"Y'all know if you do this within the next two months, Zee baby and Dray won't be able to come. She's due any day now, and it'll be too soon after the birth for Zee or the baby to travel. And you know Dray isn't going anywhere without them."

"Yeah... I know."

Denzel's squeeze of assurance to her thigh brought Dominique a little comfort.

"Don't worry, Una. We'll work something out."

Accepting Denzel's encouragement, Dominique kept her hand on his as they finished their meals. Denzel contacted his folks to arrange the time for the call, pleasing both sets of parents. Well... mostly. Although Dominique's father had stopped shooting daggers at Denzel, he was at most a sideline participant in the discussion.

Event planning wasn't his favorite thing. He normally stayed out of it until the day of, at which point he went to wherever her mother said and performed the tasks she directed him to. But, asking him to actually make a decision beyond pulling out his wallet to pay was a bridge farther than Neal Truman wanted to go.

In contrast, Denzel's father had many suggestions. Most of them had to do with the food since he and Denzel's abuela were adamant about not using outside caterers. Their ideas didn't bother Dominique. And her mother's expression shifted from a state of confusion once Denzel told them his father owned and operated more than a few successful restaurants. All establishments he started from the ground up cooking alongside his own mother for many years.

Dominique placed her foot back onto the mat, keeping her hands behind her head, concentrating on maintaining her balance on the yoga ball supporting her. Her personal trainer, Kam, was seated opposite her on an identical ball. Once Dominique had been cleared from the doctor to continue her exercise routine, she'd spoken to Kam, who'd designed a prenatally friendly regimen.

Prenatally friendly didn't mean easy. Since Kam had helped Dominique build her endurance and overall physical conditioning over the months she'd been in Logan City, she'd hoped the trainer would be able to continue. Luckily for her, Kam was also certified as a pre and postnatal fitness trainer. Having the consistency helped Dominique in the midst of all the other changes occurring in her life.

"Okay. Let's go to the left leg."

Kam demonstrated the move she wanted Dominique to perform before prompting her to mirror the exercise.

"Come on. You've got this DT. Last set."

Despite the cool air circulating in the home gym, sweat beaded on Dominique's forehead. Kam dangled the *last set* carrot in front of Dominique a minimum of four times during their sessions. It shouldn't work as often as it did to galvanize her into pushing through.

Dominique was positive the activity wouldn't have taken so much out of her if Kam hadn't made it last on the list before they moved to cool down. Considering the things the woman had her doing, pre-pregnancy, these leg raises should've been easy as pie. Completing the set, she dropped her arms, letting her hands rest on her thighs.

She still had to leverage herself off the ball without landing on her ass, so she needed a minute. As if she hadn't a care in the world, Kam hopped up from her yoga ball, walking over to the equipment storage to place it on the rack.

"Stop looking at me like that." The trainer shot over her shoulder.

"Like what?" Dominique shot back.

"Like I just tortured you or found a way to make easy things hard."

Accepting her water bottle when Kam extended it to her, Dominique uncapped it, taking a drink.

"I don't think you set out to torture me. At least not today. But, as hard as we hit things when I was working on the show, these modified exercises shouldn't be this difficult. Should they?"

Offering Dominique a hand, Kam helped her safely stand from the big gray ball.

"Your body is going through a lot of changes, DT. Growing a human is hard, energy draining, work. You can't compare your previous self to who you are right now. You're doing great."

"Of course she is. My baby is a warrior."

Denzel chimed in on Kam's pep talk as he strode into the gym dressed in his normal workout gear. Giving Kam a fist bump, he wrapped an arm around Dominique's waist before leaning down to place a quick peck on her lips.

"Thanks for the vote of confidence."

"Always, Una."

Until she cleared her throat, Dominique had almost forgotten Kam's presence as she fell into the intensity of her man's gaze.

"That's it for today. I'm trusting you to cool down on your own. I'm going to head out. I'll see you in a couple of days." Holding up her phone, she wiggled it. "I've sent you a list of safe things you can do on your own. Or with...assistance from Mr. Football."

"Thanks, Kam."

Remembering her manners, Dominique tossed out the appreciation to her trainer's retreating back. She'd barely closed the door behind her when Denzel shifted his hold, placing both hands on Dominique's ass while walking them toward the bench situated against the wall. Turning them at the last moment, he sat, tugging her onto his lap.

"Den, I'm all sweaty." Dominique squirmed in protest, but didn't put up any real fight to keep from straddling his hips and allowing his muscular thighs to support her weight.

"Since when have I ever cared about a little sweat?"

Emphasizing his statement by nuzzling her neck, he placed kisses and nibbles there, making her temporarily forget the point of her statement. Dominique saw no reason to stop him until a random thought floated across her mind. Clawing her way out of a lust filled fog, she pressed against Denzel's shoulders. Her attempt to create space only garnered her a few inches.

"What's wrong, baby?" Concern knitted Denzel's brow.

"Nothing, but why did you come down dressed like you're about to work out? Didn't you and Rob have your usual session at five this morning?"

It wasn't uncommon for Dominique to awaken to Denzel returning from his morning workout with his personal trainer. The only times they overlapped was when he exercised on his own, and she had to be up early to go in to the studio.

"Who says I'm here to work out?" Denzel punched his hips upward, allowing her to more easily feel his thickness beneath her center.

"Well, it'll be a workout, just not the one you think."

"Den!" Dominique's tap to his shoulder said she wasn't nearly as scandalized as her voice exclaimed. "Did you seriously come down here to get a little nookie? Kam and I were done. I would've been back upstairs within the next fifteen minutes."

"Fifteen minutes is a lifetime, Una. I missed saying good morning to Her Highness. You know my day doesn't get off to a good start without morning worship."

Another light shove was accompanied by a giggle. "You are so nasty!"

"You wouldn't have it any other way."

Denzel coupled his response with another pelvic tilt and a squeeze to her ass. He hadn't relinquished his hold on her posterior. Instead, he flexed his fingers, apparently enjoying the feeling of the rounded cheeks in his hands.

Giving in to the inevitable, Dominique slid her arms around him, grazing her fingertips over his shoulders before lightly scraping her nails through the short hair at his nape.

"No. I wouldn't have it any other way."

Initiating a kiss that had him growling and gripping her tighter, Dominique rocked into his hold allowing all forms of his love to wash over her. When he released her lips, she kissed her way to his ear, where she nipped the lobe before offering a counter suggestion to sex on the gym bench.

Before she'd adequately completed the sentence, Denzel was on his feet, stalking to the elevator. By the time they entered their ensuite bathroom, neither of them wore a stitch of clothing and her core pulsed with anticipation. After turning on both sets of shower heads, Denzel placed her on the bench built into the back wall of the shower.

Dropping to his knees between her spread legs, he tossed one thick thigh onto his shoulders. Pausing from his visual devouring of her pussy, he pierced her with a hungry gaze.

"It's time to keep your promise, Una. I wanna hear my high G."

Epilogue

Two months later

"Come away from over there. She's not gonna appear in the yard waiting for you. The wedding doesn't start for another three hours."

The joking tone of Carver's voice was accompanied by the hand he placed on Denzel's shoulder.

"I never said she was. I was just looking outside."

"Yeah. Whatever you have to tell yourself."

Steering him away from the window, Carver pressed Denzel's shoulder until he sat down in the barber's chair. Taking a note out of Denzel's book, Carver had arranged for a team of barbers to give them a haircut and shave. Denzel wasn't making the guy's job easy by constantly hopping up to look out the window.

The rooms Denzel and his groomsmen were using overlooked the west side of the property where they'd decided to have the wedding. At the time they selected for the ceremony, the setting sun would be the backdrop for their official exchange of vows. He couldn't wait to see the glow the sunlight placed on his Una's deep brown skin.

Denzel knew why he was antsy, and it wasn't simply because today he'd officially marry the love of his life. No. Nothing about joining his life with Dominique's made him nervous. What bothered him was he hadn't seen her in more than twelve solid hours.

When he'd agreed to a wedding time late in the day, he didn't realize they'd have to adhere to the archaic tradition of the groom not seeing the bride before the wedding. If he had, he would've extended their time together and stayed beyond midnight. As far as anyone else knew, they'd parted ways after the rehearsal dinner at eight p.m. the previous night.

It wasn't anyone's business that he'd slipped back into their suite after the other ladies left and made love to her one last time as her fiancé. Their late-night meeting was made easier by her bridesmaids being otherwise occupied. Sydney, Dominique's Maid of Honor, was the most difficult to get rid of, but she had an emergency call which cleared the way.

Getting his head back in the game, Denzel responded to the light touches to the back of his head from the barber, tilting in the appropriate directions. The man had just leaned him back to begin cleaning up his low beard when the door opened. Pablo stepped through, followed by Raffi and Andrei. Those three Denzel expected. The surprise was Vitaly trailing his brother.

"Look who we found." Pablo hitched a thumb over his shoulder, pointing to the Antonov brothers. "I had to rescue these two from Abuela. She was getting ready to put them to work."

His cousin's comment brought a smile to Denzel's face. His abuela was being true to her word. His and Dominique's wedding was a true family affair. While there were some things hired out simply due to scale and availability—like florists and such—almost everyone had a part in bringing the event together.

"Thanks, primo."

Denzel almost made a crack about how a little work wouldn't hurt them since they led otherwise cushy lives, but neither brother looked like their lives were particularly easy at the moment. He was pretty sure he knew what was up with Andrei. However, he had no clue what Vitaly's long face was about.

Andrei and Zaria had arrived amid a flurry of activity early the previous morning. Zaria was determined and adamant that she and little

Adiya were well enough to travel. Considering the entourage they arrived with, Andrei attempted to cover all the bases. Denzel didn't blame him for a second. He'd do no less for his Una.

As a matter of fact, once he'd learned about the security nanny Andrei found for Adiya, Denzel went on the hunt for someone similar. Although Dominique shook her head when he told her he'd started looking, she didn't try to talk him out of it. Not that it would've done any good. Their child would be cared for and protected in every way within his means to provide.

By the time the barber unwrapped the cool towel and was applying beard oil, Raffi was in the chair next to him getting started and Andrei looked like he was about to make a break for it. A couple of Denzel's other male cousins, from the Collier side of his family, were lounging around snacking, and chatting.

Their wedding party wasn't large, which suited him just fine. So, most of the men hanging around in the room weren't groomsmen. A few were ushers and others were just there to commiserate with him since they missed the bachelor party the previous weekend.

"Dray, where are you going?"

Cisco's question was innocent enough, but the expression on Andrei's face said he wasn't happy with being discovered trying to slip away. Also, it was well established that the big guy didn't like to answer to anyone, with the exception of his wife.

"If you must know, I'm going to check on my daughter."

"Isn't she with Zee?" Completely oblivious, Cisco sat in the chair Denzel vacated.

The glare Andrei sent his brother-in-law had been known to send men running, but it appeared to completely fly over Cisco's head. Approaching Andrei, Denzel tapped his shoulder.

"I get it. You wanna see for yourself if they're okay. I'm of the same mind, but I know the mothers aren't going to let either of us within ten feet of that door without kicking up a ruckus. A ruckus would upset them, and more than you want to be certain they're fine, you don't want to be the reason they aren't. Right?"

Andrei turned his ice-blue eyes onto Denzel, who met his glower with a raised brow. After a few seconds, he gave a barely perceptible nod and Denzel offered him a smile.

"Come on. Let's grab something from this buffet Pop laid out for us. It'll be hours before we eat again."

Later, as the sun was sitting low in the sky, Denzel stood beneath the arch decorated with flowers in the hues of golden yellow, pink, violet, orange, and white. It was elegant while injecting a little of both sides of his and her heritage. Soft music played while the bridesmaids were escorted in and everyone else took their positions.

Fernanda made the cutest little flower girl. It's possible Denzel was biased, but he didn't care. Despite her dress being made up of several layers of white gauzy material, his tia assured him the little girl wouldn't be hot. Taking her duties seriously, his youngest cousin dropped rose petals on the royal purple runner leading from the double doors to where Denzel stood with the minister on his right and Carver on his left.

Denzel didn't need the change in music to know it was time for his Una to make her entrance. Beneath the covering of his suit, the hair on his arms stood at attention and his heartbeat increased. When he lifted his gaze from Fernanda taking her place on the little bench next to his other cousin's little boy who was serving as the ring bearer, he was struck breathless by Dominique framed in the doorway. Stunning was too mild a word to use to describe her beauty, but it would have to suffice.

A tap between his shoulder blades from his best friend restarted his breathing as Dominique clasped her father's arm and stepped onto the runner. The lacy white dress lovingly draped over her form, hugged her breasts, before skimming the rest of her full figure, ending in a long train which fanned out behind her as she walked.

It was designed in such a way that it accentuated all of her positive physical attributes, but masked the bump caused by their child growing in her womb. Personally, Denzel didn't care if everyone could see the evidence of their love, but it was important to Dominique to not have her pregnancy upstage the day. Although, most everyone in attendance was already aware of her condition following the recent story in The Rumor Mill after they were seen leaving the OBGYN in Logan City.

By the time Dominique made it within a few feet of him, Denzel's body was strung tight as a bow. It was taking every ounce of self-control he possessed to stay in his spot until it was time to claim his bride. He listened to enough of what the minister said to know when it was time to take her hand in his and stand at her side. They'd decided to have traditional vows interwoven with them speaking words of love and commitment.

If there was ever a moment when Denzel's heart was full to bursting, it was when Dominique declared her love for him in the presence of their family and friends. After the exchange of rings, they stood facing one another, with their hands clasped together, fingers entwined. Dominique's expression projected her feelings, but her words left no doubt.

"Denzel Alejandro Reyes... you are the dream I was afraid to hope for. Eclipsing my expectations for what love would look like for me. I love the way you love me and I love the way you inspire me to love you. And I will spend the rest of my life basking in both."

Covering both of her hands with one of his, Denzel retrieved his handkerchief to dab at the tears threatening to fall down her cheeks. Whispering for her ears only, he confirmed his love before gathering himself.

"Dominique Latoya Truman, my Una. I've told you before, Baby, that you are my One. And you always will be. You're the one who made me want to be the best possible version of myself. Even before we started our relationship, you were the one who made me examine what I wanted my future to look like. I knew, almost from the moment we met, I wanted it to include you. Loving you, protecting you, being the man you wanted and needed. Forever."

Dominique's tears were flowing a little more earnestly, but Denzel was there to dab them away. Somehow, they managed to make it through the rest of the service. The moment the minister spoke the magic words, *you may kiss your bride*, Denzel was able to follow through with not only saluting his bride, but kissing away the tears streaming down her cheeks.

Holding her hand in his, he turned to the assembly of their family and friends as the officiant presented them for the first time as husband and wife. For Denzel, there couldn't possibly be a better moment than this—the instance when his Una completed his world.

The End

About the Author

Darie McCoy is an independent author of contemporary, interracial, romantic suspense, and paranormal/shifter romance books. A reader first, she enjoys reading books across many genres although romance holds a special place in her heart. Her experience working in a STEM field offers her a unique perspective which she uses in each story she pens.

When she doesn't have her nose in a book or her fingers on the keyboard, Darie enjoys working in her vegetable garden. A serial hobbyist, she also enjoys knitting, sewing, baking and canning. One of her favorite treats to make is salted caramel popcorn. Amongst her friends, she's known to transport the sweet treat in large quantities to share whenever they get together.

Born and raised in the south, Darie stands by the staunchly held southern sentiments that the best tea is sweet tea and college football is life.

Acknowledgments

First, thank you to the Vella Community. You choose to spend your tokens on my stories and honor me with your top fave vote each week. You're amazing!

My sincere thanks to my Darlings, Delights, Decadents and Divas. You ladies read my rough words, cheer me on, offer feedback to help me sharpen my pen.

A special thank you to Michel Prince for allowing me the use of the name of the Ryd security service Dominique mentioned using. If you'd like to meet those characters, you should check out At Her Service and Fully Covering Her, which is part of her Ryd series available in e-book and paperback.

As always, I thank my writing partners, Brianna Q. Price and Niccoyan Zheng. Without your support, I don't think I could've grown as an author as quickly as I have. There's still work to do, and I couldn't be happier to have you on this journey with me.

Last but not least, thank you to all the readers and everyone who lends me guidance and support throughout this author journey. You're amazing. I don't have enough words to show my gratitude.

Also by Darie McCoy

Central Valley Pack Series

Chosen

Healed

Reclaimed

Frost Family Series

For Real

Sano's Queen (A Novella)

Christmas Candy

Draft Pick Series

Draft Pick Season I: Carver

Draft Pick Season II: Andrei

Draft Pick Season IV: Vitaly (Kindle Vella)

Other books/stories

Involuntary

Just Kiss Me (Part of Cupid's Kiss Anthology)

Toad: Sin City MC Oakland

Controlled Desire: Fall of Desire

The Glassmaker's Helper: The Getaway Chronicles

Construction Book Boyfriend (Book Boyfriend Series)

The Rancher's Home (Silver Creek Ranch Series)

Made in the USA
Columbia, SC
25 November 2024

47147094R00237